D0389054

DEADLY SHORES

DESTROYERMEN

DESTROYERMEN

DEADLY
SHORES

TAYLOR ANDERSON

A ROC BOOK

ROC
Published by the Penguin Group
Penguin Group (USA) LLC, 375 Hudson Street,
New York, New York 10014

USA | Canada | UK | Ireland | Australia | New Zealand | India | South Africa | China
penguin.com
A Penguin Random House Company

First published by Roc, an imprint of New American Library,
a division of Penguin Group (USA) LLC

First Printing, May 2014

RoC REGISTERED TRADEMARK—MARCA REGISTRADA

LIBRARY OF CONGRESS CATALOGING-IN-PUBLICATION DATA:

Anderson, Taylor, 1963–
    Deadly shores/Taylor Anderson.
        pages cm.—(Destroyermen)
    ISBN 978-0-451-46566-5
    1. Imaginary wars and battles—Fiction. 2. World War, 1939–1945—Fiction. 3. Destroyers
(Warships)—Fiction. I. Title.
    PS3601.N5475D43 2014
    813'.6—dc23   2013042557

Printed in the United States of America
10 9 8 7 6 5 4 3 2 1

Set in Minion
Designed by Alissa Amell

ACKNOWLEDGMENTS

Thanks again to Russell Galen, the best agent in the business, and Ginjer Buchanan, who has got to be the most supportive, gracious, and forgiving editor in the cosmos. I couldn't do it without them, period. Thanks to all my friends and family who—cheerfully and otherwise—stick with me, even when I sequester myself on a writing binge to the exclusion of all other activities and considerations. An awful lot of distracting stuff happened this last year, and I particularly want to thank Fred Fiedler for his painstaking assistance in keeping things straight in the manuscript, and spotting a few really glaring goofs. Like so many of my friends, Fred is a little . . . odd (yep, another former submariner), and has an amazing eye for detail. Kind of like Courtney Bradford in one respect, he's always either staring at the sky or the ground, studying the heavens—or a bug.

Otherwise, my darling daughter Rebecca, now CO of her MCJROTC Battalion and captain of her Rifle, Color Guard, and PT teams (while still getting tolerable grades), remains the inspiration for several of the strong female characters in this story. She's at that age when she can be a different girl every time I talk to her, but her character and commitment to things she believes in are steadfast.

Finally, always remember that, no matter how weird this story gets at times, a great deal of it is at least vaguely inspired by real events. The old adage that truth is stranger than fiction finds no greater traction than in combat. Try to find a detailed account of a particular action involving the old four-stacker USS *Borie* sometime when you have the chance. . . .

CAST OF CHARACTERS

(The following does not necessarily reflect initial or even final deployments, but only those most pertinent to the events described.)

See the back of the book for details of ships and specifications.

Note:

(L)—*Lemurians, or Mi-Anakka (People) are bipedal, somewhat felinoid folk with large eyes, fur, and expressive but nonprehensile tails. They are highly intelligent, social, and dexterous. It has been proposed that they are descended from the giant lemurs of Madagascar.*

(G)—*Grik, or Ghaarrichk'k, are bipedal reptilians reminiscent of various Mesozoic dromaeosaurids. Covered with fine downy fur, males develop bristly crests and tail plumage, and retain formidable teeth and claws. Grik society consists of two distinct classes: the ruling, or industrious, Hij, and the worker-warrior Uul. The basic Grik-like form is ubiquitous, and serves as a foundation for numerous unassociated races and species.*

x

Members of the Grand Alliance

First Fleet South

USS *Walker* (DD-163)

Lt. Cmdr. Matthew Patrick Reddy, USNR—Commanding. CINCAF—(Commander in Chief of All Allied Forces).

Cmdr. Brad "Spanky" McFarlane—Exec. Minister of Naval Engineering.

Lt. Tab-At (L)—Engineering Officer.

Courtney Bradford—Australian naturalist and engineer; Minister of Science for the Grand Alliance and Plenipotentiary at Large.

Chief Quartermaster Patrick "Paddy" Rosen—Acting First Officer.

Lt. Sonny Campeti—Gunnery Officer.

Cmdr. Bernard Sandison—Torpedo Officer and Minister of Experimental Ordnance.

Lt. Ed Palmer—Signals.

Chief Bosun Fitzhugh Gray—Chief Bosun of the Navy and Damage Control Officer. Highest ranking NCO in the Alliance and commander of the Captain's Guard.

Chief Gunner's Mate Dennis Silva

Lawrence "Larry the Lizard"—orange-and-brown tiger-striped Grik-like ex-Tagranesi (Sa'aaran).

Surgeon Lieutenant Pam Cross

Gunnery Sergeant Arnold Horn—USMC, formerly of the 4th Marines (US).

Gunner's Mate Pak-Ras-Ar, "Pack Rat" (L)

Jeek (L)—Flight Crew Chief, Special Air Division.

Earl Lanier—Cook.

Johnny Parks—Machinist's Mate.

Juan Marcos—Officers' Steward.

Wallace Fairchild—Sonarman—Anti-Mountain Fish Countermeasures—(AMF-DIC).

Min-Sakir, "Minnie" (L)—Bridge Talker.

Chief Engineer Isak Reuben—One of the original Mice.

Cmdr. Simon Herring—Chief of Strategic Intelligence (ONI).

Lance Corporal Ian Miles—Formerly in 2nd of the 4th Marines—assigned to Bernard Sandison.

Salissa Battle Group

USNRS *Salissa* "Big Sal" (CV-1)

Admiral Keje-Fris-Ar (L)—(CINCWEST)

Adar (L)—COTGA (Chairman of the Grand Alliance), and High Chief and Sky Priest of Baalkpan.

Atlaan-Fas (L)—Commanding.

Lt. Sandy Newman—Exec.

Surgeon Commander Sandra Tucker Reddy—Minister of Medicine and wife of Captain Reddy.

Diania—Steward's Assistant.

1st Naval Air Wing

Captain Jis-Tikkar, "Tikker" (L)—COFO (Commander of Flight Operations). 1st, 2nd, and 3rd Bomb Squadrons, and 1st and 2nd Pursuit Squadrons remain or have been reconstituted aboard *Salissa* (CV-1).

Frigates (DDs) attached: (Des-Ron 6)

USS *Haakar-Faask***

Lt. Cmdr. Niaal-Ras-Kavaat (L)—Commanding.
USS *Nakja-Mur**

Captain Jarrik-Fas (L)—Commanding.
USS *Tassat***

Cmdr. Muraak-Saanga (L)—Commanding; former *Donaghey* exec. and sailing master.
USS *Scott****

Cmdr. Cablaas-Rag-Laan (L)—Commanding.

II Corps

General Queen Safir Maraan (L)—Commanding.

3rd Division

General Daanis (L)—Commanding.

Colonel Mersaak (L)—"The 600" (B'mbaado Regiment composed of Silver and Black Battalions)—Exec. 3rd Baalkpan, 3rd, 10th B'mbaado, 5th Sular.

5th Division

Captain Saachic (L)—Commanding. Includes remnants of First Amalgamated (Flynn's Rangers), 1st Battalion, 2nd Marines, 6th Maa-ni-la Cavalry, 1st Sular.

6th Division

General Grisa—Commanding.

5th, 6th B'mbaado, 1st, 2nd, 9th Aryaal, 3rd Sular*, 3rd Maa-ni-la Cavalry

USS *Respite Island* (SPD-1)—Self-Propelled Dry Dock #1.

MTB-Ron-1—Motor Torpedo Boat Squadron #1, 12 x MTBs (#s 4–16).

Lt. (jg) Winston "Winny" Rominger—Former carpenter's mate 3rd. Head of the "PT" project.

Lt. Cmdr. Irvin Laumer—Exec.

Ensign Nathaniel Hardee—PT-7.

1st Allied Raider "Commando" Brigade

Lt. Col. Chack-Sab-At (L)—Commanding—Bosun's Mate (Marine Lt. Colonel).

21st (combined) Allied Regiment

Major Alistair Jindal—Commanding—Imperial Marine, and Chack's exec.

1st and 2nd Battalions of the 9th Maa-ni-la, 2nd Battalion of the 1st Respite

7th (combined) Allied Regiment

Captain Risa Sab-At (L)—Commanding—(Chack's sister).

2nd and 3rd Battalions of the 19th Baalkpan, 1st Battalion of
the 11th Imperial Marines

First Fleet North

Indiaa

Allied Expeditionary Force (North)

General of the Army and Marines Pete Alden—Commanding. Former sergeant in USS *Houston* Marine contingent.

I Corps

General Lord Muln-Rolak (L)—Commanding.

Hij Geerki—Rolak's "pet" Grik, captured at Rangoon.

1st (Galla) Division

General Taa-leen (L)—Commanding.

Colonel Enaak (L) (5th Maa-ni-la Cavalry)—Exec.

1st Marines, 5th, 6th, 7th, 10th Baalkpan

2nd Division

General Rin-Taaka-Ar (L)—Commanding.

Major Simon (Simy) Gutfeld (3rd Marines)—Exec.

1st, 2nd Maa-ni-la, 4th, 6th, 7th Aryaal

III Corps

General Faan-Ma-Mar (L)—Commanding.

9th and 11th Divisions composed of the 2nd, 3rd Maa-ni-la, 8th Baalkpan, 7th and 8th Maa-ni-la, 10th Aryaal

VI Corps

General Linnaa-Fas-Ra—Commanding.

Lt. Cmdr. Mark Leedom—COFO—5th and 8th Bomb Squadrons and 6th Pursuit Squadron from *Humfra-Dar* (remains of 2nd Naval Air Wing) attached.

Ceylon

"Mackey" Field—near Trin-com-lee.

3rd Pursuit Squadron (P-40Es) Army Air Corps.

Colonel Ben Mallory—Commanding.

Lt. (jg) Suaak-Pas-Ra, "Soupy" (L)

Lt. Conrad Diebel

2nd Lt. Niaa-Saa, "Shirley" (L)

S. Sergeant Cecil Dixon

At Madras
USS *Santa Catalina* (CAP-1)

Lt. Cmdr. Russ Chapelle—Commanding.

Lt. Michael "Mikey" Monk—Exec.

Lt. (jg) Dean Laney—Engineering Officer.

Surgeon Cmdr. Kathy McCoy

Stanley "Dobbin" Dobson—Chief Bosun's Mate.

USS *Mahan*

Cmdr. Perry Brister—Commanding. Minister of Defensive and Industrial Works.

Lt. (jg) Jeff Brooks—Sonarman—Anti-Mountain Fish Countermeasures—(AMF-DIC).

Lt. (jg) Rolando "Ronson" Rodriguez—Chief Electrician.

Taarba-Kaar, "Tobasco" (L)—Cook.

Chief Bosun's Mate Carl Bashear

Ensign Johnny Parks—Engineering Officer.

Ensign Paul Stites—Gunnery Officer.

Arracca Battle Group

USNRS *Arracca* (CV-3)

Tassanna-Ay-Arracca (L), High Chief—Commanding.
5th Naval Air Wing

Frigates (DDs) attached: (Des-Ron 9)

USS *Kas-Ra-Ar***
   Captain Mescus-Ricum (L)—Commanding.

USS *Ramic-Sa-Ar**

USS *Felts***

USS *Naga****

USS *Bowles****

USS *Saak-Fas****

USS *Clark***

TFG-2 (Task Force Garrett-2)

(Long-Range Reconnaissance and Exploration)

USS *Donaghey* (DD-2)

Cmdr. Greg Garrett—Commanding.

Lt. Saama-Kera, "Sammy" (L)—Exec.

Lt. (jg) Wendel "Smitty" Smith—Gunnery Officer.

Captain Bekiaa-Sab-At (L)—Commanding Marines.

Chief Bosun's Mate Jenaar-Laan (L)

USS *Sineaa* (DE-48) Captured Grik "Indiaman," of the earlier (lighter) design. "Razeed" to the gun deck, these are swift, agile, dedicated sailors with three masts and a square rig. 130' x 32'. About 900 tons. 12 x 18 pdrs. Y gun and depth charges.

Baalkpan

Cmdr. Alan Letts—Chief of Staff, Minister of Industry and the Division of Strategic Logistics; acting Chairman of the Grand Alliance.

Cmdr. Steve "Sparks" Riggs—Minister of Communications and Electrical Contrivances.

Lord Bolton Forester—Imperial Ambassador.

Lt. Bachman—Forester's aide.

Surgeon Cmdr. Karen Theimer Letts—Assistant Minister of Medicine.

"Pepper" (L)—Black and white Lemurian keeper of the "Castaway Cook" (Busted Screw).

Leading Seaman Henry Stokes, HMAS *Perth*—Assistant Director of Office of Strategic Intelligence—(OSI).

Army and Naval Air Corps Training Center (Kaufman Field) Baalkpan

Lt. Walt "Jumbo" Fisher—Commanding.

4th and 7th Bomb Squadrons, and 4th and 5th Pursuit in extra training.

Khonashi

"King" Tony Scott

"Captain" I'joorka—Respected warrior and Scott's friend.

Among the Khonashi

Ensign Abel Cook—Commanding Allied Mission. Imperial Midshipman Stuart Brassey.

Moe the Hunter

Pokey—"Pet" Grik brass-picker.

Fil-pin Lands

Saan-Kakja (L)—High Chief of Maa-ni-la and all the Fil-pin Lands.

Meksnaak (L)—High Sky Priest of Maa-ni-la.

Chinakru—Ex-Tagranesi, now colonial governor on Samaar.

General Ansik-Talaa (L)—Fil-pin Scouts.

Colonel Busaa (L)—Coastal Artillery—commanding Advanced Training Center—(ATC).

Respite Island

Governor Radcliff

Emelia Radcliff

Lt. Busbee—Cutter Pilot.

Bishop Akin Todd

New Britain Isles

Governor-Empress Rebecca Anne McDonald

Sean "O'Casey" Bates—Prime Factor and Chief of Staff for
G-E.

Lt. Ezekial Krish—Assistant to Mr. Bates.

HIMS *Ulysses, Euripides, Tacitus*—Completing repairs.

Allied Assets/New Britain Isles

Sister Audry—Benedictine nun, and new Allied Ambassador.

"Lord" Sergeant Koratin (L)—Marine protector and advisor to
Sister Audry.

Eastern Sea Campaign

High Admiral Harvey Jenks (CINCEAST)

Enchanted Isles

Sir Thomas Humphries—Imperial Governor of Albermarl.

Colonel Alexander—Garrison commander.

Second Fleet

USS *Maaka-Kakja* (CV-4)

Admiral Lelaa-Tal-Cleraan (L)—Commanding.

Lieutenant Tex Sheider (Sparks)—Exec.

Gilbert Yeager—Engineer (one of the original Mice).

3rd Naval Air Wing

9th, 11th, 12th Bomb Squadrons and 7th, 10th Pursuit Squadrons
(58 planes available).

2nd Lieutenant Orrin Reddy—COFO.

Sgt. Kuaar-Ran-Taak "Seepy" (L)—Reddy's backseater.

Second Fleet DDs (of note)

USS *Mertz****

USS *Tindal****

USS *Finir-Pel****

Lt. Haan-Sor Plaar (L)—Commanding.

HIMS *Achilles*
Lt. Grimsley—Commanding.

HIMS *Icarus*
Lt. Parr—Commanding.

USS *Simms****
Lt. Ruik-Sor-Raa (L)—Commanding.

USS *Pinaa-Tubo*—Ammunition ship.
Lt. Radaa-Nin (L)—Commanding.

USS *Pecos*—Fleet oiler.

USS *Pucot*—Fleet oiler.

Second Fleet Expeditionary Force (X Corps)
4 regiments Lemurian Army and Marines, 2 regiments "Frontier" troops, 5 regiments Imperial Marines—(3 Divisions) with artillery train.

General Tomatsu Shinya—Commanding.

Colonel James Blair

Major Dao Iverson—Commanding 2nd Battalion, 6th Imperial Marines.

Nurse Cmdr. Selass-Fris-Ar (L)—"Doc'Selass"; daughter of Keje-Fris-Ar.

Capt. Blas-Ma-Ar "Blossom" (L)—Commanding 2nd Battalion, 2nd Marines.

Spon-Ar-Aak "Spook" (L)—Gunner's Mate, and First Sgt of A Company, 2nd Battalion, 2nd Marines.

Lt. Staas-Fin "Finny" (L)—C Company, 2nd Battalion, 8th Maa-ni-la.

Lt. Faal-Pel "Stumpy" (L)—A Company, 1st Battalion, 8th Maa-ni-la. Former ordnance striker.

Lt. (jg) Fred Reynolds—Formerly Special Air Division—USS *Walker.*

Ensign Kari-Faask (L)—Reynolds's friend and backseater.

Characters in and from the "Republic of Real People"
Caesar (Kaiser) Nig-Taak
Kapitan Adler Von Melhausen—Commanding SMS *Amerika.*

General Marcus Kim—Military High Command.

Inquisitor Kon-Choon—Director of Spies.

Kapitan Leutnant Becker Lange—Von Melhausen's exec.

Leftenant Doocy Meek—British sailor and former POW (WWI).

Lt. Toryu Miyata—Defected ambassador from Kurokawa and the Grik.

Enemies

General of the Sea Hisashi Kurokawa—Formerly of the Japanese Imperial Navy battle cruiser *Amagi*.

General Orochi Niwa—Former advisor to Grik General Halik. Now in Allied hands.

"General of the Sky" Hideki Muriname

"Lieutenant of the Sky" Iguri—Muriname's exec.

Signals Lt. Fukui

Cmdr. Riku—Ordnance.

Grik (Ghaarrichk'k)

Celestial Mother—Absolute, godlike ruler of all the Grik, regardless of the relationships between the various Regencies.

The Chooser—Highest member of his order at the Court of the Celestial Mother. Prior to current policy, "choosers" selected those destined for life—or the cook pots, as well as those eligible for elevation to Hij status.

General Esshk—First General of all the Grik.

General Halik—Elevated Uul sport fighter.

General Ugla, General Shlook—"Promising" Grik leaders under Halik's command.

Holy Dominion

His Supreme Holiness, Messiah of Mexico, and by the Grace of God, Emperor of the World—"Dom Pope" and absolute ruler.

Don Hernan DeDivino Dicha—Blood Cardinal and former Dominion ambassador to the Empire of the New Britain Isles.

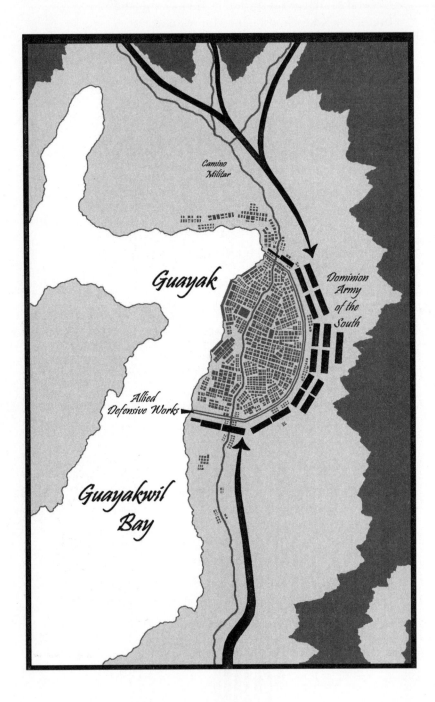

Camino
Militar

Guayak

Dominion
Army
of the
South

Allied
Defensive Works

Guayakwil
Bay

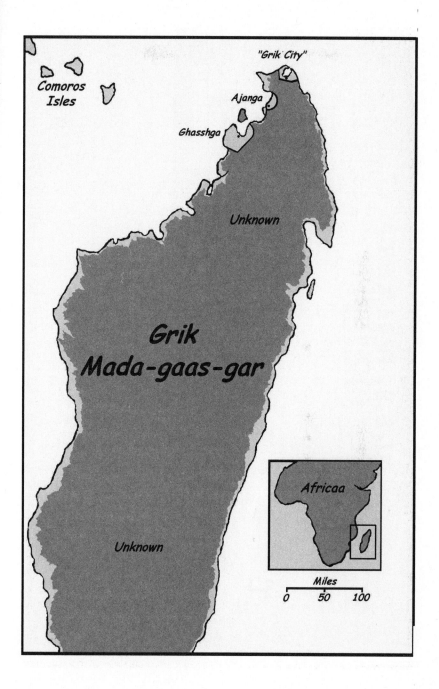

"Grik City"

Comoros
Isles

Ajanga

Ghasshga

Unknown

Grik
Mada-gaas-gar

Unknown

Africaa

Miles
0   50   100

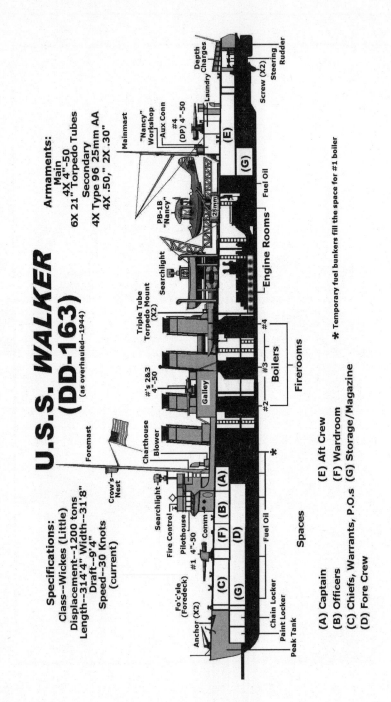

U.S.S. WALKER (DD-163)
(as overhauled--1944)

Specifications:
Class--Wickes (Little)
Displacement--1200 tons
Length--314'4" Width--31'8"
Draft--9'4"
Speed--30 Knots
(current)

Armaments:
Main
4X 4"-50
6X 21" Torpedo Tubes
Secondary
4X Type 96 25mm AA
4X .50," 2X .30"

Spaces

(A) Captain
(B) Officers
(C) Chiefs, Warrants, P.O.s
(D) Fore Crew
(E) Aft Crew
(F) Wardroom
(G) Storage/Magazine

* Temporary fuel bunkers fill the space for #1 boiler

DEADLY
SHORES

////// *Cochin*
Southwest Coast of Grik India
June 16, 1944

en days after the great battle that drove General of the
Sea Hisashi Kurokawa and the tattered remnants of
his once-mighty fleet from Madras, only two of his
little squadron of Grik-built cruisers, *Nachi* and *Tat-
suma*, remained to steam into the port of Cochin.
They'd been lashed by a terrible storm all the way
around India and Ceylon, which was probably why
they hadn't all been harried to destruction, but a third cruiser had survived the battle only to lose power and be driven ashore several days
before. Even now, the tail of the tempest plagued them, scouring *Nachi's*
deck with sheets of rain as her mostly Grik crew struggled to secure the
exhausted ship to the nearly deserted pier.

Kurokawa puffed up the companionway from below, finding it difficult to breathe the sodden air, and glanced around the harbor from

beneath the wide umbrella that Signals Lieutenant Fukui hurried to protect him with. *At least I still have* some *ships here,* Kurokawa brooded, *and their commanders have followed orders.* Six of the great ironclad dreadnaughts, and a like number of cruisers that hadn't arrived at Madras in time for the battle, were moored away from the docks, where their crews couldn't be infected by the treachery mounting against him all across India. *Conditions aboard those ships must be miserable,* he reflected, *inescapably permeated by the filth of their Grik crews, but my Japanese officers have remained loyal and have heeded Fukui's wireless warnings.* This last revelation came almost as a surprise, so accustomed had he grown to treachery—real and imagined.

Kurokawa's first intimation that he had a general mutiny on his hands came when General of the Sky Muriname's second in command, Lieutenant Iguri, sent word that warriors under orders of Grik General Halik had arrived at their aerodrome near Bombay to *seize* the remaining airships waiting there! Iguri's own Grik security forces, recognizing him as their commander and with no idea who Halik even was, drove them off after a sharp fight—but Iguri had been forced to abandon India, racing west with all his airworthy zeppelins ahead of the looming storm. He'd ordered his ground forces and all the "new" Grik troops assembling in the area—raised and trained according to Kurokawa's principles— to march south to Cochin. But there was no way to know whether they had, or if the twenty-odd thousand of them had been incorporated or slaughtered along the way by warriors loyal to Halik. Kurokawa desperately hoped they'd made it. He needed fuel for his ships, which he could get only if Cochin remained in "friendly" hands, and he wanted Iguri's Grik troops as well. His behavioral experiments had helped form them, after all, and he hoped to make them just as fanatically loyal to him as they'd always been to their bloated "Celestial Mother." Only then could he consider, from anything like a position of strength, the offers of assistance made by unknown forces watching his war.

Since they were entering port under communications silence, there was only one way to find out. *Nachi* was flying signal flags calling for a command meeting immediately. Whether "his" troops had arrived or not, he had to go ashore and present himself as the ultimate authority, the regent consort of all India and Ceylon, who, absent any direct command to the contrary from the Celestial Mother herself, every Grik in India was still—theoretically—bound to obey. Regardless of how far Halik's treachery extended, Kurokawa hoped to convince the creatures here that not only had Halik gone rogue, but he'd made unprecedented and unnatural accommodations with the Americans and their ape-man lackeys—with *prey*—and it was Halik who should be resisted! Kurokawa had no desire to direct a civil war from Cochin. He didn't have time. No doubt he would be condemned by the Celestial Mother for his defeat at Madras just as soon as ships sent from Bombay by Halik reached her, but with aircraft denied to make the trip and without wireless communications—one thing Kurokawa had providentially withheld from his Grik "allies"—it would be many weeks before an official condemnation arrived. He'd be long gone by then.

"Come, Fukui," he said as a guard of a hundred Grik led them down the gangplank and formed around them on the dock.

"Are you certain you should do this, Lord?" Fukui questioned.

"Who else could? You?" Kurokawa snorted with contempt.

Fukui looked away. He hated Kurokawa, hated everything they'd done since they came to this . . . other earth, but despite his madness, Kurokawa did have courage of a sort. He'd never risk himself if he didn't absolutely have to, but when he did, there was no apparent hesitation. "No, Lord," Fukui replied, searching anxiously in the rainy gloom for signs of a threat. Just then, a single Grik warrior dashed into view. He was unarmed and immediately hurled himself at Kurokawa's feet; this was likely the only reason he wasn't instantly slain. He began rasping rapidly in his tongue.

"Tell him to slow down," Fukui snapped at one of their party who understood spoken English. The creature didn't *speak* it, with his toothy, lipless jaws. Very few Grik could, and Kurokawa hated hearing *any* human language mangled by their tongues. Even fewer humans spoke Grik—Fukui didn't—but he could understand it if it didn't come at him too fast. The guard complied, and the messenger on the wet planks dutifully repeated himself. Fukui turned to Kurokawa. "The harbor remains in our hands, Lord," he said with relief, "and perhaps seven thousand of 'our' warriors have established a defensive position north and east of the city." He frowned. "They are all that got through. Halik's, um, 'rebels' were more numerous and had artillery, but were not of the breed that understands defense. Ours were able to break through, and have begun to move some artillery from the harbor fortifications to face them."

"I gathered that," Kurokawa said, and he probably did. He'd been "communicating" with Grik longer than any of them. He stared down at the warrior. "Are there disloyal forces in the city itself?"

"No longer," replied the messenger, before adding simply, "They were slain. But scouts report a large column approaching from the northeast, and it is said that General Shlook commands them!"

"Shlook!" Kurokawa said, and frowned. Shlook, one of Halik's disciples, commanded an army of forty or fifty thousand of the new warriors, once called the "hatchling host." No matter what kind of defense his "loyal" Grik threw up, they couldn't hold against that. "How far?" he demanded.

"Three days' march," the messenger whined. "In this weather, perhaps four."

Kurokawa nodded. Plenty of time. He looked at the creature, suddenly struck by the . . . quality of the report, not to mention how well-spoken it was, even if the words were Grik. With a flush of pride, he realized *he* was responsible for that! He'd instituted the programs that trained Grik warriors to become more than just the mindless killing machines they'd always been. Before, only Hij—members of the Grik ruling class—could've reported more than "Bad Grik come." That was about all any Uul, the warrior/worker class, could've accomplished. He congratulated himself—but then frowned more deeply. He'd also "created" Halik, in a sense, and that had come back to bite him. He'd have to tread far more carefully with the new Grik, even those loyal to him, than he ever had before.

"Who sent you?" Fukui demanded. "And why is he not here to receive us himself?"

"Commander of ten hundreds Agta leads us now. He pledges that the coaling yard is clear of enemies or traps. He hurries here afterward. Shelter has been prepared for you, if you will follow me."

The rain tapered away at last as the day wore on, but the gray sky remained and the muggy air seemed to hold just as much moisture as before. Kurokawa and Fukui had a dry place to rest, at least, while the remainder of their party guarded the entrance to the adobe-like structure where they waited. Kurokawa had ordered all his ships to move to the coaling pier and fuel as quickly as possible, but he was growing annoyed that this "Agta" did not arrive more swiftly. It was Fukui who first realized that the thunder they still heard in the distance was not thunder at all, but artillery. Kurokawa rose from the padded, saddlelike Grik chair he'd been leaning against and advanced toward the door in alarm. Just then, there was a commotion outside, and the best spoken guard hurried into the chamber.

"Agta is here with his staff," the creature announced.

"It's about time," Kurokawa ground out, relaxing slightly. "Escort him alone inside—but watch him!"

Fukui nodded. He'd had very little contact with "new" Grik, and this whole situation was most irregular. For once, he agreed entirely with his lord's paranoia. Ultimately, there was no reason for concern. Agta wasn't exactly a hatchling; he was probably elevated in much the same way Halik had been, but was very young to command ten hundreds (Kurokawa translated the rank as major), and if he didn't throw himself on the damp dirt floor at Kurokawa's feet, he did kneel and bow quite low. He was dressed in the red-and-black-painted leather armor standard for the "new" Grik, and wore the far better sword, much like a katana, that Kurokawa had designed himself. His plumed helmet was under his arm, revealing the young crest down the center of his head, now flattened in sincere obeisance.

"My lord regent," he said in his own tongue, though his words were easily understood. "I will gladly destroy myself for inconveniencing you so long, but the rebels press us closely on the main road. I desired to place the guns myself before coming to you, lest they break through and inconvenience you further."

"Well done, Agta," Kurokawa said, uncharacteristically mild. "Rise and hear my commands."

Agta stood, his eyes still downcast.

"What . . ." Kurokawa paused, considering. "What is your opinion of the situation?"

Agta's snout drooped lower, but he quickly recovered himself. "Lord, I must tell you that the force I was able to bring through can hold the rebels for a time, but cannot resist General Shlook when he arrives. I . . . I do not know how we will defeat them without more warriors. Many more."

"An honest and accurate appraisal," Kurokawa breathed with something akin to wonder. His voice rose. "We *will* defeat them, Agta, but we have a greater chore before us just now. Halik and his followers are not the only rogue elements on the loose within the very bosom of the Grik Empire! There are rebels everywhere, some that even threaten the Celestial Mother herself!" He saw the flash of consternation in Agta's upward glance. "Indeed," Kurokawa continued. "I fear the treachery here is but the distant tip of a more horrendous campaign instigated by intimates of the Giver of Life from within the Celestial Palace itself!" He looked away. "I have long admired First General Esshk, but it seems that certain ambitions have released a terrible storm. I can't say Esshk is *directly* involved himself. . . ."

"First General Esshk?" Agta moaned, and Kurokawa nodded sadly. "We must pray that is not the case," he said doubtfully, "but whether or not he leads the rebellion, his policies and ambition have sparked it just as surely as if he gave the command. Agta!" he shouted, breaking the stunned astonishment that threatened to overcome the Grik commander. "I will fuel and provision all the ships in the harbor. You must discourage the rebels sufficiently to pull your warriors back to the city under cover of darkness so I can take as many of them as possible from this place!"

"Leave?" Agta mumbled doubtfully. "Flee?"

"No!" Kurokawa assured. "We do *not* flee. But we must . . . redirect

our attack—and leave only for a time so we can move to protect the sacred, ancient lands! We have no time to lose! Even now, there are reinforcements on their way here—ships, troops. We must intercept them
before they can arrive and be infected with Halik's madness. Once that
is accomplished, we will be in a better position to crush the rebellion—
or protect the Celestial Mother. Whichever requires our most urgent
attention. Are you with me, *General* Agta?"

Agta seemed shaken by the word "general," but he slashed his head
downward in a Grik nod. "Of course, Lord Regent!"

"Excellent," Kurokawa purred. "Now obey your orders! We must
move quickly."

When Agta was gone, Fukui could only look at Kurokawa with awe.
The man was insane; few knew that better than he. Yet, for a moment,
even *he* had believed the lies.

"We will salvage this situation yet, Fukui!" Kurokawa chortled,
breaking the spell. "Now," he said softly. "*Now* you can try to contact the
'others' who have communicated their willingness to aid us. By the time
we reach our home, our 'preserve,'" he spat, "of Zanzibar, we will have
an army *and* a navy in addition to the projects we are completing there.
We will not be powerless supplicants to whoever these mysterious potential allies might be!" He considered. "Send a message to Zanzibar as
well. Instruct Commander Riku to collect all our people from the various worksites where they are employed and gather them at our enclave.
We will need them. They are free to perform whatever sabotage to the
Grik industries they can think of that will not be immediately discovered, or might bring too quick a response. We will also need time to
complete our defenses."

"Yes, Lord, but . . . what shall I tell the 'others'? They have expressed
a desire to meet, but where should that be?"

Kurokawa shrugged. "Tell them to come to Zanzibar as well . . .
when we call them, and not before." He looked at Fukui. "We must get
there first ourselves, of course!" He frowned. "If they cannot come there,
they are of no use to us in any event."

CHAPTER 1

////// Madras
HQ First Fleet North AEF

"Go . . . osh dang it!" Lieutenant Commander Matthew Reddy, captain of the old Asiatic Fleet "four-stacker" destroyer USS *Walker* (DD-163), and commander in chief of all Allied forces (CINCAF) united beneath or beside the Banner of the Trees, semi-swore. His left foot had strayed from the planked pathway and his shoe was caught in the sticky mud. The stronger curse he stifled would've been inappropriate in present company, and even uncharacteristic of him for something so trivial, but he was genuinely annoyed—at himself. It had taken only a second of inattention to stray from the boards, and his wife, Nurse Lieutenant (now Surgeon Commander) Sandra Tucker Reddy, was very good at distracting him. In this instance, it merely took a toss of her head to produce the enchanting bounce of her long ponytail. She did it unconsciously, but it was one of those little things about her that always melted his heart.

"Damn," he said, his frustration escalating as he tugged carefully against the black east Indian mud.

"Clumsy," Sandra scolded with a grin, kneeling to see if she could help him save the shoe. It was one of a new pair, specially made, just arrived from Baalkpan with the latest supply convoy. And unlike the usual Lemurian-made "boondockers," these shoes were smooth and highly polished. At least they had been. Carefully, together, they teased the shoe out of the mud, and Matt stamped his foot several times to knock off the worst of the black blob.

"Damn Clumsy!" Petey cawed, earning a resentful glare. Petey was a small, tree-gliding reptile from Yap Island. Discarded by the Governor-Empress of the Empire of the New Britain Isles, Rebecca Anne McDonald, as "inappropriate," Sandra had adopted him by default. He most often lay coiled around the back of her neck like a fuzzy, feathery squirrel—with an insatiable appetite and a filthy mouth.

"They were such pretty shoes too," Sandra said, ignoring Petey's parrotlike outburst, as usual.

"Yeah. But I guess the best thing about them is what they represent," Matt pointed out, still scraping. "Even with all the new ship construction, weapons manufacture, logistical support necessary to maintain and supply two major fleets—more than two, counting the Imperials'—we can still scrape up enough resources to make a pair of fancy shoes!" He shrugged. "Of course, we're also supporting large armies in multiple theaters, and running what's turned into a *world war*!" He nodded ruefully at the shoe that was starting to turn gray as it dried. "I don't know whether to be proud of these or embarrassed."

"Don't be embarrassed," Sandra scolded, "except for maybe ruining them. And yours aren't the only 'shiny' ones. Just be glad we've got enough shoes and sandals for all our troops. That's something to be proud of."

Matt supposed she was right—as usual. It wasn't as if the supply of ships, planes, weapons, ammunition, rations, or anything else he could think of had slowed. If anything, it was speeding up. The only real

shortage was personnel, and with more troops beginning to arrive from
the Empire of the New Britain Isles—what would've been Hawaii, California, and countless Pacific isles in the world they left—and the growing addition of Lemurian troops from the Great South Isle—essentially
Australia—even their numbers were starting to improve. But here, on
the "western front," they faced potentially *endless* numbers of furry/
feathery, somewhat reptilian, and entirely lethal Grik.

And the eastern front, aimed at the rabidly fanatical human "Holy
Dominion" in the Americas, did have serious supply problems, particularly when it came to the more modern weapons the Alliance was pro-
ducing, because of the vast distances involved. Worse, it appeared that a
major battle was brewing there, and Lord High Admiral Harvey Jenks,
commander in chief of all Allied forces in the East (CINCEAST), had
just been handed some unpleasant surprises. He was jockeying to coun-
ter them even while his forces were overextended by a strategy based on
an outdated understanding of the situation.

Matt shook his head. Jenks was on his own. Half a world away, there
was nothing Matt could do to help him, and he was about to embark on
a major, extremely risky operation of his own. He'd always believed the
old saying that "fortune favors the bold." He couldn't remember who
said it first, and recognized that history was replete with examples of
the opposite. . . . Still, though the Grand Alliance was just beginning to
hit its stride, it couldn't afford a long war of attrition against the Grik;
Grik bred much too fast, and the Allies just didn't have, and couldn't get
the numbers for that. Now was the time for a crushing blow, while the
Grik were on their heels. The Doms were bad, maybe worse than the
Grik in some ways, but they were people—well, human, at least—and
couldn't replace losses any faster than the Allies. So, if the war in the
East wasn't exactly on a back burner, the primary focus of the Alliance
was—and had to be, in Matt's view—against the Grik for now.

Jenks had a formidable, if somewhat outdated force at his disposal,
and he was getting at least a few of the new weapons. He also had General Shinya. The former Japanese naval officer who'd become Matt's
friend was maturing into an excellent infantry commander. He had a
carrier commanded by the Lemurian Admiral Lelaa-Tal-Cleraan, with

Matt's own cousin, Lieutenant Orrin Reddy as COFO (Commander of Flight Operations). Orrin had been in the Army Air Corps in the Philippines before being captured by the Japanese and also winding up here, and by all accounts he was shaping up well. Jenks also had a lot of other veterans of hard fighting under his command: Colonel Blair, Captain Blas-Ma-Ar, even a few of *Walker*'s "old" Lemurian hands. He'd do fine; Matt was sure. Right now, he had to concentrate on his own mission.

"If you're finished with your mud pies, we're running a little late," Sandra reminded him.

"Yeah," Matt muttered, and with a final scrape of his shoe, he joined her to proceed down the walkway.

The storm, a genuine "strakka,"—essentially a particularly vigorous typhoon—had battered them for the better part of a week, but now it had passed entirely, leaving the sky bright and clear. More, it was as if the great storm had finally swept away the lingering "rainy season" that had plagued the region, and made the prelude to the great Battle of Madras, or Alden's Perimeter as it was interchangeably called, so miserable for its participants. It had also hindered rescue efforts for those wounded in the jungle combat, as well as repairs to the ships damaged in the battle at sea. Now, the humidity remained terrible, but that wasn't unusual, and the Lemurian Sky Priests predicted that they might actually be rewarded with several sunny days in a row.

The storm had been a bad one, but Matt was still awed by the sheer scope of the battle—and the victory. Serious problems still faced the Allied occupation of south and east Indiaa, and there were still a hell of a lot of Grik beyond their frontier, but a major Grik army had been decimated and a fleet that took two years to build had been destroyed. Madras was the prize, though: a major port with access to abundant raw materials. North of the city were stands of trees with interlocking root systems that produced a kind of rubber that would be a great help. There were coal, copper, tin, and many other metals, minerals, and chemicals the Allies needed, and, just as important, had now been denied to the Grik. There was also iron in preexisting mines stretching like battered moonscapes northwest of town, and hundreds of tons of processed plate had been stockpiled for Grik ironclads. It appeared to be even better stuff than they'd originally used on their ships, which spoke disturbing volumes about what the enemy had achieved technologically. The earlier Grik armor was thick but brittle, and having actually captured a couple of the monster ships fairly intact at the anchorage, they could directly compare the quality. Those ships now floated, also under repair, but Matt wasn't sure what good they'd be. That was where he and Sandra were headed first—to finally inspect one of the behemoths before attending a staff meeting aboard the even bigger aircraft carrier/tender, USNRS *Salissa*. It was there that Matt would announce his decision regarding the composition of his audacious mission, and he wasn't looking forward to it. A lot of his friends were going to be disappointed.

Nearing the pier, Matt was reminded that many Allied ships had been lost or damaged in the battle as well, including his own USS *Walker*. Rust streaks marred her sides, and she was fire-blackened aft of the amidships gun platform. At least most of her more serious damage had already been attended to, and so soon after a major overhaul, they'd had a lot more to work with than usual. Brad "Spanky" McFarlane, *Walker*'s former engineering officer and now Matt's exec—as well as Minister of Naval Engineering—had assured him they'd even start *painting* over the old ship's sores as soon as the weather permitted. Matt was content with the pace of repairs, considering the constraints. *Walker* would be ready.

Other ships weren't so lucky. Poor *Mahan* (DD-102), *Walker*'s only recently reanimated sister, had nearly been sunk by one of *Walker*'s own errant torpedoes! The new weapons worked amazingly well, arguably winning the naval battle largely by themselves, but they weren't perfect. Their range remained limited to a couple of thousand yards, and they still had some guidance issues that Bernie Sandison, *Walker*'s torpedo officer and Minister for Experimental Ordnance, blamed on himself. Matt—everyone—assured the dark-haired young man that it wasn't his fault, and the torpedoes still worked better than any they'd had to use against the Japanese. It didn't matter. Bernie was working himself to death, night and day, trying to solve the problem. Part of his difficulty was that the torpedoes had gone into mass production back in Baalkpan (headquarters of the Grand Alliance on the south coast of "Borno"), and all he could manage were simple field modifications. If he figured it out, the fix could be incorporated at the factory, but he had only finished weapons to tinker with. Matt wasn't worried. The dreary sight of *Mahan* sagging at the dock, her new bow blown off, was a sad, cautionary example to them all. It also put a kink in his operational planning for the upcoming mission. But as far as he was concerned, the torpedoes were a success.

Beyond *Mahan* lay the "Protected Cruiser" (CA-P-1), *Santa Catalina*. She remained whole, but had arguably been in greater danger of sinking than *Mahan* after the beating she took. She'd been the main focus of the whole battle line of massive Grik dreadnaughts and had suffered serious casualties. Among the killed was Commodore James Ellis, *Walker*'s old exec, and Matt's best friend. She suffered even more later that night when Kurokawa and the last of the Grik fleet broke out of Madras in conjunction with a mass attack by Grik zeppelins and their damn "suicider" bombs. She'd been riddled with heavy shot at close range, and her consort, the old submarine-turned torpedo gunboat, S-19, had been rammed and sunk with nearly half her crew. It had been a terrible, shocking exclamation point to the otherwise successful operation, and Matt took savage satisfaction from the subsequent, personal destruction of every ship they could find that broke out that night. He was morally certain they'd finally killed that Japanese madman, Hisashi Kurokawa, the architect of so many of their woes, and it was impossible not to be pleased by his destruction. Matt supposed Kurokawa would never really be "dead" to him, since he'd never *seen* him dead, but considering how complete the slaughter of his force had been, he wouldn't lie awake worrying about him anymore either.

On the pier itself, they passed *Walker, Mahan,* and *Santa Catalina,* self-consciously waving at the cheering men and Lemurian "'Cats" working on board. More cheers came from the wooden-hulled steam frigates, or "DDs," beyond, and they finally reached the gangway leading aboard the dark, malignant shape of the first Grik ironclad.

The thing was huge, over eight hundred feet long, and powerfully armed. The dark iron casemate protecting its armament sloped upward and away, towering high above the harbor water, and resembled nothing more than a gigantic version of the old Confederate ironclad *Virginia*—

or *"Merrimac."* Besides being much larger, however, there were other differences. There were two gun decks instead of one, for example, and four slender funnels protruded high above the casemate. So close, the thing seemed invincible—until one observed the deep-shot dents and shattered plates, as well as the heavy streaks and blotches of rust that proved the thing was mortal after all. And of course, Matt had seen torpedoes make very short work of the massive ships with his own eyes. *No, it's not invincible,* he told himself. *It may not even be good for anything, now,* he decided. He might've considered it a dinosaur if it weren't for the fact that there were real dinosaurs on this world, and some remained extremely formidable.

"What are we here to see?" Sandra asked, somewhat reluctant to go aboard. The Grik kept captives as rations on their ships, and she never wanted to see the . . . aftermath . . . of that again.

"Actually, we're here to see Spanky, and hear what he has to say about this thing," Matt replied. "Besides, I'd kind of like to have a look. Chances are, we'll run into more of them." He saw her expression. "No, I don't expect we need to go down in the hold."

They mounted the gangplank and saluted the Stars and Stripes streaming above the perverted version of a Japanese flag, its rising sun embraced by a pair of Grik-like swords that appeared to have been adopted as a kind of Grik naval jack. They turned and saluted a 'Cat guard at the top of the gangway.

"Permission to come aboard?"

"O' course, Cap-i-taan Reddy! Mister Maac-Faar-lane is wait-een for you!"

Matt and Sandra passed through the crude, heavy hatch that, like all the gunports, had been left open for ventilation. Inside, they found themselves on a cramped, gloomy, open deck on a level with the weather deck outside the casemate. *Does that make this part of the weather deck too? Or the orlop?* Matt wasn't sure. Whatever it was, it seemed to have served as a berthing space for countless Grik, and even with the fresh air, the dark, dank interior reeked of death, mold, and rot. It would've been unbearably creepy if they'd been there all alone, but the dozen or so Lemurians working within their view helped a lot.

"Gonna have to scour this thing out with *bleach*," Spanky grouched as if reading their minds. He approached, ducking under the massive beams supporting the lower gun deck overhead. Spanky was a short, wiry guy, but the power of his personality always left people remembering him bigger than he was. "You better watch your head in here, Skipper." Matt was more than six feet tall and already had to crouch, even between the beams. "You smack your forehead, no tellin' what you'll get infected with!"

"I'll be careful. What can you show me?"

Spanky scratched the whiskers on his chin. "Well, some of it you can see right here. Look at those casemate timbers, backing the armor plate." Spanky raised a lantern. "Recognize the design?"

"Sure. I'll be derned. The timbers are diagonally laminated, just like Lemurian Homes. No wonder they can build something this size out of wood! How many layers?"

"Four below the waterline, and six on the casemate under the iron— and the way they've got the iron bolted on every few inches or so just adds to the structural strength." He patted a beam, not with affection, but respect. "Other Grik ships have always been surprisingly well made. That new Jap, Miyata, that showed up at Diego Garcia with those . . . other folks, told Mr. Garrett he'd been at a Grik shipyard on the Africa coast. Apparently, the lizards've been assembly-linin' their ships for a long time. That could explain how a buncha idiot Uul turn out a decent hull; all they need is a few of their smarter lizards, their Hij, hangin' around to make sure all the pieces go together right." He swayed the lantern at the casemate timbers. "This is the first time we've seen 'em use *this*, though. I'd say it was Kurokawa's idea, or one of the Japs workin' for him. Good thing for us they put so much faith in protection that they never gave much thought to what would happen if we did knock holes in 'em. No watertight compartmentalization at all. If they can't pump water out of the whole damn thing, they ain't stoppin' it until it *fills* the whole damn thing!"

"I take it you've got a fix for that?"

Spanky's face turned sour. "Sure. It's no big deal. Some transverse bulkheads'll do the trick. Can't really make 'em water*tight*, but they'll survive a lot bigger hole. Put in our better Lemurian pumps, and they'll only have to handle the seepage past the flooded compartment."

"You don't sound enthusiastic," Matt observed. "We've used captured Grik ships before, particularly after you and our 'Cat friends made improvements. The cut-down 'Indiamen' make good DEs."

"Yeah, but this is different." Spanky rubbed his eyes with his knuckles. "Maybe I'm too much of an old destroyerman," he allowed. "I like fast an' skinny over slow an' fat, and with the weapons we've got now, these things are sitting ducks. They're god-awful big and powerfully armed—though the guns are still rough as hell. As liable to burst as shoot. And wait till you see the power plant! The boilers aren't bad, maybe even as good as Imperial boilers, but the engines are so crude, they look like some blind Chinaman sculpted 'em out o' river mud an' baked 'em in a kiln!"

"They do seem to work, though, don't they?"

"I don't see how, unless they're constantly squirtin' gallons o' grease on 'em."

"But they *do* work, Spanky," Matt insisted sternly.

"I guess," Spanky grudged. "Some of 'em. The ones aboard here don't, and I figure that's why they left her. Same on the other 'prize,' though it was kinda sunk in the shallows too. No big holes, so we were able to pump her out. I bet some of our bombs opened enough seams that the onboard pumps couldn't handle the flow."

Matt looked at his watch, then glanced at Sandra. "Okay, Spanky. Give us the nickel tour. Then we've got to get over to *Big Sal*."

"Eat?" Petey inquired, almost politely. He'd risen from his perch, sniffing around, but the mention of *Big Sal* got his attention. He always associated her with good food.

"Soon," Sandra assured him, patting his head.

Spanky quickly led them to the engineering spaces, and Matt realized he hadn't been exaggerating. All the great iron castings were amazingly crude, complete with voids and bubbles. But the contraption had clearly worked, and he remembered that a lot of their own early machinery hadn't looked much better. They toured the gun decks and walked among the monstrous, rough-cast guns. If anything, the headroom was even more limited there. Matt paused several times to look at splintered timbers that showed where Allied shot had struck the armor on the other side. This ship must've been one of the first to arrive, a veteran of the First Battle of Madras that drove the Allies out. He wondered briefly if Jim Ellis's lost *Dowden* had done this damage. He shook his head. It didn't matter.

"Skipper?" Spanky asked in a tone that implied he was repeating himself.

"Mr. McFarlane?"

"You want to go to the bridge? Not much there but a wheel and a repeater."

"No. Not unless there's anything unusual. We really need to get going."

"Okay. Actually, the only 'unusual' stuff we found is the wireless shack, aft, I told you about already, and . . . well, I think I found the captain's cabin. Pretty sure there was a Jap in there, judging by the bed and a few personal items. Bastard must've left in a hurry."

"So your survey's complete?"

"Aye, sir."

"And your recommendation?"

Spanky spread his hands. "I don't really know. I'm tryin' to keep an open mind. The engine's junk, like I said, and so's the main armament. You probably noticed all those empty slots where guns used to be? I bet they burst, and that makes 'em as dangerous to the crews servin' 'em as to the enemy. Frankly, I gotta recommend we break her up for the iron." He paused before continuing. "That said, the hull's sound. Just because I can't think of anything to use it for right off doesn't mean our 'Cat engineers can't. One of 'em even suggested we make a kind of 'attack carrier' out of her, sorta like *Big Sal* acted like during First Madras. Protect her against long-range fire, maybe plate the flight deck, and put some of our new four-inch-fifties on her, as they come out of Baalkpan. They might even add some of the heavier rifled guns they're working on—though I don't think they've settled on muzzle-loaders or bag guns. Muzzle-loaders are easier to make, but you can load the bag guns from the breech, behind protection. Either way, make something like that out of both prizes, reengine 'em, and convert 'em to burn oil. *That* might be pretty slick."

Matt nodded, smiling. "Okay, that's what we'll do: give the 'Cat engineers their head. They know what they're doing, and they've earned the chance. God knows they're coming up with new angles on old ideas faster than we are nowadays."

"With respect, Skipper, for you and them, part of that might be because there's a lot fewer of *us* left to experiment on stuff."

"Could be, Spanky," Matt answered sadly, his smile vanishing, "and liable to be fewer after this next push. C'mon, let's get out of here."

Matt was still in a dark mood when they emerged on the gangway, back in the clean air and bright sunshine. When he turned to salute the colors again, however, he paused and pointed at the Jap-Grik flag. "Have somebody run up there and tear that damn rag down!" he told the Lemurian still stationed there.

"Ay, ay, Cap-i-taan!"

They finally reached the gangway to board USNRS *Salissa* (CV-1). The vessel had once been a great seagoing "Home" for thousands, with high pagoda-like apartments within three tall tripod masts supporting huge sails, or "wings." *Salissa*, or *"Big Sal"* as the first American destroyermen dubbed her, had been rebuilt into the first aircraft carrier on this world after her near destruction by the Japanese Imperial battle cruiser *Amagi* during the Battle of Baalkpan Bay. Ironically, sunken *Amagi*'s steel had gone into creating the thousand-foot ship's power plant, as well as much of her other machinery. *Amagi* continued contributing a great deal to the cause of defeating her former Grik/Japanese masters. Other carriers had since been converted or purpose built; two more were under repair in this very harbor. But *Salissa* was the first, and her people had been the first that *Walker*'s ever met on this world. Matt, Sandra, and Spanky were going aboard now to confer with all the commanders or their representatives on this front, but most especially their dear friends "Ahd-mi-raal" Keje-Fris-Ar, *Salissa*'s High Chief, and Adar, who, though now High Chief and Sky Priest of Baalkpan, and Chairman of the Grand Alliance, had once merely been *Salissa*'s High Sky Priest.

"Good morning, Captain Reddy, Commander Reddy, Commander McFarlane," came a Brooklyn-accented voice behind them. They turned before mounting the gangway.

"Pam!" Sandra greeted the other woman happily. Pam Cross was *Walker's* surgeon, but she'd been ashore in a makeshift hospital ever since the battle—as had Sandra. But there'd been so many wounded, several hospitals had been established, and the two women hadn't seen much of each other.

"Good morning, Lieutenant Cross," Matt said with a smile, returning her salute. "Glad you could get away." The conference was more than just a meeting of commanders. Matt wanted as many department heads as possible from the various ships, particularly those slated for the mission, to attend as well.

"At least we're not the only ones late!" Sandra giggled.

"Well, yah, maybe you are." Pam grinned. "I been waitin' down here for ya, smokin' these PIG-cigs." She grimaced and flicked one of the smoldering things into the dirty water alongside. "PIG" was an acronym for the Pepper, Isak, and Gilbert Smoking Tobacco Co. It was named after the 'Cat and two very strange men who'd perfected a secret process for removing the vile, waxy coating that prevented Lemurian tobacco from being smoked. Considering the terrible, ammonia-tinged taste and smell of the cigarettes Pepper produced (he was in charge of manufacture), the nickname was probably permanent. "Nasty, yucky things," Pam muttered. "I ain't sure if you ought'a give those guys a medal for makin' 'Cat tobacco smokable, er throw 'em in irons! Anyway, I figured I'd just wait here. The big huddle won't start without you guys." She looked beyond them. "You all by yourselves? Where's the 'Captain's Guard'?"

"We sent Chief Gray ahead, and the rest of the fellas have plenty to do. No need for them to waste time watching us." Matt chuckled.

"So Silva ain't back yet?"

Matt and Sandra both knew Dennis Silva, a powerful, dangerous, and at least moderately depraved chief gunner's mate, and Surgeon Lieutenant Pam Cross still had a "thing," even if they'd tried to hide it.

"Back?" Matt asked, realizing Silva probably would've tagged along with them as one of their more dedicated guards if he wasn't off doing something else.

Pam waved a hand. "Oh, never mind. What's it to me? I'll be happy to escort you aboard, now you're here."

Big Sal's spacious admiral's quarters doubled as a conference room, and it was packed when the four of them entered to applause. Matt's face heated. He was uncomfortable with that kind of attention, and despite all that had gone before, the level it had reached from here to Maa-ni-la was kind of new. He consoled himself with the rationalization that the recent victory remained cause for celebration and they hadn't all been together like this since. Besides, he wasn't necessarily the focus of the praise, as much as he represented—almost personified—his ship, her people, and all they'd accomplished together. That was traditional and normal, and therefore a little more acceptable to him. Furthermore, since *Walker's* participation in the most recent battle had been somewhat limited, he suspected the greater share of enthusiasm reflected the popularity of the mission they were about to undertake. Pam peeled off, and Matt, Sandra, and Spanky nodded and smiled as they moved through the crowd toward the large central table.

Keje was standing, grinning hugely. He wore his Navy white tunic and kilt without his armor for once, and his dark, rust-colored fur contrasted starkly with the fabric. Beside him, taller and much thinner than his lifelong friend, stood Chairman Adar. As always, he was dressed in what had long been irreverently referred to as his "Sky Priest suit," consisting of a hooded robe, dark purple with embroidered stars flecked across the shoulders. The metallic eyes set in the gray fur covering his face looked tired but pleased and excited. Other faces Matt knew well beamed back at him from around the table. Pete Alden, former Marine sergeant aboard the doomed USS *Houston*, and now general of the Allied armies and Marines, nodded with a smile on his haggard face. He and Matt had spoken often in the last few days. Beside him was General Queen Protector Safir Maraan of B'mbaado, commanding what remained of II Corps. Matt hadn't seen her since the battle, but he knew she'd been lightly wounded. She didn't show it, resplendent as always in a new silver-washed cuirass and black cape and kilt that accentuated her shape, deep ebony fur, and bright silver eyes that blinked happily at him from her exotic face. Matt knew she'd been informed that this meeting would confirm that she and her Corps would participate in what had originally been proposed as a strong raid, but was now shaping into something a little more ambitious. Perhaps just as important to her, she'd finally join her long-absent love, Chack-Sab-At, now preparing for their arrival at the island of Diego Garcia.

Next to her, his hand protectively on her shoulder, was General Lord Muln Rolak of Aryaal. Enemies before the Great War, they'd grown as close as father and daughter. Matt looked carefully and saw that Rolak's old, battle-scarred face did not look pleased. He suddenly reflected that Lemurians really were a lot more expressive than he'd originally thought. Their tails, ears, and patterns of blinking conveyed a wealth of body language, but after more than two years among them, he'd learned to spot very subtle facial expressions as well. Rolak, always urbane and stoic, was better at hiding even those small motions than most, but he'd doubtless heard that his I Corps wouldn't be making the trip. At least not at first.

Elsewhere around the table were other familiar faces. One of them was Colonel Ben Mallory, currently commanding the 3rd Pursuit Squadron, but still in charge of all Army and Navy air. The pride of the 3rd remained a dwindling number of P-40E Warhawks, salvaged from a Chill-chaap swamp. Matt noted that he seemed to be brooding about something. Beside him was Commander Jis-Tikkar, or "Tikker," COFO of *Big Sal*'s 1st Naval Air Wing. With them was Lieutenant Commander Mark Leedom, a hot pilot who'd once been a torpedoman, but who'd stay behind to command Pete's combined Army and Navy air. His expression was a lot like Ben's, and Matt suspected he knew the source of Colonel Mallory's displeasure.

There were more, all of them men and 'Cats Matt knew well. Just "regular guys" who'd become heroes, leaders of a generation from two worlds—or was it more? he absently asked himself—caught up in an unimaginably bitter war for survival. He loved most of them like family. They *were* his family, he realized, and far too many were gone forever. Finally, he nodded at Commander Simon Herring, their "new" director of strategic intelligence. Herring remained inscrutable to Matt. He'd started as an insufferable martinet, opposed to the raid as originally conceived, but now, apparently, one of Matt's biggest strategic supporters. He shook his head and looked around. *Where's Courtney? He should be here, and a lot of us are waiting to hear his theories about, well, a lot of recent revelations.* He frowned.

Courtney Bradford was an Australian petroleum engineer, rescued from Java during the Old War. More important, he was a naturalist and the Allied Minister of Science. He was an extremely valuable and engaging man, but if he had a fault, it was his unruly "stream of consciousness" thought process. Chief Gray, *Walker*'s "Super Bosun," once referred to Bradford's mind as a "BB in a vacuum cleaner," and it wasn't a bad metaphor. Matt had a few ideas about the discoveries Chack and Captain Garrett had made, based on his historical background, but Courtney had been hinting a lot lately about the "how" of it all. Matt sighed. *Most likely, he's on his hands and knees, following some bug around the jungle, and has completely forgotten about this meeting. As a matter of fact, that's probably where Silva is too. Protecting him. But Silva at least should've been keeping track of time!*

Adar sat, and so did everyone, quickly quieting as the conference began. "My friends, my people," Adar said, then added, "Gentlemen and ladies," for the benefit and chagrin of some of the Imperials present. Even Matt felt that jab. All Lemurians fought, male and female, indiscriminately. Many former Imperial women, once virtual slaves, were fighting now as well. Soon, the Empire of the New Britain Isles would have an integrated navy, at least. It was necessary, and only made sense—particularly as far as the 'Cats were concerned. To them, a female not allowed to do whatever a male could do was not as free as the male. It was that simple. "We are here to announce the final dispositions for what I hope might prove a decisive campaign against the hated Grik!" Adar continued. "Much has been decided already, including the straa-ti-gee and objective." He glanced at Herring. "Doubtless, many of you have guessed those dispositions already, but I must stress the need for secrecy. Not only is it sadly possible the Doms, who can infiltrate our ranks quite easily, might make use of what they learn, but we are now in almost daily contact with the Grik across"—he blinked concern at Alden—"across the cease-fire line that separates our forces from theirs in Indiaa. I do not expect the . . . truce . . . to hold for long, but in the meantime, we must guard our words!"

Alden and Rolak nodded. They'd learned a lot about the Grik from their brief talks with General Halik, and even more from "General" Niwa, Halik's Japanese friend now in their care. But Halik was sharp. He might've learned just as much from them.

"Ultimately, it is most important that Halik not know we shift any focus from him. He will only see our strength here grow, and must not suspect we divert any to another front." He blinked compassion at Rolak. "This is one reason you and General Alden must remain. He knows you both, and he could miss you from the talks if you leave. But he has not met our dear Queen Protector Safir Maraan. Besides, when we *do* strike Halik again, we will need you here," he finished brusquely. He understood why Alden agreed to a cease-fire, but the very thought of an accommodation with the Grik struck him as perverse. He wanted Alden and Rolak to resume the offensive as quickly as possible. Adar looked at Matt. "And, of course, we are not taking a great deal of our strength on this mission in any event. Cap-i-taan Reddy?"

"That's right, Mr. Chairman. We'll take more than originally planned so we'll be ready if a big opportunity pops, but with more troops coming in here all the time, the departure of Second Corps shouldn't make a difference." Matt didn't point out that II Corps had been decimated, and it too would be composed largely of replacements and new recruits, but he saw Safir's predatory grin when he confirmed she was going. He smiled at her. "I understand you want to take cavalry. I agree that's a good idea; the Grik don't seem to like it at all, and it gives us an edge when it comes to recon, rapid deployment, and screening troop movements. But I'm still not sure how that's going to work. We're talking about a long voyage. How will we keep 'meanies' from going nuts and trying to eat our crews?"

There was laughter. Me-naaks, or "meanies," were cavalry mounts indigenous to the Fil-pin Lands, and looked like long-legged crocodiles with an armored case protecting their abdomens. They were notoriously ill-tempered, and usually wore muzzles to keep them from biting even their riders in combat.

Safir smiled back at him. "It required a long voyage to get them *here*," she reminded, "and I'm told that they will remain quite happy aboard ship as long as they are well fed." She glanced at a Lemurian standing behind her. "And besides, I have grown to value Major Saach-ic's services—and valor." By all accounts, Saachic had become one hell of a "cav-'Cat," but Matt figured he would've blushed at the praise if he could.

"What am I supposed to use for cav?" Pete protested. Matt looked down the table at a large, wildly bearded man named Dalibor Svec, and raised his eyebrows. Svec styled himself a colonel in what he called the "Brotherhood of Volunteers," and even though his "brotherhood" was primarily composed of a previously unknown continental tribe of Le-murians, some of his people were obviously—somehow—aging veter-ans of what Matt remembered as the Czech Legion. From previous conversations, Matt had learned that Svec's Czechs and Slovaks had been involved in that bizarre odyssey at the end of the Great War (back home) when sixty-odd thousand of his comrades, fighting with the Rus-sians, had been stranded on the Eastern Front when the Bolsheviks made a separate peace with Germany. His people were promised safe conduct out of their positions, but when Trotsky tried to arrest them and take their arms, they rebelled. The "Legion" had been spread out up and down the Trans-Siberian Railroad by that time, and fought a series of bitter battles against the Bolsheviks to consolidate their forces at Vladivostok. Matt knew what happened next, but Svec and his two hun-dred or so riflemen never did. It was during that time they'd somehow wound up on this different earth.

Matt was fascinated by Svec's story of how his people survived, join-ing forces with Lemurians who'd once inhabited northern India—driven there, and then still farther by the encroaching Grik they didn't dare confront—and he was anxious to hear more. He was particularly inter-ested to learn why they wound up where they did and, well, *how.* Svec's people were the first they'd ever encountered who didn't come to this world by sea. Irritation flashed. That was another reason he'd wanted Courtney here! The Australian had heard of the legionnaires, but hadn't talked to them yet. Matt focused back on Svec. Infantryman or not, he and all his people, human and Lemurian, had become outstanding cav-alry, riding beasts every bit as frightening-looking as me-naaks, even if they weren't carnivores. They'd been poorly armed with crude flintlocks for the most part, built in their primitive, nomadic villages, but they also had a few old Moisen Nagants. They retained ancient knowledge of the region, as well as a tradition of surveillance. They even attacked isolated groups of Grik when the opportunity arose to do so without leaving witnesses, so they knew the country very well. They'd just "shown up" at the climax of the battle for Alden's Perimeter, after apparently watching for some time, waiting to see if the Allies truly had a chance against their hereditary enemy. Convinced now that they did, they were anxious to get on with it, and were just as frustrated as Adar by Pete's cease-fire.

"What's your current strength, Colonel Svec?" Matt asked.

"A full brigade," Svec said proudly in heavily accented English. It was good that he spoke it, since his Lemurians and Matt's could barely understand one another. "Two regiments as you count such things. More are coming now."

"Good. You've been under Saachic's command since you arrived, but can you do without him?" What Matt meant was, "Will you *cooperate* without him watching over you?" Svec smiled. "My volunteers will behave," he assured, "now that we know the fight is not over, just postponed. We understand well the need to gather one's strength!" He gestured around. "And we know you do not really make peace with the Gaarik." His expression darkened. "Our friends have made peace with our enemies before, and at first, we thought that was the case again. Now we know it is not, we will cooperate fully with General Alden, and eagerly await the day we can kill the Gaarik and drive him from this land at last!"

"Fine," Matt said, glancing meaningfully at Pete, making sure he'd caught the implied impatience. Now that Svec and his "volunteers" had powerful allies, it wasn't beyond the realm of possibility that they might precipitate an end to the cease-fire if it dragged on too long. He took a breath and resumed. "Otherwise, besides the assets already at Diego, which I won't go into, *Salissa* and her air wing will be going, of course. Repairs to *Arracca* and *Baalkpan Bay* are almost complete, and they should be sufficient to protect our naval forces with their air power, particularly with the better bombs." He looked at Tassanna-Ay-Arracca, *Arracca*'s High Chief. "As soon as possible, I'd like you to take your battle group and blockade the western ports of Indiaa." Tassanna blinked appreciation. She was still very young for a High Chief, and what Matt was suggesting amounted to her very first independent command. "As for the battle group that will accompany *Salissa . . .*" He paused, noting how the tension ratcheted up among the frigate, or "DD" skippers. "*Walker* goes, obviously, but so does . . . Destroyer Squadron Six," he announced. The statement was received by whoops and groans. It was interesting that the disappointed ones were those not going. Everyone wanted in on this show. "That's about it. We sail in ten days. With any luck, we'll get our licks in before the Grik anywhere else get a clue what's happened here." He looked at Keje. "You'll organize whatever auxiliaries we need, oilers and tenders and such?"

"Of course." Keje beamed. "I have grown good at that!" He glanced at Atlaan-Fas, *Salissa*'s Lemurian CO, and Lieutenant Newman, her exec. "Or at least those persons have!" Matt smiled back at him. In the growing noise that followed, Lieutenant Commander Irvin Laumer approached the table and stood by his arm.

"Yes, Commander?" Matt asked, a little surprised. The Skipper of destroyed S-19, who'd put so much of himself into the old sub, looked terrible. He was taking the loss of his ship and much of his crew very hard.

"What about me, sir?" he asked quietly. "I'd . . . I'd like to go."

Matt studied him. "Honestly, Mr. Laumer, I thought you'd like to have one of the new destroyers building in Baalkpan." At that moment, two nearly exact copies of *Walker* and *Mahan* were within a month or two of launching. The builders had had a lot of practice working on the ships that inspired them, and they'd even come up with improvements. It would take time to fit them out, but the ships should be ready for sea in four months at most. Matt considered the offer a reward for Laumer's conduct.

"I appreciate it, sir, but"—he leaned down to whisper—"I learned a lot using my boat as a torpedo gun boat, and I'd like one of the PTs waiting at Diego." Matt pursed his lips. The PTs were probably the worst-kept secret in the Alliance. He leaned back in his chair and arched his eyebrows. "Okay."

As soon as Laumer stepped away, Adar rose. "Just as Cap-i-taan Reddy has said, that is about it. Thank you for coming. You will receive your orders." He seemed to be trying to divert further requests, but as soon as Matt stood, Ben Mallory braced him. "So what about *me*?"

"What about you, Ben?"

Mallory eased Matt away from the table. "You're jumping right down the shark's throat on this one, sir. You're going to *need* me—and at least a few of my modern birds."

Matt nodded. "And I wish we could take them, though I think *you'd* still need to stay here. But the question is, what would we do with them?"

"Well, you can fly 'em off *Big Sal* if you have to!"

"*Once*, Ben," Matt stated flatly. "Just one time. And what then? Where will they land? They can't set back down on *Big Sal*!"

"Well . . . there's got to be someplace on the whole damn island of Madagascar—" He looked around and lowered his voice, as if one or two people in the compartment might not know where they were going. "There's got to be someplace we can set down!"

"But what if it's someplace we can't get to, where we can't fuel them, where we have to *leave* them!"

"We wouldn't leave them in one piece, Captain!"

"I don't want to leave them at all, damn it!"

"Then take that silly damn thing we put those Jap floats on!" Ben insisted. "It looks weird as hell, but it'll still be faster than anything else you have, and can carry more ordnance!" One of the P-40s had been damaged, and after the landing gear was removed, a pair of floats salvaged from *Amagi*'s hangars had been attached.

Matt grinned. "We already did. It went to Diego aboard *Respite Island*, with the PTs."

"Then I should go!" Ben repeated. "Who can fly a P-Forty or a floatplane better than me?"

Matt put his hand on his shoulder. "Not you, Ben. Things can still spin out of control here, and nothing we've got can hammer the Grik better than your Warhawks. Besides, if we wind up in a situation that needs air power to get us out, I don't care where it is, I'll rely on you to come through." He said the last almost jokingly, but he was serious, and Ben knew it.

The meeting broke up, with officers hurrying toward their commands. Matt and Sandra were stepping back down the gangplank when they caught up with Pam again. She was looking around, scanning the pier and the ruins beyond.

"So," Matt asked casually, "where did Silva go, anyway?"

"I'm not so sure now. He *said* he was goin' fishin'." She took a deep breath and shrugged.

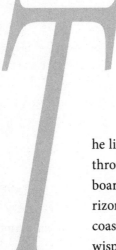he little sloop-rigged gri-kakka boat pounded briskly through the choppy sea on a stiff breeze from the starboard quarter. The sun had risen above the empty horizon to the east and glared sharp and bright at the coast of India a dozen miles off the port beam. High, wispy clouds scudded swiftly across a mostly clear sky, and it was probably barely eighty degrees. Without question, it was absolutely the finest day to play hooky that they could've ever hoped for.

The boat was only eight tails long—about twenty-five feet—and the occupants—four men, two 'Cats, and a single Grik-like Sa'aaran—were having a thrilling sail. Perhaps more thrilling than one or two might prefer. The giant Chief Gunner's Mate Dennis Silva, dressed only in cutoffs, a black eye patch, and his ever-present web belt festooned with Colt pistol, 1917 cutlass, and 1903 Springfield bayonet, stood in the bow, whooping with glee. His shouts were sometimes muffled by the packets of spray sluicing back to drench everyone in the boat. The much smaller Sa'aaran, Lawrence, or "Larry the Lizard," crouched beside him, orange-and-brown tiger-striped feathery fur soaked and plastered to his body. He didn't look as happy as Silva, but there was a predatory gleam in his eyes. He also looked much more reptilian than usual with his fur and moderate tail plumage flattened. A little farther back, Courtney Bradford, a wide sombrero tied on his balding head, stared forward with excited fascination. Earl Lanier, *Walker's* bloated, irascible cook, was in the center of the boat where he'd been ordered to remain "as ballast." He was furious, but also grimly determined not to spew. He was an obsessive fisherman, and the outing had been his idea, after all. Gunnery Sergeant Arnold Horn, late of the 4th Marines, had no interest in the proceedings whatsoever, and didn't care what anybody thought. He was leaning over the lee rail, practically in the water at times, washing his breakfast out of the black beard covering his face. The little boat's crew, 'Cat lance hurlers from one of the bigger fishing feluccas contracted to carry freight to Madras from Baalkpan, only seemed amused.

"There must be a dozen of the buggers!" Courtney gushed. "And we do seem to be gaining at last!"

Silva looked back. "What?" he roared.

"We're getting closer!"

"Damn straight! We'll be close enough to give 'em a poke di-rectly! No, Earl, goddamn it! Stay put for now. You heave your fat ass up forward an' push her head down, you'll slow us up. Boogers'll get plumb away!"

"The hell you say!" Earl ranted with an emphatic, universal gesture. "I hired this boat, an' it's my fishin' trip! I just allowed you guys to tag along."

"Hired with what? The fish we get! An' you sure as hell ain't gettin' one on your own!"

All this was true. An absolute fiend for fishing, Earl had arranged the enterprise to "catch" a gri-kakka—or the local equivalent no 'Cat had ever taken. But gri-kakka were monstrous things, a type of plesiosaur, and this particular species was about the size of a right whale. Their value to Lemurians was similar to whales as well, as they rendered their fat for oil, but also harvested their flesh. The economies of the great seagoing Homes were largely dependent on them. Fishing feluccas made their living filling their holds with flasher fish, or any of a number of smaller, edible sea creatures. But flashies wouldn't keep, and felucca skippers were always happy to get a few dozen barrels of gri-kakka oil if the opportunity arose—especially when returning empty to Baalkpan.

Earl smoldered.

"Those are '*ig* hish!" Lawrence said quietly to Silva. He understood English as well as anyone, and spoke it perfectly as well—except for words that required lips. He actively tried to avoid those.

"The bigger they are, the more satisfyin' the dance!" Silva proclaimed, but he saw Lawrence's curious gaze. "The fancier they flop!" he explained happily. "You know, like a super lizard! Damn things fall like a redwood tree!"

"You *are* crazy," Lawrence observed, then flicked his tail. "So long as they don't 'lop on us."

Silva cocked his head philosophically. "We'll just hafta be careful."

Lawrence snorted. "Care'ul, you?"

"You ain't goin' chikkin on me, are you, Larry?"

"Not chikkin. 'Ut e'en that hish doesn't 'lop on us, Ca'tain Reddy is going to, us get 'ack. He *ordered* you not to do this, long ago." He nodded back toward Courtney. "And you take Courtney too! Ca'tain'll go nuts!"

Silva frowned. Lawrence was right. This was one of the few times—in his opinion—he might've let one of his little stunts go just a tad over the top. But what it all boiled down to was that he'd been bored. Well, not *bored* exactly; he had plenty to do, but he'd been a "good boy" for an unnaturally long time, doing his duty and generally behaving himself in an entirely unprecedented manner. He no longer felt the need to disobey orders on general principle; he was loyal to the Skipper and his ship, and even the cause they fought for. He *admired* Captain Reddy. But after all, he was Dennis Silva, and a certain degree of "over-the-top" was expected of him on a fairly regular basis. If he didn't pull something now and then, he figured he was letting his shipmates down, and he rationalized that his occasional harmless stunts were important for morale. They were certainly important for *his* morale, and that counted for something, didn't it? An unhappy Silva made for an unhappy—and nervous—crew.

Then there was the whole "Pam angle" to consider. He guessed he was maybe a little in love with the spunky little broad, but part of "the deal" he made with her was that she had to quit trying to turn him into . . . anything other than what he was. He needed stunts like this now and then to emphasize to everybody, and maybe Pam most of all, that no matter what, he was still Dennis Silva.

"Yeah," he finally answered, "but that ain't my fault. Just like he's done before, Courtney found out what was up and said he'd blow if we didn't take him to watch." He glared back at Bradford. "No principles—no honor amongst scamps, so ta speak. He *blackmailed* me. Again! Ever-thing was set, an' he just showed up and jumped in the boat. Hell, you *saw*! What was I s'posed to do?"

"You should ha' thrown he out on the dock. Ca'tain's going to hear o' this any'ay. He'll just get angrier now."

"Why the hell didn't you say so at the time, damn it? I swear. What good does it do for one of us to think ahead if he don't warn the other?"

Lawrence nodded at Gunny Horn. "He thought ahead, said us shouldn't go at all."

Silva looked at his—currently wretched—Marine friend. Horn was almost as big as Silva, if not as tall. "Yeah, but he let a whole ship fall on him not too long ago."

"So did us!"

"That was different. We were inside. He was outside, an' shoulda' seen it comin'. Besides, his thinkin' ahead hasn't always worked out so well in other ways," he added cryptically, again referencing some event from the pair's past that remained mysterious. He faced forward. "An' we're here now," he said, voice rising as he became exuberant once more. "Just *look* at those damn fish!"

The closest creature was barely three boat lengths ahead now, slowly rising and falling in the swells, making a respectable four or five knots. Silva could finally get a good look at it. At a glance, he'd have thought it was a whale . . . of some sort . . . in the old days. The smooth skin on its back was a dark bluish black, and what he saw of it moved like a whale as well. On closer inspection, however, it was clear it had no long tail with flukes, but rather four massive fins that propelled it with a striking grace for something so large. There was another fin, kind of long and low, down the center of its back that didn't look very whalelike either, but the weirdest thing was how far forward the periodic, rainbow-washed spume rose in the air when it blew. Obviously, these "pleezy-sores," as Silva called them, were the type with long necks usually ending in relatively small heads, given their overall size, that were often armed with a frightening array of teeth. If that was the case, they probably weren't as aggressive as the sort without long necks. Those had been known to seek out and destroy boats the size they were in. Despite that, and despite the apparently oblivious placidity with which the pod moved, they'd learned that virtually all sea creatures on this world were shockingly dangerous.

"Oh, look!" Courtney gushed, shouldering his way forward. "Look at it move! Amazing! And there! That fin seems to extend a remarkable distance forward, perhaps all the way to the head! I predict they use it much like a rudder, or shifting keel!"

"You reckon they just naturally go whichever way they're lookin'?"

"Indeed!"

Silva grunted. That might be so, but that long neck probably left them vulnerable to the kind without one, he thought. It might also be why they didn't tend to attack large prey as aggressively.

"You better pick a good-un!" Earl shouted from amidships. "I didn't charter this jaunt to catch a minnow!"

"Draw yer fires, Earl. They're all whoppers. This first one's as big as any, I guess. You might as well come on up here an' take yer shot. Mr. Bradford, you better ease on back an' take his place. If anybody gets yanked er knocked over the side, I'd rather it was him."

Courtney reluctantly obeyed, and Earl went forward, clutching a long, wickedly barbed harpoon.

"You stick'em in front o' body," the 'Cat at the tiller reminded loudly. "Up close to neck. Lots o' blood hoses there. You stick'em in body, you pop air sack, he sink like rock. We lose! We run up on his back, you stick'eem right then!"

"In other words, don't miss!" Silva warned.

"I won't miss, you rotten skunk's ass!" Lanier sneered.

"Make ready," the 'Cat cried again. The other 'Cat bounded forward, tail high, and hooked a line on Earl's harpoon. He quickly paid out a couple dozen fathoms of the bright-colored rope, holding it looped in his hand, then took a quick turn around a heavy rounded post at the bow. With Earl's bulk forward, the boat actually was slowing, but it was time to do so at any rate. The great fish was right there, rising almost beneath them, and with a heeling jolt, the boat grounded on its back.

"Now!" cried the 'Cats.

"*Now*, you gallopin' glob o' lard," Silva urged happily.

Earl Lanier must've been practicing for this. With surprising ease, he raised the harpoon, angled the four-bladed tip downward, and launched it on a two-handed, straight-line drive deep into the flesh forward of what had to be some kind of massive shoulder blade. Earl might be obese, but no one ever thought he was weak. He had to be fairly strong just to heave himself around, didn't he?

"Hold on!" trilled the 'Cat in the bow, just as the monster exploded in a frenzy of motion. Something slammed the bottom of the boat, and white water erupted around them like a depth charge. "He gonna run now," added the 'Cat, matter-of-factly.

There was considerable elasticity in the line attached to the harpoon, and the turn around the post acted as a kind of clutch, but when the line went taut, everyone tumbled into the bottom of the boat as it practically jerked out from under them.

"Whoo-eee!" Silva roared, scrambling back to his perch amid the froth and spray.

"Down sails!" shrieked the 'Cat at the tiller in Lemurian, and the other 'Cat shouted at Silva to keep tension on the line around the post. "Let it slip some," he warned, "till that fish run outa gas. Udderwise, he yank the boat in two! Throw water on it, it start to smoke!" Not much need for that, with all the water splashing in. Silva took the line and the 'Cat scampered aft and released the halyard. The mainsail rattled down the mast. He quickly bundled it and lashed it to the boom, then lowered what the humans would've called a jib. Lawrence tried to bundle it as it flapped in the breeze, and soon the boat was bare-poled, slashing through the sea at ten or twelve knots. Most of the other gri-kakka veered away as their quarry plunged forward, but the boat suddenly slammed across the back of a beast that hadn't yet. A great head on the end of a slender, finned neck reared from the sea, striking down with a gaping mouth full of six-inch, needle-sharp teeth, ideal for catching fish. They appeared just as efficient at snatching people, and nearly got Gunny Horn.

"Goddamn!" he yelped, throwing himself away from the beam where he'd crawled to resume his misery when the boat took off. His discomfort finally in perspective, he struggled forward to join Silva.

"Damn thing nearly got me!" he accused.

Silva, still straining at the line, took in his bright-eyed anger and grinned. "Cured your sea-sick, though, didn't he? Damn, Arnie, it's about time you got in the game an' quit loungin' on the deck chairs!" He looked at Horn. "I always thought the whole reason for Marines was havin' soldiers on a boat!"

"On *ships*, you maniac. Not wood chips like this!"

"Marine pukery," Silva accused severely. "Dis-gustin'. Ain't that right up there with dereflection o' duty an' wastin' beer? Help Larry with that jib before it beats him ta death, wilya?"

Still a little green, Horn moved to comply while the 'Cat made his way forward with a bundle of long, sharp lances. He laid them down, points projecting over the bulwark.

"I thought we was just goin' fishin'," Horn grumbled, looking at the plunging monster ahead, "not hunting sea monsters!"

"Every fish in this sea is a sea monster o' some sort, you stupid gyrene. Ain't you figgered that out yet?" Earl barked scathingly. "Hell, what do you think I feed you devils half the time? Friggin' guppies? Most o' what you guys eat as *meat* started out as somethin' like that!" He pointed at the plesiosaur.

Horn hadn't been a shipboard Marine very long, and didn't know that stuff, but it explained a lot. "Rhino pig" tasted like normal pork, but a lot of what they ate didn't taste normal at all. He'd written that off to Lanier's cooking.

"He gettin' tired, run outa blood," the 'Cat judged. "Gri-kakka blood all fat an' slippery. Squirt out fast. We start heavin' in now."

The 'Cat, Earl, Larry, Horn, and even Courtney joined Silva on the line, and started hauling the boat, hand over hand, closer to the wounded monster.

"Is he gonna flip out when we get up to him?" Silva asked, his voice strained. He suspected he was doing most of the work.

"I not know what that mean. He flip boat? Maybe yes."

"Swell," Horn muttered. "I've been told that getting in the water is a bad thing?"

"You've been told right. We'll all be dead!" Silva replied cheerfully.

"Swell."

The fish didn't flip them, although it came close once. Earl's throw had been amazingly well placed and the creature was weakening fast, but a convulsive slap from a hind flipper nearly tipped them over. Earl Lanier hurled himself down in the bilge and the boat quickly righted. Ultimately, amid laughing fits at Earl's expense, they pulled right up alongside the great fish as its strokes became feebler. The line secured, Silva, Earl, and even Horn stood in the bow, lances poised.

"Up around his shoulders an' neck," Earl reminded like an expert. "Don't pop his bag an' sink him now, for God's sake!"

The first lance spurred a renewed surge from the beast, but it was short-lived, and among them, the three lancers quickly finished the fish. With a final great effort, it lifted its head from the sea and looked back, perhaps seeing its killers for the first time. Then, with a rasping moan, the great neck and head splashed back into the reddening sea.

For just a moment, they all stood there looking at what they'd done. There was pride of course; they were small and the fish was very large, and it wasn't like they hadn't risked their lives to kill it—but Silva didn't feel the visceral rush of satisfaction he often experienced after battle, or after killing a super lizard. Those were always contests between him and something trying to kill him. Even his rhino-pig hunts were fun because they'd kill him and eat him if they could. Gunny Horn might not agree, especially after one nearly got him, but to Silva, this had been more like chasing a swimming cow. He shrugged. Okay, so what? What if it was like killing a cow, for food and other things? The chase was fun—and the ride was a blast.

"We tie on quick, before flashies eat-eem up!" the 'Cat reminded. Already, a few silvery shapes were darting in to snatch away mouthfuls of flesh.

"How do we do that?" Earl asked.

"We get chain 'round he neck, just behind head. Then we make sail for Madras."

"I say, will there be enough of him left to view, at all? When we take him from the water, of course," Courtney asked.

The 'Cat looked at him like he was nuts. "We not take him from water!" he said. "We not a *Home*. We got no platform for that. We take what we get off him alongside our big boat."

Courtney frowned. "Pity. I'd so hoped . . ."

"What the hell's *that*?" Horn suddenly blurted, surprising everyone.

"What?" Silva demanded, looking around, confused.

"*That*, there in the water!"

"*Where* in the water, you nitwit? There's a helluva lot of water out there, you know."

"There, goddamn it!" He pointed. "Two hundred yards off the port bow. Don't you see it?"

"See what?" Silva insisted, squinting his eye. "I don't see shit."

Horn was still pointing, but he slumped. "It was there. I saw it. I . . . I think it's gone now."

"What the hell was it?"

"I think . . . I think it was a feather. "Isn't that what you call it? A periscope feather!"

"A periscope?" Earl goggled. "An' how the hell would you know what a periscope looks like? You're seein' things. Prob'ly just another pleezy-sore."

"I'm not making it up!" Horn stated emphatically.

"Well, perhaps it was a fin of some sort," Courtney suggested diplomatically. "A fin might certainly look like a periscope, I'm sure."

Horn wasn't convinced, and looked at Silva. "You believe me?"

"I b'lieve you seen somethin', Arnie, but Mr. Bradford's right. Prob'ly was a fish. What would a sub be doin' around here, anyway? We couldn't turn the old S-Nineteen back into a sub; no way them Jap-Griks built one from scratch!" He snorted. "An' if it was one, somebody else's, they'd've prob'ly figgered out the fix they're in by now, same as we had to. They'd've seen *us* for sure. Why not bob up an' say hello?"

Horn wasn't convinced. He *was* sure what he'd seen . . . or thought he was, anyway. He wished he felt better. Maybe his affliction had left him seeing things after all, and he couldn't answer Silva's question. Why wouldn't a sub that wound up on this world be glad to see them, and surface to say hello—unless they already knew what the situation was and they were on somebody else's side.

"C'mon," Silva gruffed. "Let's get this critter back." He looked strangely at Horn. "He'll prob'ly just write it off to your Marine-ness an' shameful pukery too, but I'll tell the Skipper you seen a periscope fish while he's tearin' strips offa me."

///// *Airborne*
Six Miles NNW of Guayak
New Granada Province
Holy Dominion
South America
June 17, 1944

Orrin Reddy's four-ship flight of PB-1B "Nancys" crossed the mountainous coastline at five thousand feet and turned north, paralleling the mighty peaks. The mountains here soared higher than aircrews could fly without oxygen, and since provisions for such were problematic for the open-cockpit Nancys, not to mention furry Lemurian faces, they formed a formidable barrier to observations of enemy activity in the interior. Certain passes could be used, but they were increasingly heavily guarded by what the Imperials called "dragons," or what the human/Lemurian "American" Navy and Marines probably more appropriately described as "Grikbirds." The things *looked* like Grik, with longer snouts and slightly different, if just as wicked teeth. Their feet sported talons better adapted to snatching prey than slashing it, and their plumage was much thicker, more colorful, and far better tailored for flight. Ultimately, the biggest physical difference between Grik and Grikbirds was that, instead of powerful arms with fingers and deadly claws, Grikbirds had broad, feathery, membranous wings, and could be very bad news for Nancys.

Nancys remained good little planes, considering they'd been in service for nearly two years with only minor modifications. They looked like miniature PBY Catalina floatplanes, from which their lines had been taken, and were powered by a single, four-cylinder, in-line "Wright-Gypsy"–type motor. The little engines were so reliable that they were being mass produced from Baalkpan to Maa-ni-la, with a new factory even setting up in the Empire of the New Britain Isles. They were used in everything from airplanes to powerboats, and heavier, more powerful versions had gone into the new "PTs," or motor torpedo boats, being built in the Fil-pin Lands. There was even talk of putting them in some kind of land vehicle.

Orrin contemplated that for a moment as he scanned the skies for enemies. His Lemurian Observer/Copilot (OC), Sergeant Kuaar-Ran-Taak, or "Seepy," in the other cockpit behind the high-wing-mounted engine and spinning pusher prop, would be watching behind them, as well as looking for troop movements on the coastal road below. Orrin wasn't sure how useful a land vehicle would be on this world. A sort of truck might be handy to haul stuff around in the cities—definitely more cooperative than the Asian elephant-size "brontosarries" they used for such things now. They might even be useful in places like the Empire, where there were good roads. He frowned. *Might use some here, if we can ever push out beyond our foothold at Guayak,* he thought. *It looks like the Doms have a few decent roads between their important cities, at least.* He shook his head. *Some kind of armored truck, or even a tank might be better for that. But making them and then getting them way the hell out here on the longest limb of the war probably isn't going to happen any time soon. Besides, given a choice, I'd rather have some of the new pursuit ships they're finally turning out!* He liked Nancys fine. They were good for what they'd been designed for, and they were even pretty good for ground attack and antiship operations. They could float too, which was a definite plus, but they *were* vulnerable to Grikbirds. They were faster than the Doms' flying lizards, but that was about it—and either the Grikbirds or their Dom trainers had figured out tactics to get around that. In response, Orrin's wing had finally received some of the new "Blitzer Bug" SMGs for the backseaters to use to keep the damn things off their backs. This was the first sortie, in fact, when every plane was so armed. And in addition to their scouting mission, Orrin hoped to find out how well the new weapons would defend his ships. He smiled ironically.

As a "mere" second lieutenant who refused a more exalted Navy rank, and actually still considered himself a member of the US Army Air Corps, Orrin Reddy was very much like Matt, his cousin, when it came to sheer stubbornness. His official rank didn't much matter to him or anyone else. He was Commander of Flight Operations (COFO) for the aircraft carrier/tender USS *Maaka-Kakja* (CV-4), and also like his cousin, he'd shouldered a lot more responsibility than the rank he'd accept would imply.

Orrin was different from Matt in other ways, many of them superficial. He was shorter, with lighter hair, considerably younger, and of course he'd gone Army instead of Navy. Since he'd been a prisoner of the Japanese in the Philippines, his arrival on this world aboard a hellish prison ship had been very different as well. As for personality, he had a lot of the "fighter jock" in him, but as a destroyer skipper, so did Matt to a degree. The biggest difference in that respect came with age, experience, and the fact that Matt had lost so many people under his command. That had given him a far better appreciation for the consequences of command. But Orrin was starting to learn that bitter lesson for himself.

"Ell-tee!" came Seepy's tinny shout through the voice tube by his ear. That was another aggravation. He'd heard the fliers in First Fleet had voice com now, and pilots could listen in on what their OCs, who also operated the airborne wireless transmitters, heard. Nobody had a voice transmitter small enough to fit in a plane yet, though First Fleet also had Talk Between Ships (TBS) capability now.

"Whatcha got, Seepy?" Orrin demanded, looking at the 'Cat in the little mirror that allowed him to see behind. Seepy was staring down through an Imperial telescope.

"More Dom in-faantry! They marchin' down that road outa the pass east o' here. We go down an' shoot 'em up? They is awful purty target!"

Orrin looked down. Sure enough, another long enemy column was snaking down out of the gap in the abruptly rising mountains. Even this high, their bright yellow and red, or white uniform tunics were clearly visible. There were lots of flags and pennants too, almost like some medieval army, flapping and flickering above the column and making it look like some fiery red and gold serpent. Although he couldn't see it now, he didn't doubt the whole force was marching behind another of the giant, grotesquely disfigured golden crosses they'd seen at the head of every arriving division. Orrin wasn't particularly religious, but he did recognize the thing for the perversion it was—and fully understood its significance to the troops behind it. He was sorely tempted to roll in and blast the thing. "No," he said with a reluctant grunt. "Not yet, anyway." General Tomatsu Shinya didn't want them bombing the Dom columns converging on Guayak. Orrin figured he wanted the enemy massed before they made such an attack, sucking as many of them into the killing field as he could before bringing on a major battle. Orrin didn't know if he agreed with that strategy or not.

First, and he just couldn't help it, but Shinya was a "Jap." He knew Matt liked and trusted Shinya, but Orrin had had an entirely different experience with the Japanese in the Philippines and didn't know if he could ever forgive them, one or all. Second, despite reinforcements from Second Fleet and the Enchanted Isles, the Allied Expeditionary Force at Guayak still numbered only about eighteen thousand men and 'Cats. There were already upward of forty thousand Dominion troops encircling the "rebel" city. Shinya and High Admiral Jenks were sure that deploying all those troops essentially *back* to this area from where they'd been drawn would weaken or at least delay the massive Dom fleet accumulating in the vicinity of El Paso del Fuego, most likely aimed at another attempt to take the Enchanted Isles. Those islands, better known to some as the Galápagos, constituted the Allies' best and most convenient staging point for operations against the Doms.

El Paso del Fuego had come as a stunning surprise, and Jenks was still trying to sort out its implications—and how to deal with them. They thought they'd destroyed the entire Dom fleet, but now they knew the bastards had a whole other one to draw from—in the *Atlantic*! The pass was a large navigable strait between South and Central America, carved through what should've been Costa Rica. It might have been caused by volcanism, or who knew what—they'd long since learned this world wasn't exactly like the old—but whatever made it, it was much, much larger than any Panama Canal. Apparently, it was plagued by terrific tidal races and was therefore only passable at certain times, but no one had ever even dreamed it existed. They hadn't been able to get close to the place with ships or planes, and if it hadn't been for Fred Reynolds's and Kari-Faask's escape from Dom captivity, they wouldn't have known about it at all until it was too late. Fred and Kari had told them a number of other interesting and useful things, but the existence of the pass was the most immediately pertinent. The two friends were still recuperating from their ordeal, but a day didn't pass that they didn't ask to be returned to flying status.

"Send it out," Orrin ordered. "Inform . . . General Shinya he'll soon have even more guests to entertain, but we've got other business today."

"Ay, ay," Seepy replied reluctantly. Orrin banked the Nancy slightly east, toward the mouth of the mountain pass the troops were flowing from. He glanced left to ensure the other planes followed his lead.

"Grikbirds! Grikbirds!" came Seepy's excited shout. "Ship number nine's got 'em, 'leven the clock high!"

Orrin looked up and a little to the left. Maybe a dozen dark shapes were hurtling down to converge on the four-ship flight. They were tucked in like stooping hawks and would've slashed through the formation, ripping wings, control surfaces, or bodies with their terrifying claws in mere seconds.

"Break right!" Orrin shouted, wrenching the little plane over. His order was unnecessary, and Seepy couldn't have relayed it in time in any case. Already alerted, the rest of the Nancys followed his lead, and the four planes quickly formed what was essentially a battle line in midair. The Grikbirds tried to compensate but were diving too fast and simply couldn't correct their angle of attack sufficiently. What resulted was much as Orrin hoped: all the creatures tried to throw on the brakes, flaring out to come at the flight from the side. Such a braking maneuver had to put a lot of stress on the monsters and was probably very painful. About half the Grikbirds gave up and retucked their wings, instinctively realizing their attack had failed. They plummeted away. The rest couldn't resist the equally strong instinct to drive their strike home, however, and for a moment they just hung there, their swoop having brought them up, their bleeding speed leaving them relatively motionless alongside the planes.

"Blast 'em, Seepy!" Orrin roared. Seepy had already yanked the bolt back on his Blitzer Bug, and he quickly sighted down the top of the tubular receiver. Almost simultaneously with the OCs in the other planes, he squeezed the trigger. Smoky tracers sprayed out with a rattling buzz. The little guns were hard to handle with their high rate of fire and heavy .45 ACP cartridges, but the ammunition was the same being issued to the new P-1 Mosquito Hawks (better known as "Fleashooters") in First Fleet for zeppelin hunting. The burning phosphorous in the base of the bullets meant to light hydrogen helped the shooters correct their fire. Two Grikbirds immediately folded, hammered by the heavy slugs. The rest beat their wings to close the gap as the shooters redirected their initially wild fusillade. Another Grikbird staggered, a shattered wing throwing it out of control. A fourth monster fell, its shrieks audible over the drone of the motors. The final two appeared to decide to go for Orrin's lead ship, probably thinking the others would scatter like any other flying prey they hunted.

"Empty!" cried Seepy, dropping a magazine out of the well of his weapon and groping for another in the vest he wore.

"Hang on!" Orrin yelled back. He knew the guns of the following planes would no longer bear. *Damn! We gotta get guns in the front of these things!* he raged to himself. His ship actually did have a .50-caliber machine gun in the nose, an "extra" that came to this world aboard *Santa Catalina*, but their current tactics wouldn't let him use it. He could never turn on the Grikbirds now; they were too close. He slammed the stick forward.

One Grikbird, terrifyingly close, barely missed snatching his port wing in its jaws. He knew all it had to do was get ahold of his plane and it would latch on, tearing it to shreds with claws and teeth even as it fell. It would jump away before the wreck hit the ground—but return to eat him and Seepy after the crash. He'd seen it before. He'd also learned very well how to combat other more maneuverable but slightly slower enemies while flying P-40s in the Philippines. In a steep dive now, he started to pull away from the Grikbirds that had tucked in to follow. Unlike in the Philippines, however, he could do something about pursuers here.

"Hose 'em, Seepy!" he shouted into the voice tube. "And make it snappy. The world's coming at us awful fast!" He was answered by a long *burrrp!* of the Blitzer Bug. A Grikbird tumbled and veered away in his mirror, but the last monster was actually closing! Just as bad, the ground was coming up fast, and Seepy wasn't shooting anymore.

"Seepy!" he demanded.

"I empty again! Gimme a minute!"

"We don't *have* one!"

"Okay! I ready! Pull up!"

Orrin hesitated. The ground was *right there*, but if he pulled up too abruptly, the Grikbird would have them almost instantly. He had no choice. Below, he saw the upturned faces of the Doms in the enemy column, watching the aerial battle overhead. They'd probably be shooting at him in a second. "Okay," he yelled. "Here goes!" He pulled back on the stick. Just as he'd expected, the Grikbird grew large in his mirror, its talons outstretched to strike. Right then, as the Nancy swooped up over the Doms just a couple of hundred feet below, and their pursuer appeared mere inches from the red-and-white-striped rudder of the plane, Seepy hosed the Grikbird right in its open mouth. Instantly, it cartwheeled and tumbled lifelessly down to slam directly into the troops below.

"Ha! I bet that kill a couple Doms too!" Seepy chortled as a surprised but vengeful patter of musket fire chased after them. Nothing hit the plane, but Orrin was quickly on the lookout.

"Swell," he shouted, relief turning to exasperation. "And we would've got even more if *we* crashed into 'em! What the hell's the matter with you? We're not playing chicken here . . . and get your eyes up! Where do you think those other Grikbirds went? They're down here on the deck someplace. So quit fooling around!"

"Hey! Take it easy, Ell-Tee! You plan worked, an' these Blitzers is swell guns! Way better than tryin' to blaast 'em with a musket an' buck-shot!"

"Yeah, but if we were back there blowing dirt bubbles, all this fun you're having would be over!"

Seepy was silent for a while as they climbed back to join the other three ships. "Could've got more of 'em too, if you thought to use *you* gun while we was divin'," he finally accused, just loud enough to be heard through the voice tube. Orrin snorted and shook his head. He hadn't been around when his cousin Matt first met the Lemurians, and he found it hard to believe they'd once been practically pacifists, almost as a race. There were exceptions. Supposedly the Aryaalans and B'mbaadans used to fight all the time, but from what he'd learned of 'Cats, they all seemed pretty bloodthirsty. Of course, it had taken the Japanese to make *him* a killer. *And as soon as this patrol's over, I'll report to a Jap! War sure is funny like that.*

The four Nancys set down on the gentle, protected water of Guayaquil Bay and motored in line like blue and white ducks over toward the pier established for their support. Beyond it was the strange city of Guayak the Allies had occupied almost without a fight, and the first "permanent" Allied foothold in the Dominion. The architecture was a combination of stone and adobe, but the adobe had been whitewashed or brightly painted. There hadn't been a wall around the city when they took it, but the Allies had raised one with a lot of local help. Beyond the wall was a broad killing ground on a vast cropland plain, and it was studded with trenches, stakes, and barbed-wire entanglements. Every-one suspected that the barbed wire, newly arrived from Maa-ni-la, would come as a very nasty surprise indeed for the Doms.

Only the 9th and 11th Bomb Squadrons of the 3rd Naval Air Wing operated directly out of Guayak, while the other squadrons continued flying off their carrier, *Maaka-Kakja*. The great ship wasn't far beyond the horizon, and Orrin alternated between her and shore. Right now, he felt more needed here because, besides his "test" that day, it was starting to look like things were about to pop. They'd only seen the one column of Doms for almost a hundred miles up the coast, and though they couldn't get through to the interior to confirm no more were coming from there, the new arrivals would increase the enemy numbers to more than fifty thousand. That was plenty, and probably more than enough to make them sure they had the edge. That was likely all they'd been wait-ing on.

Orrin gunned his engine, and the plane surged forward to settle atop a submerged truck on a broad, newly graded ramp beside the pier. When his crew chief satisfied himself that the plane was properly sup-ported, a large group of locals heaved on a line and pulled it out of the water. The fabric skin covering the Nancys was well sealed and they'd float for days, but they did tend to seep after a while. It was better to get them out of the water—particularly after an action that might have caused holes they weren't aware of—and maintenance was easier ashore as well. Once Orrin and Seepy's plane was high on the ramp, they climbed down and looked around. They'd been told that General Shinya himself would meet them. He wasn't there, so they waited. Orrin's gaze swept over the locals, toiling alongside the ground crew. They weren't what he'd expected at all. Everyone had thought all the Doms were nuts, adhering to a wildly warped, slightly Catholic-flavored religion that was probably closer to what the Grik believed than anything. Their "pope," like the Grik "Celestial Mother," was basically God, or at least repre-sented him. Orrin wasn't clear on that and didn't really care beyond the ways it influenced their enemies to fight. But the locals had their own screwy faith with a bunch of goofy gods, and what mattered to them was that, having seen the invaders tread upon the very soil of the Holy

Dominion itself, they'd be killed just as mercilessly as the invaders. Orrin wondered how the Doms would justify letting the army sent to fight them live after also seeing them there. Maybe they wouldn't? *More likely they'll cook up some new holy declaration that it's okay to see us to shoot us after we're already here,* he thought. But that left the locals, poor devils, who didn't much care for the Dom Pope either. They hadn't wanted any part of the war, but now, all of a sudden, just because the Allies chose to land at their city, they were in it up to their necks. Orrin didn't think that was really fair, but then again, it never was, was it? *Another funny thing about war,* he mused. *The civvies in the way always get stomped on, and more of them usually die than soldiers do.* The great lesson there, he supposed, was not to be a civilian when a war falls on top of you. By the look of things, the people of Guayak weren't civilians anymore.

"Lieutenant Reddy," came a voice behind him, and he turned. General Shinya and a number of others had finally approached, joining the fliers who had gathered around him.

"General," Orrin said, saluting. Shinya returned the sudden swarm of other salutes very crisply.

"I gathered from the wireless traffic that your new air-to-air tactics are a success. Congratulations," Shinya said.

"Thank you, sir. It was kind of a tight squeeze"—Orrin glanced darkly at Seepy—"but we got six of them without loss." In the past, armed only with muskets, the aircrews would've been lucky to knock down three for one, and even though a trickle of crated Nancys was still arriving with supply convoys, the losses—particularly in trained aviators—were unacceptable. "Who knows how long it'll work before they get wise," he had to add.

"It may not have to work much longer," Shinya said cryptically. He turned to the Imperial Marine Colonel Blair standing beside him. Orrin considered Blair one of the "good Brits." He was one of the few high-ranking Imperials with any land combat experience, having learned a bitter lesson in Singapore, then honed his skills alongside Chack-Sab-At. "The map, please, Colonel," Shinya asked.

"Of course." Blair took the map offered him by Captain Blas-Ma-Ar.

She was a Lemurian Marine, commanding the 2nd Battalion, 2nd Marines to be precise, and had seen a *lot* of action on every front. She was a tiny thing, and really cute in a kitteny sort of way, but Orrin often felt intimidated by her intense gaze. There were rumors about her going all the way back to the battle of Aryaal that might explain her unforgiving personality.

Blair displayed the map. "Yours was not the only reconnaissance of the day. We've had other planes up, as you know, and our cavalry actually skirmished with theirs south of the city." He paused. The Eastern AEF had cavalry with real horses, but not very many, whereas the Doms probably had a full division of horse-mounted lancers. Fortunately, they didn't use them very well, keeping them distributed in battalion-size clumps attached to infantry. "Our horse was pushed back," Blair continued, "but not before confirming that the enemy has extended his flank to cut the south road."

Orrin shrugged. He liked Blair, but despite their official rank difference, he didn't consider him his superior. "So? My guys could've told you that, and we knew they were going to do it."

"Yes, but they didn't march fresh troops up to do it, as we'd expected, and there are no more coming from the south. They merely extended their lines. The cavalry skirmish is immaterial," Blair added, waving it away, and it occurred to Orrin that it had probably been carried out on impulse by yet another Imperial officer who wouldn't be an officer much longer. "But if the column you observed is indeed the last element of the enemy army, we can expect an assault on the city very soon."

Orrin nodded. "That's what I was thinking. I'm kind of surprised they haven't hit us already."

A dark-skinned man in a strangely cut but otherwise plain robe cleared his throat. His name was Suares and he was the liaison for the local high priest/mayor/whatever he was, named Don Ricardo Del Guayak, usually referred to simply as "Alcalde." A former trader to the "Honorable" New Britain Company, Suares spoke a variety of English; no other locals did. Few locals, including the alcalde, even spoke Spanish, which everyone had always thought the universal language of the

Dominion. The lingo here was apparently based on something much older.

"They will only attack when they are positive of success," Suares said nervously. "To do otherwise courts even greater disaster than your presence here already represents!"

"That stands to reason," Orrin agreed. "When Fred and Kari came in, they said things aren't all peaches and cream in the Dom empire. Any hint of a defeat here could stir up a lot of trouble, maybe even a revolt." Orrin scratched his head. "Which I bet that spy they ran into, Mr. What's-his-name . . ."

"Cap-i-taan Aanson," Blas supplied, and Orrin nodded at her.

"Yeah, Anson. The guy's supposedly from some other 'Americans' who got here earlier than we did." Orrin's eyebrows went up. "Here since the Mexican War, in the *1840s*! How weird are they liable to be? Anyway, I bet that's exactly what he's been trying to stir up." He looked at Shinya. "Any idea how to get ahold of those people?"

"None. Mr. Reynolds suspected that contact might follow a decisive fleet action by them or us, on one side or the other of this amazing passage between the continents."

"And since we can't get eyes on what's there . . ."

"Exactly. High Admiral Jenks refuses to bring on such an action, and hopes to avoid it until our own fleet is stronger. Thus," Shinya said with a sigh, "here we remain, hopefully delaying that fleet from setting sail by occupying so large a portion of the army meant to join it!"

"All in a nutshell," Orrin murmured.

"Indeed," agreed Blair. "But, back to the original subject, I would appreciate your assessment of the enemy position. For our benefit, as well as that of Señor Suares. This will be his first briefing on the overall tactical situation." Orrin looked at him, surprised. "Yes. As you know, we've been giving rudimentary training to his people here of military age." Blair frowned. "Male *and* female," he added uncomfortably. "It's time he was allowed to inform his alcalde exactly what we all face together."

"Fair enough," Orrin agreed. He cocked his head and looked at the map. "We're surrounded, or about to be," he supplied unnecessarily, "and besides their fifty thousand troops, they've got about a hundred guns. Big suckers, some of 'em, that it took a dozen of those goofy armadillo-looking things to pull." The Doms used horses for their light artillery, but their siege guns—probably the same weapons used aboard their heaviest ships of the line—were drawn by animals that did look like giant armadillos with long, spiked tails. "Again, like their lancers, they haven't concentrated them anywhere, so they'll probably use 'em to pick at us all along the line. They might gather 'em all together for a big push someplace, which is what I'd do, but so far there's no sign of that." He looked at Shinya. "We're good for ordnance, right?"

"For the time being, at least. Our line of supply is very long, but we have significant supplies already stockpiled at the Enchanted Isles."

"Fine. Then unless they pull something really weird, we should be okay for a while." He nodded at the bay. "My biggest concern is there. It's the only place we can't really fortify, and we don't have enough ships to cover it unless High Admiral Jenks cuts more of Admiral Lelaa's screen loose—which I doubt he'll do under the circumstances. If they do get more troops and decide to cross the water, or worse, their fleet shows up and we can't stop it, we might be in trouble."

"A most succinct appraisal," Shinya complimented.

Suares looked increasingly incredulous. "If I may," he said. "I do not mean to seem rude or disrespectful, but I find it difficult to credit your confidence, Lieutenant Reddy."

"I believe what he means," Blair said with a trace of amusement, "is that he can't understand how we, with just over twenty-five thousand troops, including his militia, can hope to resist twice that number."

"Well . . . indeed," agreed Suares, "though I mean no offense."

Shinya considered. "No offense taken, and I understand your concern. But do not fear. You have not seen how we fight, and though the Doms have formidable numbers, none of those here can have the slightest idea of the monster they've marched against."

"Then if you are so confident of victory, why do you need my people to fight? Why do you not simply destroy the Doms here and then continue fighting them somewhere else?"

"That is easy," Blas suddenly interjected harshly, glaring at Suares.

"This is *your* war now too. It should be all your people's war, to rid the world of the Doms!"

"That's one consideration," Shinya confirmed. "The other is that I want the enemy to send more troops *here* for us to kill. I do not wish to chase him about. The best way to ensure that, I think, is to beat those already surrounding the city . . . and wait."

////// *USS Maaka-Kakja (CV-4)*
Flagship Second Fleet
June 18, 1944

 surprisingly cool dawn, considering the lati-
tude, swept across the vast expanse of sea be-
tween the occupied coastal city of Guayak and
the Enchanted Isles to the west. Upon that sea
sailed and steamed the greater part of Second
Fleet, broadly deployed to support Shinya's
expeditionary force ashore, as well as cover
the approaches to the Enchanted Isles from the curious, troubling passage far to the northeast. The fleet was an impressive sight, screened by
steam and sail-powered paddlewheel sloops and frigates of the Empire
of the New Britain Isles, and similarly powered Lemurian (American
Navy) screw frigates or "DDs." Beyond the screen, far beyond in some
cases, prowled small divisions of DDs or seaplane tender destroyers
(DTSs) designed to scout and fight. Within the screen were oilers, trans-

ports, freighters, ammunition ships, and colliers for the Imperials' coal-fired boilers. Recently arrived Imperial ships of the line, "battleships" or "liners" as they were called by some, nestled around the great aircraft carrier/tender *Maaka-Kakja* (CV-4).

Maaka-Kakja had been the first purpose-built carrier on this world, but despite some major changes, her basic form remained very similar to the massive seagoing, sailing Homes that inspired her. Powerfully armed and capable of operating a large number of Nancys, she was unquestionably the most powerful ship in the Pacific, or "Eastern Sea." But in some ways, though still practically new, she was already obsolete, and would be the only ship of her class ever built. She wasn't designed to operate the new pursuit ships, or anything actually capable of landing aboard her. Those modifications would be made when time and facilities allowed, but the Allied "BuShips" had settled on smaller, faster, lighter armed, dedicated carriers to provide improved capability while at the same time—hopefully—preventing another catastrophic loss such as that of the converted Home, *Humfra-Dar*. *Maaka-Kakja*, and indeed other converted Homes such as *Arracca* and *Salissa,* were in no danger of being decommissioned or released from service, but the new fleet carriers of the *Baalkpan Bay* class were the wave of the future.

"Ahd-mi-raal." Lelaa-Tal-Cleraan stepped out on the great carrier's starboard bridgewing, overhanging the broad, busy flight deck below, carrying two steaming mugs in her hands. Lemurians, at least those from within the Malay Barrier, on the Great South Isle, or in the Fil-pin Lands, were accustomed to heat, and Lelaa gladly wore her Navy tunic over her brindled fur that morning. She strode to join a tall man in a dark blue tunic with yellow facings and white knee breeches. Knee-high boots were on his feet, and long, sun-bleached hair was braided down his back. As he turned to face her, he exposed equally long, braided mustaches on a weathered face.

"Good morning, Admiral Lelaa," the man said.

"High Ahd-mi-raal Jenks," Lelaa replied with a smile. "I brought you tea."

"Why, thank you!" he said, taking one mug. He peered with distaste at the other. Lemurians were absolute fiends for iced tea, but most liked the hot variety as well. Almost none could stomach the ersatz "coffee" of this world that the human destroyermen had quickly adopted. Even when carefully brewed, it hid beneath a strange, greenish foam and tasted vile. Lemurians did use it as a tonic against extreme lethargy, but Lelaa-Tal-Cleraan was the only 'Cat Jenks ever met who drank it as habitually as any human American. Since all Navy 'Cats had taken the same oath and considered themselves members of the "American Clan," he supposed it was inevitable that some would take on a few of the Americans' more disagreeable habits. Some even chewed the disgusting yellow tobacco, and it was rumored they were even smoking the stuff in the West now! But the *coffee*? Jenks watched Lelaa's face as she sipped the brew to try once more to determine if she really liked it or if drinking it was an affectation. She smiled at him more broadly, guessing his intent, and blinked amusement.

Jenks shook his head. "You have just come from your briefing? What is the latest news?" he asked. He was always invited to the morning briefings, but a lot of time was always spent on reports concerning the daily operation of the ship, and he felt like an intruder on the family atmosphere that prevailed. Instead, he relied on Admiral Lelaa or her exec, Tex Sheider, to fill him in.

"The ship is in fine shape—if one reads between the lines of Chief Gilbert's constant complaints regarding the engineering division. None of his grievances reflect the material condition of the power plant or the combat readiness of my ship. Otherwise, there have been no reports of enemy activity in the vicinity of this 'pass of fire.'" Her tail swished. "I do wish Mr. Reynolds or Kari-Faask might have arranged some way for us to communicate or cooperate with the 'other Americans' they insist exist beyond the Dom frontier. We have no way to coordinate with them—and no real way of knowing if we even should." She blinked frustration. "Our scouts creep closer, and Grikbirds have been seen. Our antiair devices discourage them from serious attacks, and no one thinks they can actually report to their masters. Barring a confrontation that results in heavy losses on their part, I doubt the Doms will suspect we know their secret. We have encountered none of their ships.

I assume that means they intend that we continue thinking we have swept their fleet from the sea."

"But when it does come . . . we have no idea how large or powerful it may be."

"We continue to prepare and behave as if it is at least a match for us," Lelaa assured.

Jenks frowned and nodded. "What of this other report that Fred Reynolds and Kari-Faask made—that the mountain fishes of the world gather in the vicinity of the pass to feed after giving birth? Is there some way we might use that?"

"Possibly," Lelaa said, hedging. "Mr. Reynolds even proposed a desperate plan, but it would be extremely costly in aircraft and flight crews, and I cannot condone it at present."

"Yes, I remember, and I agree with your decision. Still, it is a plan we may want to 'keep in our back pocket,' as Captain Reddy would say."

"We try to plan for all contingencies, High Ahd-mi-raal, but plans do so rarely go . . . as planned."

"Indeed. And what is the latest from General Shinya?" Jenks asked, changing the subject from one he knew Lelaa was uncomfortable with.

"General Shinya is convinced the Dom force opposing him has received all the reinforcements it considers necessary to succeed. He hopes to disabuse them of that certainty within a few days of their assault."

"He expects it soon?"

"Almost immediately." Lelaa shrugged in a very human way. "Perhaps with this very dawn."

"Very well. You are prepared to support him if he calls?"

"Of course."

Jenks hesitated. "Are you . . . Are *we* also prepared to pull him out if we must?"

Lelaa blinked doubt. "We can certainly withdraw the force we landed at Guayak. I remain less sure we can evacuate the entire local population of the city, if it comes to that."

"And General Shinya will not leave the people there at the 'mercy' of the Doms," Jenks finished for her. He rubbed his eyes. "One more reason we cannot land even more troops to assist him." He looked at Lelaa. "Of course, 'if it comes to that,' Shinya's force and the local population will both be much reduced by then."

"I expect so," Lelaa said, swishing her tail in agitation and blinking a hint of dread.

Allied Center
East side of Guayak

"That's the purtiest aar-mee I ever saw," muttered First Sergeant Spon-Ar-Aak, better known as "Spook," of A Co., 2nd of the 2nd Marines. He'd gained his nickname as a gunner's mate aboard *Walker*, but he'd been a "Marine" ever since going ashore to fight in the land battles south of Saint Francis. He'd remained as liaison to then Commodore Jenks, but now he and his precious, trusty Browning Automatic Rifle (BAR) were under Captain Blas-Ma-Ar's orders in the Lemurian Marine battalion she commanded. At that moment, he was just about in the exact center of the Allied defensive line protecting the city from behind the hasty but formidable earthworks heaped up around it. Before him, across the vast, cultivated plain at the base of the mountains in the middle distance, the Army of the Holy Dominion was beginning to deploy at last.

He squinted up at the sun just now rising above the high, distant peaks. "Y'know, I bet they was waitin' till now just so the light would show us how purty they are!"

"Tryeen' to scare us," said Lieutenant Stas-Fin, or "Finny," who came from similar circumstances, but now commanded Co. C of the 2nd Battalion, 8th Maa-ni-la, deployed to the left of the Marines. Lieutenant Faal-Pel, better known as "Stumpy" and another of their old *Walker* shipmates, was on the far end of the 8th, commanding its Co. A. Both of them still had '03 Springfield rifles. For a while they merely watched as the enemy maneuvered on the plain.

"Is it working?" Captain Blas asked dryly, suddenly appearing beside them.

Spook gave her a long, appraising stare. "Nope," he said at last, spitting a stream of yellowish tobacco juice in his best imitation of Spanky McFarlane. Lemurians couldn't spit as elegantly as humans, but he'd practiced a lot and accomplished a very creditable squirt. Some of the 'Cat infantry nearby even cheered and stamped their feet.

"They have many flaags," Blas observed. "More than we, for the same number of troops." She gestured at the gold-embroidered black standard of the 8th, and the Stars and Stripes of the 2nd Marines. Each flag fluttered beside the stainless banner of the Alliance. "We got regimental flaags, but I bet they got 'em for every company, maybe every plaa-toon. Makes it look like there's more of 'em than there is. An' all their flaags are the same, see? That red field with the rough, sideways X on 'em in gold—just like the sails on their warships!"

"Let's watch an' see what they do," Finny suggested.

It was quite a spectacle, and none of them had ever seen anything like it. The Grik came to war as a swarm—at least that was the way those at Guayak remembered it. They knew things had changed, but they doubted the "new" Grik paraded into battle like the Doms were doing now. The sound of drums was thunderous, and bands with horns played a dirgelike, but markedly martial piece. All the while, columns of troops marched across the front and took positions opposite the defenders. Artillery was brought to the front with equal pomp, drawn by the lumbering armadillo-like things, their shells now garishly painted and draped in bunting.

"Think a lot of themselves, don't they?" Spook finally managed.

"There's a lot of 'em," Finny replied softly.

"Not as many as it looks like, but still a lot," Blas admitted, blinking thoughtfully. "Them spreading out there, not far beyond musket shot, I think not a single one of 'em's ever faced *us* before." Her tail swished and her sudden grin turned feral. "They're gonna learn some things today."

"Look there!" Finny exclaimed. "What the hell they doin'?"

Blas blinked. A column of lancers had advanced, right out between the armies. Some stopped, facing forward, while others dismounted and began erecting a colorful pavilion removed from a wagon that followed them out.

"Beats me."

"Captain Blas!" came a shout behind. Blas turned and saw Colonel Blair riding a dark horse behind the line. "A mount for you is coming. I recall you enjoy riding horses?"

"Ay, Col-nol," Blas replied. "Where are we going?"

Blair pointed at the rising pavilion.

"Out there. General Shinya, you, I, and Mr. Suares will represent the Allies at the parlay."

"Paar-lay? You mean we're gonna *talk* with them before we kill 'em?"

"I'm told they always do such things," Blair said with a snort. "God knows why. Proper form, I suppose. Come along."

Blas looked darkly at Finny and Spook. "If they kill me, you mugs kill an extra bunch of them, hear? Talkin' with the enemy! What a shaam!"

General Ghanan Nerino had been born for this. He'd commanded the Army of the South since he was twelve years old, and in the forty years since donning the broad, feathered hat of his office, he'd never been granted anything like a *real* battle to test his military genius. He drilled the standing, permanent portion of his army to a perfection unmatched in all the Dominion, he thought, but aside from occasional clashes with rebel heretics that rarely required more than a squadron of lancers to scatter, there'd been little to amuse him. Sometimes, when the great dragons threatened important cities, he deployed his infantry and artillery against them, but they were mere beasts with no notion of how a proper army should move, no appreciation for the intricate dance of formal battle. He'd often despaired, despite the bishop's devout assurance that his army would be tested someday, if not against the weak armies of the Empire of the New Britain Isles, then certainly against Los Diablos del Norte. It was inevitable, he'd said. General Nerino had not been so sure. Soon he would retire and his eldest son—already past thirty—would take his place. He hadn't doubted that war would come; that *was* inevitable, but he'd grown increasingly convinced it would wait too long for him to enjoy it. But the bishop had been right all along.

"Come, come," he scolded a staff officer, arranging a cherished tap-estry from Nerino's own villa against the bright morning sun. "We must do this properly! How often are we afforded the opportunity to enter-tain such a foe?"

"But General," the officer complained, "it is said they are barbarians, and even fight alongside *animals*! Our scouts have confirmed this!"

"What difference does that make, fool?" Nerino snapped. "We shall observe all civilized proprieties regardless! Let us appreciate them even if the enemy cannot!"

"Of course, General."

General Ghanan Nerino settled his short but ample frame on an or-nate chair and sipped from a golden goblet of spiced, melting ice. Slowly sculpting the pointed whiskers on his chin with his fingers, he watched the enemy position for any sign his invitation had been accepted. How tragic it would be if they did not come. He hated the thought that he might destroy his first true enemy in his first real battle after all these years without ever even meeting its leaders.

A short column of cavalry suddenly cantered through a fleeting gap in the enemy lines, and he smiled.

"How does this work, Mr. Suares?" Blair asked.

"I am not sure. I am no military man," Suares replied, trying to stay on his horse. "I think we are to approach with roughly equal numbers, as we are, then we four should continue alone and unarmed to join the enemy commander for refreshments."

"*That* ain't gonna happen," Blas said, fingering the sling of her Baalkpan armory musket.

Shinya glanced at her. "What is this supposed to accomplish?" he demanded of the Guayakan. "Will he offer terms?"

"Terms?" Suares asked.

"Yes. Ah, conditions for surrender or something."

Suares looked blank. "There can be no surrender," he stated flatly. "This is a . . . what? A 'social call.' That is all."

"I see."

"About what we've come to expect, Gen-er-aal," Blas said. "No quarter asked or given. Why do we do this?"

"I want to meet him," Shinya said simply.

"If there is treachery . . ."

"Then others will take our places," Shinya assured. "We have not built such a fragile force that it cannot survive without us. And we might learn a few things about the enemy."

Blas was silent, not sure she agreed with Shinya's reasoning. He was probably right that they'd get some useful insights, but she doubted that Suares could be replaced so easily. And as for Blair and Shinya, Blair was the only high-ranking "Impie" she really trusted on the ground, and Shinya . . . well, she hadn't actually fought with him yet, but she'd seen plenty of evidence of his competence and tenacity. His forced march across the width of New Ireland to reinforce Chack's and Blair's command at New Dublin had arrived too late for the fighting, but it had been a stunning achievement.

They advanced to a point roughly equal in distance to the pavilion that the Dom lancers had reorganized beyond it, and Shinya, Blair, Blas, and Suares went on alone. Stopping before the gaudy shelter, they dismounted and strode beneath its shade. Several officers wearing the bright yellow and white of Dom regulars were already standing. A figure in a long red robe they took for some kind of Blood Priest was present as well, but none of the fanatical "Blood Drinkers," the elite infantry of the Dom Pope, seemed to be there. A short, plump man with a dark complexion, jet-black chin whiskers and mustaches, dressed in a highly decorative, heavily laced version of the "regular" uniform rose to greet them.

"It is at times like this I most miss Captain Reddy," Shinya murmured. "Or even Chief Bosun Gray. They both have such amusing ways of dealing with awkward confrontations." They stopped a short distance from the Dom leader, and if any of the enemy noticed they were armed, they gave no sign. The Dom in the fancy uniform set a goblet aside and took a step forward.

"I am General Ghanan Nerino," he said in passable English, to the surprise of all. He gestured around with an affected modesty his next words didn't support. "I have the honor of commanding the invincible army arrayed before you at the orders of His Supreme Holiness, Messiah of Mexico, and by the Grace of God, Emperor of the World. It is by His decree I must destroy you for the terrible sin of treading upon the sacred land of His Holy Dominion." He paused and smiled. "But I would beg you to accept refreshment and conversation before the . . . unpleasantness must commence."

"I am General Tomatsu Shinya, commanding the Allied Armies." Shinya considered, then added, "In this hemisphere," thinking that should be suitably vague, and perhaps even intimidating. "With me are Colonel Blair, of the Empire of the New Britain Isles." He stopped again, thinking. "Vice Alcalde Suares, of Guayak City," he exaggerated, "and Captain Blas-Ma-Ar of the American Marines. You are most considerate," he finished. "We accept."

Nerino beamed and waved to his attendants who brought three chairs. Only three. Shinya looked at them curiously.

"This can only be a conversation among people," Nerino explained. "Your animal may remain, but it cannot sit with us."

Blas bristled, but said nothing. Shinya's face lost all expression, however, and he turned abruptly away. "Come," he snapped. "We are finished here."

"Wait!" called Nerino, stunned and surprised, and Shinya stood still. "You would forsake the pleasantries of battle for the sake of an *animal*?"

"I will not speak with anyone who shows such appalling disrespect to any officer under my command—particularly one as courageous and honored as Captain Blas-Ma-Ar," he said coldly. "Perhaps you do not understand that we consider *you*, sir, and all you represent, the true animals on this field today! I had hoped this meeting might encourage *us* to reconsider that." He sighed theatrically. "There is no honor in slaying animals!"

"Please do reconsider, General Shinya!" Nerino almost pleaded. "I have so looked forward . . ." He stopped. "I apologize. Your . . . *officer* may certainly sit with us!"

The Dom holy man snapped at Nerino, but the general waved him away.

Shinya turned back. "In that case, we shall remain. But what shall we talk about?"

* * *

"That guy is one weird duck," Blas said as they rode back to the Allied lines.

"He is an amateur." Blair snorted, then looked apologetically at Blas. "Even more so than my people once were."

"You are right," Shinya agreed. "An amateur playing a role. He moves his troops well enough, to prepare for a set-piece battle, but only against an army such as he himself commands." He chuckled. "Anyone can learn to do that with the years he said he's had to practice! He seems most excited by the prospect of a 'real' battle, but doesn't have any idea what he's gotten himself into. That's largely what I hoped to confirm."

"It will be interesting to see how quickly he adapts, or if he even can," Blair mused.

Suares was watching them, his face still pale. "How . . . How can you all remain so calm, so confident, after what that terrible beast said?" He'd been wrong. After an interesting and bizarrely courteous conversation that lasted nearly half an hour, Nerino did indeed offer "terms." He gave his word that if the Allied forces at Guayak agreed to surrender, they would all be honorably and mercifully shot, despite the great expense in powder and shot (he'd likely have to pay for himself), that such a benevolent act would entail. If they chose to resist, however—something he fully expected and even encouraged them to do—sadly, all survivors would have to be impaled. He had no discretion there. The Holy Decrees of His Holiness himself clearly prescribed such punishment for enemies who spilled the Sacred Blood of His noble soldiers within the Dominion itself. Apparently there was some leeway for expeditionary commanders during foreign conquest, to facilitate occupation, but he had none here. All the people of Guayak, however, every man, woman, and child, must be impaled regardless. They'd broken far more terrible commandments by succoring enemies of God.

Shinya looked at Suares. He had no doubt now that the people of Guayak would be firmly bound to the cause. "Because we're not going to lose," he said simply. "Some of your people will die in battle, but none will be impaled."

CHAPTER 5

////// Battle of Guayak
June 18, 1944

hundred Dom guns, many quite large, commenced firing one after another at almost exactly noon. A great, rolling billow of white smoke eventually obscured the entire enemy line, and the deep-throated roar was tremendous. Heavy roundshot crashed into the soil and stone earthworks around the city, but many shrieked overhead to impact the buildings beyond with the clattering crash of shattered masonry. Only six batteries of "light" Allied guns, thirty-six in all, plus a few heavy Dom guns taken from the harbor fort opposed them, but they replied immediately, snarling defiance from prepared embrasures in the works. Mostly twelve-pounders, and Imperial eight-pounders, the Allied guns were light, highly mobile field artillery pieces, but they possessed several key advantages. All of them, even the "Impie" guns, were provided with more than just solid roundshot now. At this range, and with the enemy in the open, exploding spherical case shot snapped above and among the Doms, spraying them with musket balls and hot shards of iron. The Allied gunners didn't even have to aim particularly well—impossible through all the smoke at any rate—they just had to keep firing at the same elevation, with fuses set for the same time of flight for the well-observed range.

Shinya was on top of one of the taller buildings near the eastern line with a relatively small staff, observing with his binoculars. They didn't have any of the new field telephones in the East yet, but they'd had plenty of time to string telegraph wires to numerous command posts around the city. If lines were cut by the bombardment, a number of locals stood by to act as runners. Besides the runners, however, the only locals present were Suares and the alcalde in his robes and goofy headdress. Both looked nervous, and they hadn't spoken since having arrived together. The rest of the city's population, those not on the line and armed with Dom muskets from the fort armory, had taken shelter in cellars beneath the more-imposing structures. That was good, Shinya realized, because no matter how destructive his own fire must be to the enemy, the Doms' heavy shot would ultimately pulverize the city.

A big ball struck the building he was standing on, near street level, and the dust swirled up to engulf them four stories up.

"Damn," he said. "I can see nothing from here!"

"You won't see better anywhere else," said Fred Reynolds. He and Kari-Faask remained weak from their ordeal, and Orrin still hadn't cleared them to fly. But they knew more about the Doms on the continent than anyone else—or at least that was the excuse they used to get Shinya to let them "tag along" with him. They hadn't needed an excuse. Shinya remembered Fred as the youngest member of *Walker*'s crew, and the kid had always been friendly to him when almost no one else was. His carefree, California attitude had also aroused nostalgic memories of Shinya's own college days at Berkeley, which may have even facilitated his "Americanization" on this world. He liked Fred—and Kari—and was glad for their company.

"I suspect you're right," Shinya grudged. "This artillery duel may go on for some time, so you may as well elaborate on some of the points you began to make earlier. You still believe they will strike first at the center?"

"Yessir." Fred nodded. "I'm no infantryman, and I'm sure no strat-egy or tactics guy, but those people"—he waved toward the enemy—"they're really arrogant, y'know? And I don't mean the kind of arrogant some folks get when they've done a lot of stuff they're good at. It isn't *earned* arrogance, if you know what I mean. I'm not saying that kind of arrogance is any prettier, and that it won't bite you on the ass, but folks can kind of understand it." He shrugged. "Their kind isn't based on anything other than they know they're right because they've been *told* they're right—*commanded to accept they're right*—so long that they don't dare question it. They think God's on their side, period."

"But they have built formidable armies and navies, and they handle them quite professionally," Shinya objected.

"Sure, they move 'em around just fine, but that's all drill. Rote train-ing. From what I've heard, they don't fight 'em very well once they lock horns. I mean, the troops fight hard, sure. They won't hardly quit. But you guys marched rings around 'em on New Ireland, and the Skipper and *Walker* stomped their whole fleet with just a few other ships to help. They're not . . . flexible."

Shinya didn't entirely agree that things had been quite so one-sided on New Ireland. The Doms had devised a good and dangerous plan—based on inside information, it turned out—and they'd executed it very creditably. But they hadn't reacted well when the Allies changed their tactics in response, had they? As for Captain Reddy's victory off Saint Francis, that was more complicated as well—but maybe it really wasn't when all was said and done.

"Straight at us, you say, right up the middle," Shinya mused.

"Keep it simple," Fred agreed. "I'm not saying they won't give us a shove here and there in other places; that would be expected by all the brass over there. Let everybody have their little part in the big dance."

Shinya looked sharply at Fred, remembering Nerino's flowery speech at the end of their parlay in which he said something to the effect of "Let the glorious dance of battle commence!" He nodded at where Suares and his alcalde had stepped away to view the panorama from a different position. "Would you ask Mr. Suares—or his alcalde—if they agree with your assessment?"

"I'll try." A few moments later, he returned to Shinya. "They don't know, sir. I guess they're even less 'tactical' than I am. Even more edgy too. But I think I'm right."

"Signalman," Shinya snapped. "Send: each regiment, but particularly those along the southern line, will stand ready to shift one company in three to the center at my command."

Moments passed while the bombardment continued, amid a continuous thunder of guns and crash of shot. Most of the Dom shot was falling in front of the earthworks now, striking the soft earth and skating upward to fall almost harmlessly behind the defensive lines and their reserve detachments as well. The Allied gunners had laid timbers beneath their guns to keep their elevations consistent, but the Doms hadn't taken time for such, so their wheels would be digging deeper in the earth with every shot and recoil; if their gunners couldn't see what they were shooting at, most were probably not compensating for lost elevation. As if the enemy realized this, and even expected it, his guns slowly stopped firing, allowing the battlefield to clear a bit. The Allied guns didn't stop, however, and for the first time, Shinya saw the carnage they'd been wreaking. Mangled bodies writhed and crawled or lay completely still on the hazy ground among and beyond the enemy guns, some of which had been dismounted. Ragged gaps had been slashed in the ranks of the infantry, and it appeared stunned, for a moment, by what the clearing smoke revealed. Distant shouts erupted, and the lines started closing up. Even as he watched, a case shot exploded above the Dom ranks, mowing down half a dozen men.

"The artillery will cease firing and replenish ammunition!" Shinya ordered.

"But we killin' hell outa them!" Kari-Faask protested, her keen eyes needing no binoculars.

Shinya looked at her and spoke gently. Few people had suffered worse than she had at the hands of the Doms. "We are, but we will do far more when they advance, I promise. And I do not want to discourage them from doing so."

"I get replies from all but Sixth Impie Maa-rines!" the signals 'Cat announced. "We must'a lost that line."

"Send a runner. Inform Mr. Reddy that his squadrons may lift off now, but they must wait for my order to attack.

"Ay, ay. What about *Maaka-Kakja*'s planes?"

"Not yet. I don't want the Doms to know we have anything at our disposal beyond what they see here."

Captain Blas-Ma-Ar was coughing dust. "Daamn," she finally managed. "That last one was close."

"Right on the other side o' the heap," Spook agreed. He'd taken off his helmet and was shaking out his near-white fur. A few of the Imperial militiamen from the Saint Francis region, leaning on their long guns, watched him with amusement. "You think they comin' now?"

Blas peered over the earthwork, blinking, her eyes wet. "Yeah. C'mere, First Sergeant. You gotta see this." The rumble of drums had replaced the artillery fire, and now a loud, strange, martial tune began to play. With hundreds of red flags streaming above them, perhaps ten thousand Doms, across a half-mile front, stepped off. Above them, now that the smoke was clearing, Grikbirds—more than she'd ever seen—swooped and swirled. She doubted the things would be much of a menace on a battlefield, particularly once the smoke returned. Everyone now knew they didn't like smoke at all. But the scary-looking things, so obviously in the power of the Doms, were an intimidating sight.

"Can we start shootin' now?" demanded a militiaman. He was taller than most Impies and had a long dark beard. Imperial Marine regulations allowed just about any form of mustache a man could imagine or achieve, but no beards. The militia from the continental colonies generally obeyed "sensible" orders but paid little attention to that sort. They wore no uniform either, unless a kind of apparently universal hunting frock might be considered such, and didn't participate in close-order drill. Their large rifled weapons that would've even impressed Dennis Silva were well designed to kill some very large continental monsters, but had no provision for a bayonet. For close-up work, they carried two-handed "hunting swords," longer and heavier than any military sword

Blas had ever seen. Blas already knew their rifles were accurate enough to kill a specific man at the roughly three hundred tails to the enemy.

She looked back at the advancing Doms. *Hell, our aar-tillery canister would even be effective at this range!* Baalkpan and Maa-ni-la Arsenal smoothbore muskets were still the standard infantry arm in the East and would probably remain so for a while longer. They had tight enough tolerances to be effective at two hundred yards, and fairly accurate at a hundred. Impie flintlocks weren't quite as good, but all of them could already be taking some toll. These particular Doms had never fought the Allied armies before, however, and had clearly formed to fight an enemy equipped just as they were. Blas wondered if they'd be foolish enough to do so again after today. Apparently, Shinya wanted to reinforce their misconceptions a little longer, and had something other than just a slugging match in mind—at least she hoped he did. In any event, she hadn't yet received orders to open fire.

"Soon," she promised the militiaman. "When we get started, though, I want you Saint Francis-aans killin' officers, savvy?"

"An' them damn Blood Priests too, I hope?" the man asked. Blas nodded. "My pleasure, Cap'n," the man said. "They're easy enough ta spot!" It was true. Lemurian troops had always dressed the same, first by clans, then regiments, and now almost universally. Lemurian Marines still wore their blue kilts in battle, and Safir Maraan's personal guard regiment, her "600," retained their house colors as well, but with the exception of stripes and other rank devices—much smaller now on combat dress—officers were indistinguishable from privates. Even the Imperial Marines, once given to a degree of pomp, had adopted the practice, even if their tunics remained red, at least here in the East. But Dom officers, like General Nerino, were easily distinguishable—as were the bloodred-robed priests that accompanied them.

"Captain Blas!" came a cry from behind, and again Blair appeared atop his horse, followed by a larger staff than before.

"Sur?"

"That music they play is most disagreeable," Blair announced loudly enough to be heard by hundreds. "Their notion of melody is quite grating on my ears. Pray, is there anything you can do about it?"

"May I?"

"By all means, Captain."

Blas hurried to a 'Cat commanding a section of guns to her left. She remembered him from the fighting on New Ireland and knew he was good. "Can you silence that screeching band, Lieuten-aant?" she demanded, just as loudly as Blair.

"Wit much happy!" Most Lemurian-Americans spoke passable English now, or the near-universal patois that had sprung up. Some still relied on a kind of pidgin. "Action front!" The 'Cat roared memorized commands to his two grinning gun's crews, their embrasures about twenty-five yards apart. "Load case, target dat skeechy band!"

"Two fifty!" chorused the chiefs of each piece sending the appropriate ammunition forward. The gunners pierced their fuses for one second, fudging them a bit shorter still. Lemurian cannoneers rammed the fixed charges down the barrels and then stepped back, leaving the gunners and one other to quickly aim each piece. When the gunners were satisfied, others pierced the charges through the vents and primed them. It all took mere seconds before each gun was ready and waiting. The section chief was still watching the stately, plodding advance of the enemy, and when the target neared the estimated range, he took a breath and roared, "Fire!"

Linstocks slapped down, and both guns roared as one, rumbling and jangling back across the planked overlays. An instant later, two gray and white clouds burst nearly amid the enemy band, and the musicians were swept to the ground, either by fragments of metal or the concussion of the twin blasts. Cheers erupted up and down the earthworks, and somewhere far to the left, where several entire companies of continental militia were gathered, strange, yowelly music such as Blas had never heard squawked to life.

"Oh dear," Colonel Blair said with a false frown. "We've awakened the bagpipes! Pity we can't silence them so easily!" Another cheer rose, but Blas listened to the pipes. Whatever they looked like—she had no idea—they didn't sound that different from some of her own people's instruments. Maybe louder. She decided she rather liked them.

They may have slain much of the enemy's main band, but the drums still thundered, and the Doms continued inexorably forward.

"They're gettin' awful close!" Fred Reynolds murmured to Kari.

"Indeed," Shinya agreed sourly. "I did not expect so many Grikbirds. Look at them all! I wanted COFO Reddy's planes to have a clear view of their targets, to avoid hitting any of our own people, but his planes may *collide* with Grikbirds if they remain so thick and low!" Decisively, he lowered his binoculars. "This to all commands," he said tersely to the signal-'Cat. "Commence firing, but do not, repeat, *do not* employ mortars!" He looked at Fred. "We don't want Reddy's aircraft to collide with them either!" He stepped to the 'Cat, already tapping out the message. "The Grikbirds should rise with the smoke and the bombing squadrons will strike low, beneath most of them, I should think. Mr. Reddy's machine-gun-armed craft will drive through first, hopefully scattering any Grikbirds that remain." He paused. "My desire is that the attacking division or corps, or however the enemy designates such things, should be annihilated, but no plane will drop without a visible target. We can afford no accidental gaps in our defenses! Pilots without such targets may drop on the enemy reserves, but they must clear the airspace above the battlefield as soon as possible so I may use my mortars. Subsequent air strikes will focus on the enemy reserves and rear areas."

"What about those parts of the line the Doms aren't coming at yet?" Kari asked.

Shinya's brow rose. "All commands may shoot at whatever they think they can hit! The more smoke the better, I suppose."

"Hold yer mortars, but commence firing! Commence firing, but hold yer mortars!" shouted an Imperial Marine on Blair's staff, galloping down the road behind, and parallel to the works. Blas nodded. The word about the mortars had already arrived via messenger from her comm shack. The final word had awaited only this runner, and guns north of her position, closer to the bay, had been pounding for several moments already. A crackle of musketry was growing to a roar. She glanced at Lieutenant Finny, who'd remained nearby with his adjoining company, and blinked an irony Finny caught with a swish of his tail. Neither was anxious for what was to come; they'd seen it often enough. But the waiting only intensified the dread, and they were glad it was over. "Mortar sections, hold," Blas trilled. "Aar-tillery sections will load caanister!" She stared down the line of expectant faces turned to hers, "gun 'Cats" and Marines poised by and with their weapons. "Commence independent fire!" At this range, careful aim was more important than the stunning effect of a volley—and the approaching Doms ought to be sufficiently stunned by something else directly.

"Jeez! Look at that!" Orrin Reddy shouted at his OC through the plane's voice tube. He'd seen battles from the air before, first against the Japanese in the Philippines, then against the Doms on New Ireland, but never had they been so concentrated and on such a scale. The whole city seemed surrounded by a gigantic, rising doughnut of smoke, and he and his two squadrons of Nancys, racing in at low altitude after a swing around the bay, were headed right for it.

"I say jeez too—for all the Grikbirds!" came the reply.

Orrin sobered. Seepy was right. There were hundreds of the damn things, rising above the smoke and kiting on thermals over the city like monstrous reptilian vultures. "Yeah, and we have to run interference." Orrin was personally leading the 9th Bomb Squadron on this mission. Their ship and Lieutenant Ninaar-Rin-Ar's (CO of the 11th Bomb Squadron) were the only ones armed with .50s in the nose. Every plane in both squadrons had Blitzer Bugs, but they'd be of limited use on a bomb run. But four more ships had been designated as "top cover" for the attack, and would follow Orrin and Ninaar straight in to blow a hole for the others.

"Remind everybody to be extra careful where they drop!" Orrin told Seepy one more time. The two bombs each Nancy carried were terrible things—one hundred pounds of gasoline mixed with obstinately flammable sap from the gimpra tree. The stuff didn't stay mixed very well, but it didn't really have to. Detonation, or a high-speed collision with the ground would recombine the substances sufficiently to provide an expanding inferno of sticky gobbets of flaming sap that could land as far as seventy-five yards from the detonation point. Other compounds had been considered, of course, as had airbursts, but fusing remained an issue in the second case, and in the first—what was the point? In any event, every aviator in the 3rd Naval Air Wing was more terrified of accidentally dropping one of the weapons on his own people than he was of death. Orrin was confident there'd be no accidents.

"Here we go!" he announced. A gaggle of Grikbirds had noticed them and was swooping down in front of them, still just above the battlesmoke. Ninaar was off his left wing and Orrin glanced down. He had his landmarks, and stabbing flashes of cannon fire confirmed his line. His eyes twitched to his mirror to confirm that both squadrons remained tucked in a tight column of twos behind the lead ships. As soon as he gave the order, Seepy would press his telegraph key and hold it down—until he had to start shooting. That would send the bombers diving through the smoke, and into the attack.

"Tally ho!" he shouted, and Seepy jammed his key. Immediately, eighteen Nancys dove, and Orrin centered his crude sights on the Grikbirds ahead and fired.

"Their artillery is disturbingly effective, considering its size," General Nerino observed, maintaining an urbane façade. In truth, he'd been terrified when the heretics' shells began exploding among his advancing troops, and even disconcertingly close to *him*. The armies of the Holy Dominion used exploding shells in their monstrous twelve-inch mortars, but they had none of those here. They had nothing, in fact, that fired anything but solid shot and grape. Ramming a lit projectile down the long barrel of a field piece before firing it was considered far too dangerous and unpredictable. He wondered how his enemies had solved the problem with such apparent safety to their crews, and precision of effect. There'd been proposals that simply firing a gun would serve to ignite a fuse, he remembered, but few hereditary officers had given the notion much credibility. They might have to rethink that. At last, however, the guns had fallen silent, and his heart no longer raced as he sat on his gilded chair and watched his first shell-torn Corps, or "El Mano del Papa," march across the broad gap to grasp the enemy at last. The red flags made a seamless, protective river of divine blood above his host, and the thundering drums echoed the pulsing rush of blood in his ears. The band advanced as well, providing a stirringly devout martial accompaniment to the dance of war. So thrilling! All his life, General Nerino had waited to see such a sight! He felt like falling to his knees and joining his priest in thanks to God and His Holiness for this opportunity.

He might have actually done so if two gray shell bursts hadn't suddenly, deliberately, slaughtered the noncombatant musicians.

"*Qué terriblemente grosero!*" he exclaimed, stunned. Never had he imagined anyone capable of such rude behavior on a battlefield! An instant later, a great cheer built among the enemy, joined by an appalling squealing sound. Then the distant guns spat fire and smoke, and a rising crackle of musketry erupted.

"They do not even wait for the exchange of volleys!" the priest seethed. "They are *animals*, my general!"

"Perhaps not all," Nerino said defensively. "The enemy army is a mixed force. Perhaps many are amateurs. To foul their weapons at such a hopeless distance certainly does not *seem* very professional!" The standard musket of the Holy Dominion was wildly inaccurate and couldn't strike any specific man-size target beyond seventy or eighty paces. Nerino had no reason to suspect Imperial muskets were any better, and frankly suspected the Imperials had armed what he considered their animalistic allies with spears at best. It never occurred to him that the Lemurian "Americans" might have their own, even better weapons. "Our noble Salvadores will show them what discipline in the ranks may achieve." He paused. "But what is that absurd buzzing sound? Not more of their odd flying machines, I hope! Surely we have sufficient dragons above us to protect against any mischief they may cause?" He turned to his aide, the sound growing more insistent. "Captain, what . . ." Something flashed in the corner of his eye, and he turned back to the battlefield in time to see a great, sprawling mushroom of fire, crowned by greasy black smoke. "What?" he murmured again, just as an enemy machine darted past the white smoke of battle and climbed up and away to the south. Then there was another terrible, orange flash—and another! Even from where he sat, the screams were clear. Obviously, the heretics were dropping some kind of bomb, in much the same way that dragons had been taught to attack ships, but these were not the large rocks or roundshot the dragons carried, but some kind of demonic incendiary device.

"They are burning our army!" Nerino shrieked, standing from his chair. *Whump! Whump! Whump!* went the bombs and more screams mounted, even while the fire from the enemy earthworks redoubled. More flying machines roared by, rising in the sky. Nerino saw one, diving down to the north. Two pointed cylinders fell away and tumbled to the ground, igniting among his terrified, surging troops. He continued watching as it too pulled up and away, but then saw several dragons slash into the thing and carry it tumbling to the ground.

"They only have the two bombs each," he cried. "Doubtless, they go back for more, but it will take time. We must push the next Hand of the Pope forward immediately!"

"It is already formed, my general!" the aide assured him.

"Send it!" Nerino waved his hands manically. "Send *everything*! I want a general attack around the entire perimeter at the rush!"

"Wow," said First Sergeant Spook. "Lookie at 'em burn!"

"They're not all burnin'," Blas muttered. "Them flyboys were maybe a little too careful not to hit us. A buncha Doms were already past the drop point!" Even as she watched, a second Nancy staggered in the sky as a pair of Grikbirds fastened onto its port wing and sent it into a helpless spin. It impacted on the other side of the line of fire, and as far as she could tell, the Grikbirds never let go. She felt bad for the brave aviators she'd just seen die, but she had more pressing problems. Thousands of Doms were literally running at them now, partly to escape the fire, no doubt, but also to come to grips with their tormenters. She raised her voice. "Let 'em have it! Keep firing! Chew 'em up! Kill 'em!"

"Load double canister! Load and hold!" the section chief to her left cried out, and she nodded on hearing his words. The Doms were coming fast, and the lieutenant's guns would get only one more shot before the wave hit. Clearly he meant to make the most of it. At that moment, another rider galloped past on the road behind. "Commence firing mortars!" he yelled, over and over. Almost instantly, the distinctive *toomp!* sounds stuttered behind the lines. Blas turned back to her troops, tightening her helmet strap. "Fix bayonets!" she trilled.

"Comin' just like Grik!" Spook shouted over the growing roar.

"No! These Doms have minds, and they'll fight with 'em—if we don't change 'em first. Take your Bee Ayy Arr and cover the gunners after they fire. Maybe they can keep shootin' if you keep the Doms off 'em!"

"Ay, ay, Cap-i-taan Blas," Spook replied, then blinked irony. "Watch yer tail!"

Blas unslung her Baalkpan arsenal musket and affixed the bayonet. In seconds, she'd be needed more on the firing line than standing back, giving orders. She disagreed with Spook in more ways than she'd had time to explain, however. Wild as the Dom charge had become, no similar Grik assault ever came at her with more than a single thought behind the onslaught. These Doms, these *men*, each had their own thoughts just as surely as her troops had theirs. Did that mean they'd be easier to break—or fight even more ferociously than any Grik she'd ever faced? On the other hand, from what she'd heard, the Grik were fighting with their minds now too. . . . Added to this was the conflict many Lemurians faced, a lingering discomfort at the prospect of killing humans with the same ruthlessness they killed Grik. It was hard sometimes to reconcile what this war had become with how it started. "Shields up!" she roared at her Marines, who still carried the things, and stepped into the line. "Brace for it!"

Horns sounded and loud cries of *"Alto! Alto!"* rose above the tumult, even as the defenders continued pouring in loads of "buck and ball" at a mere thirty yards or so. Sluggishly, like an animal goaded beyond endurance, the charging horde managed to arrest its sprint and try to dress its ranks in the face of the withering fire. *"Escopetas aplomo!"* came another repeated shout. One officer, just across from Blas, never finished the command, thrown back by the heavy slug of a militiaman's rifle. Around him, however, gasping, bloodied Doms raised their muskets and took a wavering aim.

"Down!" Blas shrieked, ducking behind a Marine's angled shield. *"Disparar!"*

A ragged but thundering volley churned at the earthworks, pitching Marines backward amid a hail of *vipping* balls and screaming rocks and gravel. A ball whacked the shield just in front of Blas's face and moaned away overhead, and just as suddenly as the volley came, the screams of her own troops filled the air. She noticed a stinging pain in her left thigh and glanced down to see the twisted tang of a buttplate, a jagged splinter of wood still attached, sticking out of her leg. She'd been hit by a piece of a musket, struck by a Dom ball. She yanked it out with a gush of breath.

"Up! Up! Fire into them! Let 'em have it!" she roared in that peculiar Lemurian way that carried her voice so far. Immediately, those around her started firing again, tearing paper cartridges with their teeth, pouring powder, and forcing .60-caliber balls topped with three pieces of buckshot down their barrels with iron rammers. Even as they died, the Doms were obeying unheard commands to draw their long, swordlike bayonets, and jam them in the muzzles of their muskets. Unlike the defenders with their socket bayonets, the Doms would no longer be able to fire their weapons, but soon, a good pike or spear might be just as dangerous. Another horn blew, and the Doms lowered their weapons with a desperate yell and charged. With a thundering crash, they slammed into the upraised shields of the Marines, and the first rank bowed back under the blow. The second rank stabbed at the enemy over the shields with their bayonets, while the third rank kept firing. Spook's BAR opened up with a *Wham! Wham! Wham!* staccato, punctuated by another blast of double canister to the left, its yellowish smoke swirling and mixing with the white smoke of the muskets. Almost unheard, the stutter of exploding mortar bombs began.

Pushed into the second rank, Blas stabbed at anything that showed itself beyond the shields. The sharp point of her bayonet skated off a nose and found the wide eye of a Dom. She literally *felt* the scream

through the wood and metal of her weapon. That, of all the events she'd ever experienced in combat, sickened her, but there was no time to contemplate it. Killing was killing, after all, and nothing she did could possibly compare to the agony the firebombs had caused. She fought on, quickly losing the extra breath to shout any orders, but further such were pointless now at any rate. Her whole world became the thrust and parry of the bayonet, the grunting of Marines straining to hold the shield wall, the screams and wails of the wounded and dying, and the foamy sweat that leached down from the leather band in her helmet to sting her eyes.

It seemed to her that they were holding, even though the greater mass of the enemy corps must have chosen her section of the line to concentrate, but she had to wonder how the rest of the line was faring. Only the Marines, and a few other Lemurian regiments had shields. They were heavy and cumbersome, and would only turn musket balls at a certain angle or until badly dented. The Imperials didn't like them at all. She knew they'd been mostly done away with in the West, against the Grik, but the troops there had breech-loading rifles. Even then, recent experiences had indicated that shields still had a place. They were helping here, no question, and if the pressure might not be so great on other parts of the line, she suspected they were having a bad time without the extra protection.

"Mortars are gettin' louder!" a 'Cat next to her huffed, breaking her metronomic reverie.

"They're walking back this way," Blas confirmed breathlessly. "The fires from the bombs must be going out, and I bet the Doms're sending more troops at us here. Mortars are prob'ly trying to break 'em up!"

"Well," the 'Cat—a corporal—gasped, "they gonna hafta get through the ones we killin' *now* to get at us!" Spook's BAR was hammering away, and the pair of guns he protected thundered again. More guns were firing now, Blas suddenly realized, meaning the pressure must be easing a bit—somewhere besides here, anyway. "They ain't gonna like it if they do," she promised grimly.

*　　　*　　　*

For the next three-quarters of an hour, the battle convulsed like a tor-tured snake all around the perimeter, except along the bayside docks. Kari Faask was practically hopping up and down, trying to see through the smoke obscuring the eastern line. The Doms were attacking every-where, but it was at that point that the heaviest blow had fallen—perhaps twenty thousand troops funneled into a front barely a mile wide. Of course, nowhere near twenty thousand had made it all the way to the Allied defenses. The mortars still churned the rear ranks of the second corps, and shredded the bodies strewn across the field be-hind it.

"Mortars say they runnin' low on aammo!" A comm-'Cat fretted, approaching the command staff that had remained on the roof through-out the fight. "Dom guns have opened up again, even wit their own troops under the shot, an' its dis-ruptin' replenishment!"

"Where's Colonel Blair?" Shinya

"He tryin' to bring up the reser⸱⸱⸱⸱⸱⸱ pie M'reens to rein-force Cap-i-taan Blas."

"He had better hurry. What's Lieu⸱⸱⸱⸱⸱ status?"

"He takin' off again now, rearmed ar⸱⸱⸱ ⸱ut he down to he call 'baker's dozen' ships. Grikbirds chas⸱ way back to bay. He say there maybe not so many Grikb⸱ ⸱⸱ ⸱ough, either. They Blitzer Bugs shoot ⸱⸱ ⸱own in ⸱⸱ches⸱

Shinya nodded. They d seen that; qui⸱ few of the terrifying crea-tures had even fallen in the ⸱⸱⸱⸱ ⸱ several planes.

"We, Kari and ⸱⸱⸱ted grimly.

"Are you fit to fly⸱ f you re, there are no extra aircraft. You are cer⸱⸱ ⸱⸱p ⸱me. I honor your desire to fight, Lieute⸱⸱ nare it most strongly. But we must all do what we are able, ⸱⸱ our duty requires. Right now, your duty requires you to heal—and ad⸱ise me on matters concerning aviation. Tell me, what should Lieutenant Reddy do now?"

Surprised, and a little suspicious that Shinya was only pretending to need his counsel, Fred concentrated. "Mr. Reddy can't target the enemy infantry this time," he said. "It's too closely engaged. I'd suggest he con-centrate on the Dom artillery and reserves." He paused. "If he sees any-

thing that might be General Nerino's command post, he might take a whack at that."

"An excellent recommendation, Lieutenant," Shinya said. He turned to the comm-'Cat. "Send it."

"Ay, ay."

"What is happening? I cannot see!" General Nerino thundered, rising to pace and stare at the unprecedented chaos of the battlefield, before self-consciously returning to his gilded chair.

"I do not know, my general," his aide almost wailed. "The smoke is too thick to see even the signal flags. The mortars . . ." He paused. Hundreds, *thousands* of deadly little bombs still blanketed the Army of God, sometimes dangerously close to where he stood. They had to come from some kind of mortar, t̶ had no idea how the heretics could have shipped so many of s weapons so far, and brought them ashore. Scouting l̶a ibed sr all, lightweight tubes within the enemy positio̶n lays but surely *they* could not achieve the range and destru of the rain of bombs he was watching! "It *must* be mortars though how . . ."

"What is that demanded, pointing. The aide peered through the smoke. A steady woun had been stumbling or crawling out of the fight in front of enemy works, bu ow men were *running* from the battle, appare and many unarmed. Nerino's face purpled as he reco m̶y personal guard," he snarled, "to push those m If they will not go, kill them!"

The aide signaled the guard captain, w ed to be expecting the command. Fifty lancers wearing red capes and gold-washed helmets and cuirasses quickly formed a line and advanced across the field.

"We have no more lancers near, my general," the aide reminded nervously. "The rest are on the flanks. And your guard may be sorely diminished amid that storm of fire."

Nerino looked at him. "I still have my army to protect me, Captain, at least what remains of it."

"But . . . how much is that?" A droning interrupted him, and they both stared at the northern sky. The flying machines were returning, this time in a staggered formation. Some clearly meant to burn the battlefield where Nerino's guards had just gone—but others seemed to be aiming right at *him*! Dragons swirled above them, but seemed hesitant to descend into the dense smoke of battle. "Even our own demons have deserted us," he murmured as the bombs tumbled to the earth.

Captain Blas's line was beginning to falter. The shields had been battered into uselessness, and almost no one was firing anymore. The line had thinned too much to maintain a third rank, much less the luxury of loading their muskets. The fight in the center had essentially turned into a stabbing match of bayonets, and despite the skill of the Marines, they were exhausted by a full hour of constant, physical combat. There were just too many Doms. Spook's BAR still fired sparingly, allowing "his" guns to spew canister, but that couldn't last much longer. Blas rammed her bayonet through the chest of a burly Dom in front of her, but she had trouble pulling the sticky blade free. A Dom sword banged her helmet, and she stumbled to the side. A roaring shout rose around her, and, in her disorientation, she thought the enemy had broken her line at last. Shapes rushed around her, and she waved her musket, fending them away.

"Easy there, Cap'n Blas!" came a voice she vaguely remembered from another time, as hands took her by the shoulders and steadied her.

"Corporal Smuke," she said dully, remembering the Imperial's name. Against her will, she sagged heavily, the last of her strength fleeing her legs, and she blinked away the gummy tears that started to fill her eyes. "I haven't seen you since New Ireland," she murmured. "What are you doing here?"

"Me an' me lads've come to *your* rescue fer a change," Smuke said. "Have a taste o' this!" He held a canteen to her mouth. She coughed on water grogged with something strong she didn't recognize, but her weary wits were returning. Imperial Marines streamed past her, filling gaps in the line and firing muskets directly in the faces of their attackers.

"Col-nol Blair has reinforced us!"

"Aye," Smuke confirmed, scooping her up in his arms. She struggled weakly, indignantly.

"Put me down this instant, Corporal! I'll have you on a charge!"

Smuke laughed. "Charge all ye like, Cap'n Blas, but the colonel hisself bade me take care o' ye, an' if ye dinnae notice, ye've taken a wee scratch ain yer leg! Now trouble me nae further. Colonel Blair'll stop me grog if I leave ye—an' ye'd never allow 'im ta do sich a heinous thing!"

Shinya's arms hurt from holding his binoculars to his eyes for so long. Just moments before, Lieutenant Reddy's Nancy squadrons had gone in again, their firebombs erupting far beyond the closer battle for the most part, though a few gushed flames extremely close behind the second attacking force in the center. Shinya winced when he saw yet another Nancy cartwheel out of the sky, Grikbirds bolting away from it just before it impacted in the smoke-hazed field. The crumpled corpse of the plane immediately burst into flames. He winced again at the sight of a lone smoldering horse, probably a lancer's mount, galloping aimlessly, panicked or wild with pain. Beneath its hooves, the cropland beyond the perimeter was covered with butchered, bleeding bodies.

"Colonel Blair's going in," Fred said quietly at his side, and Shinya refocused his binoculars.

"At laast," Kari breathed with relief. The pressure was becoming unbearable in the center, and it had looked like Blas and her Marines were about to fold. A stutter of musketry, so long quiet there, suddenly erupted, and flashes of orange fire stabbed at the Doms. Shinya handed his glasses to Fred, resting his arms, and Fred raised them gratefully.

"That's done it!" he shouted triumphantly. "My God, the Doms are pulling back!"

"No troops, ours or theirs, can withstand such horror forever," Shinya said. He didn't add that he'd seen such intense, sustained fighting only once before, at Aryaal, and that time it had been Allied troops that finally broke. But he'd gained a new regard for their eastern enemies that day, if not outright respect. Nerino's troops had advanced, and then stood and fought in the face of far superior weaponry, and even while being savaged in front and behind by other weapons they'd never faced before. He didn't know if they were motivated by courage, fear, or simple fanaticism, but it made him question his fundamental strategy of drawing as many Doms down on them as they could. A breakthrough in the center could've probably been contained and there'd been little real pressure elsewhere, but a more thoughtful attack supported by greater numbers might've overwhelmed them here at Guayak.

"Keep at it! Pour it in!" Fred grated excitedly. "Shit! There they go!" He urgently handed the binoculars back to Shinya. "They're breaking!"

Shinya took the glasses and watched the Dom line. It had pulled back in the face of Blair's fresh troops, but with bayonets jammed in their muzzles, they couldn't return the renewed firing that scythed them down. Shinya understood perfectly what began to happen next. Incapable of advancing and unable to stand any longer—or even withdraw in an orderly fashion under such a hail of bullets and increased artillery fire—the Dom line appeared to spontaneously shatter. What had been a disciplined, cohesive force a moment before, teetering on the edge of victory, suddenly became a wild mass of terrified individuals, streaming to the rear as fast as their exhausted legs and lungs could take them. A great cheer resounded from the Allied line, and clumps of men and Lemurians actually leaped the earthworks and started chasing the fleeing Doms.

Whistles and horns immediately sounded the recall, and most of those who'd been carried over the works by their passions began to halt, but as he watched, Shinya continued to wonder if he didn't need to revise his overall strategy to some extent.

"They're pulling back everywhere, Gener-aal," Kari said, her voice almost drowned by the exuberant exclamations of Suares and the alcalde. Shinya focused his binoculars beyond the battlefield, at the smoldering gun emplacements, the scattered ranks of reserve troops, broken up by Reddy's bombing run—and particularly at the area he suspected Nerino had been watching the battle as intently as he. The whole Dom army was recoiling, folding back, pulling away from the radically expanded killing field in disarray.

"I wanted to draw the Doms here, army by army, and destroy them as they came," he said softly, "but I think now that such a plan will not work." He gestured across the field. "Whatever the Grik have become, there was a time when such a repulse would have ruined many of their warriors that fled in such a way—but these are not Grik, and I must stop equating this enemy with them. Those Dom troops, those *men*, no matter how terrified at present, will eventually take control of themselves. They will re-form. They will not be surprised by our weapons again, and may gain even greater confidence for having survived them. They will pass their knowledge to others, and we will face them again."

"What're you saying, General?" Fred asked.

"Only that my every instinct has always compelled me to pursue a beaten enemy and drive him without pause." He smiled. "I believe I have objectively convinced myself that I should follow those instincts in this case after all, despite what I originally thought. That gives me a measure of satisfaction on this otherwise terrible day."

Fred looked out at the battlefield. "Chase 'em? Wow. That's a tall order."

"No. We will chase them hard for a distance beyond this field, far enough that they know they are chased." He frowned. "Because I did not prepare for it in advance, we can do little more at present, but I won't allow them to imagine later that they *chose* to leave on their own."

"Just so long as we don't wind up like the poodle that chased the bear—until it stopped running," Fred muttered.

"You think of Colonel Flynn, and his fate beyond the Rocky Gap in India?" Shinya asked.

Fred hesitated, then nodded. "Sure. How can I not? I didn't know him well, but Billy—I mean Colonel Flynn—was a right guy by all accounts. Hearing what happened to him and all those others . . . It came hard."

"I'm sure it did," Shinya agreed, "but I can assure you we shall not share his fate, Lieutenant. Do you know why?"

Fred and Kari both shook their heads.

"Because we're facing men, for one thing. Granted, the Doms are very *strange* men, but men nevertheless, and they strike me—so far—as more predictable foe than the Grik have become. We also have the two of you." He smiled. "And Colonel Blair, Lieutenant Reddy, and such as Captain Blas. There is also me, of course, and I have the honor of commanding a largely veteran army that has trained together extensively." He shrugged. "Behind us are Admirals Lelaa and Jenks. That is a good team, I think." He grew somber. "And we do have Colonel Flynn's example. Not only of how he was lost, but of his courage and determination. Our enemy fought better than I expected today," he allowed, "but for all the treachery of their leaders, their commanders cannot match our technology, determination, or experience." He straightened. "Our greatest asset is our experience, and we must deny the Dom survivors the experience they gained today. The only 'experience' I want them to take from this field is that we *mauled* them, and then chased them until it suited us to stop."

"*Where* will we stop, Gen-er-aal?" Kari asked.

Shinya smiled. "At a most interesting and convenient place for our next encounter!"

General Ghanan Nerino moaned softly in the black night atop the battered ammunition cart as the wheels jounced across scattered rocks. The many layers of his elaborate uniform coat and the aide who'd covered him with his own body had protected Nerino to some degree from the sticky, obdurate flames of the enemy bombs, but his head, hands, and lower body had been badly burned. If he hadn't been drugged into near senselessness, the bumpy ride would've had him screaming as piteously as the few other wounded being carried down the track. The loyal aide, and all those around him, had burned to death.

Normally, the rocks would've been heaved aside by troops detailed for that purpose, and the general would've barely noticed them in his elegant carriage protected by gentle springs. Now, even if the carriage hadn't been destroyed in the bombing and subsequent counterattack by the heretic horde, it was certainly in their hands. And frankly, Nerino was lucky to have the cart. Few vehicles were saved during the nearly complete rout that ensued when the enemy, flushed with victory, charged out of its earthworks around Guayak and slammed into the shattered, terrified, and disorganized Army of the South. The counterattack had been stunning in its barbaric relentlessness, and only a full commitment of the thus far reserved, but limited regiments of elite Blood Drinkers had slowed it enough to get anything out. Little, if any of the army's artillery had been withdrawn, and though they fought like the fiends they were, the sounds of battle to the south that dwindled with the day made it likely that even the Blood Drinkers had been destroyed at last.

Some hoped that the brief, relative quiet meant the rear guard had been successful and this long, terrible day might end at last. What remained of the army would retreat to a position where it could re-form and establish a defense. But then the night resumed crackling with musketry as enemy skirmishers regained contact with the ragged column and began applying pressure once more. Worse, a few of the enemy flying machines remained aloft, still battling dragons, but occasionally swooping to drop one of their terrible bombs. Even when they burned nothing but grass and trees, the remorseless, unnatural assault from the sky further unnerved the defeated troops—and sometimes, a hideous chorus of screams arose with the roiling flames. The loitering menace above prevented any lights from being made along the line of retreat, and that added even more confusion and misery to the defeated force. Few could've imagined a worse, more terrifying hell in the flaming caverns beneath the earth than they were now enduring.

Nerino understood little in his drug-hazed state. He knew pain, of course, but he'd lost his connection to the unfolding events. He could hear voices, and recognized what was being said, but he couldn't relate any of it to his own unpleasant situation. Very quickly, anything he heard was forgotten. He became aware that a squadron of lancers had appeared in the darkness alongside his cart and managed to raise himself up slightly to see. He couldn't focus, but his eyes were drawn south toward a pulsing glow. *A fire,* he thought muzzily. *A fire back there where I was today. How lovely it is, yet so dreadful as well. Why is it dreadful? Because it hurts! It has hurt me!* He lay back with a moan.

"Quickly, you four men—get those armabueyes out of their traces! Replace them with your own mounts. We must get the general out of here at once!" cried an authoritative voice Nerino didn't recognize.

"But these are not draft animals, Colonel!" a man protested. *One of the lancers,* Nerino assumed. *Quite right,* he agreed. Lancers often sprang from landed families, and not only were they responsible for providing their own mounts; the beasts were some of the finest horse-flesh in all the Dominion! "Ridiculous!" he exclaimed.

"Do it now, or I'll give you to the priests!" the colonel warned, ignoring Nerino.

"Oh, all right! No reason to get nasty! We'll have to ride them, though. They've never been harnessed before."

"Of course. Take these other lancers with you as a guard, but don't hesitate to change horses when they tire."

"Don't worry about that!" the lancer assured, his tone implying the other men in his squadron better not refuse to do their part.

"Go as quickly as you dare," the colonel urged, "and try to get him through the pass before daylight."

"But won't that just kill him? And what if he starts screaming?"

"My healer priest will ride along in the cart. He says the general may live if the pain doesn't reach his heart. He will ensure that General Nerino gets as much medicine as he can bear."

"All right. But after today, the Pajaros Rojos will just have him flayed anyway."

"Perhaps," the colonel allowed, "but I hope not. General Nerino may be a *fatuo,* but he's smart, and he may be the only one who can sort out what happened to us when his wits return. Now hurry! The heretics are getting closer."

Fatuo indeed! Nerino fumed silently through the mounting waves of pain. Then his wandering mind fastened onto something else he'd heard. *I would so dislike being flayed. I do so hope that I can sort out whatever it is that has happened!*

////// *Empire of the New Britain Isles*
New Scotland
June 21, 1944

er Majesty, Rebecca Anne McDonald,
Governor-Empress of the Empire of the
New Britain Isles, was working diligently at
her murdered father's desk. Around her, in
Gerald McDonald's expansive Government
House library at Scapa Flow, reposed every
"original" prepassage book that came to this
world aboard the three East Indiamen that brought her ancestors here.
They'd been her father's most prized possessions, and though expensive
reprints were available throughout the Empire, Gerald had considered
his guardianship of these precious links to the old world one of his most
sacred trusts. Now they, and all the interesting gadgets and contrivances her father had tinkered with in the chamber, remained just as

he'd left them: essential links between an idolized father and his griev-
ing daughter.

Rebecca supposed she probably ought to be at Government House
across the strait in the capital of New London, on New Britain Isle, particularly now that the "Time of Treachery" seemed to have passed, but
she felt much more comfortable in what had been her childhood home.
Besides, Scapa Flow was a Navy port and a Navy city, and its people
were unreservedly devoted to her. Some might be uncomfortable about
the Decree of Manumission she'd recently issued, giving full citizen-
ship to women and officially ending the age-old practice of female in-
denture, but women had always enjoyed better conditions in Scapa Flow
than elsewhere in the Empire. They'd been Navy auxiliaries, skilled
yard workers and shipwrights. Some had even been entrusted with real
authority within those occupations. That made their transition from
virtual slavery to legal equality less tumultuous across New Scotland
than elsewhere. Even there, however, some stodgy traditionalists railed
about "slippery slopes" and remained horrified by the notion of allowing women in the Navy itself. But they were careful not to criticize the
young empress's reforms in general terms. Despite her tender age, and
having established the framework for the restoration of the Courts of
Directors and Proprietors, Rebecca Anne McDonald had snatched back
a great deal of executive power that had been seeping away for generations. She'd also shown herself to be a courageous, determined leader
when the Empire needed one most, as well as a ruthless enemy to her
foes—foreign and domestic.

His Excellency Sean Bates, once known to the Lemurian/American
powers in the Alliance as "O'Casey," had advanced from the status of
outlaw protector of a young, shipwrecked princess to become Prime
Factor to the Governor-Empress. He remained her legal guardian as
well, though most recognized that post as a fiction. He'd continue to
guard her, with his one mighty arm until the day he died, and he'd always counsel her, if allowed, but he couldn't—wouldn't—exercise any
legal restraint on her. She'd proven herself sufficiently mature beyond
her fourteen years to fully assume her duties, and his only real concern
was that she'd been forced to grow up too quickly—and far too vio-

lently. That showed in the degree to which she'd begun to suppress her sweeter nature, and isolate her emotions from those who loved her most.

Sean passed her yet another page to sign—a naval commission for the master of a former Company ship—and glanced at the clock on the mantel above the cavernous fireplace in the library.

"Sister Audry'll be along directly, lass," he said quietly.

Rebecca finished signing her name for perhaps the hundredth time that morning, and sighed. She looked at the clock as well. "She's probably already waiting, poor thing. Please do see if she's in the hall, won't you?"

"Of course, Yer Majesty." Sean's chair creaked as he stood to step to the heavy door. Opening it, he peered outside. "Aye, there she is, with that evil Sergeant Koratin, as usual," he said with a grin. Then he paused, his grin fading. "An' they seem to've brought that . . . visitor we discussed."

"I see," Rebecca murmured. "Well, don't leave them waiting any longer. Let them in."

"I'm still nae sure ye shid see 'im without a guard," Bates hedged.

"I'm confident you and Sergeant Koratin can protect me, even should he sprout wings and fangs and go for my throat," she said dryly. "You've both protected me from far worse before. And if Sister Audry, a far greater threat to his soul than I, remains safe in his presence, I should have little to fear."

Grudgingly, Sean opened the door wider. "Her Majesty'll see ye now," he said, then stepped aside. Sister Audry, wearing a new duplicate of the habit she'd worn to utter destruction, hurried into the room, an enthusiastic smile on her face. She was Dutch, a Benedictine nun, carried away from Java in the Old War to shepherd a number of children of diplomats and high-ranking officers aboard the old submarine, S-19. Rebecca had known her since they had all been stranded together on Talaud Island a couple of years before. She was very attached to the young straw-haired woman who believed she'd been called not only to spread the "true faith" among the Allies, but perhaps more important, salvage the tortured souls of those enslaved by the twisted faith of the Dominion.

She'd gone among the Dom prisoners taken during the New Ireland campaign, along with ministers of the British Church, preaching and explaining how the Catholic faith of the Spanish element of their culture had been so hideously perverted. Dom regulars were professional and competent soldiers, but only their officers could read—essential for passing orders and dispatches, and completing the paperwork required for any army—but there was no acceptable literature other than devout treatises and holy writs in the Dominion, and their entire cultural and religious indoctrination came from the fearsome Blood Priests. After learning as much about the Dom faith as she could bear to hear (since she had an active imagination, even verbal descriptions gave her nightmares), Sister Audry found it relatively simple to refute much of its twisted, contradictory dogma. Her teachings were far more compelling and attractive, particularly to defeated soldiers who'd been raised in such a repressive, unforgiving, and impulsively cruel society. She believed, and had reported, that she'd made significant breakthroughs at last.

Following her through the doorway was a slender man in the tattered but clean uniform of a lieutenant of Dominion "Salvadores," or expeditionary regulars. The expression on his dark, handsome face was guarded—except when he glanced at Audry for reassurance. Then it turned to something that bordered on . . . worshipful. He paused before Rebecca and bowed very low.

Bringing up the rear was a short, muscular, wizened Lemurian with quick eyes that gave the impression he was constantly evaluating threats—or opportunities. The fur beneath his white Marine dress armor had streaks of white as well, from middle age and battle scars. Rebecca stood and received Audry's kiss on her cheek, nodded at Koratin with a smile, then regarded her other visitor curiously.

"May I present Teniente Arano Garcia?" Audry gushed. "He has been selected to represent nearly eight hundred souls that have surrendered their lives to God, and to your service in the cause of liberating their people from the evil infesting their home!"

"Eight hundred, indeed?" asked Rebecca with a tentative smile. "How charming."

"Eight hundred out'a more'n four thousand prisoners," Bates gruffed.

"My—our—mission has had little time to reverse *lifetimes* of lies," Audry defended, "and more are coming around. But Teniente Garcia has staked his life on the loyalty of the men he represents!"

"We've all staked our lives on the defeat of his country, which will result—has *already* resulted in the deaths of thousands on both sides," Rebecca said softly.

"He understands that," Audry insisted. "He wants to help!"

"I know you speak some Spanish, but do you speak enough to fully evaluate his motives?" Rebecca asked, a polite way of inquiring how Audry could be sure Garcia wasn't lying.

"As a Salvadore, I have had intensive instruction in the English," Garcia said quietly. "Many Dominion officers have. It is deemed important to communicate with conquered peoples," he added with apologetic irony.

Rebecca looked at Sergeant Koratin. The Lemurian had once been a lord of Aryaal, and by his own admission an "expert" on treachery. He'd had a traumatic epiphany, however, and had actually been one of Sister Audry's earliest Lemurian converts to Catholicism. "What do you think, Sergeant?"

Koratin blinked thoughtfully. "I have come to know Lieutenant Garcia," he said, "and I think I believe him." He shrugged and swished his tail. "But I have believed others before, to my . . . disadvantage, who had less reason to mislead me. I am—was—perhaps better at deception in my old life than at discovering it. And as an enlisted Marine, I have grown . . . rusty, yes? Rusty at intrigue. I have come to prefer much more straightforward confrontations." Rebecca nodded. There was no doubting Koratin's valor.

"But ye do think he wants tae fight fer us?" Bates demanded.

Koratin regarded Garcia a moment before nodding at last. "I do. And I have made very clear to him and his men how I would personally prosecute any hint of infidelity."

Audry shuddered, then sighed. There were whispered rumors of how Koratin had "prosecuted" the treacherous, upstart king of Aryaal. "Really, Sergeant . . ."

"Good," Bates agreed. He looked at Garcia. "So you want to fight?"

"I do. My people do." His stoic expression suddenly went adrift, and he looked at Audry with eyes that reflected a tortured woe. "I cannot express, can hardly comprehend . . . My people, my race—the hideous lies that torment us from our very birth—"

"Very well," Rebecca interjected gently. "I'm glad to hear it. I will give you your chance to fight, perhaps sooner than you might imagine."

Bates looked at her. "Yer Majesty?"

Rebecca regarded every face, then took a long breath. "Please, everyone, be seated."

Refreshments were brought, and they talked lightly for a time. Much of the conversation was directed at Garcia, of course, and Audry described conditions in the prison camp and the rebuilding efforts underway on New Ireland. Many prisoners had been set to work assisting in that respect, and others were employed harvesting the charred timber of the great valley forest. It was hard work, but the prisoners universally considered themselves lucky. They were sheltered, well fed, and undoubtedly better treated than Imperial troops in their position ever would've been.

Finally, Rebecca took a sip of watered brandy and spoke. "The information I am about to relate must not go beyond this chamber," she said, deeply serious. "Perhaps that will serve as a final test of Lieutenant Garcia's loyalty?" She eyed the man. "Beyond those here, the only others who know what I am about to tell you are the Lemurian Marines entrusted with our most sensitive codes. If you speak of it, I *will* know." She sipped again. "High Admiral Jenks has sent word that General Shinya and the Allied Expeditionary Force in the East have won a great victory over the Doms at the coastal city of Guayak. Not only that, but he has hounded a Dom army numbering upward of fifty thousand troops to virtual annihilation." She let that sit a moment, examining expressions. Bates already knew, of course, but the revelation was news to everyone else. "General Shinya has now stopped and begun fortifying a crossroads vital to the enemy, without which they cannot mass more troops against him from east of the mountains, nor can they approach from north or south without exposing themselves to continuous air attack. He retains firm lines of supply, and contact with the coast. From there, he will consolidate his gains and prepare to resume his offensive." She noted with satisfaction that Garcia leaned forward with a predatory gleam in his eye.

"Good," she murmured, then raised her voice. "Despite the imperatives in the West, the time has come to support Admiral Jenks and General Shinya more fully. Having sent so many troops west, we have little left here but our strategic reserve and home guard. That said, I believe the Isles are safe from attack, and the time has come to use those troops."

"Yer Majesty!" Bates protested, but Rebecca held up her hand. "The Isles will not be left naked. My sister, Saan-Kakja, High Chief of all the Fil-pin Lands, will soon arrive for a state visit, accompanied by two thousand Maa-ni-la infantry. She has already sent enough of her people to fight our enemy, so they will remain here—but that frees more of *us* to fight."

Bates sat back, a little less alarmed. He deeply admired Saan-Kakja, and knew the extraordinary Lemurian had already sent more assets east than she was comfortable with. Her profound friendship with the just slightly younger Rebecca was probably the only reason she had. Rebecca had called her "sister," in the Lemurian way of addressing other High Chiefs, but Bates knew she trusted and regarded Saan-Kakja at least as closely as she would any real sister. Just as he'd begun to calm a bit after her earlier statement, however, young Rebecca stunned him with what she said next:

"It is my belief that Saan-Kakja means to travel from here to the eastern front of the war. She once promised to go west with the troops she sent against the Grik, and she has long been frustrated by her inability to do so. She has implied to me that, with as many of her people now in the East as in the West, at least with the Army, if not the Navy, she now feels equally drawn there." She stared defiantly around. "If she goes, I shall go with her."

"Nay, lass! I ferbid it!" Bates thundered. "Tis much too dangerous!"

"You *forbid*, Prime Factor Bates?" Rebecca asked softly, icily.

Bates paused, gathering himself. "I *counsel* strongly against it, Yer Majesty," he revised, face red. "The situation here in the Isles is better, aye, but nae yet fixed in stone. Ye cannae risk yersel' so. All we've worked tae achieve could wither away!"

"Not if you remain here, as regent, to prevent it," Rebecca said reasonably, but Bates's eyes bulged from their sockets at the suggestion she might go without him. "I will have sufficient protection," she assured before he could speak, and looked squarely at Sister Audry. "Particularly now that *you* have raised me yet another loyal regiment of already seasoned troops!"

"*I* didn't raise them, Your Majesty," Sister Audry demurred modestly before she caught Rebecca's intent stare. "But . . . you cannot mean!"

"Indeed. It is *your* regiment, Sister Audry, yours to lead and command!"

"This is utter madness, my dear!" Audry exclaimed. "I have no notion whatsoever of military affairs!"

"You know who the true enemy is," Rebecca countered relentlessly, "which is more than many of my more formally trained commanders did for some time." She looked at Garcia. "And who better to lead them? Whom do they revere more?"

Garcia seemed stunned as well, but finally nodded. "Sister Audry came to us as a prophet, and she raised our souls from the sickening pit in which they dwelt. Speaking for myself and all my men, you could not appoint another leader over us to whom we would be more devoted. We will follow and protect her like the prophet she is!"

"Never fear," Rebecca added to the flabbergasted nun. "You shall have sufficient help. I'm sure Sergeant Koratin, for one, will be pleased to remain with you and can certainly deal with many of your administrative and training duties."

"Of course," Koratin said, blinking amusement. He wondered if he alone recognized the brilliance of the Governor-Empress's scheme. With Audry commanding the regiment, not only would the chance of treachery from the ranks be even less likely; Audry had the chance to redeem not only the former Doms under her command, but her very church in the eyes of the Imperial subjects. There was no real association between the true Catholic Church and the superficial similarities the Doms had adopted, but far too many of Rebecca's people didn't understand the distinctions.

"It's all settled, then," Rebecca said grandly. "Factor Bates? Would you kindly send for more refreshments?" She smiled at Sister Audry with a trace of her old, girlish enthusiasm. "We must propose a proper toast to the formation of our newest regiment. I wonder what we should call it."

////// *First Fleet South*
1100 Miles South of Ceylon
June 30, 1944

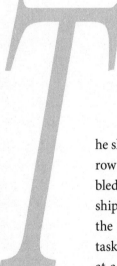

he sky remained dazzlingly clear for the third day in a row above the white, gust-swept wave tops that marbled the cerulean sea. Most of the DDs and support ships constituting USNRS *Salissa*'s battle group and the other accumulated vessels that rounded out the task force plodded creditably through the brisk swells at a modest but workmanlike eight knots. From the surface, the collection of ships appeared a formidable force. To one of the Nancy floatplanes returning from a long-range scout, however, the task force looked more like a scattered, lonely atoll in the center of an endless, empty sea.

The DDs and all sail DEs could've easily made much more of the strong, southerly wind. Even *Salissa*, lightened as she'd been, could've comfortably made ten or twelve knots. But the tenders—and particularly the oilers—were having a little trouble. Some of the screening DDs could gallop along unrestrained, scouting ahead or on the flanks of the task force, pounding the depths with powerful sonar pulses to deter any lurking mountain fish that might pose a threat to the fleet. But the ship most grievously inhibited by the poky advance at the moment was USS *Walker*. She was steaming carefully alongside *Salissa*, her helmsman straining to match her every move and compensate for the suction, the thumping waves, conflicting wakes, and the old destroyer's erratic pitching. Matt was on the port bridgewing, watching the narrow gap between his ship and *Salissa* with apparent calm. If someone had noticed his right hand gripping the rail beside the Morse lamp, however, they'd have seen his knuckles were white.

Their own experiments, and others performed before the Old War that Matt was aware of, had shown that steaming this close was actually easier at a greater speed of ten to fifteen knots, when the ships could more easily compensate for the suction generated between them. But Matt was determined that they practice the maneuver at all speeds and in various sea states. So far, the results were decidedly mixed.

"No, no, *no*, goddamn it!" roared the terrible Chief Bosun Fitzhugh Gray down on the fo'c'sle below. "Who told you to secure those taglines? Cast 'em off!" For an instant, some of the mostly Lemurian detail just stared at him, but then a couple scampered to obey. Fortunately, the lines were still slack, but the instant they were released, *Walker*'s bow pitched down and some of the lines—and a fat cable hawser—whipped up into the sky like flying snakes, and then lashed the sea alongside. Gray's face was purple with rage. "What the hell do you think you're doin'?" he ranted. "You can't *secure* the goddamn hose to the ship! How many times've I gotta pound it through your pointy little ears?"

"But it get away!" a tall 'Cat cried back in frustration, gesturing over the side.

"*Course* it's gonna get away, the way that stripy-assed idiot strikin' for QM's steerin' the ship!" Gray bellowed with an almost pleading glance back up at the captain. "But if it wants to get away that bad, you gotta let it go! We've got a springline on it an' it won't get *plumb* away. But you secure it to the ship and it's liable to part—or worse!" He closed his eyes. "When I look again, you better be outa my sight! Go secure your twitchy tail to a *signal halyard* an' hoist your stupid ass to the foremast yard!" He opened one eye to find the dumbfounded 'Cat just staring at him. He sighed. "Too many newies," he lamented. "Too many old hands got sent off to *Mahan*, right when we need 'em most." He whirled. "You! Gyrene! What was your name?"

"Lance Corporal Miles, Bosun. Ian Miles," answered a tall, thin man with dark hair. Gray remembered Miles's name perfectly well, but wasn't impressed. He'd been with Commander Herring in the Philippines, along with Gunny Horn, but he acted like that still meant something. Horn had slipped into the role of Silva's chief minion, an association he'd obviously been comfortable with in a previous life, but if that didn't necessarily recommend him, it made him useful. Miles struck Gray as a slacker, with no intention of truly becoming part of *Walker*'s company. Gray took that personally. Also, despite Herring's apparent conversion to the cause and his sincere desire to become a "real" destroyerman, Lance Corporal Miles maintained an oddly confidential relationship with him that Commander Herring didn't seem to discourage. Maybe that was normal, after all they'd been through together, but Gray suspected Miles was milking it. He didn't reflect on his own close friendships with officers, and indeed the very highest ranking leaders of the Grand Alliance. He always kept that in perspective, and diligently ensured that it never interfered with the chain of command.

"*You* take over the detail," he ordered, "and you better do it right. You've sat on your ass an' watched it done often enough. Make yourself useful for a change. Ain't no full-time Marines on *this* ship, with their dainty gloves an' such! Clap onto that hawser when they shift it back—I mean the 'hose,' damn it! And pretend there's a storm comin' an' we're slap out of fuel!" He rounded on the others. "If there's any more mistakes, they better come from the pilothouse, an' not my damn division!"

Matt smiled faintly as he watched the little drama, thankful that amid all the change they'd endured in the past couple of years, Chief Gray was always there to provide a sense of continuity.

"Not going so well?" asked Spanky, rather delicately, over his shoulder.

"No, no, it's fine. Just a few bugs. Mr. Rosen?" he said, turning to

Chief Quartermaster "Paddy" Rosen. "Take the helm, if you please. Mr. Herring, you still have the conn."

"Aye, aye, sir. I still have the conn!" Herring announced a little self-consciously. Matt nodded reassuringly at him, and caught himself *liking* Herring at last. He was glad the pedantic intelligence officer was genuinely doing his very best to learn the art of shiphandling. He hoped the new attitude would help him become a better, more levelheaded analyst as well. Rosen stepped beside the foam-sweaty 'Cat at the big brass wheel. "I relieve you, sir."

"I staand veery relieved!" gasped the 'Cat, and Matt had to stifle a grin. Looking up, he watched as one of *Big Sal*'s seaplane-lifting booms raised the heavy hawser back out of the sea. The hawser was standing in for a fueling hose for this drill. Slowly, carefully, the boom came down, leaving the end of the hawser dangling just in front of the bridge. Chief Gray roared again, and taglines brought the heavy cable near where a fueling hose would have to be in order to transfer oil into the ship's bunkers. Miraculously, this time, they managed to maintain station for almost eleven minutes. Miles held the cable end coiled on the deck while others on both ships worked to keep the proper tension on the "hose" and boom as *Walker* capered alongside the relatively motionless *Salissa*.

Suddenly, *Walker*'s bow took another unexpected plunge, and seawater coursed across the fo'c'sle, knocking a couple of 'Cats to the deck. Miles was almost yanked off the ship before releasing the cable, and he watched it whip into the sky. Then he shot the Bosun what might've been a resentful smirk before he shrugged.

"Well," Matt said, looking at his watch in disappointment. "Eleven minutes. That's something. Secure from underway fueling. Mr. Palmer, signal *Big Sal* and thank Admiral Keje for his cooperation. Tell him we're finished for now, and we'll resume our screening pattern."

"Aye, aye, Skipper," replied Lieutenant Ed Palmer, moving behind the Morse lamp as Matt stepped back into the pilothouse. A light flashed on *Salissa*, and the young signals officer grimaced. "Admiral Keje says 'anytime,' and 'we must all do what we can to avoid the tedium of this voyage,' and his people 'enjoy fishing for *Walker* very much!' His words, sir."

"Oh crap," Spanky grumbled. "That's just mean. Look, sir, you know how I like my—I mean *Tabby's*—bunkers: fat an' happy. But we already proved we can replenish when the sea's not up so high. And we've been doing it alongside *Big Sal* when she's stationary for two damn years! Why've we gotta keep humiliating ourselves? Hell, nobody back home had even really perfected a stunt like this when we left!"

"No, but they'd been working on it for twenty years because it's a valuable capability." Matt frowned. "And maybe I just don't like the idea of being a sitting duck. We're going an awful long way from home again, and nobody we know has even been there to tell us what to expect this time—except one lost Jap. Besides"—Matt shrugged—"like Keje said, it passes the time."

"Keje asks if you'll be over to dine with him—and your, uh, 'mate'—this evening," Palmer interjected.

"It's my pleasure, as always," Matt replied in a softer tone. "Now," he said, more businesslike, "resume standard screening pattern, if you please, Mr. Herring. You have the deck and the conn. Mr. McFarlane and I will be in the wardroom."

"I have the deck and the conn," Herring declared. "Standard screening pattern, aye."

Matt nodded and turned toward the stairs at the back of the bridge.

"I know what you're really worried about," Spanky gruffed quietly, conspiratorially, following him down the metal steps, and then down the companionway leading between the officers' staterooms toward the wardroom.

"I don't know what you're talking about," Matt grumbled. As always, the smells assailing them as soon as they left the open air were overwhelming. Sour sweat and mildew were all-pervading, but so were other things like hot linoleum, fuel oil, and those vague but distinct odors of brass, iron, paint, and rust. They were used to the smells, of course, but that didn't mean they never noticed them. Worst of all perhaps, as they passed through the embroidered curtain into the wardroom, was the stench emanating from the officers' coffeepot as they drew near.

"Sure you do," McFarlane insisted.

Instead of replying, Matt, his expression grim, raised the lid on the pot and looked inside. "My God. I know it's against tradition to wash

these things and all, but it's not like Juan has real coffee to ruin. Juan!"
he shouted, being uncharacteristically harsh. A few moments later, Juan
Marcos, the peg-legged, self-appointed chief steward for the commander in chief of all Allied forces, stumped into the compartment
from the chief's quarters forward, his small, Filipino face aggrieved.

"Cap-tan?"

Matt calmed himself and closed the lid. "Could you make some
more coffee, Juan . . . and maybe slosh a little of the foam out of this
thing first?"

"Of course, Cap-tan," Juan said, a little stiffly, taken aback. Juan
treated Matt and all the officers very well, and nobody ever criticized
him but the fat cook, Earl Lanier. But suddenly, Matt's tone and expression implied reproach. Juan snatched the pot and stumped out of the
wardroom with remarkable poise and agility, considering his condition
and the continued pitching of the ship.

"Kind of hard on the little guy, weren't you, Skipper?" Spanky said.
"Yeah," he decided. "You're worried about that pigboat Silva saw!"

"I'm not worried about something that's probably not even out
there," Matt denied.

"Who says it isn't? Why can't there be another pigboat somewhere
on this creepy world? Hell, *we* used to have one!"

Matt took a breath, glad Laumer was on *Big Sal*. He was still taking
the loss of his sub-turned-torpedo-boat hard. "Then I guess what I'm
saying is, we don't know what it was—if it was anything. And Silva
didn't see it. Frankly, weird as it sounds, I'd feel better if he had. Gunny
Horn seems reliable enough, but when has he ever seen a periscope?
Silva's likely right. It was probably some kind of fin. All those idiots
were mixed up with a bunch of weird fish at the time. Who knows what
kind of fin might've been sticking up?"

"Courtney didn't think it was a fin," Spanky reminded.

"He didn't see it."

"No, but he said there wasn't anything around that had a fin any
'thinking being,' as he said, could possibly mistake for a periscope."

"So, he's insulting Horn *or* Silva—not that either would care. But
whose side is he on?" Matt demanded, frustrated. He'd been furious

when he heard about the latest "Silva Stunt," and it had put him in a bad position. Dennis Silva had just recently out-heroed himself and deserved all their gratitude—but then he turned around and disobeyed a long-standing, direct order; something Matt had been fairly sure Silva wouldn't ever do again. That Lanier was the instigator didn't even signify. He was a lost cause; only marginally useful—any of his mess attendants could take over as cook—and only barely tolerable anymore. But Matt had grown to rely on Silva far more than he'd realized, and Courtney's reckless, irresponsible participation had been icing on the cake. That was why Courtney was on *Big Sal* right now instead of *Walker*: he was on probation. Not that such a banishment was really a punishment; *Big Sal* was much more comfortable, and there was a great deal more for Courtney to do aboard her. But the implied threat was that he had better shape up if he wanted to join *Walker* again when something "interesting" was in the works.

Matt still had to figure out what punishment he'd inflict on the other miscreants—right at a time when they'd embarked on perhaps their most audacious, precarious, and with Adar along, potentially *ambiguous* operation of the war! For obvious reasons, he had a lot on his mind. His, and the other ships in the task force were in reasonably good shape, but they'd been handled roughly very recently. He had every confidence in Chack-Sab-At, and was sure his Raider Brigade and the PT "mosquito fleet" would be ready to go when they reached Diego Garcia, but he wasn't sure exactly what else he'd find when they got there. "Lemurian" aborigines! Representatives of an extremely strange power also opposing the Grik! A Japanese refugee from *Amagi*, who claimed actual personal knowledge of Grik Madagascar! How would all that come together?

Other things nagged at him. He visited Sandra aboard *Big Sal* nearly every day, coincidentally crossing to confer with Adar, Keje, and the staff of First Fleet South, but shortly after leaving Madras, Sandra had grown suddenly cryptic, even distant to a degree. That confused and hurt him. In addition, Adar increasingly used the terms "take" and "liberate" instead of "raid" in connection to their mission to the prehistoric birthplace of his people, and everyone around him, even Keje, seemed affected by his rhetoric. Then, of course, besides the recent episode, Courtney Bradford was acting even more strangely than usual, becoming short-tempered and rebellious as he apparently wrestled with what he'd begun calling his own "unified theory of here." Matt took a long breath. *And there's this "periscope fin" to consider.*

He'd planned this expedition, worked for it, done everything he could to convince everyone it was *right*, and he still believed that. But he felt increasingly hemmed in by alterations, unexpected developments, and what appeared to be the changing aims of all the other participants. He was used to improvisation, and was honest enough to realize that his ability to adapt to situations, either strategically or in a slugging match, had certainly saved his ship many times. It had maybe even saved the whole war. But for the first time in longer than he could remember, he was beginning to feel uncertain, even overwhelmed. There was too much happening all at once, and he had far too little control. Worse, right when these feelings began to mount, when he most needed Bradford's advice, Adar's steady purpose, Sandra's quiet strength and love—and even Silva's loyalty, damn it!—he sensed a growing gulf between himself and all those things.

"Sounds like Courtney's either saying Horn's an idiot for claiming a periscope, or Silva is for not believing him," Spanky mused, thankfully oblivious to Matt's thoughts.

"Yeah," Matt agreed, looking at his watch. It was 1649 hours. "I think it's time we asked him which it is. That, and a lot of things."

"When? Tonight when you go over to *Big Sal*?"

Matt thought it over, then shook his head. "No. Not in any big way, anyhow." He smiled. "We'll be at Diego in five or six days if the weather holds. Let's see just what the hell is going on with our new friends from this 'Republic of Real People' before we pin him down. That may be the last card he needs before he lays his hand on the table."

The hard-used, once-drowned general alarm squawked horribly through the overhead speaker, and Matt and Spanky looked at each other.

*　　*　　*

"Cap-i-taan on the bridge!" trilled the diminutive 'Cat talker named Min-Sakir, or "Minnie." Matt reflected again that the little Lemurian really did sound like Minnie Mouse.

"As you were," he said. "Report, Mr. Herring."

"Jarrik-Fas on USS *Tassat* has a mountain fish contact."

"Mountain fish," "island fish," or just simply "Leviathans" as the Imperials called them, were utterly tremendous beasts. They were many times the size of a blue whale, but they were similar in the sense that they were air breathers and filter feeders—of a sort. Those were about the only similarities, however, if one discounted the obvious fact that they swam in the sea. Entirely unlike blue whales, mountain fish were aggressively territorial, at least part of the time. They did apparently migrate to breed—during which time they were as passive as monstrous lambs, according to new information from Admiral Jenks in the East—but little more about their nature was known. And their method of "filter feeding" wasn't passive at all, gobbling anything that would fit in their mouths as they cruised along, including plesiosaurs and the humongous sharks in these waters. They could even be dangerous to vessels the size of *Big Sal*.

Matt's brows rose. "Really." Usually, the monstrous fish avoided the punishing sound pulses used by the screening ships and rarely hung around long enough to be detected. "Where's *Tassat*?"

"Dead ahead, Captain," Herring said. "Two two zero degrees. I took the liberty of steering toward her."

"Very well." *Walker* was the fastest ship in the fleet, maybe in the world, and her job when it came to mountain fish encounters was to sprint toward whichever ship detected one, just in case it didn't go away. "All ahead full. Have Mr. Fairchild commence underwater search."

"Ay, ay!" called Minnie. Every steam-powered DD in the West had very crude sonar now, but *Walker*'s set, primitive as it was by modern standards on the world she left, was at least capable of providing the general position of an underwater target. The accuracy of that position plummeted in direct proportion to her speed, however; the faster she went, the worse the return. This was problematic against submarines, of course, but all she had to do was get near a mountain fish. The huge creatures clearly used some kind of natural sonar themselves, and were extremely sensitive to the electronic lashing *Walker* could deliver at close range. They almost always fled.

Walker quickly built speed, and the blower behind the bridge roared louder, forcing more air into her fiery boilers to burn the sudden gush of additional fuel oil. The fuel flared against the water tubes to generate more, quicker steam, to spin up the lovingly maintained Parsons geared turbines in the ship's two engine rooms. Twin shafts turned faster, and the screws churned the sea beneath the propeller guards. Matt took a step to the left and glanced aft, past the charthouse, and saw hardly a puff of extra smoke haze the top of two of the ship's four funnels. Lieutenant Tab-At, or "Tabby" as everyone called her, had become a fine engineering officer. Of course she had the aid of Chief Isak Reuben, one of the original fireroom Mice, and no doubt he was watching the burner batters like a hawk . . . *or some other, stranger creature,* Matt reflected. He turned back forward to watch the sea sluice up past the fo'c'sle in ragged gouts of spray.

Ahead, just over a mile now, was USS *Tassat. Tassat* was a fine-looking ship, practically streaking along with her sails taut, and white spray cascading back from her sleek black hull. She was one of their second-generation square rig, screw steamers of the *Haakar-Faask* Class. Displacing 1,600 tons—heavier than *Walker* herself—she was all wood except for blisters of armor plate to provide some protection for her engineering spaces. Even with the add-on weight of the armor, she could make fifteen knots on steam alone—somewhat more when all sails were set and she had her favorite wind. She still carried the older thirty-two-pounder guns, but had twenty of them, along with her Y guns and depth charges. Her captain, Jarrik-Fas, was Keje's cousin, and Matt had known him almost as long as any Lemurian. He and many of his 226 officers and enlisted crew had come from *Salissa* herself. Matt smiled when he noted only the merest wisp of smoke from *Tassat's* single tall funnel just forward of the mainmast.

"Tell Captain Jarrik to ease off on the gas," Matt instructed his talker. "We'll be up with him soon enough. If his contact wants to be stubborn, no sense making it mad all by himself. We'll chase it off together."

"Sound room has the con-taact," Minnie reported. "Con-taact bearing two four seero!"

"Very well. Inform *Tassat*. Right standard rudder, Mr. Rosen. Bring us to two four zero."

"Two four zero, aye."

Tassat altered course and slowed slightly while *Walker* caught up; then both ships proceeded toward the contact in line abreast, about six hundred yards apart, at twelve knots.

"Sound room has firm contact," Minnie announced. "Faar-chyd reports taargit course two seero seero now, bearing two two seero!"

"Range?" Matt demanded.

"Eight hundred."

"It's not running away," Herring observed, a trace of tension in his voice. He'd never seen a mountain fish up close before, and didn't really want to.

"No," Matt agreed. "But it's not coming at us either." He looked at Spanky. "We can't let it just hang around out here, though. We're not far off the path the bulk of the task force will take, and it's sort of frustrating when you get that many ships to alter course around one of the damn things, and then it just swims back in front of 'em again." He stared out the pilothouse windows, then continued for Herring's benefit. "Normally, we prefer to leave the big boys alone if they leave us alone. They can be . . . a handful when they get annoyed." He scratched his nose. "But this one's being unusually persistent."

"Maybe he's got a head cold," Spanky quipped, and Matt blinked mild amusement in the Lemurian way.

"Could be. Well, we'll either cure him or make him worse. Tell *Tassat* we'll both crank up the volume and hammer him hard." He grinned at Herring. "Which might *really* hack him off. Mountain fish have a temper. We'll ready the Y guns and have the main battery stand by for surface action if the fish comes up. Pass the word to Mr. Campeti."

"Aa-spect change!" Minnie trilled. "Sound says the con-taact moves away, goes deeper! It still not in any hurry, though."

Spanky's brow furrowed, and he motioned at the chartroom with his head. *Walker*'s chartroom served multiple functions. It was the sound room as well as the captain's sea cabin where he kept an uncomfortable cot. Matt nodded, and they stepped around to the starboard side of the structure to peer through the hatch.

"Whatcha got, Wally?" he asked Wallace Fairchild, *Walker*'s chief sonarman. He was one of the few men aboard who still had almost the same job he'd started with. His duties had expanded, of course, and he was most responsible for all the advances they'd made in "AMFDIC," or anti-mountain fish countermeasures.

"I still got him," Wally muttered under his dark mustache, eyes intent on the squiggly screen.

"Well, what's he doing?" Spanky demanded, impatient. He was a mechanical genius, but electricity in general, and sophisticated equipment like Fairchild's in particular might as well have been voodoo as far as he was concerned.

"He's turned away, going deep, but we're gaining fast." Big as they were, a mountain fish in full flight—or charge—could sprint at eighteen to twenty knots for a short distance. He frowned.

"What's the matter?" Matt asked.

"Well, sir, it's hard to say. Everything about this contact is just, well, screwy."

"Screwy, how?"

"Mountain fish are big, sir," Wally said, excitement rising in his voice. "They bounce back a helluva signal, but its, well, kinda . . . diffused. Sorta . . . mushy, sir, if you know what I mean."

"Mushy," Spanky grated. "Because they're meat instead of metal?"

"Not exactly, sir, though I can see why you'd think that. Actually, the sound pulse doesn't bounce back off the animal, but the air inside it. Mountain fish carry around a lot of air, in their lungs and air bladders, I guess. Sorta like trim tanks or something."

Matt was nodding. "So what's different about this one?" he asked, a strange prickling sensation climbing his back.

"It's a . . . harder contact, I think. It's fading now"—he pointed at the screen—"but I think that's because it's deeper, going under a layer, I bet."

"Harder? Like a sub?" Matt asked. The air in a sub wasn't diffused.

Wally screwed up his face. "Well, maybe . . . But where would a sub come from? Besides"—he pointed again—"no matter what kind of return we got, it's too big to be any sub *I* ever saw. It may not be the biggest mountain fish, but it's too big to be a sub."

"Are you sure?"

"No, sir. But I'm not sure a mountain fish can't make a hard return like that either." He shrugged. "Beats me. And whatever it is, it's fading." He stared at the screen and turned a large dial back and forth. "Gone, sir."

"Gone," Spanky grunted. "Like a fish would."

"A slow, hard fish," Matt said softly.

"Yes, sir."

"Thank you, Mr. Fairchild," Matt said briskly, turning out of the charthouse. "Let me know immediately if it comes back."

"Aye, aye, sir."

Matt and Spanky stepped back into the pilothouse. "Minnie, instruct *Tassat* that we'll circle here for a while before returning to our patrol stations. Secure from general quarters, but maintain condition three."

"Is everything all right, Captain?" Herring asked.

Matt nodded slightly. "Sure. As far as I know. Oh, Minnie? Please inform *Salissa* that we investigated an . . . indeterminate contact, but we're going to stay on our toes for a while. Extend my regrets to the admiral and my wife that I'll be unable to dine with them this evening."

"Ay, ay, Cap-i-taan."

///// *TFG-2*
USS Donaghey *(DDS-2)*
Indian (Western) Ocean

aptain of Marines Bekiaa-Sab-At leaned on USS *Donaghey*'s port fo'c'sle rail, staring down at the foaming sea beneath the bows as the ship slanted south-southwest across a choppy gray sea. But Bekiaa didn't see the froth, or feel the stiff, salty breeze. Instead, at that moment, she stood on the southern slope of North Hill once again. The chaotic white foam had become the urgent billow of cannon smoke, and the marching waves were a relentless tide of Grik warriors surging, hacking, *swarming*, against the meager defenses and precious lives atop the otherwise insignificant little hill.

As always, when this memory, this . . . reality . . . swept her back to that other time and place, her pulse thundered, and her heart hammered at her breastbone, her stomach clenched with dread, the bile of hopeless anguish rose in her throat—and she was afraid. The fear actually stunned her. She'd been in desperate combat many times, often when the likely outcome appeared very bleak indeed, but she'd never truly been afraid. Even stranger, even as she relived that awful moment when she realized, for the very first time, they'd never break *this* Grik charge no matter how savagely they mauled it, a detached, analytical fragment of her mind recognized she *hadn't* been afraid, not like this, at the moment she'd returned to. It was later, when the enormity of the concept of disciplined Grik finally registered, that she knew that she and every member of Colonel Flynn's scratch division surrounded on North Hill were doomed. Worse, that . . . other self who'd been there, miraculously survived, and reported to the "self" she'd since become, understood that despite all the horror and trauma she'd endured since, it was that earlier moment, not even decisive in itself, that summoned and focused all her dread. Somehow her mind and memory had arranged it so that the Bekiaa who stood on *Donaghey*'s fo'c'sle now associated that particular instant with the birth of a fatalistic realization: that the extermination of her beloved comrades in Flynn's Rangers had come to represent the Alliance as a whole. It had become the moment she began to fear the war itself—and everything she loved—was lost.

To most aboard *Donaghey*, Bekiaa was almost a legend. She'd fought the slimy Grik-toads at Chill-chaap until both sides apparently decided it was better to be friends—particularly the kind of friends that never saw each other again. She'd fought alongside Captain Garrett on the Sand Spit when *Donaghey* was driven ashore on Ceylon. And, of course, she was one of only a handful to survive the slaughter of Flynn's Rangers beyond the Rocky Gap in Indiaa. She'd recovered from the wounds she suffered there by wandering the trenches of Alden's Perimeter sniping enemy officers, or Hij, until Greg Garrett requested her by name to command his Marines on this expedition.

A few on the ship, particularly some of her Marines, thought Bekiaa was mad. She knew she wasn't. True madness was very rare among Lemurians and poorly understood, so she could see how people might be confused. Usually, madness drove Mi-Anakka to suicide, and she had no desire to take her own life. She wasn't even "controlled mad" like Saak-Fas had been. He'd been the mate of Keje's daughter, Selass, and after a period of captivity among the Grik, he'd certainly wanted to die, but he'd managed to make his death matter in the end. Bekiaa knew she was perfectly sane, because she didn't want to die at all. She'd gladly *accept* death, if it came to her while she was killing many Grik, but most people she knew would make that trade. There was a difference.

"Good day to you, Cap-i-taan Bekiaa-Sab-At," came a pleasant voice beside her. Bekiaa started, surprised, and a little disoriented by her sudden return to the present. She blinked embarrassment at the strange Lemurian who'd joined her. "Good afternoon, Inquisitor Choon," she said hastily. She still didn't know if she should salute Kon-Choon or not, and didn't really know what to think of him or any of his people, human, Lemurian—or whatever else might reside in his land. Choon was odd enough. He had sharp features beneath a slightly mottled, stone-colored fur. Surprisingly large eyes, even for a Lemurian, protruded from his face. Most striking of all was that the eyes were pale blue, like some humans she knew, but never before had she met any Mi-Anakka with eyes like that. He spoke well enough, but she wondered if his ancestors had been from some tribe that never made it as far eastward as her own. She glanced at the brindled fur on her arm, so common among the Sab-Ats. Many of Choon's Mi-Anakka comrades they'd met at Diego Garciaa were colored just like any other People she knew, but none were brindled. It interested her.

She forced a friendly grin despite her Marine's pride being chastened that Choon had managed to sneak up on her so easily. She knew Captain Garrett wanted to make a good impression on their new . . . acquaintances from the southern African Republic of Real People.

"Forgive me for disturbing you," Choon said as if reading her mind, and she wondered briefly if he had. He was the Royal "Inquisitor" for his "Kaiser," Nig-Taak, after all. Supposedly, his title meant he was head of the Republic's equivalent to the Office of Strategic Intelligence that Commander Herring had established in Baalkpan . . . but did that mean it was more or less likely he could actually read minds? She shuddered at the thought. "I saw you here," he continued, "and this is the first oppor-

tunity I have had to compliment you on the professionalism and bearing of your Maa-rines when you parade them on deck in the mornings."

"Thank you, sir," Bekiaa said. She commanded sixty Marines on
Donaghey, all of whom had other duties alongside the rest of the two
hundred officers and enlisted personnel aboard, when they weren't
training or at drill. Most were qualified to man the ship's guns, but
some made passable topmen, or "wing runners." The rest performed duties 'Cats considered appropriate for "Body of Home" clans, though the
human term "deck ape" was gaining universal acceptance. *Donaghey*
had no "snipe," or engineering division. She was the sole survivor of
three ships in her class, considered "first generation" frigates, or "DDs,"
that had been built on this world, and relied entirely on the wind in her
sails for propulsion. She was small compared to the latest sail/steam
hybrids as well, measuring only 168 by 33 feet, and armed with
18-pounders—the lightest guns left on any DD. She had twenty-four of
them, though, all tied into the latest—if still primitive by *Walker*'s
standards—fire control system. She had the same sonar set as any DD in
the West, powered by wind or gasoline generators, and carried a battery
of Y guns and a depth-charge rack—all essential for her semisolitary
voyage through such a hostile sea. Finally, her stunningly successful
hull shape and sail plan meant not only was she uniquely qualified for
her long-range mission, but she remained the fastest ship in the Navy
with a kind wind, other than the new PTs assembling at Diego—and
USS *Walker* herself.

"I am most impressed by the close-quarters combat drill your Maa-
rines perform," Choon continued, blinking genuine admiration. "Our
legions know the bayonet, but hardly the sword or shield. We have had
breech-loading firearms longer than you, I understand."

Bekiaa nodded. She'd seen the single shot, "bolt action" rifles some
of Choon's people carried, and understood they'd had the things for at
least a decade. They looked unnecessarily complicated compared to the
Allin-Silva breech-loading conversions of the muzzle-loading Baalkpan
Arsenal rifled muskets her Marines used. "Yes, we have only recently
taken that step." Her smile faded. "But against the Grik, a cutlass"—she
patted the guard of the Baalkpan-made copy of the 1917 Navy pattern at

her belt—"remains a most handy tool, I assure you. And after once discarding our shields, *my* Maa-rines, at least, will not do so again," she added tonelessly.

"You have your reasons, I'm sure," Choon granted. "You have much greater experience against the Grik than we. I meant no offense, I merely observe—and speculate perhaps." He lowered his ears in self-deprecation. "I speculate quite a bit. It is my primary occupation, after all." He blinked an expression Bekiaa didn't know. "Your Colonel Chack-Sab-At, commanding the brigade gathering at the strange island where we met your people, as well as our ancient, mutual kin . . . Colonel Chack is your cousin, is he not? There is a slight resemblance." Bekiaa nodded with a genuine smile. "I thought so. Obviously a most formidable warrior, as are you, I'm sure. In any event, his 'Raider Brigade,' destined to assault Mada-gaas-car itself, trains much the same. I hope he will instruct"—he blinked annoyance—"that they will *allow* him to instruct the few legionaries we brought with us aboard the War Palace, so they might teach your Grik fighting ways to others of our people."

The "War Palace" was actually SMS *Amerika*, an old ocean liner, of all things. She'd been fitted with a few guns and commissioned as a commerce raider for the Imperial German Navy during an earlier war than the one *Walker* had been fighting. At least that was what Bekiaa understood. *Amerika* had also been swept to this world in much the same way as *Walker*, apparently, but she, her German crew, and mostly British prisoners had found a home with the Republic of Real People, who'd garishly decorated and painted the old ship. Her people technologically contributed to that society just as *Walker* had done for Bekiaa's folk. Since it was protected from the Grik by an uncomfortably cooler climate, however, the technological transformation of the Republic had not been nearly as urgent—or unsettling—as at Baalkpan and elsewhere.

"We'll do the same when we reach your home, if you like," Bekiaa offered.

"If there is time," Choon said, "I hope that you may." He looked at the sea ahead. "If there is time."

One of Bekiaa's Marines scampered up and slammed to attention, her tail rigid behind her. "Cap-i-taan Gaar-ett's compimimps, an' would the two ob you care to join him on the quarterdeck?"

Bekiaa looked at Choon.

"Of course," Choon said, looking back at Bekiaa. "Shall we?"

"Wind's getting weird," Lieutenant Wendel "Smitty" Smith grouched, wiping his prematurely bald head with a rag. He was *Donaghey*'s gunnery officer, and he'd just reported that all the ship's guns were doubly secured in case things got frisky.

"It's boxing the compass," Captain Greg Garrett agreed. He was tall and dark haired, and the gangliness of youth remained to a degree, but his soft Tennessee drawl was far more assured than it once was. His body could only mature so fast, but the man had long since been made. He glanced at *Donaghey*'s consort, USS *Sineaa* (DE-48), pounding along companionably, if a little less comfortably, about a mile to leeward. *Sineaa* was a "razeed" Grik Indiaman, captured at Singapore. With the same rig as *Donaghey* and her hull cut down to the gun deck, the smaller, lighter ship was almost as fast as Greg's. She carried only twelve guns, however, and the stores in her hold were her primary purpose.

Greg looked back at his gunnery officer. He liked the guy, and knew he had plenty of guts. He'd started out as *Walker*'s gunnery officer himself, before becoming what many considered the premier "frigate skipper" in the Alliance, and he fully approved of Smitty's precautions. He'd likewise just directed that the fore and main topsails be reefed. "I wish the wind would figure out what it's going to do," he added.

"We may not approve of its decision," said Lieutenant Saama-Kera, Greg's exec. He was blinking concern at the darkening sky. "Sammy" wasn't a Sky Priest or "Salig Maastir" as most American Navy execs had been at first. He *was* a master sailor, who could read the weather as well as any Sky Priest, and was very nearly as good a navigator—considering he hadn't studied the Heavens since birth, as true Sky Priests were expected to do. "We have little to go on regarding the weather in this region," he continued. "Though a few hints from my . . . ancestral cousins on Diego Garciaa describe some of the storms approaching from this direction as extreme." He glanced at Garrett. "They did not name them such, but they do bring the strakka to mind."

Greg nodded with a frown. Strakkas were cyclones, but the different conditions on this world often spun them up into monsters that defied comparison to any hurricane or typhoon Greg Garrett had heard of. He hoped Sammy had misunderstood the "aboriginal" Lemurians of Diego. That was possible, since their once-common language had changed significantly over time. Some believed they must retain a culture most similar to what all Lemurians shared before the ancient exodus from Madagascar, due to their isolation, but Greg wasn't so sure. The language of the southern African 'Cats who'd made it there aboard *Amerika* wasn't much different from that spoken by Mi-Anakka from Jaava to the Fil-pin Lands, and as far south as the Great South Isle. If anything, Greg figured the people on Diego—also smaller than other Lemurians— had probably regressed culturally as well as physically. It was possible they retained myths, legends, even actual accounts of what it had been like where they came from so long ago, stories otherwise lost. Maybe Courtney Bradford or Adar—or somebody else—would sort all that out someday, but that wasn't Greg's problem. His mission was to scout some of the islands his old world charts said existed east of Madagascar to discover whether the Grik had any presence there, report his findings, then proceed to the Republic of Real People with Inquisitor Choon. Beyond that? He could continue his expedition of discovery into the Atlantic at his discretion.

The weather worried him for its own sake, of course, but they were drawing uncomfortably close to where a couple of those eastern islands, specifically the Mascarenes—Mauritius and Reunion—were supposed to be. He didn't like the idea of discovering them too abruptly in the middle of any kind of storm, much less a strakka. He blinked and realized that Captain Bekiaa and Inquisitor Choon had joined them by the windward rail. "Inquisitor." He nodded. "Hi, Bekiaa." He and Bekiaa didn't exchange salutes. That happened during the morning parade of her Marines in the waist. He still looked at her for a moment, however, trying to ascertain her mood. He didn't know everything she'd been through in Indiaa, but he knew it was a lot—and very bad. He'd been in a tough spot with her himself, in the Sand Spit fight, and that hadn't shaken the Lemurian Marine. All he knew was that whatever she'd endured since had shaken her pretty bad, so as scary as the Sand Spit had been, her more recent experiences must have been even worse. He wouldn't try to imagine what she was going through, and since he was her commanding officer, it wasn't his place to ask, as long as she did her duty. But he'd be there as her friend if she needed him.

Choon bowed slightly. "I am at your service, Cap-i-taan Gaar-ett."

"I've got a couple of questions," Greg informed him.

"Of course. I will answer any I am able."

Greg smiled, recognizing the word "able" implied any number of limitations. The guy was a snoop, after all.

"You've seen our charts and know where we're headed. Any idea what we'll run into?"

"My people have almost no knowledge of this sea, or much of anything at all east of our home. We have quite a bit more knowledge of what lies west of us than perhaps any other power on this world, I daresay; better, more current charts of the Atlantic, and the various coastlines. All that was gathered by the War Palace"—he flicked his ears—"SMS *Amerika*, before she came to us." He shook his head sadly. "But our best charts of this region came with her as well. They are no better, and even older than yours."

"But you came looking for us."

"As has been explained, Lieutenant Miyata told us of you and that you had defeated the Grik attack against your Home at Baalkpan. He knew little beyond that, but his words gave us hope that we were not alone against our enemy. In addition, our people have wireless technology. We do not transmit; to do so would perhaps draw unwanted attention, but we do listen." He blinked admonishment. "Your people transmit perhaps a little too much information 'in the clear,' I believe you say, in the heat of . . . exciting situations. In any event, that is how we learned that you had not only defeated the Grik, but advanced against them; we presumed as far as Indiaa, though we could not be sure. We made for Baalkpan regardless. Lieutenant Miyata was a navigation officer and had been there before. It seemed the best choice.

Sadly, *Amerika* could not complete the journey without the repairs now underway at Diego Garciaa—we were fortunate indeed to find that place!"

"So it all worked out when we stumbled on you there," Greg murmured, "but my question is, did you ever sight any of the islands we're looking for now?"

"Sadly, no. We meant to make a straight transit across this 'Indiaan Sea,' and find you through the place you call the 'Soon-daa Strait.' We could not make it."

"Diego's a good bit north of that course."

"Yes, but we had no choice other than to look for it and hope it was there. We could go no farther."

"And it *was* there," Sammy supplied.

"Fortunately."

Sammy looked at Garrett. "So it stands to reason the Maas-carenes will be there as well."

"It would," Garrett agreed, "if we hadn't already found so many islands where they shouldn't be—or none where they should be, before."

"But that has always been in the Eastern Ocean—the Paa-cific, where so many are smoking mountains. You have said yourself that they might sprout anywhere."

"I guess. But why not here? And how come so many volcanic islands in the Malay Barrier are in the right place?"

"Not all are. Is not . . . Kraak-aa-toaa still there, when it should not be, according to your old charts—yet Talaud has destroyed itself?"

"Sure, but Talaud might've blown its top 'back home' by now, for all we know." Greg rubbed his eyebrows, then gestured around. "I guess I'm just trying to dip my toe in the water before I jump in. It might be freezing or boiling—or full of rocks."

Saama-Kera laughed. "So this trip is different from others in what respect?"

Greg chuckled back at him, acknowledging the point.

"You have other questions?" Choon asked. Garrett started to reply, when suddenly something struck the ship like a ragged broadside, slamming into the hull with a clattering, thudding staccato they could feel in the deck beneath their feet. Then something whipped by over the bulwark, something . . . amazing.

"Down!" Garrett roared. "Everybody down! Take cover!"

"What the hell!" Smitty bellowed, but Bekiaa dragged him and Inquisitor Choon to the deck just as a . . . flock of . . . things . . . soared over the ship from starboard to port. Sammy cried out and flung himself down as well, clutching his shoulder where one of the things struck him. His hand came away from the fur with blood on it.

"Flyin' swordfish!" Smitty yelled. "What next?"

"They're not swordfish," Garrett said, a mix of concern and wonder in his voice. The creatures were hitting the ship continuously now, and the hull drummed with their strikes. Some hit the rigging, parting lines in some cases as they passed, or rebounding onto the deck to flop and squirm. Others actually ripped holes in the sails!

"My God!" Greg said. "They're *squids*! Or something *like* squids!"

"*Squids?*" Smitty demanded. "Flyin', saber-toothed *squids*? What the *hell* next?"

The fusillade went on for perhaps a minute, all while *Donaghey*'s crew took cover as best they could. Even so, there were several shrill screams. Greg didn't know if his people were being hurt, or simply screaming in terror at the sight of the live, high-velocity projectiles. They *were* ugly, and the deck was filling with gray-blue, wriggling shapes. Quite a few fell near Garrett and his group, and he stared at them. *Squids, sure enough,* he thought. *But not like any squid I ever saw!* The animals' bodies were about two feet long, not counting the cluster of short tentacles at the rear—bottom?—of their abdomens. They also had huge, stunningly sensitive-looking eyes that rolled and gaped in panic as they flailed. In those respects at least, they appeared similar to ordinary squids. But like everything else Greg Garrett had seen on this world, they'd adapted to somewhat different circumstances. Instead of little fins near the top of their cylindrical bodies, these creatures looked like they'd crossed with a manta ray at some time. Their "fins" had become flexible, rubbery-looking wings. What propelled them at such velocities were organs much like ordinary squids as well, but on a larger scale. That actually didn't surprise Garrett that much. They'd encountered other creatures that squirted water at greater pressures than they'd ever known before. Doubtless, Courtney Bradford would be astounded and fashion some new theory about that. What made these things dangerous to people, and even Greg's ship—besides their size and speed— was a sharp, bony, spearpoint-looking thing poking out of the tops of their heads! That was obviously what cut Sammy, and had allowed the things to shred so much cordage and sailcloth.

The bizarre assault was tapering off, and carefully, crewfolk began to peer over the side.

"Deck there!" came a cry from the masthead. Garrett looked up. Apparently, the things hadn't flown any higher than the courses, and everyone aloft had scrambled above them.

"What is it?" Greg called back when there was no report.

"Some-teeng's in de waater, longside de ship!" Greg raised himself and peered over the rail. For a moment he was stunned by what he saw. Dozens, *hundreds* of "squids" covered the starboard side of his ship, dangling and squirming, feebly flapping their wings, their "spearpoints" imbedded in the stout timbers. For each squid, there were probably twenty or more bloody, bony spearpoints sticking in the ship, wrenched from the heads of the animals on impact, or as they struggled to escape. His gaze swept downward. The sea was getting rougher so he couldn't see beneath it, but he recognized the short, broad fins of quite a few of the more ferocious sea monsters he'd grown accustomed to. They looked a lot like giant porpoises, or maybe even big killer whales, but they had long snouts full of knitting-needle teeth. Even as he watched, one rose to the surface and snatched a floating squid. It was suddenly quite clear what had driven the strange creatures to flee in such a manner. He shuddered and backed away, remembering. Scary as the big fish were, they didn't bother ships. They *were* known to eat small boats with people in them. . . .

"Damaage control!" Sammy roared, rising as well, his tail swishing in agitation. "Bend new canvas, and get to work cutting and splicing! This is *still* a Navy ship, and we have ugly weather coming. On your feet, and twist your tails! Chief Laan, form details to clear these foul things away; over the side with them! Pass the word for the carpenter to report any leaks!"

Greg smiled and nodded. He'd been about to shout the same commands, but *Donaghey's* exec *was* her first lieutenant, and damage control
was his job. Bosun's whistles squealed and 'Cats set to work. Lemurians
couldn't do a bosun's pipe, but a series of whistle toots worked just as well
on shipboard or the battlefield. Bekiaa was helping Choon to his feet and
Smitty was already up, poking one of the squids with his shoe.

"Rocket powered, flyin' arrowhead squids," Smitty mused. "I wonder if you can eat 'em."

"Not me," Bekiaa said seriously.

"Sammy?" Greg gestured at the 'Cat's shoulder. "Get below and have
that tended. See what other casualties we've had."

"Ay, ay, Cap-i-taan, but it's just a scratch."

"I know, but these damn things might be poisonous for all we know.
Go ahead. I've got the deck."

"Ay, sir."

Choon had recovered himself and was looking around with interest.
Finally, he turned back to Garrett. "Ah, you said you had more than just
the one question, which I was sadly unable to answer to the satisfaction
of either of us. What else did you want to know?"

"Well, I was going to ask more about your land, your 'Republic.' That
can wait till later, though." He smiled ironically. "Mostly, I was going to
ask if you ran into anything, well, weird, on your own voyage across the
Indian Ocean."

Choon stooped to examine one of the squids. It was dead now, its
skin already beginning to wrinkle and parch, but still staring up at him.

"'Weird' is such an interesting word," he said cryptically. "And so
subjective, so dependent upon perspective. I never saw creatures such as
these before, but are they truly 'weird'? That is difficult to determine.
They are different from other squids I have seen, so they are unusual,
certainly." He looked at Greg. "But your people and mine do not yet
know each other well enough to agree with confidence on any definition
of 'weird.'" With that, he nodded politely and stepped away.

"I hate it when he does that," Greg growled. "He talks more than anybody I ever saw, except maybe Courtney, without saying anything at all."

Bekiaa watched the strange Lemurian step carefully through the dead squids and the activity around him and half smiled. "I find it . . . amusing."

Greg snorted. "Maybe a little, but also kind of, well, *sneaky*, if you ask me."

Bekiaa shrugged. "He is a 'snoop.' Like Mr. Braad-furd, it is his nature to gather knowledge, but he does not share it well. Even with his friends. He thinks that since he must *earn* information, so should everyone else. It is almost . . . a game."

"Do you think he's a friend?" Greg asked bluntly. "Because half the time, I really don't know."

Bekiaa smiled more broadly. "Yes," she replied. "But even with his friends, he plays his game."

///// *First Fleet South*
Diego Garcia
July 8, 1944

eneral Safir Maraan, commander of what remained of II Corps, and Queen Protector of the
Island of B'mbaado, raced like a giddy youngling down the gangway from *Big Sal* to the
newly built pier. She wore her usual silver-
washed breastplate, black cloak, and leather armor, but today she was unusually stunning,
with a radiant glow of joy. Waiting on the pier was a strange assortment
of folk. The Lemurian commander of USS *Respite Island* (SPD-1) was
there, as were Lieutenant (jg) Winston "Winny" Rominger, commanding Motor Torpedo Boat Squadron #1 (MTB-Ron-1), Major Alistair
Jindal of the Imperial Marines, and Captain Risa-Sab-At. Standing a
little to the side were two men, one quite elderly, and both in the dark
woolen uniforms of the Imperial German Navy. Beside them was a

pepper-blond, bearded man wearing a bronze cuirass, plaited leather kilt, and polished bronze greaves. With him was yet another man, apparently Japanese, dressed similarly to the first two men. Also waiting were two very short Lemurians wearing almost nothing, and blinking with a mixture of anticipation and deep concern. None of those had Safir's attention at present, however. She had eyes only for a broad-shouldered, brindle-furred 'Cat in the immaculate dress of a Lieutenant Colonel of Lemurian/American Marines, standing close beside Risa-Sab-At. The 'Cat swept his dented but freshly painted "doughboy" helmet from his head and bowed deeply as Safir approached, but amid raucous hoots and cries of approval thundering down from *Big Sal*, Safir Maraan tightly embraced him.

"Oh Chack," she practically purred. "I have missed you so! Through all our battles, so far apart, I have begged the Maker for this moment with every breath!"

"As have I, my love," Chack-Sab-At replied softly. Suddenly aware of the circumstances again, he stiffened slightly. "I mean General Maraan—Your Highness. . . ."

"Don't be ridiculous," Safir admonished, nuzzling him and lightly touching his fur with the tip of her tongue. "To you, I shall always be simply 'Safir'!"

"I will remember that when you give me orders!" He laughed. "You outrank me!"

Safir made a throwing-away gesture. "Even if that is true, we have always been equals in battle." She snorted. "And besides, you have an independent command!"

"Subject to your orders, my love," Chack reminded with a toothy grin. "Not that I mind." He stepped back. Even while this long-delayed reunion was taking place, others had descended the gangway of the great ship. Keje escorted Sandra and her former Imperial "steward," Diania, down the long ramp, closely followed by an ecstatic Courtney Bradford, who gaped all around, his head jerking this way and that like a turkey. He saw the great, newly refloated liner, *Amerika*, with her bizarre, but highly ornamental paintwork. New docks were everywhere, as well as several large storehouses. But beyond all that was the lush tropical jungle he couldn't wait to explore—not to mention the natives he was eager to observe. Adar descended the ramp next, dressed in his flowing High Sky Priest's robe. He was attended only by Captain Atlaan-Fas, and *Salissa*'s COFO, Jis-Tikkar, or "Tikker." No Marine guards accompanied them. Chack had plenty of those on the pier, and there was no doubt they were among friends. Chack saluted the new arrivals, and after they returned the salute, Adar, Keje, Sandra, and even Courtney embraced the young Marine.

"My heart swells with gladness at the sight of you, Colonel Chack!" Adar said. "And I am so proud of your accomplishments here! I regret it has taken us so long to arrive."

"You had battles," Chack said simply. No other explanation was necessary. "I am only glad that they ended well enough that you could join me now." He waved to the others close by on the pier. "Excuse me, but I think you know Lieuten-aant Rominger? Then allow me to present Kap-i-taan Aadler Von Melhausen, commander of SMS *Ameri-kaa*—also known to the Republic of Real People as the War Palace." Von Melhausen saluted and bowed very low with a briskness that belied his apparent frailty. "The large, dark-bearded man is Kap-i-taan Leut-naant Becker Laange, Kap-i-taan Von Melhausen's executive officer." Lange saluted and bowed as well. "Lef-ten-aant Doocy Meek commands *Ameri-kaa*'s, ah, 'Maa-rines,' though all the Republic's military persons are referred to as 'legionaries.'" Meek saluted sharply, palm out. Chack nodded at the Japanese man. "And as I'm sure you have guessed, this is Lieuten-aant Toryu Miyata, late of the Jaapan-ese Imperial Navy Battle Cruiser, *Amaagi*. It is he more than any other that brought us together with our new friends from the Republic—and has, perhaps, given our current mission its greatest chance for success."

Miyata bowed low. He knew these people had no reason to love him; he'd been aboard *Amagi* when she savaged their city of Baalkpan, after all. When he rose to face them, however, he was surprised—and gratified—to see the returned bows of greeting.

"Finally," Chack continued, "I must present our hosts." He flicked his ears respectfully at the two short 'Cats. "These, Pukaa and Sikaa, are sons of the High Chief that rules this land and has nobly joined our cause against the Ancient Enemy. They are not warriors," he reminded, stressing his previous recommendation that they never be used as such. They were simple people, almost like younglings, and Chack considered it his duty to protect them as much as possible from the horrors of this war. "But they have graciously allowed us to use their land to stage troops and supplies for the pending operation." He looked specifically at Adar. "I'm sure, once you get to know them, you will agree that their contribution to the cause has been sufficiently generous."

"No doubt," Adar said, closely studying the natives. He and Courtney had so much to learn from them! But he suspected Chack's assessment was accurate.

"We . . . good you here," Pukaa managed. "Happy us! Meet gone cousins. Happy us!"

"Oh! They've learned to speak!" Courtney chortled. "That will make communicating with them much, much easier than I feared!"

Adar blinked exaggerated patience, which caused a few chuckles. "It is indeed convenient that they have learned to make themselves understood by us. We must make an equal effort to learn *their* doubtless ancient and very rich dialect," Adar said dryly. He'd already been informed that the language spoken by the people of Diego Garcia, or "Laa-Laanti" as they called it, was . . . similar to that used by most allied Lemurians. The primary difference was syntax and a severely garbled pronunciation of common words. He was sure communication would swiftly grow easier. Looking at one of the natives, he blinked sincerity. "Thank you, ah, Pukaa. We will try to disrupt the lives of your people here as little as possible, and your help in the cause of defeating our ancient foe shall never be forgotten!"

Pukaa blinked and looked at his brother. Finally, he waved his arms. "Happy us!" he said again.

The little tree lizard, Petey, had made himself as small behind Sandra's neck as he could till now, when he finally peered out from under her sandy brown hair beside her right ear. "Happy us," he repeated softly; then more insistently he crowed, "Eat?"

"We'll eat soon enough, you gluttonous thing," Sandra assured, patting the reptilian head. She waved out to sea. "Captain Reddy will bring

Walker in as soon as he's scouted around the island." She frowned. "He's been a little concerned about an undersea contact they made several days ago as well."

"Yes," Keje agreed, troubled. He looked at *Respite Island*'s captain. "We'll have to bring all our screen in, eventually. Is yours sufficient to guard against the approach of . . . unexpected visitors?"

"Indeed, Ahd-mi-raal. I will see to it."

"Good. Then I propose we adjourn to a more comfortable setting. We have much to discuss, but it will wait until Cap-i-taan Reddy joins us with his officers."

Adar strode into *Salissa*'s admiral's quarters and everyone rose to attention. He took a long breath and sighed. "Please, be seated!" Aside to Keje as he joined him at the long, broad table he murmured, "I shall never grow accustomed to this! Everyone popping up and standing like wooden carvings whenever I enter a chamber. It is embarrassing!"

"You are chairman of the Grand Alliance," Keje said simply with a smile.

"In name only, at present. Mr. Letts stands as such in my stead at Baalkpan, more ably than I as well, I am sure. Perhaps the people there will recognize that and officially acclaim *him* chairman in my absence, particularly if the convention to form a true union of the allied powers is successful!"

Keje looked at Adar and blinked unease. Not for the first time, he suspected that more than banter lay beneath his friend's words. "We could do worse," Keje probed.

"Indeed." Adar looked and saw Captain Reddy still standing, Sandra at his side, and smiled to himself. Safir Maraan was sitting with Chack, and even Chief Bosun Fitzhugh Gray was sitting next to the young— exotically beautiful, for a human, he understood—Diania. The girl was only a fraction of Gray's age, but that wasn't an issue among Lemurians. He wondered why it seemed to bother Gray so much. He mentally shook his head. He was happy for them all, pleased by every reunion their voyage had made possible. He chuckled inwardly. All except one, perhaps, and not because he disapproved, but because their new friends from the Republic of Real People evidently cherished rather strict taboos concerning certain fraternizations between humans and Lemurians. He'd never thought of . . . whatever existed between Dennis Silva and Risa-Sab-At as anything other than amusing, but Von Melhausen and Becher Lange in particular had been horrified to see the way Silva and Risa embraced when they met. Some of Greg Garrett's reports hinted there were even some kind of human/Lemurian hybrids living in the Republic, and Adar had to admit he'd never imagined such an . . . outcome was possible. He still didn't, as far as Silva and Risa were concerned. He knew they were great friends, but they also gloried in "getting the goats" of others, whatever that meant. He sighed again. Besides, he also knew one of the least well-kept "secrets" in the Alliance: Dennis Silva and Nurse Pam Cross were practically betrothed.

Captain Reddy at least pretended to remain blissfully unaware of the situation, but if he was, he pretended very well. Adar had to wonder if Matt truly was that obtuse when it came to relationships of that sort. Most likely it was pretense, Adar decided. Matt needed Silva, and with Sandra traveling aboard *Salissa*, he wanted the next-best available physician on his ship. He couldn't surrender Silva or Pam, but his precious regulations, not to mention his sense of duty and example, might be compromised if he officially recognized the affair.

As for Silva's theatrically amorous reunion with Risa-Sab-At on the docks, Adar remained amused. In spite of her deep friendship with Risa, Pam was one female who would never allow such a spectacle as Silva and Risa performed to go unavenged if she thought it represented more than play. He looked at Matt. Captain Reddy, also aware of the sensibilities of their new friends, had been furious, however, and Adar wondered what punishment Silva would endure. "Yes, Cap-i-taan Reddy? You have a report?"

"Yes, Mr. Chairman," Matt replied. "We steamed all around the island. Interesting place. Not like anything we expected from our old charts. We didn't pick up anything unusual, though. Never have after that one anomalous contact, as a matter of fact, so it was probably nothing after all. But I wanted to make sure."

"Thank you. I am relieved to hear it. Now, shall we dine? I know we have much to talk about, but let us enjoy this gathering for a time before we return our thoughts to war." He nodded at *Amerika's* elderly commander. "Kap-i-taan Von Melhausen has supplied a number of interesting delicacies from both here and his homeland for us to sample. Shall we?"

Reluctantly, Matt nodded and sat. He'd wanted to make his report, but he also wanted to apologize to the people of the Republic for Silva's behavior. Adar hadn't given him a chance, and he wondered why. *Probably didn't want to make a big deal of it,* he thought. *Besides, even Adar knows Silva's too valuable to hang, and hanging's about the only thing that might tone him down.* All Matt could really do at present was restrict the maniac to the ship. Belatedly, he realized there'd been a time when he would've apologized—or said whatever he wanted to say—whether Adar shushed him or not, and he caught himself questioning what had changed. *I have, of course, and so has Adar. I'm more comfortable letting him run the show, and he's more confident doing it now.* He shifted uneasily, grasping Sandra's hand under the table. Her "distances" seemed to come in fits and starts, but tonight, everything appeared fine between them. *Should I feel more comfortable, though?* he asked himself, watching Adar more closely. He'd always tried to defer to the "civilian" authorities—as much as possible, and as much as their understanding of the situation allowed—ever since they came to this world. He did *not* want to be a king! He was beginning to worry, however, that he might have . . . abdicated a measure of responsibility.

Adar wanted sole strategic responsibility for the conduct of the war. That was fine, and it was his duty as Chairman of the Grand Alliance. But his actual role was growing a bit more tactical than Matt felt easy with, and he suspected that was probably his own fault. Inwardly, he knew he practically *yearned* for less responsibility himself, after all they'd been through and lost. It simply hurt too much. *But that never really works out, does it?* he asked himself bitterly. *The oldest rule in the book is that you can delegate authority, but never responsibility—not even to* higher *authority.* He realized he'd been slowly doing exactly that—letting Adar "test his wings" a little too soon, and perhaps a bit too thoroughly. He hadn't encouraged it, exactly, but he hadn't actively

discouraged it either. He'd *warned*, but that wasn't really enough, especially where this operation was concerned. The "prize," to go for the
whole enchilada, had to be awfully tempting—particularly for Adar. He
sighed inwardly, wondering if he was worrying about nothing—and if
there was anything he could do about it now, even if he wasn't.

Dennis Silva sat on the director's "bicycle" seat of the number two gun
atop the amidships platform. The big 4"-50 was secured fore and aft, and
he had an unobstructed view to port, past the safety chains. Across the
water, *Big Sal* was outwardly dark, despite the confab underway aboard.
Every ship in the vicinity was dark, but that didn't mean they were invisible. The stars shone brightly, and the horizon was ruddy with the
gleam of a nearly full moon preparing to rise above the sea. More light
flickered from the interior of the jungle isle, from native fires near the
lagoon, no doubt, and it served to silhouette the ships even further. Silva
could see all of them quite well—as would any lurking spectator.

The white wakes of Winny Rominger's torpedo boats crossed the
waves to seaward. Irvin Laumer had been given command of a two-boat
section, and was getting the hang of the new craft. Several DDs cruised
even farther out to sea, but Silva wasn't sure how much good any of
them would be if there really *was* a pigboat creeping around out there.
Captain Reddy obviously didn't know what to think of Horn's supposed
periscope sighting, but the screwy contact they'd investigated on the
run down from Madras had left him cautious. Chances were, they'd left
whatever it was far behind. *But hell*, Silva thought, fishing his tobacco
pouch out of his pocket. *I'm feelin' cautious too, an' I don't even b'lieve
there* was *a periscope!* he fumed. *But I was there when the numbskull
spotted it, and dope that he is, Horn's no idiot.*

Silva trusted Horn far more than he'd ever admit, but the guy was a
Marine—and not just *any* Marine! Silva had nothing against 'Cat Marines, and he considered Chack one of his very best friends. Besides, he
figured he'd helped create the Marines on this world and you had to call
them something. *Let Marine 'Cats and Navy 'Cats have a fresh start
here, like lions and lambs and such,* he mused, then chuckled. *Or maybe*

lions and tigers is a better comparison. But Horn was an old-world *China Marine!* It was the nature of whatever cosmos they were part of, wherever they were, that Silva and Horn should be contentious—at least for appearances' sake. He shook some of the yellowish "tobacco" leaves from his pouch, the sugary flavoring meant to counteract the vile, waxy taste sticky on his fingers, and crammed the wad in his cheek.

As if summoned by his thoughts, Gunny Horn suddenly joined him by the gun, preceded by a fog of "PIG-cig" smoke.

"I was just thinkin' about you," Silva accused, as if Horn were directly responsible, and the very act might pollute his mind. "Think o' the devil an' up he pops—my ol' granny prob'ly used to say."

"Probably?" Horn asked with a grin around the smoldering butt between his lips.

"Never knew the dame," Silva confessed, "but ain't that what all grannies say?" He coughed. "Brung yer own fire an' brimstone along too, I see. Damn, but I wish you'd quit smokin' them ass-wipe paper rolls o' loco weed. Smell like you stuffed rat pellets an' roaches in them papers an' lit 'em."

"I didn't roll them. They come from Baalkpan ready-made." Horn took the smoke out and looked at it, before nodding at Isak Reuben, leaning on the rail below them next to the big freezer. Isak was smoking too. "And for all I know, those 'Mice' fellas, as you call them, might use that exact recipe. They are pretty awful."

Silva stood and spat over the rail, the stream describing a solid, graceful arch. "You oughta take up a respectable, genteel, *fireproof* vice, like me. No smokin' lamps to worry about, ash holes in your clothes—an' why darken the ship against make-believe pigboats, then hop around like a buncha damn fireflies!" Even as he spoke, a match flared on the aft deckhouse, and he cursed. Matches were great, and it was good to have them again. They'd been a by-product of efforts to create friction primers and fuses. But the 'Cats, ordinarily very sensible when it came to open flames aboard any ship, thought they were practically magical and often played with them whether they smoked or not. That had to be watched and discouraged. He looked around. "Who's got the deck? The Skipper'd throw a fit!" He raised his voice so it could be heard aft. "The next—

anybody—who makes a light is on report!" He spat again. "Damn snipes. That's them back there, I know it. Play with fire mor'n anybody aboard. Maybe we'll see just how much they like it. I already got a score to settle with some of 'em," he growled.

"What kind of score?" Horn asked.

"A *sore* score." Silva glared at Horn in the dark. "*Black* teeth too, fer God's sake," he continued, as if his rant had never been interrupted. "Like you chew betel nuts all day. You'll be sharpenin' them scum columns into *points*, next." He sniffed. "An' o' course you smell like smolderin' rat pellets all the time." Warming to his tirade, Silva put his hands on his hips, aping Spanky's habitual pose. "You think wimmen crave snugglin' with a giant rat turd? Not here, or in any world *I* ever been to." He lowered his voice. "Which I figger the Asia Station counts for at least one. Alabama's another, so I'm calculatin' that wimmen would reject cavortin' with rat turds on at least *four* different worlds."

Horn laughed. "I won't argue with that. Not a lot of dames aboard to impress, though."

"A lot more than there ever used to be," Silva argued, slightly aggrieved. "Which you'd know if you hadn't missed the worst o' the 'Dame Famine,'" he accused. "'Cat gals've been with us since we met 'em, but now there's a corny-copia o' human broads scamperin' all over the ship, compared to back then. *Five* of 'em, not countin' Pam," he stressed. Horn was one of the few who "officially" knew Pam and Silva remained sweet on each other. "An' with only eighteen old-time destroyermen aboard," Silva continued, "meanin' them without tails an' fur, why, that's a downright momentous increase in proportionism if you ask me."

"I didn't know there were that many," Horn mused.

"The other five, all of 'em, are fireroom snipes," Dennis explained. "They're ex-pat Impie gals, an' hardly ever creep out on deck." He furrowed the brow over his good eye. "You know? I bet Tabby *recruits* 'em down there, so there'll always be somebody waggin' sweaty boobs at Spanky when he goes below—just like she used to do. Drives him nuts! And now that she's engineerin' officer, there's not much he can do about it."

"She *still* s'eet on he," Lawrence announced, padding up to join them, the claws on his feet scritching on the deckplates.

"Tabby's sweet on the *exec*?" Horn demanded, staring at Lawrence.

"Yeah," Silva confirmed. "Always has been. Ain't natural," he added piously.

Horn snorted. "Then what was that you were doin' with that 'Cat gal—a *Marine officer*—when we touched at the pier this morning?"

"That's Risa," Silva said, as if that explained everything. "We was just funnin', is all. We're old pals."

"Your fun got you restricted to the ship."

Silva shrugged. "So?" He pointed at the dark shape of *Big Sal*. The moon was rising, and soon she'd be even more obvious against the dark jungle of the island. *Too bad she's too big for the lagoon the little munchkin cat-monkeys got here.* "If I wasn't here, I'd be over there listenin' to the brass argue an' bump their gums about all the stuff we already know about." He cocked his head. "Some of it, anyway. An' what's the use? Nobody's gonna attack the Skipper over there, an' I thought Pam was gonna stay aboard here. . . ."

"So that's it! You were hoping to spend some time with her!"

Silva thought about it for a moment, then nodded. "Sure. Why not?"

"But *she* got called over to meet with the Skipper's wife. Some kind of fleet medical powwow."

"Yeah," Silva grumped, then looked at Lawrence. "Hey, where've you been, anyway?"

"I's looking at the 'ish Lanier caught."

Earl didn't just go for monster plesiosaurs; he dropped a line over the side whenever *Walker* anchored anywhere. Some of his catches were unusual to say the least, and a few had very nearly caught *him*. The thing he'd pulled aboard just before sunset actually seemed fairly straightforward for a change, even edible—at least at first glance. Perhaps the best way to describe it was as a kind of rainbow-colored flounder, since it had two eyes on the side of its head. What made it weird was that it wasn't particularly flat, and it had two eyes on the other side of its head as well.

Silva rolled his own eye. "Yeah, that thing ain't right. Booger has *four* eyes, an' I only got one. I bet that'd come in handy, though, havin' good depth perception in all directions." He peered at Lawrence. "You could see other boogers comin' at you better."

"Still," Horn prodded, "if you hadn't gotten uninvited to the meeting on *Big Sal*, you'd know all the details about what we're headed into."

Silva looked at the tall Marine and grinned. "An' then I could tell *you*." He chuckled. "I'll get another chance. The locals are throwin' us a big 'so long' bash, though I can't imagine where they'll put everybody. We prob'ly got more sailors an' Marines aboard these ships than there is folks livin' on that whole island." He paused, contemplative. "But the word is, that's when Mr. Bradford's gonna unwrap his big notion. His 'theory of ever'thing' he's been workin' on. That's what I'm waitin' to hear. As for the 'details' of 'what we're headed into' "—he spat again—"I already know mosta them."

"So? Spill 'em."

Silva's grin widened. "Why, we're gonna jump down the hole right in the Grik's front parlor, kickin' hell outa whatever yellow jacket nest we land on with both feet—an' we'll all be lucky to live through it. What other details do we need, you and me?" He ruffled Lawrence's crest. "Or you, you fuzzy little salamander."

Lawrence backed out of reach with a hiss, but seemed pleased by Silva's confidence. Dennis raised his gaze slightly to watch a moonlit shape move away from the gathering where Lanier was filleting the strange fish beside the port 25-mm gun tub, just aft of the number two torpedo mount. He saw a cherry brighten as that man also leaned against a stanchion to stare out to sea, and realized he was smoking one of Isak's vile cigarettes as well. "Or maybe, if you really want to know, you might just ask your ol' buddy down there," Silva grouched.

Horn followed his gaze. "Lance Corporal Miles?" he asked skeptically. "Why him? What would he know?" Ian Miles had been attached to Bernie Sandison in Experimental Ordnance after his arrival in Baalkpan with Horn, Herring, Conrad Diebel, and Leading Seaman Henry Stokes. Like many of the survivors of *Mizuki Maru*'s old-world mission as a slave-labor transport, he'd been given a job he seemed suited for. Stokes was running Allied Intel while Herring was away, and

Diebel was flying P-40s for Ben Mallory in Indiaa. After his adventures with Silva in Borno, Gunnery Sergeant Horn was basically assigned to him in Sonny Campeti's gunnery division (which seemed appropriate). He was still a Marine, of course, but not considered part of *Walker*'s small Marine contingent. Likewise, Lance Corporal Miles remained under Sandison's authority, though some suspected he still truly answered only to Commander Simon Herring.

"Why don't you ask him?" Dennis repeated. "He's your pal, an' he's prob'ly oozin' all sorts o' dope Herring's fed him."

Horn stared at the other Marine thoughtfully for a moment. He knew Miles and Herring had remained close after their ordeal together, closer than one might expect considering their wildly divergent attitudes toward rank. "Miles is a good Marine," he defended, "and a good guy to have at your back . . . in the situation we were in after the Philippines fell." He shrugged. "Sure, he had a chip on his shoulder in China. Played the sea lawyer too, sometimes. But he straightened up. Hell, you know the type. You were much the same yourself."

"I never was the type to toady up to a tin Tojo type like Herring," Silva stated flatly, and Horn frowned. He had to admit Silva had a point. Gunny Horn had admired Commander Herring while they were in the hands of the Japanese, but he'd been disappointed by the way Herring tried to throw his weight around after they joined the Grand Alliance here. Sure, he was chief of strategic intelligence now, along to see the Grik "elephant" for himself. But after the hellacious fight with Kurokawa's battlewagons, he did seem to be trying to become a "real, live" naval officer at last. He'd also clearly changed his opinion of Captain Reddy, and completely embraced the scheme to hit the Grik where they lived.

"Commander Herring's not like that now," Horn defended.

"No? Then how come him an' a lowly shoestring corporal like Miles is always promenadin' our decks an jawin' about stuff—an' clammin' up whenever I . . . whenever *anybody* wanders by?"

"Maybe they don't like it when fellas spy on them," Horn retorted, "or make such a fuss about them being pals. Neither one is easy to be friends with; trust me, I was with them long enough." He took a long drag on his PIG-cig and coughed.

Silva's eye widened. "Say, you don't s'pose they're *special* pals, do ya?" Horn glared at him. "Hell no! What's the matter with you?"

Silva rolled his eye. "Just a thought. An' dis-gustin' as that notion is, it'd worry me less than the one I'm really stuck on."

"And what's that?"

"Those two are up to somethin'," Silva stated firmly. "Somethin' the Skipper won't like."

///// *East Indiaa*
The "Western Front"
July 8, 1944

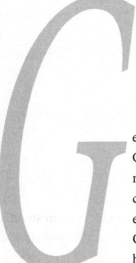

eneral of the Army and Marines and acting
CINCWEST, General Pete Alden, rode his me-
naak alongside General Muln Rolak as they
carefully picked their way through the Allied
entrenchments at the west end of the Rocky
Gap. Gleefully sitting atop another me-naak
behind them was Hij Geerki, an ancient Grik
bookkeeper, as best they could interpret. They'd captured him at Raan-
goon, and he essentially belonged to Rolak now, body and soul. He was
along to translate. The trio was surrounded by a full company of Colonel Enaak's 5th Maa-ni-la Cavalry, and accompanied by the colonel
himself. The day was dreary, breathless, and hot, with a heavy overcast
lingering above. Alden's "weather weenies"—mostly Lemurian Sky
Priests—were confident it wouldn't rain, but then no Lemurians had

any long-term experience with weather this far west. Alden took their assurances with a grain of salt.

"Yah!" he snapped, kicking at his me-naak's head when it suddenly swung toward his left leg as if intent on taking a bite. The beast was muzzled, but that couldn't prevent Pete's instinctive reaction. Me-naaks, or "meanies," might be fine cavalry mounts, but they looked like long-legged crocodiles with a protective, almost bulletproof case around their abdomens. They were notoriously ill-tempered, and though oddly loyal to their long-term riders, they were fickle, notional creatures, not above occasionally attempting to snatch a snack—particularly when carrying someone they weren't used to.

"Gener-aal Aal-den," Rolak chided, "you'll hurt his feelings!" Rolak was old and scarred, but singularly charming in an aggressively mischievous sort of way. He'd been a warrior long before most Lemurians were and had quickly earned a rare war-wisdom that had been uncommon for his race. He also possessed an unusually dry wit that complemented Pete's earthier humor.

"I don't give a damn," Pete retorted tautly. "It kinda hurts my feelings that he wants to eat me!"

"He just playing," Colonel Enaak assured, blinking amusement. "He tease you. He know . . . what you say? He know 'mud marines' when he smell them."

"Is that so?" Alden challenged, preparing a bantering reply, but just then his party passed through the final Allied trenches and barbed-wire entanglements, and into the shattered no-man's-land moonscape beyond. Just a hundred yards ahead across the denuded plain stood a large, open-sided, octagonal marquee. The canvas was painted against the weather; not colorfully, as Lemurians usually preferred, but in a somber gray similar to that used on *Walker* and the other iron ships. The earth here had once been picturesque, Alden had been told, but now it appeared tortured and dead. There were no deep craters such as those that pockmarked France and Belgium during the Great War, but the land was scarred and gouged by roundshot, withering musketry and canister, flames, and thousands of feet that had churned the slowly drying, but still-damp ground. Despite the best efforts of both sides to remove them, it had proven impossible to retrieve all the dead. Bones picked clean by the skuggik-like local carrion eaters still protruded, jagged and forlorn, from the firming morass like broken stumps of scrub.

The harsh, smoky odor of Lemurian funeral pyres still lingered, and Pete knew the Grik had burned their dead as well—at least those that had lain too long to eat—and in that one small respect, his army, his *people*, had finally found common cause with the Grik. Whether for morale, to prevent disease, or simply because the stench had grown too great to bear, neither side wanted such festering heaps choking the killing ground between their positions.

Ominously dominating the destroyed landscape were the two small hills, respectively called simply "north" and "south" where all the forces that wound up under the command of Colonel Billy Flynn made their last stand. It was nothing short of a miracle that any of them made it out alive, but most didn't. The hills' current, ostentatious occupation by Grik warriors made Pete wonder if the Grik General Halik was experimenting with some newly developed sense of human-Lemurian psychology. The hill forts contributed little to Halik's defensive line and were vulnerable to air attack. They might be good places to install heavily protected batteries, but if Halik wasn't short of warriors, gathered from all over Indiaa, his artillery reserve was pretty skimpy and likely to remain so. Madraas had been the center of heavy industry in Indiaa, and the Allied Navy was patrolling off every port where more artillery might be landed. Pete suddenly realized his first impression was probably right. Unfortunately, Halik was no idiot. He *must* have left the hills occupied for the sole purpose of reminding Pete and his army what happened there. He clenched his teeth. *As if I could forget,* he thought. *But if that bastard thinks being reminded of a traumatic but ultimately small defeat will shake us, he's still got a lot to learn!*

"Looks like hell around here," he said at last, breaking the short silence.

"If my understanding of your concept of 'hell' is correct, I would have to agree." Rolak nodded, blinking unease. "And the quiet. That no one is shooting while we all remain poised, just waiting for the slaughter to resume, adds an even more menacing aspect to the scene. Let us get this over with. Much as it fascinates me to study General Halik and some other members of his staff, I do not like it here. The fighting around our perimeter was tortuous, and the land around it came to resemble this place far more than I care to remember. Your 'trenching' provides an admirable defense, but Halik has learned it. I do not relish the notion of attacking trenches from trenches!"

"Neither do I, old buddy," Alden growled. "And much as I want Halik to think we will, when the time comes, I don't have any intention of doing it!"

Rolak and Enaak both glanced at him, blinking speculation, as they arrived at the marquee. Halik and his party were already there, glaring . . . covetously? Pete wondered, at Enaak's meanies. The Grik didn't have anything like them.

Halik strode forward while Pete and Rolak dismounted. The Maa-ni-la Cav dismounted as well, forming a line facing the Grik guards, their weapons held at the ready. As always, Pete was impressed by the odd Grik general. He wasn't any taller than the average Grik, but older, of course, and unusually muscular. He also . . . carried himself differently, almost like a man, Pete reflected. Of course, he'd been around that Jap, Niwa, long enough for a few mannerisms to rub off, but he'd clearly picked up quite a few notions as well. These meetings, to discuss grievances and try to patch up misunderstandings and downright violations of the truce, had been *Halik's* idea. Both sides knew this was just the calm before the next bloody storm; actual peace and coexistence weren't an option either could even contemplate. But Alden's and Halik's forces had both fought to a shattered nub, and the tactical situation at the time had made it clear that neither could possibly win, so they'd simply quit fighting—for a time. Since then, both armies had secured their lines of supply, at least as far as victuals were concerned, and both had swelled in numbers as well. Halik still had greater numbers by far, but Pete had the edge in artillery, air, and small arms. He also kept a distinct edge in training, he thought. Some kind of "new" Grik, trained and conditioned to defend, had bolstered Halik's lines, but he was sure Halik was still burdened with a preponderance of "ordinary" Grik, which were only good for mindless charges and melee combat. At least he *thought* he was sure.

No salutes were exchanged when the leaders met, but Pete was tempted to hold up a hand and say "how" like they did in the Western movie pictures. That wouldn't do, he realized immediately. Among Lemurians, the gesture was called the "sign of the empty hand," and meant you held no weapons or grudges. Such was not the case here at all. For an instant he wondered if the similar sign in the pictures meant the same thing among American Indians once—or if indeed it was based on anything other than some screenwriter's notion. It didn't matter. He held plenty of weapons and grudges for the Grik, and since nobody was around who'd appreciate the irony, the gesture would only confuse things.

"Whatcha got, Halik?" Pete asked instead. "You wanted this meeting, so what's the dope?"

Geerki translated, though he didn't really need to. Halik couldn't speak English, but he'd learned to understand it from Niwa. Geerki spoke regardless, to apply his better understanding of Alden's slang. Then he'd tell Pete and Rolak what Halik said. Halik snapped, clacked, and hissed in his own tongue for a moment, and Geerki turned to Pete.

"He says the Czechs are at it again," Geerki explained. With the Lemurian-American example already set, everyone had begun considering all the "Brotherhood of Volunteers" under Colonel Dalibor Svec's command as the "Czech Legion." The somewhat odd continental 'Cats didn't seem to mind. "They're still raiding isolated Grik garrisons at either end o' Halik's ar'y."

"Still picking at the flanks, eh?" Pete commiserated solemnly, speaking directly to Halik. He shrugged. "Nothing I can do about it. Let's see if I can explain this in a way you'll understand. The Legion joined *our* 'hunt' against you, the same way that bastard Kurokawa and his Japs once joined your hunt against us. The Czechs only agreed to follow the orders they like, and right now they don't like it when I tell 'em to leave off killing your guys when they see an easy mark. If you don't like it, beef up the garrisons they're targeting."

"But they sneak across the mountains through passes we do not know!" Halik complained.

"Then it seems to me they're doing you a favor," Pete stated sourly. "They're showing you all the places I might try to sneak *my* army across! Don't you think I'd stop them if I could?" In point of fact, the Legion was doing exactly what Pete wanted: forcing Halik to spread out and defend an ever-growing number of passes while very carefully not revealing some of the better ones.

Halik stared hard at Alden before jerking a nod. "I can appreciate your frustration in that regard. It seems we are both plagued by other hunters with their own agendas. Our now mutual enemy, Kurokawa, tasks me still as well."

Pete's ears pricked up at that. Kurokawa was dead . . . wasn't he? Maybe Halik just didn't know, and was referring to Kurokawa's inability to protect the sea lanes—or maybe he really had heard from the crazy Jap. "Yeah? What's he been up to now?" he asked casually.

Halik snorted. "I shall not tell you that, General Alden. But like your Czechs, he does not . . . cooperate. And ironically, his actions aid you at present more than they do me—unless he should somehow encounter those elements of your fleet that sailed several days ago. Surely you understand why I will not tell you how that may be if you do not already know."

"Can't blame a fella for asking," Pete murmured, mind racing. He had to get word to the Skipper that Kurokawa might not be dead after all—and he might now be entirely on the loose, and utterly unpredictable!

"What other complaints do you wish to advance?" Rolak asked, and Halik's intense, reptilian eyes turned to him.

"Your flying machines. They fly over us at will, scouting our positions and watching our every move. They *are* under your control, and I understood that none of us was to cross the cease-fire line."

"Shoot 'em down, if you can," Pete said. "Or try to scout us with your zeppelins if you like. We'll shoot *them* down if we catch 'em, though."

Halik could only nod. He didn't have any zeppelins left. Those few that had remained airworthy after the last battle had vanished from India before or with Kurokawa, but he wasn't about to admit that.

"Could be we've missed a few, or you wouldn't know part of our fleet has sailed—but that only proves you've been spying on us, so I don't want to hear any more whining about cheating."

Halik said nothing. He had his spies, certainly, but they were on the ground, lurking in the dense jungle along the coast south of Madras. Contact was sporadic, however, and he wasn't getting nearly enough reports on troop movements. Even worse, what he did get was often confusing or made no sense at all, and that left him anxious. Sometimes he wished he was like other Hij, born into the class, and able to remain dispassionate, almost disassociated from events surrounding them. First General Esshk had been his role model after his elevation, but Halik knew Esshk wouldn't know what to do under these circumstances. He was a designer of battles in the same way that a master swordsmith might instruct an apprentice how best to shape a blade. He was responsible for how it turned out, but wasn't personally invested in its creation—and had little interest at all in how it was used. Halik couldn't lead like that, couldn't even *think* like that anymore. Battles had become very personal things for him, and he was entirely invested in their outcome.

He had no doubt that the current peace was a fragile thing, and hostilities could resume over any provocation. They'd resume anyway, just as soon as either side thought it had a decisive advantage. When that finally occurred, he and his new . . . fraternity . . . of officers would lead their troops in ways that Esshk never could: with passion and complete commitment. They were determined to achieve victory, and to accomplish it with as little loss as possible. That was another thing that set Halik aside from other "born" Hij officers. He'd started out as a lowly Uul himself, and if he could grow into what he'd become, why couldn't others? What a terrible waste was the old way of war!

In addition, though, somehow, his new awareness had taught him to consider it a terrible shame that hostilities must resume. To his amazement, he even caught himself actually admiring this foe—Alden and Rolak in particular. But for whatever reason, the Giver of Life had decreed that all non-Grik not associated with the Great Hunt must be exterminated as prey, and it was not his place to defy the Celestial Mother. To that extent at least, he was as dogmatic as any Grik ever hatched.

"Come, General Halik," Rolak said. "None of this is new; we have haggled over these same details before. What is the real reason you asked to speak with us?"

Halik's crest rose and he glared at the old Lemurian. Then he puffed a breath through sharp, clenched teeth. "Two reasons, I suppose. First, to inquire after the health of General Niwa yet again. You have given me no news about him for some time, and I find myself . . . concerned about the possible reasons for this. Second, honestly, to take your measure. Without General Niwa to rely on for counsel, I must keep my own—and at times, I must admit, I feel as if I understand you better than I do my own people. Perhaps I trust my *sense* of you, that you are not poised to strike, better than I trust my spies, or the words of the representatives you usually send in your stead."

Pete blinked consternation in the Lemurian way, then looked at Rolak.

"What does your 'sense' of us tell you?" Rolak asked quietly.

"That you are not prepared to attack me yet, but will be soon," Halik stated simply. He stared at Pete. "*You* now think, 'Ah! Halik does not expect us, so now is the time!' But after reflection, you will decide that I would not have invited attack by confessing I did not expect it if I was not ready to receive it! Is this not an exciting way to think?" Halik paused. His expression didn't change, but his tone was deeper when he resumed. "I miss talking with Niwa thus, and you, my enemies, are the only ones with whom I can share such conversations and insights. So tell me true, does Niwa yet live?"

Pete and Rolak looked at each other again. *Holy shit!* Pete realized. *The damn thing's lonesome!* Finally, Rolak nodded at him.

"Yeah," Pete admitted. "He's alive. He ain't out of the woods yet, and he's weak, but I expect he'll live. We visited a minute or two before we came out, in fact, and I guess I was going to tell you that he asked if I'd pass on his regards."

Halik's mouth opened slightly in what apparently passed for a smile, but didn't seem so friendly with all those teeth. "You would not mistreat him?"

"Of course not!" Rolak stated emphatically. "We question him, of course, and he has told us of his friendship toward you. But even as we care for him, we treat him as the prisoner of war he is. We will not break our agreement about prisoners as long as you do not."

Halik jerked another nod. "I have none of your people prisoner now, but when I catch them, they will not be eaten!"

Pete grimaced. "Same here. Like in the deal."

They were silent awhile as they rode back toward their own lines, and through the zigzag trenches and bombproofs at the front. "I'm kinda glad we didn't let that Jap croak after all," Pete finally said. "I figger he'll stick to the deal on prisoners as long as he's alive."

"Perhaps," Rolak hedged. "But we should probably let them meet before we resume the offensive, just to make sure."

"Good idea. You know? That Halik gives me the creeps. He guessed exactly what I was thinking, damn it! I hope he doesn't guess anything else."

"Most perplexing," Rolak agreed. "But your hu-maan face moving gives much away. You must guard against that."

"I try."

"Yes, but he has learned it well. Not as well as I," Rolak bragged, "but well enough, I fear." His ears stood erect in concentration. "I have noticed that Grik faces move more than Mi-Anakka—Lemurians, but I can make little sense of it. Perhaps, for that reason, the concept of wearing one's thoughts on the face is easier for him to grasp and interpret. What do you think, Hij Geerki?" Rolak asked their Grik companion.

"I ser' you, Lord!" Geerki crowed piously, before quickly answering. "You could say right, though. I don't know. Human faces got thoughts all on they. You ask I, he'd know iv you told he that Ni'a alive and he not."

"Another good reason he didn't croak, then," Pete said. "And of course it doesn't hurt that, out from under the Grik's or Kurokawa's thumb, he seems to be coming to his senses a little." He frowned. "Jeez, what a mixed-up kid!"

"So it does *seem*," Rolak agreed cautiously. "But whatever common cause he might share with us regarding the Grik in general, and Kurokawa in particular, he also knows he is now 'under *our* thumb,' as you said. And do not forget, however it came to be, he has formed a very real attachment to General Halik. Most strange."

"Damn strange," Pete agreed, "but understandable, I guess, with nobody else to talk to for so long."

"Perhaps, but we must be careful how we use him. He has told us much about these 'new' Grik we face, and to truly gain Niwa's trust, we really must attempt to capture Halik alive—as we've promised—when we resume our offensive."

"*You* promised," Pete stressed. "And it'll take more than a 'Yeah, Grik are bad, and I'm sorry I helped 'em kill your folks' before I'll trust Niwa as far as a snail can fly." Rolak glared at him, blinking reproach. "Oh sure. We'll *try*," Pete retorted, rolling his eyes. "Hell, I'd like to study the bastard. Figure out how the hell he turned Grik into real soldiers! But if he gets dead in the fighting, that's the breaks."

"Just so long as we try," Rolak prodded.

"We will. Let's go talk to Niwa and see if we can squeeze him for what Kurokawa might do now."

"If Kurokawa actually lives. I find it difficult to believe Halik just let that information slip."

Pete pondered that. "Me too, but you know? How would he even know we thought he was dead in the first place? We didn't blow, beyond telling him we won the fight at sea. That much he could figure out on his own." Pete's face hardened. "Halik has to have had recent news of, or contact with the bastard, and maybe that didn't just slip. It's obvious he hates Kurokawa's guts. Understandable, if he actually bumped off the vice regent—or whatever the hell he was—and basically set himself up as king of India, like Niwa said. I'll bet Halik *wants* us to catch him, and that just about clinches it for me that the slippery little bastard really is still out there somewhere!"

CHAPTER 11

////// Diego Garcia
"Laa-Laanti"
July 13, 1944

he sun was setting on Diego Garcia as the last officers of First Fleet South were rowed or motored ashore, to join those already there. The High Chief of the island, more a king really, when his status was compared to the High Chiefs of other Lemurian Homes, had invited his new "allies" to a ceremony meant to bless their endeavors in the eyes of the Heavens. (To them, the stars were the very eyes of their ancestors, watching from above.) The High Chief, Gin-Taaor, had known he'd have many guests for the festivities, but he blinked what looked like near panic from atop his throne of mountain fish teeth when he saw just how many were actually coming.

Only about a third of the people from all the ships had been allowed ashore, but Adar thought it was important for as many of his people as possible to meet the Laa-Laantis, both for cultural reasons, and to quell any "why should we fight for them if they won't fight for themselves" muttering. They could then spread the word through the fleet. It had been a good call from his perspective, and it was clear that most of those who came ashore and saw the small, inoffensive natives for the first time, were beginning to get it.

Gin-Taaor saw it differently. His people anxiously regarded the sheer number of strangers, and strangers were something they weren't used to at all, having met none for as long as their oral history recalled. Some even thought the strangers must be gods, given their size, purpose, and magical technology. Gin-Taaor knew they weren't gods; he'd already been convinced of that in the months since the great "serpent fish ship" (*Amerika*) had arrived, followed quickly by *Donaghey*, *Sineaa*, then an ever-growing collection of visitors. But that didn't mean he was entirely comfortable with their power—or their appearance right out of the most ancient myths. That could pose a problem. He dared not insult his new "allies," but it was dawning on him at last that just those who'd come today nearly outnumbered all his folk on the island combined. He hadn't grasped that the Allied ships, big as they were, could hold so many people, and he was increasingly worried how he was going to feed them all.

Matt, Sandra, Adar, Keje, Courtney, and Becher Lange were the last to come ashore, in one of *Salissa*'s motor launches. They were accompanied by Chief Gray, in his capacity as "commander of the Captain's Guard," and several members of his detail. For this event, that included Silva—who'd sworn he'd behave—Lawrence, Gunner's Mate Pak-Ras-Ar (Pack Rat), and Diania, who, besides being Sandra's personal steward, had been receiving intensive combat instruction from other members of the guard, including Gray himself. He thought she was ready, at least for this. Together, they gathered with other friends under the trees in the dwindling light and stared around.

"Isn't it remarkable?" demanded Courtney, who'd been ashore almost constantly over the last few days. He and Adar had practically lived among the locals since they arrived, spending most of their time with Gin-Taaor's wiry "wizard," who served much the same purpose here as a Sky Priest. They'd devoted themselves to learning as much about the locals as they could in the time they had. At present, Courtney was holding out his hands and gesturing around as if he'd discovered the place. "Utterly remarkable," he emphasized.

The main, central village on the island of Laa-Laanti was a sprawling affair, nearly encompassing the broad, relatively shallow lagoon. Dwellings were simple, framed with the bones of greatfish, and covered with their skins. The basic, somewhat domed architecture appeared nearly universal, but the bones and skins came from a variety of different species. The overall impression was one of ingenious utilitarianism, but it was also quite smelly in an old, dry-fish sort of way. That was understandable, since the People here obviously depended on the sea for the greatest share of their livelihood. Smallish, clinker-built fishing boats with crab-claw-shaped woven mat sails predominated, but there were larger boats, presumably used to hunt the biggest fish. Even so, two of the steam/sail DDs of the Alliance dominated the harbor on a beach near the northwest headland, where the natives had allowed them to be careened to clean their hulls. The rest of the ships of First Fleet South that needed it, would enter the floating dry dock that was *Respite Island* to have their hulls cleaned before the whole small armada finally moved on its objective.

"It's *sumpin'*," Silva groused quietly, and Matt gave him a warning stare.

"Well, Skipper, it ain't exactly Shanghai—or even Baalkpan, for my first step ashore in so long."

"Quit complaining," Matt ordered. "You're lucky to be ashore at all."

"Sumpin' eemarkable!" Petey cawed on Sandra's shoulder. The little tree-gliding reptile had exposed himself more fully than usual. He wasn't comfortable with crowds, but was getting over his reticence—not always a good thing, with him.

Courtney shuffled his notes nervously. "When would it be most appropriate for me to speak, Captain?" he asked. Matt looked questioningly at Adar.

"You speak quite a lot, whether appropriate or not." Adar blinked fondly, then sobered. "And I do remain unconvinced this is the proper time and setting for you to reveal your theory. There shall be a time set

aside for you tonight, as I promised. Even High Chief Gin-Taaor is anxious to hear what you have to say. But for the sake of . . . clarity, I do
wish you would consider a postponement."

Courtney frowned. "But I'm ready *now*!"

"Perhaps, but are you sure your audience is?" Sandra cautioned.

"You may have a point," he conceded glumly. "I don't mean to be
rude, but much of what I have to say assumes a certain level of technical
understanding. I've tried to keep it as uncomplicated as possible, ridiculously so, in most respects, but . . ."

"I'm not nearly as concerned that you will cause offense as I am
about other things," Adar said. "These people know we are different,
and most of what we do or say requires explanation. Time would bring
them to understand what you say."

"As if *anything* he jabbers on about can ever be understood," Silva
mumbled aside to Pack Rat.

"But in this context," Adar continued, "at this time, I find it likely
that your theory may only confuse the issue when we all have so much
more to focus on."

"You're probably right," Matt agreed, "but the issue's already pretty
confused. These people have had an awful lot to get used to in a short
period of time. If Courtney's theory can clear up any of the confusion,
for any of us, that might be a good thing. And this could be the best
time of all to roll it out." He grinned at Bradford. "No pressure."

Adar blinked thoughtfully. "Perhaps. Perhaps you are right." He
looked at Courtney. "Is there *any* chance what you say tonight may
more likely reassure folk than alarm them?"

Courtney blinked. "Well, yes, of course! My observations cannot
possibly cause alarm! And as Captain Reddy has said, explanations, by
their very nature, dispel confusion! Have no fear, my dear Adar!"

The group moved toward the center of the village with more of
Walker's officers and POs who'd joined them. On the way, they picked
up Chack, Safir Maraan, Laumer, Rominger, and several others. Wading through the throng of sailors, Marines, and even quite a few locals,
they finally reached the circle around the throne of teeth, just as the sun
disappeared completely. Pukaa and Sikaa attended their father, the

High Chief, as did the wizard and some of his acolytes, who were lighting a large heap of wood.

"Our way of receiving guests is *much* more dignified," murmured
Keje, referring to the grand processions visitors took to the Great Halls
aboard ship or on shore.

"But not terribly different," Courtney observed. "There's always a
great deal of jostling in any event. The traditions obviously spring from
the same, ancient source—as do others."

Adar immediately proved Courtney's point by advancing into the
circle of increasing light, provided by the growing fire. His hand was
raised in greeting, but also as a sign recognized even here as a symbol
that one's hand grasped no weapon. Gin-Taaor returned the sign and
stood. He wore a headdress of fish skin, of a type possibly related to the
creature Earl had caught, since the polished scales glittered in the fire-
light like all the colors of a rainbow. Hundreds of small bones dangled
from the headdress, jostling softly together to make a sound like the sea.
His long loincloth was made of the same glistening skin, and even his
tail was decorated with the bones. He wore no other adornments, and
was clearly a young, healthy specimen of the Laa-Laanti People. He
waited a moment while the crowd's sounds diminished, then grinned at
Adar and spoke: "Well-come," he said, with a self-satisfied blink. He
gestured around. "You all well-come here!" He paused, having apparently exhausted his supply of words all the strangers would understand,
and leaned down to speak to one of his sons, who nodded slightly. It was
Pukaa, the elder and his father's successor.

"The great Gin-Taaor begs you to make you selfs at home. Eat, drink,
be happy," Pukaa said. Matt leaned forward and whispered to Chack.
"Is this the same kid that's been hanging around you guys since you got
here? He could hardly string three words together when we met him a
few days ago."

"Indeed," Chack whispered back. "His newfound fluency is surprising." He shrugged. "But how long did it take me to learn your speech? Less
than the months we have known Pukaa, certainly." He grinned. "That he
would hide his fluency actually encourages me to some extent."

"Why's that?" Matt asked.

"Because, my dear Captain Reddy," Courtney interrupted, "it shows these people are far more, um, sophisticated, I suppose, than we have suspected before. But that is a good thing! Think on it; they have been listening to and understanding our unguarded speech for quite some time. We have no secrets from them and they know it! They doubtless already fully understand our cause and our goals, and know we mean them no harm. Quite the contrary. I'm sure they've gathered by now that we mean to protect them as best we can!"

Matt nodded, and finally smiled. "I guess nobody likes being spied on, but in this case I suppose it's for the best. At least it eliminates the need for us to constantly reassure them that we come in peace!"

"Toward them, at any rate," Sandra said.

"Of course," Courtney agreed.

Pukaa had been speaking in his own tongue during this exchange, and Gin-Taaor had more to say as well, but finally Pukaa invited Adar to speak to the assembly. "I will . . . exchange your words for our people," Pukaa explained. "They already know who you are."

"Thank you, Pukaa," Adar said, throwing back the star-embroidered hood of his deep purple cloak to reveal his silvery fur. He laid back his ears in respect. "And thank you, Your Excellency," he said, bowing to the High Chief, "for your hospitality and assistance at this historic time." He stepped forward so he could turn slightly, symbolically addressing all those present. "As you certainly know by now, the people I have the honor to lead, people of various species but of one mind and heart, have embarked on a great quest to smite the Ancient Enemy that drove us from our collective ancestral home." He waited while Pukaa spoke, quickly translating his words before he resumed. "That terrible enemy, those we call the 'Grik,' was not content to expel us from that place, but has sought, through the ages, to pursue us to extinction. Great battles have been fought and many victories have been achieved, but the contest remains dangerously balanced and unresolved. Our quest, now joined by other long-lost cousins from the southern lands beyond our ancestral home, is designed to tip the balance and carve a pathway to victory at last. This you know," Adar stressed to those who'd grown quiet to listen.

"Yet to one not accustomed to the pathways of the Heavens, not steeped in their mysteries or attuned to their purpose, the happy re-union of our peoples here after so many ages might seem merely a fortuitous accident," he continued, shaking his head. "I do not believe that is the case. That our new friends and cousins from the Republic of Real People should be saved from their distress by finding this tiny island in the uncharted vastness of the Western Ocean is coincidence enough. That our people, led by the intrepid Cap-i-taan Gaar-ett, should then quickly find you *both* here as well, makes me skeptical that mere chance can have been responsible. That the people here can be so willing to join the cause of ridding the world of the Grik menace forever, and that this island, Laa-Laanti, is so perfectly situated as a staging point from which to launch our quest . . ." Adar paused and took a breath in the utter silence that had descended, and raised his hands to the stars above. "Surely only the Heavens themselves could have arranged such a 'coincidental' convergence of course and purpose!" he stated forcefully, and the assembly roared with delight.

"We fight Grik!" Gin-Taaor bellowed with his fist in the air, and his folk roared even louder.

"No," Adar said. He hadn't shouted, but the simple word had the same effect. Gin-Taaor spoke harshly to his son, and Pukaa blinked questioningly at Adar.

"The High Chief asks why we not fight. We 'aallies' now, yes? Aallies fight together, not so? You make aallies with others here"—he waved at the Germans and 'Cats from the Republic—"to fight with you. Why not Laa-Laantis?"

"You *are* our allies, our very firm friends," Adar assured, "but you are not warriors. I do not doubt your courage. The bones that frame your homes are proof enough that you can and will fight monstrous beasts, but the Grik are different. Far different." He looked almost imploringly at Matt, then continued. "By the Heavens, I wish I could better explain, but I beg you to accept my word that before you can hope to fight the Grik, you must first learn *how*. We lost . . ." He glanced quickly at the sky. "We lost more people than are gathered on this entire island just *learning* to fight the Grik," he explained softly, "and many who were not slain were horribly wounded." He blinked great sadness. "In some battles—the times when we gather to fight—we lose more people than are gathered here in a single *day* even now, all because the enemy has changed how he fights and we must learn again. I would not—*will not*—allow your people here to suffer like that." He gushed a sigh. "We will leave trainers here, and you can learn to fight if you wish. That is only right, in case the Grik ever find this place. Perhaps some few of you might even join us in distant battles someday, but not many, I . . . I beg you." He forced a smile. "You are the last, you see. The very last of our people that we know of that remain unbloodied by this terrible war, and we would prefer to keep it that way."

"But . . . if we are aallies, what will we do?" Pukaa demanded.

"What you have been doing," Adar said. "And perhaps a bit more. Help us here. Work on the docks, unload ships and reload others. Repair ships, fuel them—things that many of your people have already volunteered and learned to do. More ships and troops will come this way, more supplies and weapons. With your people here, we do not need to bring forward more of those whose job it would be to help us as you have, which means we can bring more warriors to the fight!"

"We work, but not fight?" Pukaa asked doubtfully.

"In this war, those who work so others can fight perform as great a service as any. You have my word." There was an uproar over this when Pukaa explained, but Adar continued. "If my word is not sufficient to convince you, consider the circumstances!" he said loudly, and the clamor died away. "My people were never warriors. . . . *Few* of us were, I should say," he added, catching the firelit eyes of Safir Maraan. He gestured at Matt. "But the arrival of Cap-i-taan Reddy and his destroyermen aboard the swift, slender ship of iron changed that at precisely the right moment for us to defeat the first Grik tentacles that reached for us, and set the course that ultimately brought us here. I consider that no more a coincidence than any other great event I have described. He and his people prepared us for the task ahead, just as Kap-i-taan Von Melhausen and Becher Lange, and all the people of *Amer-i-kaa* have done for the Republic they serve." He blinked irony. "Nor do I find coincidence in the name of that mighty ship—and the fact that ours is the

Amer-i-caan Navy!" He shook his head. "There are forces at work here, upon our world, that I do not understand. His Excellency, Courtney Bradford, claims to have explanations based on science—a kind of learning—and he has come to deliver them tonight as well, but regardless of the various faiths that guide us, that we seek comfort and direction from, I am personally convinced that no 'science' can explain much, if any, of what I have said tonight." He stared upward. "Science is a wonderful thing and it has helped us greatly; there is no doubt. But beyond science, beyond everything, I see the paths of the Heavens, directed by the Creator of All Things, and believe it is He who brought us all together with our ships, our warriors, our resolve; this land and its people"—he grinned at Courtney—"and our science, at this time, in this place, and for this purpose." His voice rose again. "And *that* is why, with the help of all those gathered here, prepared to contribute in the ways they are best prepared, I am sure we *will not fail!*"

"Where'd Courtney wind up?" Matt asked. He, Sandra, Chack, Safir, Becher Lange, and Chief Gray were walking on the sandy beach under the moonlight on the northeast shore of the island. As usual, Lieutenant Toryu Miyata was Lange's virtual shadow, but he remained several paces back. He knew feelings among the new arrivals were mixed at best toward any Japanese, particularly after what *Amagi* had done, not to mention other recent events. But he trusted the tall German, and doubted he had much to fear from *this* group in any event. They believed he truly did have valuable information regarding their objective, and Lange had convinced them, with the tale of his arrival in the Republic and his role in bringing them here, that regardless of the past, Miyata was honor bound to the destruction of the Grik. For his part, Miyata was certain that this "Grand Alliance" shared that goal, and from what he'd learned of Captain Reddy before they even met—specifically the man's command of the defense of Baalkpan against seemingly impossible odds—he couldn't question Reddy's honor.

The sea was calm, but the surf made a constant roar they had to speak over. Silva, Pack Rat, Doocy Meek, and a couple of Republic 'Cats tagged along behind, there to protect them in the unlikely event they should require it, but out of earshot.

"Braad-furd sulks," Chack said, his tone thoughtful but subdued.

"He is drunk," Safir added distastefully.

"He's in a drunken sulk," Gray confirmed.

"I don't know what he expected," Sandra said, almost wonderingly. "Especially after Adar's speech. Courtney bounced up with that ridiculous sombrero on his head and started in about stuff I'm not even sure *he* understands. Did he expect everybody to just sit and listen raptly like he was addressing the Royal Society? Of course nobody was listening by then."

"I was listening," Matt said thoughtfully. "And so were you," he told his wife. Sandra nodded uncomfortably. "So were a lot of people who give a damn," Matt added, looking at Gray, Chack, and Safir in turn.

"I did not understand him," Safir defended, "but Mr. Braad-furd is always interesting."

"And just as often nutty as a forty-acre goober field," Gray proclaimed, but without his usual conviction.

"Maybe," Matt agreed, "and not all of what he said was new. He's still convinced that whatever . . . phenomenon brings people here has something to do with electromagnetism and energy. Storm energy and a freaky squall in our case, I guess." He nodded at Becher. "Maybe yours too." *Amerika* had crossed over in a storm at night, unnoticed by her crew who were trying to save their battle-damaged ship. Matt paused and looked to the sea, his eyes scanning the silhouettes of the warships anchored offshore. There was *Walker,* lying dark and low.

"His invocation of the sun as a source for the energy was new,"

Chack said, looking at Safir, "and it certainly captured the imagination of some." The People of Aryaal and B'mbaado believed the sun *was* God. Safir blinked annoyance, but leaned tightly against her betrothed. She and Chack had made no formal announcement, as they'd once planned, but that no longer mattered after their long separation. It was now simply understood that they were and had always been bound to each other.

"Of course the sun affects the weather," Gray grumbled. "Even Petey probably knows that." He nodded at the fuzzy reptile draped around Sandra's neck. The creature glared back with bright, moonlit eyes and burped. "So maybe he's right," Gray conceded. "But what about all that other stuff he went on about?" he prodded. "What the *hell* about that? Look, I get that this is a different world; I guess a whole different *universe* than the one we came from—that the Japs chased us out of," he added with a sour glance at Miyata. "I—all of us—figured that out a long time ago. An' I'm not even sayin' it's a bad thing we wound up here." His brows furrowed. "It was curtains for us in the Java Sea. But it *was* hard for me—for the fellas—to get a grip on the notion that there's two, ah, 'universes' overlappin' like this. Bein' so much alike, but so different too, adds a whole other degree of weirdness, but that's obviously the way it is. Now Bradford comes up with this new brainstorm that there ain't just *two* 'universes,' but maybe gobs of 'em! That's creepy as hell. It can't be true, can it, Skipper? I mean, with swarms of screwy places folks could've come from, what else are we liable to run into? What if there's some earth where Martians took over, an' *they've* wound up here?"

Sandra covered a smile by rubbing her chin. "I don't think you need to worry about *Martians*, Mr. Gray. If Mr. Bradford's 'radio metaphor' is right, such a historically distinctive 'frequency' should not be received . . . here."

"But what if they just now showed up?" Gray persisted.

"That's enough, Boats," Matt said sternly. He'd never seen Fitzhugh Gray flinch from anything, but everyone had his limit. Apparently, for Gray it was Martians. "Look," he said more softly, looking at his old friend. "Speculation of that sort won't do any good at all. We'll keep dealing with whatever we run into, whatever it is. So Courtney threw out some possible answers. Maybe they helped, and maybe they just raised more questions, like Adar thought they might. It's hard to explain, but I guess I do feel better." He snorted. "It's funny, but even if not much of what Bradford said made sense by itself, it *all* sort of made sense, if you know what I mean. There's more than one head working on it now, so maybe he did make things less confusing in the long run. I particularly liked his radio comparison, when you think about all the similarities—and differences. Mr. Palmer must've helped him with that part, so maybe he can explain it better than Courtney did."

With the existence of the Republic of Real People in hand, particularly the accounts of the odd diversity of histories incorporated there—everything from ancient Chinese explorers, Ptolemaic Egyptians, *tenth-century* Romans—and Lemurians, of course—Courtney Bradford had finally decided that this world was not only the dumping ground for the refuse of their old one, but it had somehow collected "specimens" from multiple earths over time. He remained convinced that a combination of electromagnetism and a titanic discharge of energy on a scale not easily imagined provided the actual mechanism of transportation but now believed this world was connected to the rest by means of something similar to radio. At least radio provided his metaphor. Essentially, "this" earth was a receiver, and all the worlds that fed it were transmitters of a sort. Most likely, the receiver was "tuned" to the "frequency" of the world the destroyermen left, at least at present, judging by the number of recent familiar "receptions."

He proposed that it was possible that the frequency "hopped about" on occasion, allowing crossovers from "different" earths, but even then he believed it was more like one frequency "bleeding over" onto another. The tenth-century Romans who helped build the Republic were the most extreme example of this they'd encountered yet. Probably—and perhaps hopefully—wildly different histories, and the worlds they built, created frequencies on a different wavelength entirely—too different to cross over at all. He still didn't know if this world was also a transmitter as well as a receiver, however, and the very stark differences between this world and the one they came from left a few gaping holes in his theory.

He had more, but by the time he reached that point in his presentation, he realized he'd largely lost his audience. He almost petulantly bid everyone a good night and scurried quickly to where the barrels of seep and beer had been brought ashore. Little was seen of him after that, so no one could get him to expand on his theory, but what he'd said was enough.

Matt appraised Becher Lange. "But you kind of knew all this stuff already, didn't you, Mr. Lange? Different worlds with different histories. That's the only explanation for the way things have wound up in your Republic. I studied history a little," Matt admitted, slightly self-conscious, as usual. "*Our* history," he amended, "and I have to wonder if time affects the adjustment of Courtney's 'frequencies' to some extent. It does seem—sometimes," he cautioned, "that the further back in history you go, the bigger the differences are. But even as 'close together' as we came through, my ships and yours, just twenty-five years or so, there're differences. For example, you said your *Amerika* fought *Mauretania* hammer and tongs before you wound up here." Becher nodded and Matt shook his head, staring back at his ship. "Two elegant ocean liners, armed with a few guns and fighting it out. It must've been a sight." He looked back at Lange. "The only thing is, in *my* history, it never happened. Sure, *Mauretania* was converted to an auxiliary cruiser, but *Amerika* was in the States when the Great War started, and stayed there until the States jumped in in 1917. After that, she was seized and converted to a troopship." He smiled apologetically at Lange. "She still was one, last I heard, but she never fought for the Kaiser."

Becher said nothing for a long moment, but then spoke in a falsely cheerful tone. "In that case, Kapitan Reddy, we may as well assume that our countries at least, from our apparently separate worlds, never did go to war. So we need not concern ourselves with any lingering animosities, no?"

Matt smiled and extended his hand. "Not against each other, anyway. The Grik are another matter."

"*Ja*," Lange said, and took Matt's hand.

"But that only confirms Courtney's theory!" Sandra said, frustration seeping into her tone. "I seriously doubt you had descendants of tenth-century Romans in the world *you* came from, Mr. Lange."

"No," Becher agreed. "We did not. Yet they are here. And though I do not know 'radio,' I understand the 'frequencies' Herr Bradford described. His is a rather elegant interpretation of much that has puzzled our people, in fact. The Republic has its history, but the histories of many of those who found themselves there over time do not always agree, and we have long suspected the existence of multiple, ah, sources. Herr Bradford has finally described one way by which those various sources might converge." He smiled, but his lips were hidden by the gray-black beard and the darkness. "Personally, that makes me feel better as well. I have always been more interested in the how than the why. I am an engineer, after all."

"'Why' still bugs the hell out of me," Gray grumbled, "but I *ain't* an engineer."

"Perhaps there is no 'why,' only a 'how,'" Chack said suddenly. "Or perhaps Chairman Adar explained it best before Mr. Braad-furd even spoke." He looked at the puzzled expressions, grinned, and flicked his tail. "Could it not be that the 'how' and 'why' are both the work of the Maker after all?"

They digested that for a time as they walked, and though many questions still plagued their minds, perhaps Adar's *was* the best explanation. They might never discover all the hows and whys for sure, but the Grik remained, and they were very real. For now they must focus on that.

"Lieutenant Miyata," Matt said at last, "will you join us, please?"

Miyata trotted forward. "Of course, Captain Reddy. What may I do for you?"

"Help us when we hit Madagascar," Matt said simply, "but there's something I thought you"—he nodded at the others—"all of you, should know." He frowned. "General Alden's latest dispatch has me a little concerned." By the clipped tension in his words, that was clearly an understatement. "I won't go into all the details, but it now seems possible, maybe even likely, we didn't get Kurokawa after all."

Sandra gasped, and Gray took a breath and straightened.

"Lieutenant Miyata told you about Kurokawa?" Matt asked Lange, and the German nodded grimly. "Well, in spite of everything, Pete Alden believes the slimy bastard might've slipped through our fingers.

Again." He looked quizzically at Miyata. "You don't mind my calling the 'General of the Sea' a 'slimy bastard,' do you, Lieutenant?"

"No, Captain Reddy. I consider him worse in Japanese, but I do not have the words to call him such in English."

"Fine. But the point is, if he is alive, he's still got some powerful ships and maybe even an army of sorts. In addition, he's apparently on the outs with the Grik. What do you think he'll do?"

Miyata considered. "Sir," he said at last, "Hisashi Kurokawa is quite mad. He is . . . *evil* mad. I fear that if he has those things and anywhere secure to take them, he will become even more unpredictable, and perhaps even more dangerous."

Matt nodded grimly. "That's what I thought."

Commander Simon Herring, chief of Strategic Intelligence, and watch standing "supernumerary" bridge officer, returned early aboard USS *Walker* from the party ashore. A few entirely sober Lemurian sailors had hitched a ride in the motor whaleboat so they'd be back in time for their watches. They'd conversed quietly in their own tongue, largely about Courtney Bradford's strange theory, from what Herring could pick up, but they didn't speak to him. That was just as well. When Herring ascended the accommodation ladder and saluted the Lemurian OOD, he was relieved there were no other humans in sight. Quickly, he descended the companionway under the bridge overhang and made his way to the wardroom. Juan Marcos was in there, supervising a Lemurian assistant fussing with the plates in the cabinets, but other than a curious nod, Juan paid him no mind. Herring stifled an instinctive reprimand, reminding himself that *Walker* was no Pacific Fleet battleship moored in Pearl Harbor before the war, or even his more familiar office in Washington. Regardless of how much he'd endured in China, the Philippines, and in Japanese hands, however, he still found the casual approach to military courtesy aboard this ship somewhat jarring. He shook it off. This was Juan's domain, as surely as the engineering spaces belonged to Lieutenant Tab-At. And given Herring's ambiguous status aboard, he was content not to draw too much attention. Picking up a cup, he poured himself some of the vile fluid masquerading as coffee and retreated back down the short passageway. Pushing a green curtain aside, he entered the cramped, starboard-side stateroom he shared with Bernie Sandison and found Lance Corporal Ian Miles already there. The China Marine was reclining on a metal chair, looking at one of Bernie's many sketches of torpedo components, his feet up on the small writing desk. Herring suppressed another surge of irritation, but it must have shown on his face. Reluctantly, Miles lowered his feet to the deck, but he didn't stand.

"You're early," Herring snapped quietly, closing the curtain but leaving a gap so he could see if anyone passed. He sat on the lower rack that Sandison had kindly insisted he take. "What if Mr. Sandison found you here?"

"I'd just tell him I was waiting for you. We're old pals, remember?"

Herring grimaced. "That fiction only goes so far, Miles, and won't hold up to as much scrutiny as it is beginning to draw. Nor," he continued, "does it give you license to take so many liberties. We may have a common cause, you and I, but we are not 'pals.' Do I make myself clear?"

"Clear as can be, Commander," Miles replied, falsely cheerful. "My 'cause' is survival, plain and simple. I don't give a damn about this ship, or any of the deluded, monkey-lovin' dopes aboard. And as for the monkeys . . ." He snorted. "I don't even care about their stupid war, or even who wins it, except for how it affects my own precious life, see?" He shrugged languidly. "Your scheme seems to offer the best chance of preserving my life, in the long run, so I'm helping you. That's as far as it goes for me too. I'm no hero, and as long as you bear that in mind, we'll stay square."

Herring's lip curled in disgust. "My 'scheme' as you call it, remains a last resort. I was wrong about Captain Reddy, nearly as wrong as I was to take you into my confidence."

Miles chuckled quietly. "No, you were right to trust me, Commander. I'm just as anxious to save the world as you are, so I'll have a place to live. I don't know why your little secret mission should be a 'last resort' all of a sudden, though. I haven't seen any reason to change the plan."

"The plan has changed *because* of Captain Reddy, you fool."

Miles looked at him wonderingly. "You've got to be kidding. You really think he can pull it off!" Miles shook his head. "A handful of Asiatic sailors and a few boatloads of monkeys and throwback Brits and Krauts against who knows how many Lizards and Japs, and you think they might actually *win*?"

"They *have* been winning," Herring stressed forcefully. "And after the action against the Grik battleships, when I saw Captain Reddy at work for the very first time, I won't underestimate him again. He may not have as much strategic sense and polish as I would prefer, but there is no doubt his combat instincts are superb." He paused. "And having met the other commanders he surrounds himself with, I do indeed think there is a chance he may succeed." He sighed. "Despite your derogatory comments, even you must see by now that these people—all of them—are noble folk in a terrible war. They have not been through what we have, though," he added darkly, "and they haven't lived through the aftermath of defeat. I understand there is no living with defeat by the Grik, but I remain unsure they truly understand all that would mean, besides their own deaths. My ultimate task—and yours—is to prevent defeat under any circumstances, and I a▓▓▓▓▓red to do what I must. But as long as any chance for victory exi▓▓▓▓▓eep my personal plan in reserve. The likely consequences of p▓▓▓▓▓the crisis that would ensue are simply too great to embrace e▓▓▓▓▓t resort. Again, do I make myself clear?"

"Yeah," Miles answered. "Clear as clea▓▓▓▓▓▓e be clear: if things fall apart and you wait too long to pop your pills, you'll be doing it by yourself."

Herring nodded, accepting that. "So you went aboard *Salissa*?" he asked, changing the subject.

"Yeah. Got back half an hour ago."

"And the cargo? It hasn't been disturbed, I assume, or you would have mentioned it immediately, precluding the necessity for our previous, tedious conversation."

"All secure and undisturbed. Nobody's likely to shift a few heavy, copper drums labeled 'Dietary Supplement for Grik Prisoners to be mixed one part in fifty with fish hash' except to throw them over the side." For the first time, Miles showed genuine respect for Herring.

"Any problems at all?"

"Just one," Miles admitted. "You said our little 'fiction' won't stand up forever, and you're right. Some of the monkeys may be spying on us—I can't tell—but one *guy* in particular is getting wise. That big chief gunner's mate with one eye, the one who's all chummy with Gunny Horn, has been snooping around. In case you haven't noticed."

Herring scratched his chin. "I've noticed. A remarkable fellow, actually, but he does have a habit of sticking his nose in things."

"You, ah, think I ought to do something about him?" Miles asked, and Herring glared at him. "Absolutely not! The man is a valuable member of Captain Reddy's team, and his motives, however questionable at times, are far more honorable than yours! Besides," Herring added, "if you did try something against him, I wouldn't be at all surprised if he didn't 'do' something about you."

Three days later, after a h⬛ ⬛ quall pounded the sea to a glassy tranquility, USS Walk⬛⬛⬛r and sped o⬛ to sea. There'd be no more TBS traffic ⬛⬛⬛th advanc⬛ on its objective, so *Walker* exchanged s⬛⬛⬛ng steam ⬛ ⬛s patrolling west of the island. Sure th⬛⬛⬛ seen ⬛ vicinity, she raced back and signaled ⬛⬛⬛fle⬛ still a⬛⬛⬛ng off the little harbor on the north e⬛⬛⬛anti. Ponde⬛ USNRS *Salissa* and her battle group pr⬛⬛⬛course of t⬛ ⬛ zero, a pair of Nancys already lofting from⬛ ⬛ deck to scout even farther out to sea. Almost half of Safir Ma⬛ I Corps was crammed aboard the mighty carrier. The other half was split among the massive self-propelled dry dock (SPD) USS *Respite Island* and the swarm of transports that had brought them here. SMS *Amerika* had been combat loaded with Chack's Raider Brigade, and *Respite Island* had also taken aboard Winny Rominger and Irvin Laumer's little "mosquito fleet" of torpedo boats, as well as the oddly float-equipped P-40E. Together, they joined the mob of auxiliaries that would advance within another cordon of DDs.

A large percentage of the population of Laa-Laanti lined the shore to watch the mighty fleet sail westward, leaving only a handful of ships and support personnel behind. Doubtless they wondered if they'd ever see them again. Tales of the dreaded Grik that drove all Mi-Anakka from their ancestral home had survived here, as everywhere. And if the Grik had become creatures of myth and legend, their existence was never doubted, and the dread they inspired had likely only grown with time. Always there had lurked, through countless generations, the primal understanding that the Grik were out there, somewhere, and the peaceful utopia of Laa-Laanti might not escape their notice forever. Lawrence had shown them roughly what the Grik really looked like, and friendly as he was, most had been too terrified to approach him. They couldn't reconcile the notion that he meant them no harm. That was probably for the best, in retrospect. There was no sense in confusing the natives further with ideas that not all "Grik" were bloodthirsty monsters. They understood enough to realize, however, that their little island represented a great turning point in the sea of history for all creatures everywhere. The world had found them at last, and despite Adar's best intentions, their lives would never be the same. And if the great fleet of strange ships and folk that had gathered among them for a time didn't succeed in destroying the Grik, it was only a matter of time before the Grik return, causing more destruction.

///// *TFG-2*
Mauritius Island
July 16, 1944

*F*ortunately for USS *Donaghey* and her crew, the sailing DD finally managed to scud into a somewhat protected anchorage of sorts, on the southeast coast of the island under her jib and forecourse. In that place of relative shelter, she escaped the height of the storm that had lashed the sea for the better part of a week. Since she was still pitching madly at her moorings, her crew spent nearly *another* entire week in utter misery, but no one was lost and the stout, veteran ship suffered amazingly little damage. Now the weather had turned at last, and the day dawned breezy but blue, and the clearing water of the small protected bay was flattening nicely.

Captain Greg Garrett, who had been staring out to sea as the new day defined it, was currently fighting a superstitious chill that threatened to give him the shakes. Beyond the mouth of the little bay was an almost solid line of breakers where the more tumultuous waves still crashed against some kind of reef. He had no idea how they'd missed hitting it themselves in the stormy gloom, and he knew if they had, his ship, and likely everyone aboard, wouldn't have survived. He managed a slight smile. *Donaghey's always been a lucky ship,* he thought. *Pounded in battle, nearly sunk, and even beached and fought over before, she's always come back, repaired, and better than ever.* He knew her survival was a testament to her design, inspired by an early American shipwright named Humphries, and the innovative craftsmanship of the Lemurians who'd built her. *And of course her dedicated crews,* he added forcefully.

Turning, he stepped to the port side of the quarterdeck and joined Lieutenant Saama-Kera at the rail. His exec was glassing the shore through a tarnished telescope. "Anything yet?" he asked a little anxiously.

Sammy shook his head. "Mornin', Skipper. No, not yet. Buncha small colorful birds. Maybe lizardbirds; I can't tell from here. They're not flyin' much yet, but the trees is full of 'em. Maybe they still dryin' their wings? That's it, though." The 'Cat hesitated. "I see well why folks'd stay sheltered during the storm, but if they was anybody here, sure they'd come out to gawk at us by now."

"You'd think," Garrett agreed. He'd expected to see *some* kind of people or creatures—most likely Grik—gathering with the dawn on the brilliant white beach to stare, even though they'd seen no other boats at all, or any evidence of a village. But apparently, *Donaghey* was utterly alone in what appeared to be a pretty agreeable little natural harbor. *Of course, that scary reef might have something to do with that,* he considered. Still, it was unnerving. Miyata had told them the Grik avoided the open sea beyond Madagascar, and there was ample evidence of that. But Greg never believed Mauritius, nestled so close to the Ancestral Home of his Lemurian friends, and the supposed seat of the Grik Empire, could've really remained undiscovered through the ages. "Huh," he grunted, turning to gaze up at the masts where the lookouts were posted. "Any sign of *Sineaa*?"

"No, sir," Sammy replied, flicking his tail in concern. "Not since we lost sight of her the night before we made it here."

Greg nodded, sure Sammy would've reported any sighting of *Sineaa* first thing, but he'd had to ask.

"We could always, you know, try to contact her. At least with the TBS," Sammy suggested, but Greg shook his head. "You know we can't do that. No matter what Miyata said, we have to assume the Grik might hear us. He was away from them a long time, remember, and even if Kurokawa never gave them radio back then, he might have since. Even the TBS is too chancy." Greg couldn't risk any communications until the time was right.

"Yes, sir," Sammy agreed, blinking frustration.

Greg smiled. "But we'll have our Nancy brought up out of the hold and assembled, if you please. Our pilots have been bored out of their furry skins the entire voyage. We'll send a few Marines ashore in the motor whaleboat to have a look at the beach, but I want an aerial scout of the island before anybody goes out of sight of the ship. The pilots can look for *Sineaa* too."

"You want they should go on to scout Reunion Island? Maybe *Sineaa* wound up there."

Greg considered it, then shook his head. "If our old charts are even close to right, and there's no guarantee—these islands are volcanic after all—Reunion's nearly a hundred miles west-southwest. The plane's got the range, but that's just too damn far right now. Remember, that's a hundred miles closer to Madagascar too, where we *know* there's a helluva lot of Grik." He waved around. "We got here by accident, and apparently by luck. I'd rather have sneaked up and had a look from a distance first. That's what we'll do at Reunion."

"But if *Sineaa* is there . . . ," Sammy began.

"She's already done for if she ran into Grik," Greg stated grimly. "Risking a plane, or running over there hell for leather won't change that."

"Ay, ay, Cap-i-taan," Sammy agreed reluctantly, closing his telescope. "I'll see to the Naan-cee immediately."

A brand-new PB-1-B "Nancy" flying boat, its blue and white paint and distinctive darker blue, white star, and red dot roundels not yet faded by the sun or stained by the sea, was hoisted from the hold in three pieces. Great care was taken not to puncture the stiff, bowstring-tight fabric covering the rigid, laminated bamboo frames. Nancys were amazingly strong and light, but it didn't take much to poke a hole in one. The broad wing came up first and was carefully secured to the starboard bulwark. Next came the crated engine, to be bolted to the wing once it was attached to the top of the fuselage by numerous complex supports. The fuselage itself, which looked like a narrow cigarette boat with an airplane tail attached, appeared last. Greg watched with satisfaction as the two pilots and crew chief commanded and organized the assembly operation like they'd done it a dozen times. They had, in a way. Neither pilot, straight from training at Kaufman Field in Baalkpan, were veterans, but they'd been well-trained and they'd drilled their detail for this operation almost daily when the weather permitted. In less than an hour, the plane was fully assembled, lowered to the water alongside the ship, fueled, and the engine run up. Garrett knew Nancys were designed with this capability in mind, but he'd never seen it performed. He wondered if they could take the thing apart and strike it back down in the hold nearly as fast.

"I want to go on the scout," Captain Bekiaa-Sab-At told him while the pilots were preparing to go over the side. It hadn't been a request, and Greg stiffened, surprised by her tone. The pilots heard her and paused, blinking at Greg. "You have enough spare parts aboard to assemble another plane, so it makes no sense to send both pilots on this flight," Bekiaa explained. Her tone was still determined, but she laid her ears back in apology. "I am a better choice to go as an observer," she added.

"The commander of my Marine contingent is more expendable than another pilot, you mean?" Greg said, raising an eyebrow. "How do you figure that?"

"I can be replaced," she said simply. "Lieuten-aant Ra-Saan is an experienced officer, and a capable successor to me. I have already instructed him to take the squad of Maa-rines to the beach. Your only other pilot *cannot* be replaced. At least in the foreseeable future. Besides, I doubt you will find a more experienced observer of terrain aboard—particularly with my . . . intimate familiarity with the kind of threats that may lurk within landscapes that seem benign to less, aah, educated eyes."

"Hmm. And of course you're implying you'd also be better at *protecting* the plane itself from a threat, I suppose."

Bekiaa shrugged and actually grinned. "Any such implication should be unnecessary to *you*, Cap-i-taan Gaar-ett."

Greg nodded. She was right. "Okay, but be careful. You'll have a Blitzer Bug and the usual loadout of hand-dropped bombs, just in case, but don't forget: this is a scout, not a combat mission!"

"Ay, ay, Cap-i-taan. But you of all people know how quickly a mere scout can turn into combat!"

Greg frowned, but had to agree.

"But which of *us* will go?" asked one of the pilots, blinking open discontent.

"You will, Ensign Kaar-Raan!" Bekiaa glanced at Greg. "If the cap-i-taan has no preference."

Garrett shook his head, still looking at Bekiaa. "Nope. Just remember what I said, Captain. Just now, and some time ago. You can't be replaced as easily as you think either!"

Lieutenant Ra-Saan and his detail descended the port side of the ship to the motor whaleboat, conned by a Navy 'Cat coxswain, while Kaar and Bekiaa scampered over to starboard. They boarded the plane one at a time. Too much weight on the wing might sink the float and overturn the craft. Kaar dropped in the primary pilot seat, a little cockpit forward of the wing. Bekiaa went to the aft cockpit, located disconcertingly close behind where the pusher prop would spin. Before she could sit, she had to wait for Kaar to yell "Con-taact!" and then manually prop the engine herself. She'd never done that, but she'd seen it often enough that she did a creditable job. The motor blatted up, and she sat behind the little windscreen, pulling the goggles she found on the seat over her head. With a final salute, and looking kind of like a bug with the oversize goggles over her eyes, she shouted into the speaking tube beside her. Kaar advanced the throttle, and the little plane wallowed away from the ship, picking up speed.

"The whaleboat's away," Smitty reported, having come aft to watch the takeoff with Inquisitor Kon Choon. "She'll be fine, Skipper," he added, nodding at the little blue seaplane. "They'll both be fine."

"A remarkable machine," Choon exclaimed. "And such a pretty color. Ingenious how you have painted them to resemble the sea from above, but the clouds from below. But building them to float *and* fly—I never tire of watching them."

"Never tire of watching aircraft? Or just *our* aircraft?" Greg probed. The Republic was an ally, but so far of necessity rather than of complete trust. Just as there remained a few things Matt didn't want to share with them, such as torpedoes, armor-piercing shells, and the new fire-control system aboard *Donaghey*, for example; they kept secrets too. One such secret was whether they had aircraft of their own. There was no doubt they had the technology. Greg suspected that, as Captain Reddy, Adar— and Herring, of course—got to know Von Melhausen, Lange, Meek, and others, they'd probably start blabbing all sorts of things to one another. It was in everyone's interest to know one another's capabilities, after all. But Choon was enigmatic and secretive by nature, so he might not have told even if allowed. It mattered little to Greg, and he'd find out for himself when *Donaghey* reached the Republic. Trying to get Choon to open up had begun to amuse him as much as it did Bekiaa, though, just as Choon still seemed to delight in playing his own game of evasion.

"We have no air-craaft like *those*," Choon said, blinking to acknowledge the ongoing sport. "Nor have we any like the smaller planes, the 'Flea-shooters,' I think you call them, that fly off the deck of *Salissa*. What need have we of such? With the sadly poor exception of the War Palace, ah, *Amerika*, we are not a high-seas naval power."

Greg grinned. SMS *Amerika* was still decrepit despite her repairs; her old hull was awfully thin. But she did have some teeth, and she was at least twice as fast as anything the Grik had—that they'd seen. Greg knew that any "naval power" might have a hard time entering a Republic port uninvited, however. Lange had very matter-of-factly described the powerful harbor gunboats they maintained, and Miyata had appeared free to discuss them as well. Sadly, given the descriptions of the weather off the cape, no one seriously thought they could be brought to bear against the Grik. Apparently, barring something unrevealed, the

Republic's greatest contribution would be some excellent, if somewhat gaudy, infantry and cavalry, and some good artillery as well—although what manner of artillery they possessed hadn't been much discussed either.

"You may not get a good look at how effective our air can be before we reach Alex-aandra, Inquisitor," Greg said as the Nancy roared into the sky, "but I bet Captain Von Melhausen and Mr. Lange will."

"Oh, splendid!" Choon exclaimed with a clap of his hands, his eyes on the plane.

Lizard birds swirled from the trees on shore to take flight in great, convulsing clouds at the startling thunder of the Nancy, and perhaps the sight of the giant blue bird they'd never seen before. The plane banked to avoid the swarm that seemed equally intent on avoiding it, and clawed for altitude.

"But you already know how effective they can be, if you have any of your own," Greg said almost absently, suddenly focusing on the bird-things of Mauritius. Thousands—*millions*—of them were erupting from the jungle.

"Indeed I do . . . if we do," Choon replied. He was watching the lizardbirds with keen interest now as well. Waves of the colorful fliers continued to surge randomly about, the rising plane apparently already forgotten. Greg raised his own glass to watch. *Random at first,* he realized, but the collective behavior grew more organized. And despite the passage of the plane, he got the impression he was seeing some kind of purposeful, morning ritual. The creatures were indeed "ordinary" lizardbirds in form, though the riot of colors was more spectacular than any he'd seen before. Many had longer heads as well, some with slender jaws full of tiny teeth, and others with genuine beaks. He also began to realize that animals of similar form and color tended to throng together, and that was something kind of unusual too. Then, as the swarms appeared to sort themselves out, they began to pursue very specialized behavior. One type of lizardbird descended on the beach, overwhelming it with their numbers, and started gorging on whatever the storm and surf had washed ashore. Other fliers of various types slashed down in the shallows, chasing baitfish or other swimmers. Their impacts on the water threw up stabbing splashes like automatic weapons fire. With a tidbit in their mouths or beaks, these fliers then bolted back into the sky to consume their meal before repeating the process. Even in this melee of "bird bullets," as Greg thought of them, he was amazed to see the various species maintain a kind of separation. He'd never seen anything like that at all. Similar creatures on Borno and other places always commingled and often fought viciously over the slightest morsel, or even ate one another. There *was* some of that. One species, larger than most but few in number, struck victims out of the teeming multitudes and carried them screeching back to the trees.

"I wish Mr. Bradford could see this," Greg murmured.

"He shall, if we determine this is a good place for another 'staging point' as you put it," Choon said. He'd borrowed Sammy's glass and was raptly watching the colorful, chaotic drama. Greg felt a prickly suspicion, however, as he watched the line of bird splashes edging toward his ship—and the whaleboat that had slowed almost to a stop.

"I don't know," he murmured. "Sammy," he said louder, suddenly decisive, "signal the whaleboat to return to the ship at once! Fire a gun to get their attention if you have to."

"Ay, Cap-i-taan!" Sammy replied, a new urgency in his tone. Smitty went to prepare a gun.

Greg raised the glass again, even as the signal raced up the halyard. Bekiaa had been right—her lieutenant knew his stuff. He'd already ordered the boat about. In a sick instant, though, Greg realized it wouldn't make any difference. New explosions of water erupted on the bay, from below this time. Apparently, the birds had chased their prey to a dropoff or other underwater feature guarded by something like flasher fish— voracious, tuna-size predators that congregated in virtually every shallows they'd visited. Here, they began snatching the swooping lizardbirds in their jagged teeth even as the fliers slammed the water with even greater determination to eat their fill before the baitfish, or whatever they chased, escaped their grasp for another day. Caught in the middle of this sudden confluence of savage appetites was the whaleboat.

Flashies started hammering the boat with their hard, bony heads, probably going for the brightly spinning screw at first. The coxswain, standing in the sternsheets at the tiller, was pitched sprawling into the sea. He nèver even surfaced. A growing number of lizardbirds dove on the Marines, snatching bites from furry arms or bouncing off helmets and leather armor. Somebody, probably Lieutenant Ra-Saan—it was impossible to tell at this distance—opened up with a Blitzer, the muffled report reaching them seconds later. The lizardbirds recoiled from the unfamiliar sound, but they quickly renewed their attack. Screams began to reach the ship.

"Fire a gun, Smitty!" Greg yelled in desperation. Almost immediately, one of the eighteen-pounders directly below in the waist roared, spitting fire and a dense cloud of white smoke that swept swiftly downwind. Greg focused his glass, but quickly saw the great gun had no effect. Either the lizardbirds were so used to thunder or the booming surf on the reef, or they simply didn't care what transpired beyond their apparent boundary, and they flocked around the boat in countless numbers. The whaleboat itself, now settling due to the battering the flashies had given it, had become a heaving mound of colorful lizardbirds, frantically feeding on the unfortunate Marines. As the boat flooded lower, it looked like a little flowery island in the calm water of the bay, surrounded by white, splashing breakers of its own. If anyone was left alive to scream by now, the sounds were mercifully drowned by the raucous roar of feasting birds.

"Lookouts and topmen below! Get out of the rigging!" Greg bellowed. "Clear for action!"

"Rig the overhead netting," Sammy added. "Marines will draw shotguns, but all others will go below and batten down!"

Greg nodded agreement. Some of the smoothbore muskets had been converted to breechloaders with the same Allin-Silva technique as the standard-issue rifles, essentially becoming 20-gauge shotguns. They might be effective, but to use them, they had to get as many people out of the way as they could. He stared back at the colorful swarm as 'Cats slid down stays and bare feet thundered on the deck.

"They are not coming," Choon said mildly. "They have stopped." Greg felt an irrational surge of anger at the Republic snoop, but it quickly vanished as he realized his rage was misplaced. He *wanted* the lizardbirds to come on so he could kill them for what they'd done. But that was nuts. There weren't enough shotshells in the entire ship to put a dent in the swirling mass, and *Donaghey* would be lucky to escape an attack with no worse than shredded rigging. He sighed with belated relief, but he had to wonder if Choon really was as unaffected by all this as he appeared. Shaking his head, he stared toward shore. Slowly, like a receding wave, the swirling clouds of lizardbirds had begun edging back toward the island. Already, the explosive splashing of the flashies had ceased. A couple of orange, black, and green fliers still stalked the gunwales of the whaleboat, the only part still visible, but when it finally slipped under entirely, the lizardbirds flapped their furry, membranous wings and joined others of their kind surging back toward the trees.

"The island is theirs," Choon observed. "And the waters to a point. There is no food—or life for them—beyond where the water belongs to the fish, so they do not cross." He regarded Greg with his big, sky blue eyes. "Quite fortunate for us, I suppose."

"Yeah," Greg agreed hollowly. "But I guess Mr. Bradford won't see this place after all. Not much point."

"No."

"Now we know why nobody lives here, though," Saama-Kera softly agreed.

"Secure from battle stations, but keep a sharp lookout," Greg told his exec. "And run up a signal Captain Bekiaa and Ensign Kaar can see when they return. Tell them, whatever they do, to stay the *hell* away from that island when they set down!"

CHAPTER 14

///// *Above Mauritius*

ekiaa-Sab-At had flown before, in one of the big lumbering "Clippers." But those had four engines and enclosed passenger compartments. Flying in the Nancy was an entirely different experience. The takeoff had been weird—and wet—and the mass of swirling lizardbirds had actually frightened her. She hadn't thought that was possible anymore, and she was frankly encouraged that it was. She didn't know how much damage hitting one of the creatures would do to the plane, but imagined there'd be some. As little as she knew about aircraft and flight in general, even she knew that hitting *hundreds* of the things at once would not be survivable. Ensign Kaar was a good pilot, though, and he'd managed to avoid the mass of flying creatures that seemed to rise just as the plane did. She briefly wondered about them and hoped everything was all right back at the anchorage, but she also began enjoying herself for the first time in longer than she could remember. Flying—this kind of flying—was fun!

The view was stunning and unforgettable. There were little islets scattered around "Maar-ishus," some little bigger than *Donaghey*. Only one was as large as *Salissa*, and it was merely a barren black rock. Nothing else but the subsiding sea was visible on any horizon, and the sky was a brilliant, cloudless blue. Mauritius wasn't very large itself, but it was charming enough from the air. Shaped much like a flattened squash on this world, it was roughly fifteen miles wide, east to west, and twenty or so from north to south. The neck of the "squash" was on the northernmost end, jutting into the sea and curving east and slightly south like the neck of a goose. There was a broad savannah in the north, but the rest of the island was largely blanketed by dense jungle. Bekiaa remained amazed by how many of the colorful lizardbirds there were, flowing in swarms as if controlled by a single mind, but they stayed down close to the treetops and didn't venture near the plane flying a couple of thousand feet above them. They didn't go far out to sea either, and she watched as they churned the shallows for food. There seemed to be a threshold though, beyond which they didn't go, and she wondered about that. She also wondered why they didn't fish the reefs that almost completely surrounded the island, and took note.

"Any sign of *Sineaa*?" she shouted through the voice tube, suddenly ashamed of her inattention. She should've been scanning for their consort herself.

"I haven't seen her," the tinny voice of the pilot responded.

"I haven't seen any Grik, or any settlements of any kind either," Bekiaa said. "Let's fly back south, over the ship, and see what's down that way," she suggested a few minutes later. "Then we'll head north again, along the west coast."

"Ay, ay."

The plane banked right and flew down the eastern shore. Before long, *Donaghey* was in view, still anchored in the picturesque little bay. Bekiaa had never seen the ship from the air, and though it looked quite small, she felt a surge of admiration and affection. Then she squinted.

"There's a signal," she announced. "It says to not land close to shore. I wonder what that's about."

"Maybe they seen something there we didn't."

Bekiaa didn't answer, but still stared at the ship as they flew overhead, and it slowly grew smaller behind them. Finally, she turned around. The southern end of the island was dominated by a high, sheer, rocky monolith that drew her attention. It didn't seem to belong on the otherwise gently rolling landscape. "Let's have a closer look at that," she directed.

The plane turned a little to the right and aimed for the high, flat-topped feature. "It must've been a vol-caano," Bekiaa exclaimed. "I bet that's all dead laavaa. Maybe the earth around it has blown or fallen away over time."

"The wind might get funny around it," Kaar said. "I'll just fly over the top, okay?"

"Sure."

They got closer. Bekiaa hadn't brought a telescope. The Imperial-made instruments were far more numerous in the fleet than binoculars, but they weren't exactly disposable. Each ship had a few, but only a few. There were four on *Donaghey*. Bekiaa thought she caught a hint of movement on the dark crags ahead, and wished she could make out what it was. Normally, her keen eyes didn't need assistance. "Wait," she warned uncertainly, leaning out to the left to get a better look past the spinning prop and the pilot beyond. "There *is* something moving on that mountain!" Size was deceptive at a distance, and their elevation altered perspective as well, but she was sure now that something—numerous somethings and all fairly large—were clinging to the sheer cliffs ahead, and it looked like there were more of whatever they were crowding along the ridge at the top. "Let's turn away," she ordered, perhaps half a mile short of the peak.

"You sure? I don't see anything."

The first creature launched itself into the sky, great wings unfolding from its side and catching air. Others quickly followed, beating their wings and rising toward the plane.

"The nose blocks your view!" Bekiaa cried. "Those cliffs are crawling with *really* big lizardbirds, and some are coming for us! Turn away at once!"

The plane banked hard left, back toward the coast, and Bekiaa twisted around to look. "Uh-oh," she murmured to herself. She'd never seen the "Grikbirds," or "dragons," as the Imperials called them, that the Allies had to contend with in the east, but she understood they were aptly named. They looked and acted like Grik Uul, displaying limited intelligence and a pack mentality, and were about the same size. The main difference was that they had wings instead of arms, of course, and a longer tail. The creatures rising toward the Nancy were similar, Bekiaa supposed, but much larger, possibly two-thirds the size of the plane! There were other differences. These had long, narrow, toothy jaws—well suited for snatching fish, or perhaps other fliers—and almost more striking just then, they were blue and white!

"They think we're one of them!" Bekiaa shouted.

Ensign Kaar had finally seen the things as they turned, and his voice came shrill through the tube. "Is that good or bad?"

"How should I know?" Bekiaa demanded. "Step on it! They are gaining!" She snatched the Blitzer Bug from its spring-loaded rack beside her, inserted one of the Thompson-style twenty-round magazines, and yanked back the bolt. Her stomach flew into her throat. "No, no!" she yelled. "Do not dive! We may be faster, but you shorten the distance they must climb!" Kaar had instinctively pushed the nose down to gain more speed, but realized his mistake as soon as Bekiaa pointed it out. Quickly, he pulled up—just as one of the creatures shot past the plane. *They* are *fast!* Bekiaa realized. *Maybe faster than us!* Another monster slashed by, and Bekiaa started to fire, but hesitated. *Surely they would have slashed through us if they meant to attack. What if they really do think we are one of them?* She had no doubt the jagged snouts and long, thinly curved claws could've just made short work of the Nancy. She leaned out. Maybe a dozen more of the things were still climbing, but they were struggling now. *They* wouldn't catch them. That just left the two that had. She looked forward and saw the beasts, flapping their wings for all they were worth and trying to maintain the leading formation they'd taken. They couldn't succeed. Their mouths were hanging open now, and their oversize chests were sucking and expelling air with every beat. One creature glanced at her as the Nancy crept past, its yellow, slit-pupiled eye bulging almost indignantly. She still held her fire. "Do not fly straight to the ship," she warned. "Let us lead them out to sea. My guess is, they'll abandon the chase."

"Ay, ay, Cap-i-taan!" Kaar replied, apparently relieved, for the first time, to have someone tell him what to do. Before long, the pursuers did give up. But instead of turning back to their rocky roost, they dove down toward the breakers formed by the reef.

"They *had* to think we were one of them," Bekiaa mused through the speaking tube. "Perhaps they noticed we were larger, oddly shaped, and somewhat noisy, but that may have inspired a sense of competitiveness!" She shrugged. "Or maybe they were just trying to herd us back to the cliff."

"Could be they were males, and they thought we were a female," Kaar offered, a hint of humor cracking his tension.

"Or the opposite, Ensign," Bekiaa stated more formally. "Just as possible. Either way, I wonder what would have happened today if the Navy, in its wisdom, had not decided long ago on such a fortuitous paint scheme for its aircraft."

Ensign Kaar didn't respond, and Bekiaa leaned out to stare down once more. The frightening creatures were far below now, but already rising from the turbulent breakers. Each had a large fish—perhaps a flashy?—clutched in its formidable claws and was beating its wings with considerably less gusto than before. No doubt they needed to replace the energy they'd just expended. Bekiaa could sympathize. "Let's return to the ship and report this interesting encounter. I could use a meal myself." She smiled. "I may even compose a letter of thanks to Commaander Letts and Col-nol Maalory. I believe it was they who chose the colors for the Naval Air Corps!"

Bekiaa wasn't smiling later when she stepped aboard *Donaghey* and learned what had transpired in her absence. Nor was she particularly hungry anymore.

"There'll be no more scouts from here," Captain Garrett said grimly. "We'll bring the plane aboard immediately, but won't strike it down just yet. It'll be a pain working the ship with it in the way, but if the weather holds, we'll use the plane to scout Reunion Island as soon as we raise it, and before we bring the ship in range of any more flying lizards!"

"Ay, ay, Cap-i-taan," Bekiaa said, looking at the shore her Marines never reached. It was a shore *she'd* have never reached if she hadn't been so intent on going on the scout—yet another source of guilt for her.

"When will we leave this place?" Sammy asked.

"With the tide, if the wind holds like it is," Greg said forcefully. "There's nothing for us here, Lieutenant. I'll want the launch to precede us through the reef, taking soundings all the way, but we'll use volunteers only, in case those bigger lizardbirds Bekiaa ran into like to use that time to hunt the breakers." He snorted. "Maybe if they do, they'll leave us alone with the Nancy on deck." He looked away. "Every shore," he muttered.

"What's that, Cap-i-taan?" Bekiaa asked.

"Oh, nothing," Greg replied, forcing a brittle smile. "It just seems that every shore we touch on this goofed-up world is even deadlier than the last, with the exception of Diego."

"I understand there have been others, not so inhospitable as well," Choon encouraged.

"Sure," Greg agreed, "I guess. But I can't help worrying that when our people hit the beach at Madagascar, they're going to find the deadliest shore of all."

///// *Second Fleet*
Off Guayaquil Bay
Aboard USS Maaka-Kakja *(CV-4)*

"O h my God," High Admiral Harvey Jenks, CINCEAST, practically moaned when Admiral Lelaa-Tal-Cleraan handed over the message form. He read it for himself to make sure he hadn't somehow misunderstood. They and a large percentage of the flag staff were standing on *Maaka-Kakja*'s spacious port bridge-wing while aircraft were trundled across the flight deck on launching trucks that would be hooked to the hydraulic catapults. Air ops had been ramped up ever since a pair of Dom frigates swooped out of the night and pounded hell out of an Imperial frigate on picket duty north of the fleet. There'd been other scouts, single ships apparently groping around for the location of Second Fleet, but two ships together seemed to prove that the monstrous Dom fleet assembling near El Paso del

Fuego might be getting ready to do something. Both Doms were crippled in the fight and easily destroyed by Allied air the next morning, but the Impie frigate had to be abandoned and scuttled as well. Jenks knew perfectly well where the Dom fleet was but had no idea how large it had grown. He was certain he couldn't afford to exchange one of his ships for every two of the enemy's, however.

"The child has gone entirely mad," Jenks stated with utter certainty.

"The 'child' is your Governor-Empress," Lelaa reminded, blinking amusement, "and as such, it is my understanding that she may do as she pleases."

"How can you take her side in this?" Jenks demanded.

"How can you not?"

"Because . . . as Governor-Empress of the Empire of the New Britain Isles—and as a child—her Highness Rebecca McDonald has no business coming *to* a war that we are doing our very best to keep away from her and our country!"

"You would not have objected so strongly—if at all—to her father's coming to the war, had he lived," Selass-Fris-Ar accused. She was Keje's daughter and chief surgeon of Second Fleet. She'd also become a very vocal advocate for female rights within the Empire.

"Of course I would!" Jenks fumed, absently twisting his braided mustache. Then he grimaced and nodded politely at Selass. "Object, that is," he corrected, "though perhaps not quite so strenuously, as you say. The fact remains, however, that we are in a difficult spot. General Shinya has advanced ashore, but we remain impotent at sea." He looked at Orrin Reddy, who'd returned to the ship after the Battle of Guayak. "We still know almost nothing of what the Doms have gathered against us at that phenomenal passage Lieutenant Reynolds and Ensign Faask observed. Even better armed, our aircraft simply can't penetrate the swarms of dragons guarding the place without prohibitive losses. Too much remains mysterious for me to be content with the Governor-Empress's presence here."

"How could she not come?" Lelaa demanded. "I may know her even better than you, after we were marooned together so long, and her will is strong. Besides, Saan-Kakja of Maa-ni-la comes as well, and those two are as sisters."

"Adar's off with Matt, going against Madagascar," Orrin said. "With Rebecca and Saan-Kakja coming here, nearly all the Allied heads of state will be on the front lines somewhere. I don't much like the idea of that."

"Well said, Mr. Reddy," Jenks agreed, then took a long breath. "And there is this other matter: the troops our Governor-Empress brings!"

Lelaa blinked agreement to that. "Sister Audry I know well too. Though she is strong in faith and character, I cannot imagine her commanding a regiment in battle."

"Yet that is precisely the plan!" Jenks objected. "And not just any regiment! Doms! It is madness!"

"I don't know about that one," Orrin said thoughtfully. "Seems like having Doms on our side is working okay for Shinya, what with his Guayak Militia, and they barely know their left feet from their right. I hardly know Sister Audry, but if what I hear is true, she's the perfect dame for the job of leading a buncha converted Doms. So what if she doesn't know how to fight 'em? Her troops are pros, who nearly took New Ireland away from us. I was there," he added. "They can fight themselves, and I bet Her Highness wouldn't've put Audry in charge of 'em if they wouldn't do what she says." He grinned. "And I bet Shinya wouldn't mind having some highly trained and motivated ex-Dom troops to leaven the locals—though I'd love to see his face when they come marching up!"

"How long until they arrive?" Selass interjected.

Jenks grunted. "That, my dear, annoys me perhaps most of all. There was no discussion about this—none. And they are already on their way!" He smoldered a while longer, then took a breath, apparently bowing to the inevitable. "I will be glad of the ships they bring, and General Shinya will no doubt rejoice to have the troops, Dom and otherwise," he said reluctantly. "The new ships will help in that respect as well. I simply won't commit the rest of our army without the ships to take them off, if need be, as long as the Dom fleet remains a threat. But more ships mean we can land more troops."

"And perhaps other things," Lelaa murmured thoughtfully. "I wonder what kind of ships they are, and what they carry."

"What do you mean?"

Admiral Lelaa-Tal-Cleraan patted High Admiral Harvey Jenks affectionately on the arm. "Surely you do not believe that Her Majesty Rebecca Anne McDonald and High Chief Saan-Kakja would come all this way simply to bring us more of what we already have? If the Dom fleet does not move against us before they arrive, I suspect we may soon have the means to move against it!"

"Who told you to stop digging?" Gunner's Mate Spon-Ar-Aak, or "Spook," bellowed in his persona as a first sergeant in the 2nd Battalion, 2nd Marines. The fact that he was no longer in A Company, 2/2, but had been placed in charge of a mixed company of Guayakans stiffened by Impie and Lemurian Marines, didn't make any difference to him. First sergeants ran their companies on a day-to-day basis anyway, so not much had really changed—so far. Currently, he stood atop a growing berm being built to encircle General Shinya's entire army, and a Guayakan looked up at him as if wondering what had provoked his wrath. "Yeah, you, you witless, furless, tailless dope!" Spook raged. "Must be brainless too. That fine piece o' Imperial ironwork an' wood you is leanin' on is called a *shovel*! You s'posed to poke it in the ground an' heave dirt up *here*!" He stamped the berm impatiently, but the man just stared. Spook knew he was being monstrously unfair to the local conscript. The kid couldn't possibly understand the human/Lemurian patois he was using. But Spook's curriculum was based on the example set by Chief Bosun Fitzhugh Gray, and he knew the "Super Bosun's" verbal rants had definitely encouraged *his* understanding. If it was good enough for him, it was good enough for these guys. "By the Heavens!" he roared. "Somebody grab his stupid head an' point his stupid eyes at real work so he can see what it looks like!"

They'd planted the AEF and every Guayakan who could bear arms at the strategic north, south, east crossroad about thirty miles north of Guayak, blocking the coastal road from the north, and through the high mountains to the east. There, instead of continuing to pursue the shattered Dom army, they were building even more formidable defenses than they'd left behind, and daring the Doms to hit them again. Not everyone was happy with that strategy, and Spook was one of them. But orders were orders, and if he and "his" company had to defend this section of the works, he wanted it as tall and thick as possible.

"I wish ye'd explain what firin' steps are to these buggers," one of his Imperial corporals complained. "Ever' time my party makes a go of 'em, them other nits down lower bury 'em up again!"

"Explainin' the fine points o' my celebrated design is your job, Corporal," Spook replied grandly, swishing his tail. "I'm the idea guy in this outfit."

Captain Blas climbed up the outside of the berm where she'd been inspecting the entanglements. She paused when she saw him.

"First Sergeant," she said.

Spook spun at the sound of her voice and saluted. "Afternoon, Cap'n!"

"As you were." Blas waved, looking down the length of the earthwork that curved gradually back around to the south. Shovelfuls of dirt rose in the air as far as she could see, like thousands of grawfish were kicking mud out of their tidal-flat homes. There were more than a hundred guns in view as well, many that had once supported the Doms, and they were being placed in wood-decked embrasures with timber and earth protection overhead. Behind, the greater part of the army drilled or lounged in the orderly tent camp erected on a slight rise that was now protected by the growing defenses. Flags fluttered here and there, but the one that drew her eyes stood outside the 2nd Battalian, 2nd Marines command tent: the Stars and Stripes. She looked back at Spook and showed her teeth. "A fine pit we are building, is it not?"

"Sure," Spook hedged. He lowered his voice. "But I don't like fightin' in no pit. I wish we could 'a kept chasin' the Doms. It worked swell up north."

Spook, Finny, and Stumpy had been in the running battle that chased the Dom land forces away from the Imperial colony of Saint Francis, forcing their retreat from "Caal-i-forniaa." He would've preferred a similar strategy here.

"I'd have enjoyed such a chase as well," Blas agreed, "until it lost all steam."

Spook blinked confusion and she shook her head. "I'll always use Navy thoughts, now," she apologized. "Think like this: Steam takes fire, an' fire takes fuel. Our fuel lines are still mighty skinny, an' they all come from the sea, right? The farther we get from the sea, the longer an' skinnier the fuel lines get. Pretty soon, we don't get enough fuel to keep the fires lit, an' we run outa steam. Got it? The Doms got all the fuel in the world, an' soon as they relight their fires, they'll have plenty o' steam. When they come back, we'll bust their damn lines for 'em."

"But what good'll that do?" Spook asked. "As long as we keep givin' 'em time to relight their fires, they'll just keep comin'. All the fuel, fire, an' steam the fleet can give us won't do no good once our maa-chin'ry gets too busted up." He snorted. "Look, Cap'n, I ain't no youngling that you gotta talk to me like that. I know the score, an' I been in plenty o' fights on sea an' land." He lowered his voice further. *"Cap'n Reddy'd chase them Doms, I know it."*

Blas looked at him sharply. "I don't know that he would, but he's not here, so what he'd do makes no difference. Generaal Shinya's in command here, and he's got to plan our battles based on what High Ahd-mi-raal Jenks lets us have. Right now that means we gotta give the Doms the kind of fight they want; that they expect. We'll keep smearin' 'em," she said with a confident blink, "an' they ain't gonna like that. But they'll keep thinkin' we like to fight just like they do. Sooner or later, though, we're gonna get to kick this invasion into high gear, and I bet Generaal Shinya and all of us are gonna jump up an' surprise the hell outa them Doms then." She could tell by Spook's blinking that she wasn't getting through. She grunted, sitting down on the berm. "Look," she said. "You're right. I don't hafta talk to you like that—but it *is* true." She waved at the massive works. "Generaal Shinya don't like this kinda fight any more than us. Not anymore. But I've already been 'round this tree with Col-nol Blair myself. We did chase the daamn Doms a long way, after all, before we stopped, and we'd still be after 'em if Shinya had his way, but Jenks pulled the plug. The way Blair explained it, it's pretty much like I said. Jenks don't know what the hell's buildin' out there, and we *will* run outa steam fast if the Navy gets chased off!" She shrugged. "I'm not sure it's the right call either, but it's probably the smartest call." She took a drink from her canteen and put the stopper back in the bottle. "So this way, maybe it takes a little longer. Maybe we have another big fight right here around this stupid pit. But eventually, we'll get all the 'steam' we need—so I wouldn't build a home behind these earthworks if I was you."

A flight of three Nancys roared by overhead with bombs slung under their wings. The lead ship waggled its wings. Blas waved back. "That's Fred an' Kari!" she cried with glee. "They're flying again! Ain't that swell?"

"Sure is," Spook agreed truthfully. Fred and Kari had been very popular aboard *Walker,* and their apparent loss had been hard on their friends. Spook was somewhat amazed they were willing to fly again so soon after their captivity and escape from the Doms, particularly since they knew what awaited them if they were ever captured again. He took off his helmet and waved it vigorously at the planes, now receding toward the great mountain pass. "But they're both crazy," he added.

Some time later, after Blas had moved along, a faint booming echoed down from the distant pass. The planes must've found targets for their bombs. *Probably scouts,* Spook decided. *Whatever's left of the Dom army we chased outa here is likely still holed up in them mountains, waitin' for reinforcements. Or maybe it's scouts for* another *Dom army.* Spook had no idea. *Land battles take a awful long time to set up, compared to sea battles,* he reflected. It was interesting that Fred and Kari dropped their bombs, though. *Maybe they're just practicing, after so long on the ground?* There was little point in concealing the ground-attack capability of their planes anymore, and it made perfect sense to kill any Doms they saw coming or going. But finding *enough* Doms to drop bombs on in the pass was kind of unusual lately.

No doubt the planes found some Grikbirds too, and Spook hoped COFO Reddy's air-to-air tactics were still holding up. He shook his head, staring east. Blas's explanation of Shinya's strategy had been simplistic, but Spook had to admit it made sense. The Doms would come, he was sure, and whatever infantry they sent here couldn't board ships for the Enchanted Isles. That was a "big picture" dividend he could understand. But this fort they were building was liable to draw one *helluva* lot of Doms, despite all the bombing they pasted them with. And eventually, there'd be one helluva fight. "Keep digging," he grouched down at his men below, who'd paused to look east as well. "A little thunder in the mountains don't mean nothin' to you."

////// *Baalkpan, Borno*
July 20, 1944

ommander Alan Letts, acting High Chief of Baalkpan and temporary (thank God) chairman of the
Grand Alliance, left Adar's Great Hall with Lord
Bolton Forester, the ambassador from the Empire
of the New Britain Isles, and Commander Saraan-
Ghaani, ambassador for the Great South Isle,
who'd just recently returned from the fighting at
Madraas. With them were Commander Steve Riggs, the Allied Minister
of Communications and Electrical Contrivances, and Henry Stokes, the
assistant director of Strategic Intelligence. Tagging along, as usual, was
Lieutenant Bachman, Forester's aide. Together, they strode through the
former Parade Ground that had become a growing cemetery, its mani-
cured lawn and flowery hedges bordering pathways through the stone
markers for the dead. Burial was not the Lemurian way, but a surprising
number of 'Cats had chosen it so they could lie forever with their ship-

mates. Even so, there weren't that many separate markers yet—largely because literally thousands of dead still remained where they fell, either cremated in the traditional way, or in temporary graves. One day the cemetery would be full, as Letts grimly recognized, but for now the greatest losses were symbolized by large bronze plaques with many hundreds, sometimes *thousands* of names engraved upon them. One, starting to turn slightly green now, represented the carrier *Humfra-Dar*. Others bore the names of those lost at Sin-a-pore, Raan-goon, and even Baalkpan itself. The newest, brightest marker was also the largest, with all the names they'd confirmed lost during the battles for Madraas. Beside it were smaller plaques, just as new, for the ships and crews destroyed there as well. Alan paused in front of one headed by the legend: s-19. Other plaques were dedicated to USS *Mahan*—again—and USS *Santa Catalina*. Though the last two ships had survived, many of their people hadn't, and Alan personally knew a depressing number of them. It seemed this war would never end, and he didn't know how much longer he could bear its toll in sadness.

"Jim Ellis should've had my job," he said, finding his friend's name on *Santa Catalina*'s plaque. "He was always good with people, and a natural leader too," he murmured.

"Jim had a job he was damn good at," Riggs reminded. "And given a choice between his and yours, even now, which one do you think he would'a picked?" Alan didn't answer, but took a long breath and clasped his hands behind his back.

"I never had the pleasure of meeting your Commodore Ellis," Ambassador Forester said softly, "so you may be right about his qualifications. There can be no doubt that he was a gifted naval officer if all I have heard is true. But it has been my experience that such talents do not necessarily translate well to diplomacy, and I sincerely doubt he could have done a better job of uniting that fractious . . . congregation back there," he added, gesturing back at the Great Hall and the other delegates beginning to filter out.

"No way," Riggs agreed confidently. "We ought'a be down at the 'Screw, hoisting a brew in celebration. Not moping around in a graveyard."

Alan looked at him sharply; then his face relaxed. "Maybe so. I just needed to come here . . . and look these fellas in the eye. I like to think they would've wanted this."

Adar had left Alan Letts with a daunting assignment: to serve as chairman during the ongoing negotiations aimed at transforming the Grand Alliance into a genuine national union. The obstacles had seemed insurmountable. Each Lemurian Home, whether on land or sea, had distinct laws, traditions, customs, and interests, and was accustomed to perfect autonomy. In the face of this dreadful, world-encompassing war, however, and the uncertain future that might lie beyond it, no Home, no matter how powerful, could hope to stand alone. Baalkpan and Maa-ni-la had been pulling the heaviest load from the start, but even they couldn't succeed without the influx of troops and workers supplied by all the rest. Tremendous compromise was called for on all parts to create a kind of republic within which each Home had representation. Letts had advanced the Constitution of the United States as a model, and it was well received—once it was fully understood. The language of the preamble and certain portions of the Declaration of Independence were seized upon with great enthusiasm, with the substitution of "people" for "men" in all cases. It was fully understood by now that beings did not need to be human, or even Lemurian, to be considered "people."

But the biggest hurdle had been allowing for proportional representation, because two congressional bodies were deemed superfluous by nearly everybody. A single representative council, such as had already existed, was considered sufficient. That meant that even if it was admitted as a "state," no seagoing Home with three or four thousand people could possibly have the same say as Baalkpan, for example, the population of which had ballooned to nearly half a million. Even the various Homes were brought to understand how ridiculous that would be. As a consequence, a number of the great floating cities were scurrying to form alliances with like-minded sisters so they could collectively join the union as coequal states. This began a cascade of sparsely populated land Homes doing the same. That was confusing for everyone and caused considerable clan posturing, but it seemed to solve the problem—

until the Great South Isle, called Australia by the human destroyermen, expressed a willingness to join.

Austraal, as the people there called their land, based on the "Terra Austraalis" bestowed on it by the Prophet Siska-Ta, boasted the largest homogenous population of Lemurians known, perhaps nearly two million. They lived in numerous cities, mainly in the North, which was densely wooded with a kind of tall pinelike tree on this world. Its people were famous seafarers with all the trees in the world to build fine ships, but with an island so large, they didn't build the great seagoing Homes— at least not for themselves. Some were built there for other clans, but not very many. The thing was, like the Empire of the New Britain Isles, the Great South Isle, or Austraal, for all its size and population, had a single ruler and was essentially too big to join the union as a state—at least not based on the formula for proportional representation they'd worked so hard to solve. They'd come to a profound agreement, however. Austraal would join the union for the duration of the war, at least, so long as the prosecution of the war remained the primary agenda. Her people knew they were late to the fight and felt they had a lot to make up for. After the war, they'd "sort out the details," to the extent of Austraal splitting itself into a number of smaller states, if necessary, but that could be decided later.

"I met Commodore Ellis a few times," Saraan-Ghaani said quietly, absently smoothing the symmetrical pattern of white and brown fur on his arm that covered an old wound. "And I know he would be proud of what you have accomplished, Mr. Letts. I think he would be proud of us all."

"I hope so," Alan allowed. He cocked an eyebrow at Forester. "Even prouder if we could get the Empire to join."

Bolton Forester grimaced. "I cannot say that will never happen. And I am encouraged by what I've seen. But you must understand that my country has experienced quite enough political upheaval for a time, and must digest that before we plunge into more. The Empire will remain staunchly allied to whatever nation emerges from your negotiations, but as a *separate* nation at present. I have no authority whatsoever to say more than that—but of that you may rest assured."

"I have no doubt," Alan stated. Left unstated was the obvious fact that the Empire needed the Grand Alliance—or whatever it would eventually call itself—for its war against the Dominion far more than the Alliance needed the Empire against the Grik. That could certainly change, but that was the way it was just then. "And I don't really blame you," Alan confessed. "Some might say all we've really managed is to glue a bunch of monsters together by their tails—and each one has a separate mind for every finger and toe." He managed a grin. "I've got a feeling we're going to find out what it would be like to hitch a hundred little critters like Petey to a plow. We're not even as organized as the old Articles of Confederation!" Only Riggs understood Alan's historical reference, but all had "met" Petey at one time or another and rightly suspected he meant the new union was far from perfect. A lot of work remained.

"It's a step, though," Henry Stokes encouraged, then grinned at Saraan. "And I for one am glad to have more Aussies on our side, even if they all have tails!"

The idea of a beer seemed a good one, and they proceeded toward the Busted Screw. With all the new industry in Baalkpan, no part of the harbor front was visible from the Parade Ground anymore, but as they neared the open-sided café reserved primarily for Navy and Marine personnel, they entered the very heart of the massive naval-building establishment this part of the city had become. "My God, they're almost finished!" Letts proclaimed, pointing at a pair of ships some distance away. For all the world, the two vessels, moored side by side beneath several tall cranes, looked exactly like USS *Walker*. That was understandable, since they were near-perfect copies of her, made largely of salvaged Japanese steel. There were a number of differences, mostly internal, but few of them showed.

"I told you," Riggs said, glancing at Forester. "You've been spending too much time cooped up with all these puffed-up foreigners!" Alan rubbed his eyes and managed a grin. "I know. Karen says the same thing." Karen Theimer Letts was Deputy Minister of Medicine. Second only to Sandra, she'd become de facto chief of her department and worked just as hard as her husband. Added to her burden was a young daughter named Allison Verdia whom neither of them could be with as much as they'd have liked. "And I know you told me," Alan agreed, "but to *see* them . . ." He chuckled. "The first new four-stacker destroyers to enter service in twenty-odd years. It would seem like a step back if I didn't know what it took to do it."

"It's a big step forward here," Riggs confirmed, "and now the yards have some practice, we'll have four-stack cruisers, and even genuine 'gold platers' next! Just had to draw 'em up. Spanky poked around some *Farraguts* once. Might've even served on one for all I know. I was on the *Dewey* before I went Asiatic. Anyway, Spanky left designs for some fifteen hundred tonners that look pretty slick. Someday we'll build 'em. We already had plans for those." He pointed at the familiar ships.

"They look swell," Alan said, scratching his chin. "And it seems you told me they'll be ready for sea trials soon?"

"A month yet. Maybe more. Lots of little tweaks to make. The 'Cats are awful proud of 'em."

"They have every right to be. Pass the word that I want the sea trials as comprehensive as possible. Their shakedown cruises'll be into the war zone." They paused under a corner of the roof of the Busted Screw, and Pepper, the Lemurian proprietor in Earl Lanier's absence, blinked questioningly at them from behind the bar.

"Beers," Steve Riggs shouted over the lunch-hour rush, and steered them to a table a buxom ex-pat Imperial girl was clearing away. They sat.

"What else have I been missing during my diplomatic sequestration?" Alan asked wryly.

"Well, we're still trying to figure out what's wrong with the torpedo-guidance mechanism. You know, after what happened to *Mahan*," Stokes supplied.

"Sure. Anything yet?"

Riggs shook his head. "Not on this end. Bernie had some ideas, but he can't do much but tinker with what we send him where he is. And now, of course, we can't talk to him at all."

"Can't we figure it out without him?"

"We can keep trying, but Bernie's 'the guy.' And far as we've come, this ain't the Newport Torpedo Station in Rhode Island."

"That might be a good thing, considering the crap torpedoes they sent us before the war," Alan interjected bitterly.

"Maybe," Riggs agreed. "I bet they're better now. Doesn't matter. We're doing what we can."

Alan sighed. "I know."

Pepper himself negotiated the crowd with a tray of mugs. "Here's beer!" he called loudly. That was all he ever served during normal "duty hours." The stronger "seep," made from the ubiquitous and widely useful polta fruit, was served only at night. "You wanna eat?" Pepper demanded. "I got good steaks, fresh. Rhino pig an' pleezy-sore both."

Alan looked at Ambassador Bolton and smiled. "How about rhino pig and pleezy-sore both?" he repeated, glancing at Riggs. "Like you said, we do what we can. And I can't do another damn thing until I eat something substantial."

///// *First Fleet South*
July 21, 1944

USS *Walker* loped across a smooth sea at eighteen knots, cruising ahead of the fleet to inspect a target the patrolling Nancys had spotted nearly an hour ago. It hadn't been reported immediately since the pilots and observers thought it was just a young mountain fish, too small to be very harmful. The sonar of the approaching fleet would doubtless drive it away. But Captain Reddy still couldn't get Gunny Horn's periscope out of his mind and decided to investigate when the word trickled down via Morse lamp from *Big Sal*.

Dennis Silva didn't know or care why the blower wound up and the stern crouched down, sending a convex slice of water curling back from the sharp, straight bow. Nobody had sounded general quarters, so it made no difference to him why *Walker* suddenly outpaced the rest of the fleet. It was an unusually pretty day, if just as humid as ever, and he'd already spent most of it drilling the gun's crews to a limb-numbing proficiency. Now he had other things on his bored mind, things he couldn't ignore as long as the gnawing itch in the crack of his ass tormented him so. Folding his favorite "whittlin' knife," he tucked the little ship model he'd been shaping for two days under his arm. "Howdy, Earl," he called as he passed the galley beneath the amidships gun platform. "What kinda sea serpent you got for supper this evenin'? I hope it ain't got any suckers this time. I can't *abide* eatin' critters with suckers all over 'em!" Earl ranted something in reply, but Silva didn't stop to listen. It wasn't expected that he should, anyway. Further aft, he strolled, past the port and starboard torpedo mounts, the searchlight tower and the 25-mm gun tubs on either side of the catapult with its Nancy floatplane perched atop it. "Whatcha doin', Jeek?" he called, spying the Lemurian crew chief's tail poking out of the plane's cockpit. Jeek's head replaced his tail.

"I's strappin' the 'stensions back on them rudder pedals," he grumped. "Commaander Hee-ring was playin' around in here this mornin', pertendin' he knowed how to fly. I had to take the 'Cat 'stensions off, so now I'm puttin' 'em back. Only real pilots we got on this trip is 'Cats."

"*Can* he fly?" Silva asked.

"How I know?" Jeek demanded. "Looked like he pertendin' to me."

"Huh." Silva wiggled his fingers at him. "Well, do carry on. The Skipper might wanna ee-mergency launch the damn thing any second, an' you'd be stuck flyin' it yerself. Can *you* fly, Jeek?"

"Hell no! Ain't my job. They as good stick you in here as me!"

Silva chuckled. "Oh, I bet I could *fly* it fine," he replied. "Gettin' it back to you in one piece would be the trick." Jeek blinked stunned curiosity at him as Silva ducked under the wing and proceeded toward the aft deckhouse.

Scuttlebutt had it that this wasn't the first reference Silva ever made to having once controlled an aircraft of some sort in some fashion, and like most of the rumors that followed Silva throughout the various fleets, nobody knew how much truth there was to any of them. Jeek didn't know Silva all that well, but he knew plenty of people who did.

Unlike most, he knew there was at least some truth to *all* the rumors. He shook his head and returned to his task.

Through the forward hatch, Dennis found Bernie Sandison instructing some 'Cats on the lathe in the torpedo workshop, but the man hardly noticed him pass. The dryers in the ship's laundry were rumbling sympathetically with the screws and shafts below as T-shirts and kilts rolled and tumbled inside. Passing through another hatch, Silva entered the aft crew's head and was reminded of one of the numerous changes wrought aboard by the inclusion of female crewfolk. A partition had been placed in the center of the compartment that separated the portside of the crapper from the starboard to create some meager privacy for those doing their business there. Silva dutifully entered the starboard stall that males were supposed to use, pulled down his breeches, and plopped down on one of the double-plank seats spanning the down-angled trough beneath. Water flowed through the trough from starboard to port, washing waste from beneath each seat, and eventually out the side of the ship. It was a primitive arrangement, but novel to the 'Cats of Baalkpan who considered it the height of convenience.

A similar system had served the entire city of Maa-ni-la for a very long time, running through most homes and beneath an arched covering in the open, until it too emptied into the sea—or Maa-ni-la Bay in that case. That was pretty slick, Silva thought. 'Cats in Baalkpan used ordinary outhouses like those he'd always known before he joined the Navy, but instead of toilet paper, or even a Monkey Wards catalog, they used a bunch of stupid leaves. Silva's expression darkened. Apparently, the old rivalry between the engineering (snipe) divisions, and the deck (ape) divisions had finally been revived full force aboard USS *Walker*, and he, as well as a number of other above-deck types, had been tricked repeatedly into using some particularly inappropriate leaves for a very delicate task. A large percentage of *Walker*'s snipes were female now, but female or not, no snipes had been afflicted with the ailment. Silva knew, since Pam had confided to him how strange it was that only the deck apes had complained of discomfort. That was all the proof Silva needed, and the time had come to exact his revenge.

A striped 'Cat, from the second, aft deck division, was watching him apprehensively, several seats over. Silva took a chaw and smiled benignly. "This used to be *my* crapper, you know," he said conversationally. "The whole thing. All mine." The 'Cat quickly finished his business and scampered out the aft hatch, leaving Silva by himself in the starboard stall. All he had to do now was wait. Sure enough, within minutes, a virtual herd of females crowded into the portside stall. He'd timed his attack for the end of the watch for that very reason since it was then, he'd observed, that Tabby's female snipes dashed to the water butts and then went straight, en masse, to the aft head. If he was going to do this, he might as well do it right—making sure it was the engineering division that he victimized.

For an instant, while he pulled up his breeches and readied his trusty Zippo, he contemplated the arbitrary nature of fate. There was no guarantee that anybody on the other side of the partition had anything to do with, well, anything. That was a shame. Naturally, he'd have preferred that only the guilty suffer, but in a battle like this, there was bound to be collateral damage. It was regrettable, but that was just the way it was. Word *would* spread that certain pranks were beyond the pale, and a disproportionate response must be expected. Taking the ship model, a crudely shaped thing, but obviously meant to resemble one of the great Grik ironclads, he quickly lit the four cigar-shaped protuberances arranged like the smokestacks on the enemy ships. These were made of a different kind of wood than the rest of the vessel—gimpra wood, to be precise. And the dried sap inside caused the little stacks to blaze like signal flares. Carefully setting his little dreadnaught in the torrent of water, he let it go, and as nonchalantly as possible, retraced his steps.

"You wanted to see me, Skipper?" Silva asked when Chief Gray practically shoved him into the pilothouse. He was suddenly on edge. There were several officers on the bridge, including that weasel, Herring.

"No, but *she* does," Matt said, nodding at Lieutenant Tab-At, who stood beside the chart table, her tail rigid with fury. By the hint of scorched fur wafting through the bridge, she'd been one of those on the

"Dames" side of the partition, and Silva cringed slightly. He hadn't expected that. He had nothing at all against Tabby and knew she'd suffered some pretty bad steam burns before. That was likely to make her a
little extra sensitive to his stunt.

"I want that . . . *fiend* . . . in the brig!" Tabby demanded, her voice
hard as granite.

"We don't have a brig," Matt mildly reminded, then turned to his
talker. "Anything on what the scout planes saw yet, Minnie? Does Mr.
Fairchild have anything on his scope?" He really didn't have time for
this right now. Something screwy might be stalking his little fleet at that
very moment. Chances remained it was nothing to worry about, though,
and he had to stifle the very real problem brewing on his ship before it
escalated, as such things were liable to do. He suspected he needed to
make time to deal with this at once.

"Nothing yet, Cap-i-taan. Mr. Faar-child reports 'no contact.'"

"Tell him to keep at it. The fleet's catching up."

"Ay, ay," Minnie replied.

Matt looked back at Silva.

"Then chaineem up in the bilge," Tabby insisted. "He ain't fit to be
around people!"

"That may well be," Matt replied reasonably. "Silva? Just what is it
that's wrong with you? Chasing sea monsters, terrifying the snipes.
How can anybody be such a credit to the Navy one minute, and such a
disgrace the next? I thought you'd improved."

Dennis never even considered lying to Captain Reddy; nor did he
contemplate one of his convoluted justifications. One of the few things
that really mattered to him was Captain Reddy's trust. He wasn't exactly sure how he'd endangered it—he'd just been being himself, after
all—but apparently there really was a line he shouldn't cross. He'd expected to have to account for himself at mast, or something, but this
public, "drumhead" chastisement—particularly in front of strangers
like Herring—was a surprise, and just a bit ominous. "I *have* improved,
Skipper. Honest. And I don't know what got ahold o' me." He glared at
Tabby. "Somethin' needed doin' about certain things, an' I guess I've got
sorta used to doin' things that need doin'."

"Setting fire to people in . . . that situation *needed* doing?" Tabby demanded, almost shrill. "Somebody could 'a got hurt baad!"

"Nuh-uh," Silva denied, "not the way I set it up. Not past a little scorched fur, anyway. You think I ain't seen that same stunt a thousand times? It's one of the oldest standbys in the book." His jaw clenched. "Though maybe some folks had a little indignification comin'!"

"What's that supposed to mean?" Tabby growled.

"Ask Pam—I mean, Lieutenant Cross, what's the commonest aggravations the deck apes've been seein' her about!"

Matt looked at the Bosun, who grimaced but nodded. "He's right. The 'butt blisters' ain't hit the chiefs or officers' heads, but there's been a rash—s'cuse me, Skipper—o' complaints from those that frequent the aft crew's head."

"A *rash*!" Silva practically choked.

"Shut up, you!" Gray seethed.

Minnie suddenly interrupted the testimony. "Mr. Farr-child has a underwater contact bareen seero eight seero, relaa-tive!" she cried. "Range two t'ousands! It jus pop up there, he say."

Matt whipped his gaze to starboard, but saw nothing but the mild sea. Whatever was out there had somehow managed to slip past Wallace Fairchild's sonar gear and was still headed toward the fleet! No mountain fish had ever done that. "Right standard rudder," Matt barked. "Steady on course zero four zero. All ahead full. Sound general quarters." Amid the raucous cry of the general alarm, Matt turned back to Minnie. "Signal to Admiral Keje on *Big Sal* that we've got an unidentified target on an intercept course with the fleet. We're preparing to engage." Just like that, the "contact" had become the "target."

"What kinda signal . . . TBS?" Minnie asked.

Matt took a breath. Chances still were it was no big deal, and fleet lookouts would've been alerted by *Walker*'s sudden maneuver. They'd be watching her. "Flags and Morse lamp, but make it snappy."

Silva and Tabby started to bolt for their stations, but Matt stopped them. "One second. Silva, I don't know what it is with you, but you can't keep acting like this. People look up to you, damn it! You think I won't bust you? Think again. One more stunt like this—or anything else your creepy brain cooks up—I'll bust you to third class . . . and I'll throw you off my ship. Is that clear?"

Silva didn't care about the rank, but leave *Walker*? He couldn't believe his ears. But the Skipper was serious this time; there was no doubt about it. He gulped. "No, sir—I mean, aye, aye, sir. And no, sir, it won't happen again!" Matt glared at Tabby. "And you. You're an officer now, damn it! Keep control of your division, or I'll find somebody who can."

Tabby was equally stunned and blinked furiously, her big eyes beginning to fill.

"Now get out of my sight, both of you," Matt practically whispered, and man and 'Cat bolted for the ladder aft.

"Kinda hard on 'em, weren't you, Skipper?" Gray asked quietly as Matt raised his binoculars, looking for what? A fin? A *periscope*, God forbid? "At least on Tabby," Gray pressed.

"No, Boats, I wasn't," Matt replied. "Morale's one thing, and rivalries aren't all bad, but stuff like that can get out of hand. If this mission isn't for all the marbles—and maybe it is—it's for a hell of a lot of them any way you slice it. I *will not* tolerate anything that pits one half of the crew against the other right now, no matter how silly or innocent we've treated such things before. This job's just too big for silliness. Period. You'll make sure of that, won't you?"

"Of course, Skipper."

"Sound's losin' the taagit," Minnie warned. "We go too fast."

"What's the last Wally had on the target?"

"Range twelve hundreds an' closin'. Down doppler. Taagit course estimated one two seero, speed five knots!"

Matt had hoped to get around in front of whatever it was, but it must've surged ahead for a while before slowing back down. *Walker* had come up behind it. "Estimated range between the target and the closest DD screening the fleet?"

"Ah, eleven t'ousands," Minnie replied after repeating the question to Sonny Campeti on the fire-control platform above the bridge.

"Make your course one two zero," Matt instructed Chief Quartermaster and acting First Lieutenant "Paddy" Rosen, who'd quietly taken the helm.

"Making my course one two zero, aye," Rosen replied. "My course is one two zero," he said a few moments later.

"Very well. Slow to two-thirds. See if Wally can find the target again. Y-gun crews will stand by to throw a couple of eggs out in front of it. That should chase it away," he added to Gray.

"You think it's a baby mountain fish after all?" Gray asked a little worriedly, and Matt looked at him. Apparently, the rogue-sub scuttlebutt was gaining currency.

"I sure hope so, Boats. We don't know much about the little ones. Maybe they're extra curious, or aren't as susceptible to our sonar. I guess we'll find out."

"Lookout says there's screwy fishes, er somethin', jumpin' outa the water!" Minnie suddenly cried. Matt raised his precious Bausch & Lomb binoculars. Sure enough, just a few hundred yards ahead, strange creatures were leaping out of the water. From this distance, they looked like giant bullets—battleship shells—with wings. He snorted. "They're squids! Some kind of flying squids! Look at 'em all!" Spanky had joined them on the bridge. His normal battle station was atop the aft deckhouse, at the auxiliary conn, but there was no reason to expect a surface action and he'd always joined his captain on the bridge unless otherwise directed. "I think you're right, Skipper!" he confirmed, staring through his own binoculars. "Flyin' squids! I'll be damned. Look! They're glidin' across the water a pretty good distance before they flop back in it." He sobered. "Act like somethin's spookin' 'em from below!"

"Minnie?" Matt demanded.

"Mr. Faar-child got a contaact—a big one—but he don't know what it is."

"Must be a whole swarm o' them critters underwater," Spanky speculated, then brightened. "And you know? I bet *we're* the ones spookin' 'em!"

"You think that's what we've been chasin' all along?" Gray asked. "A big school of creepy squids, cruisin' along, all bunched up?"

Matt felt the tension ebb. Of *course* that was what it was. It was far more probable that his recent concerns had been initiated by yet more weird marvels native to this very weird world, than that they were being haunted by an enemy submarine from the old one!

"Secure the Y guns," he said. "Slow to one-third. No sense in steaming right through that mess. There's hundreds of them, and they're big enough to hurt somebody if they hit us."

"Might even dent our plates," Spanky agreed.

Walker began to slow, and sure enough, the frantic leaping and soaring of the flying squids diminished—until they suddenly erupted again, even more violently than before.

"What?" Matt muttered, raising his binoculars again.

"Skipper!" Minnie shouted. "Crow's nest say them, them 'skids,' is jumpin' in a straight, fast line, right toward the fleet!" She held the earpiece to her head under her helmet. "There's two lines now! *Three!*"

For just an instant, Matt stood watching for himself. The explosion of squids was following several unnaturally straight and rapid lines of advance, and he could fathom only one explanation. "All ahead two-thirds," he suddenly barked. "Y guns and aft racks stand by!" He looked at Spanky. "Go aft," he said bitterly. "Looks like you were right the first time, but now we've got *torpedoes* scaring the squids! Signal Keje that he's got torpedoes inbound. Multiple torpedoes, from directly in front of our position—use the TBS, damn it."

"Should I maneuver, Skipper?" Paddy asked desperately.

"No. If whoever's out there fired at us, we're better off threading the fish. Tell Mr. Fairchild he better pick something out of that mess below for me to kill right away!" he shouted back at Minnie.

"He say some-teeng comin' outa the return cloud. Range, seven hundreds. Course one, two, seero. Ten knots, down doppler. He's startin' a plot!" Bernie Sandison already had his own plot going on the chart table in the pilothouse, frantically pushing a grease pencil alongside a straight edge while Commander Herring stared at his watch. Minnie's voice rose. "Lookout gots tor-peedoes comin' at *us*! Two tor-peedoes! Ah, they's four headin' for the fleet now!"

Matt stared through the windows ahead, watching the panicked squids betray the approach of the mysterious undersea weapons screaming straight at him. "Come right two degrees," he told Rosen tersely. "Now, steady! Steady as you go." Suddenly, he stepped briskly toward the starboard bridgewing, just as a gliding flock of big-eyed squids jetted past dodging crewfolk on the fo'c'sle, or ricocheted off the hull. He looked down in time to see a long, sun-dappled cylinder streak by the starboard beam less than a dozen yards away, leading a white, steamy wake.

"That was the close one," he explained, charging back to stand beside Rosen. "Make your course one one zero, all ahead full. Set depth charges for one fifty!"

"That deep, Captain?" Herring asked, and Matt jerked a nod. "The target will have been at periscope depth to launch," Herring persisted.

"Yeah, but Wally's a good sound man. If he says the target's making ten knots underwater, I believe him. What's more, whoever shot at us had to see us, so they have to know what we are and that we'll come after them. My guess is they'll go deep, try to get under those squid things. If they do, they'll get there quick at ten knots!" He pointed at a spot beyond the dark line on the chart. "One fifty, right here."

"Range four hundreds," Minnie reported shortly. "Three hundreds . . . We losin' 'im! We too fast again!"

"Jesus," Paddy suddenly exclaimed. That's all he had to say, because everyone on the bridge immediately saw what caused his outburst. Most of the ships of First Fleet South had held their course. Wild maneuvers in such a congested formation were just as dangerous as torpedoes, and there hadn't been time at any rate. *Big Sal* had adjusted her course just enough to thread the wakes herself, and though she'd probably been the target, nothing hit her. One of the DDs wasn't so lucky. A massive plume of dirty spray erupted into the sky, and the ship beneath the rising column simply ceased to exist. A dull boom reached them several moments later, racing across the water with a physical jolt that shook the windows in the pilothouse. Tragic as the loss of the as-yet-unknown ship was, Matt was just beginning to feel a sense of relief that it hadn't been worse, when two towering columns of water rocketed into the air at the side of *Respite Island*.

"Keep your eyes on your course, Mr. Rosen!" Matt ordered sharply.

"But . . ."

"Captain Reddy," Herring interrupted, his voice strained, "there will be people in the water over there! And *Respite Island* may need assistance!"

"And there's a whole fleet over there to give it," Matt snarled. "We have other business first."

Everyone but Rosen was still looking at the distant cataracts of water collapsing down on the massive SPD. "Here," Matt snapped, stabbing his finger down on the Plexiglas-covered chart. "Now!" Most heads turned to him. "He'll wait till we're nearly on top of him, then turn," he explained grimly, mostly for Herring's benefit. "But he won't be expecting this." He raised his voice. "Y guns will commence firing! Stern racks, roll four, at three-second intervals."

The Y guns thundered, and the "Roll one! Roll two! Roll three! Roll four!" was repeated on the bridge. Shortly after, the sea astern spalled and shook, and an opaque white mound of water and smoke convulsed beneath the clear afternoon sky.

USS *Walker*'s Y guns weren't exactly like the weapons that inspired their creation but served essentially the same purpose. Improved over the first models, these could each throw two depth charges off either beam, at forty-five and ninety degrees relative to the centerline of the ship. The hefty black powder charge that propelled the (vastly improved over the early model) three-hundred-pound depth bombs could throw them only about a hundred yards, but that was sufficient to prevent underwater damage to *Walker* at any depth, really, although it did leave a large gap directly under the ship. The aft racks took care of that, rolling more charges off the stern directly in the wake. The sinking pattern of explosives, designed to detonate when the water pressure at the preselected depth actuated the fuse, was ridiculously simple, but the addition of the Y gun made it far more effective than the stern racks alone—which was all *Walker* had been equipped with before. Against the Japanese, she'd had to virtually run right over her target to have a chance of inflicting any damage. The likelihood of that wasn't great, considering her primitive, glitchy sonar. Now, with the addition of the Y guns, all she had to do was get close. Chief Gray, no supporter of depth charges, said it doubled their chances. But since two times zero was still zero, he wasn't optimistic. Wallace Fairchild, Bernie Sandison, and even Spanky believed their old chances of damaging a target were more like five or ten percent, depending on the sea's state, the size and speed of their target, and the skill of the sub's skipper, of course. If the Y guns doubled their chances, they'd certainly take ten to twenty percent. Captain Reddy wasn't considered a variable. By now, everyone just assumed that if it could be done, he could do it. Matt would've laughed at that confidence, considering his inexperience at ASW.

Whatever the chances, whether it was skill, better weapons, or just insanely good luck, the results of their third pattern, laid just eleven minutes after the first, had a distinct impact on the target. A ghostly return had somehow flashed feebly through all the underwater tumult and columns of water displacing bubbles of smoky gas, across the green-lit cathode ray tube Wallace Fairchild worshipped so intently, and USS *Walker* mercilessly hammered it.

"It's comin' up!" Minnie squeaked over the thundering blower and the rush of the convulsing sea. "Spanky thinks the taagit's comin' up!" she repeated. "He sees 'oily air gushin' up,' an' gots debris in sight!"

"Where?" Matt demanded.

"Starboard quarter, about one six seero, relative!"

"Right standard rudder," Matt ordered. "Pass the word for all gun batteries to stand by for surface action, starboard!" He stepped out on the bridgewing and focused his binoculars. The lookout already there was scanning as well. Bernie raced to his precious torpedo director, ready to confirm Campeti's ranges and bearings.

Several minutes passed while *Walker* described a gradual arc in the sea. Her 4"-50s, .50 and .30 cals, and twin 25 mms aft, were all trained out toward a growing, roiling oil slick about six hundred yards off the starboard beam. Suddenly, what looked like the knife-edge bow of a fair-size ship roared up from the depths, streaming water, laced with all the colorful hues diesel fuel could give it.

"Get a load o' that!" Bernie gasped. The thing was obviously a submarine, but it was huge! Twice the size S-19 had been. And it wasn't shaped like any sub he'd ever seen. Gradually, the bow came down as the boat leveled out and a conn tower—or something—emerged from the sea. The first part that rose into view was a pair of very large guns protruding from a rounded housing of some sort, followed by what appeared to be a relatively normal conn tower, complete with periscopes and light weapons. But the conn tower didn't seem to end; it just kept coming up, exposing a long, arched structure aft. Finally, it did end, about the time an ordinary deck gun emerged from the sea.

"I'll be . . . ," Matt muttered, confusion evident in his tone. "That thing . . . ," he started, but stopped when men appeared atop the conn tower, looking back at him. Other men, dressed in shorts and cotton shirts, dashed from the side of the tower toward the deck gun aft—just as the boat began turning toward his ship and the two massive guns forward began to twitch. "Commence firing!" he roared up at the fire-control platform above.

"But Skipper," came Campeti's stunned voice, "that's . . ."

"Commence firing *now*, damn it! *They're* about to!"

The strange submarine showed obvious damage: warped railings and washboarded plates. And the arched structure aft had taken a particularly brutal beating. The stern never came completely up, and the bow, with its four torpedo tubes, never lowered all the way back into the sea. The thing was sluggish, but still maneuvering, still clearly trying to fight. Before it could turn all the way to face USS *Walker*, however, bringing those giant, apparently fixed guns to bear, the salvo buzzer rattled and three 4"-50s barked as one. Only one round struck the boat on the first salvo, the others launching towering columns of water just beyond, but the target was barely moving. The next three rounds exploded against and within the odd conn tower a few moments later, and the 25-mm gun tubs and machine-gun tracers were already reaching for it. Flames vomited out of the rounded casemate housing the two guns forward, and the weapons seemed to actually droop as blue-yellow flame jetted out between them. Matt suspected they'd punched through the light armor and ignited the powder train as ammunition was brought up to the weapon from the handling room below. Somebody probably closed the hatch just in time because the magazine didn't blow, but already, it didn't matter. The strange, belligerent submarine had been a sitting duck—*its officers had to know it was a sitting duck!* Matt suddenly realized with a sick certainty—and *Walker*'s veteran crew of men and 'Cats made short work of it. Its apparent intention to make a fight only doomed it a few minutes later than its attempt to claw its way to the surface had delayed its fate.

"Cease firing!" Matt yelled. "Cease firing all guns!"

The conn tower and pressure hull shattered like a basket of eggs under the point-blank hammering of *Walker*'s common shells—none of the new AP rounds were kept in the ready lockers—the enigmatic submarine dove once more, smoking and hissing, back beneath the sea. With her bow again pointing at the sky, she seemed to be rising in reverse, except now the oil and diesel around her were alight, and black smoke piled into the clear afternoon sky. Just like that, the very real submarine that Gunny Horn probably really did see, that had haunted them from Madraas to Diego, and across half the Western Ocean, disappeared forever.

"My God," Herring muttered at Matt's side. "I see no survivors."

"We'll have a closer look, nevertheless," Matt said. "I'd sure as hell like to know what that was all about. Then we'll head back there"—he gestured toward the fleet where another tall column of smoke stood in the sky—"and find out how bad it hurt us. Boats?" he called toward Gray. "Have our damage-control parties rig out all our firefighting gear and stand by for rescue operations. Mr. Rosen? Take us over there for a quick look around. Then we'll shape a course back to the fleet, if you please."

Sonny Campeti joined them, still puffing from his slide down the ladder. "I can't believe it," he gasped. "Didn't you see?"

"Of course I saw," Matt replied. "But they shot fish at us and our friends, and they were about to keep shooting at us!"

"I know! And that's what doesn't make sense!"

Herring was looking at them questioningly.

"That sub," Matt explained, "was the *Surcouf*—or something from the same class. One of the biggest boats ever built—fast, long legged, and powerfully armed. Those guns she was trying to point at us were eight-inchers—*cruiser* guns!"

"I've heard of *Surcouf*!" Herring defended. He started to remind them he'd been—was—an intelligence officer, after all, but something about Matt's and Campeti's expressions stopped him—that, and the fact that he was a different man than he'd been just a few short months ago. Then it came to him. "But *Surcouf* is French!"

"Right!" Campeti declared.

"Must've gone Vichy," Bernie speculated. "Collaborating with the Krauts. Why else would they attack? They had to see our flag—and nearly every ship in the fleet flies the Stars and Stripes!"

"I don't doubt they saw our flag," Matt said, "and these four-stackers've been around long enough that everybody in the world—our old world—is familiar with our lines. They may've been confused by the rest of our fleet flying the Stars and Stripes; couldn't know it's the Navy clan flag, but they had to know who *we* are. But I thought even the Vichy French kept the tricolor. You didn't see her flag?" he asked.

"She wasn't flying one."

"It was painted on her conn tower, and I've got no idea what it meant."

"I saw it," Bernie agreed. "Looked more like an emblem of some kind."

"What was it?" Campeti demanded.

"A red octagon with a white field, and what looked like a blue cross with rockers on each side," Matt told them.

"Looked like a big, fat, blue swastika to me," Bernie added darkly.

With the TBS barn door having been opened, it was pretty jammed up with traffic by the time *Walker* rejoined the rest of First Fleet South. It was daytime, with a clear sky, so maybe the signals wouldn't travel far, but it was still a mess. They learned from snippets of excited reports that the DD that had been destroyed was USS *Naga*, one of their newest, that had transferred from Des-Ron 9 to Des-Ron 6 for this mission. As expected, there'd been no survivors. They also quickly learned that USS *Respite Island* was sinking, but they could see that for themselves. She had a serious list to starboard and was low by the stern. A mass of ships was gathered around her, taking off her crew and the troops she carried, while they joined with those left aboard in fighting a raging fire amidships. Matt wasn't sure even *Big Sal* could've survived two torpedo hits as long, but *Respite Island*, due to her nature, had more watertight compartments and better pumps than any Allied ship. She had to have them to maintain her trim and perform her duties as a floating dry dock. Regardless, she was clearly doomed. All they could do was prolong the inevitable while they evacuated her people—and as much of her cargo as possible.

Several of the torpedo boats had apparently launched themselves as the cavernous dry dock flooded, and they were busy towing others clear, ferrying survivors to ships that kept their distance—like *Big Sal*—and trying to save as many of the stacked, dory-shaped landing craft aboard the ship as they could. Matt hated to contemplate all the other supplies and equipment they simply couldn't save; tons and tons of food and ammunition and as much as half of II Corps's light artillery would be lost. Carefully, he directed *Walker*'s approach into the chaotic jumble so he could bring her own firefighting equipment to bear. Soon, streams of rainbow-infused water were arcing across the gap between the ships to play upon the flaming SPD. Steam rose within the gray cloud of woodsmoke.

"Look at that!" someone called as one of the PTs gingerly towed the fire-scorched P-40E-turned-floatplane clear of the settling stern. The fabric control surfaces on the tail had burned away, leaving the skeletonized framework in view, but the plane was in one piece and should be salvageable. Matt applauded the initiative of whoever commanded the little boat. With all the Nancys in the fleet, a "sport model" floatplane might seem superfluous, but there was no sense in letting it go down with the ship.

"Minnie, have Mr. Palmer signal all ships to quit jamming up the phone. We have to get organized here. Ask Admiral Keje to double our aerial scouts. Keep some close in case there's something else sneaking around out there, but push some farther out too. We need plenty of warning if we have to untangle this mess and get ready for a fight."

"Ay, ay, Cap-i-taan!"

"Skipper!" cried a 'Cat on the port bridgewing. "Morse lamp signal from *Salissa*; Ahd-mi-raal Keje's compliments, an' he asks that we move us away from *Respite Island*, in case she blows up. He also asks that you come aboard *Salissa* as soon as possible."

Matt frowned. "Send my respects to the admiral, and tell him I'll be happy to attend him as soon as I'm sure we can render no further assistance here."

aptain Bekiaa-Sab-At sat perched on the topgallant yard, nearly as high on the foremast as she could get. She'd been a wing-runner on *Salissa*, like her cousins Chack and Risa, before her old Home gave up the wind and became a carrier of aircraft. Heights held no terror for her, particularly after her exciting flight in *Donaghey*'s Nancy. Her perch was more precarious than it had ever been on *Salissa*, and the motion of the much smaller ship kept her swooping all over the sky, but she felt . . . *cleaner* here, less disturbed by all the real terrors she'd known.

Donaghey had finally reached the point where she was supposed to rendezvous with First Fleet South a few days before, and had spent the time slowly cruising up and down a longitude just one hundred fifty miles east of Mauritius, across the fleet's expected line of advance. There was no guarantee they'd meet; the Western Ocean was vast. But with the weather remaining mild and the visibility so good, there was an excellent chance they'd spot something the size of *Salissa* and her battle group spread across several miles of ocean, or *Salissa*'s planes would find *Donaghey*.

"Smoke!" came a cry behind her, from the main masthead. "Smoke on horizon! West-nor'west!"

Bekiaa squinted, noting the distant haze, and chastised herself for letting someone else spy what she should have seen first. Shouts came from below, but she paid them little mind at present. She supposed it was possible they'd spotted an enemy force of some kind, but they'd know that long before she needed to concern herself with preparations below. She caught a glimpse of a sunlit shape above that quickly resolved into a copy of the Nancy floatplane they'd finally struck back down into the hold. She blinked with a small sense of triumph as she hollered down: "Allied aar-craft approaching, twenty degrees off port bow!" She'd seen that one first!

Time passed, and soon dark shapes could be seen rising above the distant horizon to join the boiler smoke. It wasn't dark smoke, but she expected Captain Garrett would tactfully rib Captain Reddy about it when they met, regardless. She reached back to grab a tarry backstay and slid down it, all the way to the bright deck below. "What's wrong?" she asked Smitty, when she saw his troubled expression. "We've found First Fleet South."

"Sure. But so did somebody else. The TBS is goin' crazy."

Aboard USNRS Salissa *(CV-1)*
July 22, 1944

"You know, of course, my aviators came very close to blowing your fine ship to splinters, Cap-i-taan Gaar-ett?" *Salissa*'s COFO, Captain Jis-Tikkar (Tikker), told Greg ruefully. As usual, he was absently polishing the 7.7-mm cartridge case thrust through a hole in his ear with his sable-furred fingers. He had to speak up too, because this wasn't a formal conference in Keje's vast quarters, but a hurried gathering of anxious friends on *Big Sal*'s hangar deck. Others were still arriving, but that was as far as anyone got before the questions started to fly. The hangar deck was a loud place under normal circumstances, but the need for greater security after the torpedo attack, as well as the fleet's growing proximity to its objective, called for an increased pace of air operations. The space had been crammed with "Fleashooters" since they left Madraas, since the little pursuit ships were rarely allowed to fly so distant from land. Only a few were kept ready for emergency defense. But now nearly half the 1st Naval Air Wing's Nancys were below at any given time, undergoing the constant maintenance they required. Added to the noise and general bustle were large numbers of troops rescued from *Respite Island*, who had no choice but to sway their hammocks on the hangar deck. The lost ship's crew had been distributed throughout the fleet and easily fit in wherever they went. The troops were mostly from land Homes, however, and it was all they could do to stay out of the way.

"I considered that possibility, Tikker," Greg replied, glancing at Bekiaa and Inquisitor Choon. They'd accompanied him aboard. "That was why I was flying my battle flags—and every signal flag I could combine into any variation of 'Don't shoot me' I could find!"

"You painted your hull red, like a Grik ship," Admiral Keje-Fris-Ar observed. "Does that mean what I think it does?"

"We'll be painting it black and white again, just as soon as we part company with you, Admiral. Trust me. But yeah, we actually cruised within sight of Madagascar."

There was a hush, at least within the immediate gathering. No one except the Japanese sailor Miyata had viewed the ancestral homeland of—most likely—all the Lemurian People in untold ages. Miyata had described the Grik capital there, but almost nothing was known of what he called the "wild regions."

"Was . . . Was it beautiful?" Adar almost whispered.

Greg looked curiously at the Chairman of the Grand Alliance. "You could say that, I guess. It was . . . different." He didn't elaborate on that. "We didn't get real close, just sailed north along the eastern coast until we got within fifty or sixty miles of the port city Miyata told us about." He nodded at the Japanese sailor who'd arrived at the meeting with Irvin Laumer, Safir Maraan and Sandra. Irvin had suddenly found himself elevated to command the entire little "mosquito fleet" of torpedo boats, though the number had been reduced by nearly half. Just seven PTs survived the sinking of *Respite Island*, and they were currently stowed in the water-level docking bay. Their creator and former commander, Winny Rominger, had been killed trying to save an eighth, and his loss was a terrible blow. It was also a sad irony since the man hadn't really wanted back in the Navy in the first place after all he'd been through as a prisoner of the Japanese. He'd been willing to design and build PT boats, however, and ultimately—reluctantly—agreed to command the first squadron completed. Laumer was new to PTs and had expected a lot more time to learn about them. Now he was in charge. He'd been faced with adversity before, though, and nobody thought he'd have any trouble adapting—except maybe Irvin Laumer.

"You didn't send your scout plane to observe more closely?" Adar asked wistfully.

"No, sir," Greg replied. "My orders specifically stated that I was to avoid detection at all costs. Even painted red, I wasn't going to get too close with *Donaghey* either. Her rig's definitely not Grik, and if anybody got a good look, they'd probably figure that out."

"Did you see any ships?" Sandra asked.

"No, ma'am, but after we determined how inhospitable all the seaward islands were, I'm not too surprised. Most traffic's likely to move off the western coast, between the island and the continent, or maybe some of the northern islands."

Adar noticed that their discussion was drawing more and more attention from the troops as well as from the air and ground crews nearby. He nudged Keje. "Perhaps we should take this conversation to the appropriate place, where there are scrolls—charts—to view, and a bit more privacy. Mr. Braad-furd is already there, and I would value his views. Kap-i-taan Leut-naant Laange is en route to join us with Chack and Risa, and Cap-i-taan Reddy should be alongside directly. Come."

"I'll wait here for Captain Reddy, if you don't mind," Sandra said. "Of course."

"As will I," Safir announced. Everyone knew she wanted to greet Chack. He, Risa, Lange, and Doocy Meek were met by a side party soon afterward, and along with Safir, escorted away. Sandra smiled to see Safir and Chack almost—but not quite—holding hands, and their tails touching, caressing each other as they walked.

Sandra didn't know why Matt was the last to arrive—he had the fastest ship, after all—but when the side party piped him aboard, he was wearing whites, and her heart soared at the sight of him. He hadn't been aboard since they left Laa-Laanti, and she'd missed him terribly. Commander Herring was with him, which made sense, she supposed. He was their Chief of Strategic Intelligence, after all. He still kind of gave her the creeps, though. Last aboard was Chief Gray—with his captain, as always. Sandra hoped he and her young stewardess, Diania, might find time to spend together. She knew they'd grown crazy about each other, but Gray still wouldn't make his move because of the vast age difference. She shook her head. She'd keep working on that.

Without hesitation, or care for what anyone thought, she stepped forward and embraced her husband. He stiffened in surprise, but then wrapped her tightly in his arms. Mischievously, Sandra stood on tiptoe and planted a healthy kiss on his lips. Lemurians might not be able to manage wolf whistles, but a hearty cheer rose above the noise on the hangar deck.

"That's . . . nicer than I expected," Matt whispered in her ear. "Sometimes lately . . . I wonder if you're mad at me."

"Don't be ridiculous," she whispered back. "Just a lot going on—and a lot on my mind." She shook her head, smiling, when he raised a questioning brow. "Not now," she mouthed, stepping back.

"Peese com dis waay," a 'Cat said, gesturing. "De ahd-mi-raal, chaarman, an' ever'body else is waitin'."

Warm greetings were exchanged when Matt and his companions entered the expansive meeting room adjacent to Keje's offices and quarters. A 'Cat steward maneuvered him and Sandra to seats beside Keje and Adar, and Herring and Gray were ushered to others. Diania stood behind Matt and his wife, ready to serve them or fill their mugs, but she flashed a smile at Chief Gray as he sat. In a flustered response, he managed to strike the table with his chest when he shifted his chair forward, rattling everything on it. Keje gently knocked on the table several times with his knuckles until he had the silence he needed, then spoke to Greg Garrett, seated a short distance away.

"Cap-i-taan Garrett. I'm sure you have already heard a great deal of what has transpired since we parted company. The encounter with the strange submarine being the only incident of note, we shall return to it after you share your report. Only then may we speculate further about it."

"There is plenty to speculate about already, Admiral," Herring stated, drawing frowns.

"Indeed. But Cap-i-taan Garrett's report may add context." He looked at Greg. "Please proceed."

Garrett recounted what happened at Mauritius, and told them that the circumstances at Reunion Isle were essentially the same.

"So there's no way you can imagine us using either place as a staging area?" Matt prompted.

"None, sir. I've never seen anything like it. I don't see how anything that can't fly could live on either island."

"Perhaps nothing does," Courtney Bradford exclaimed absently, peering into his already-empty mug. The steward behind him blinked helplessly until Matt caught his eye and held up a single finger. One more for now. He wanted Courtney sharp.

"And you never found any sign of *Sineaa*?" Matt asked.

"No, sir." Garrett glanced down at the table. "I guess we have to assume she foundered in the storm."

"Or was captured—or grounded on enemy shores," Becher Lange interrupted. He'd been unused to the free-flowing way his new allies discussed things, but he appreciated how valuable an unfettered exchange of ideas might be and had quickly embraced the practice. Kapitan Melhausen was less approving, but he was unwell again, so Lange—and now Choon—would represent the Republic once more.

"She wasn't captured, sir," Garrett insisted to the bearded German. "I'll vouch for that." He saw several grim nods. "No skipper or crew of an American Navy ship on this world would ever let their ship be taken by the Grik," he added with certainty. "And as I said, there was absolutely no enemy traffic between the islands and our objective. Even if they did catch *Sineaa*, or found her aground, you'd think they'd come snooping." He looked around the table. "And if there were any survivors at all . . ." He cleared his throat. "The Grik brass understands written English, at least, and we all know how . . . remorseless the enemy can be. People, *any* people can take only so much. If they had *Sineaa* or any of her survivors, they would've learned about us and come looking."

"So you think, whatever happened to your consort, the Grik remain ignorant of our approach?" Adar demanded intently.

Greg hesitated only an instant before nodding. "Yes, Mr. Chairman, I do."

There was a rumble of conversation before Keje wrapped the table again. "Unless, of course, the sub-maa-reen that sank *Naga* and *Respite Island* was somehow in league with them," he added darkly, looking at Adar and voicing all their concerns. "We cannot discount that possibility."

Adar stiffened on his stool. "Nor can we let mere speculation deter us from our mission," he said forcefully.

Matt felt a familiar sinking feeling in his gut. He knew Keje was as keen to strike the Grik as anyone, but in the face of Adar's expanding ambitions, Keje had become the voice of caution. For the first time since he'd known the two Lemurians, he sensed tension between them. He couldn't let that spread, and it was high time he stressed his own views once more. Reluctantly, he cleared his throat. "Mr. Chairman," he said, "you're the head of state—of whatever state Alan Letts has put together in our absence." There were a few murmurs. Right on the heels of the encounter with the mystery sub, even while *Respite Island* was slipping beneath the sea, they'd picked up a transmission about the formation of the new "union" back in Baalkpan. Under the circumstances, the momentous achievement hadn't been received as joyfully as it would other-

wise have been. Matt continued. "But Keje commands First Fleet South, and it's his duty to look out for it." Matt's brow arched. "And in his capacity, he answers to *me*, Mr. Chairman, not you. Last I checked, I'm still High Chief of the Navy clan, and Supreme Commander of all Allied Forces. You tell us what you want to do and we figure out how—or whether we *can*." He nodded at Keje. "Speculation is an important first step in that." He shrugged, looking at Kon Choon and then Commander Herring. "Hell, without proper recon or intelligence, sometimes speculation is all we can do." He looked back at Adar. "But as long as I'm Supreme Commander, it's my duty to decide if we proceed with the mission, and if, even through speculation, we determine there's a high likelihood it's been compromised, I'll say it's time to think up something else." He shrugged. "If you don't like that, you can replace me in the top slot, but the Navy's my 'state,' and you can't replace me as *its* High Chief."

Adar blinked at him, but then lowered his eyes. "Of course. Please forgive me. Sometimes I find myself . . . overly enthusiastic for our cause."

Matt studied Adar and examined other faces around the table. 'Cats were so hard to read! He thought he'd properly redressed the decision-making process, and hoped that was all it would take. He feared that if he went further, hounding the various commanders for commitments to "follow the rules," he'd wind up insulting and alienating them, in addition to undermining Adar at a very bad time. He was walking a narrow tightrope, and wasn't sure what more he could do. He managed a conciliatory smile. "I don't think so, Mr. Chairman," he denied, "but we do need to get things straight." He leaned back in his chair. "All that said, *I* don't personally believe the sub was acting with the Grik. Think about it. If Gunny Horn really saw its periscope off Madras, and I guess he must have after all, it tailed us all the way from there to the point it attacked us. If it was working for the Grik, why wait? Why not strike where we were. It had more targets too, all at anchor. Hell, it could've got *Big Sal*, *Arracca*, *Baalkpan Bay*—who knows how bad it could've hurt us there. We sure weren't looking for *it*. Instead, it waited until our only possible destination was Madagascar. Why?"

That brought another round of discussion, but Courtney knocked on the table this time, with a flourish, peering about with his caterpillar eyebrows arched. He waited for silence, then looked at Matt. "The device you described on the vessel's conning tower—do you know what it was? I do."

Matt arched his own eyebrows in response.

"In short, it is an emblem I remember as having represented a faction of what essentially evolved into French *fascists*, known to have collaborated with the Nazis quite enthusiastically." He shook his head, eyes still wide. "Though this is the first I've ever heard of the symbol being displayed on any enemy ship or vehic e."

"Mr. Campeti was right," Chief Gray growled. "They were French Nazzys after all!"

"For all intents and pur ses," Courn ed.

"Maybe," Mat. ac ughtfully, bu nec

Gray grunted. "Well, if it really wa boat fulla French Nazzys, maybe it *did* just us because of lag

"But again, why wa t so long if that s th " Courtney pressed. "As Captain Reddy , there were far mo Madras flying the same flag."

"Perhaps it was ec ause, if ot necessarily in gue with our enemies, whoever was ab the vessel had so on to desire that this fleet draw no nearer m," Inquisitor Ch peculated. Everyone looked at him, consid g the implications.

"Hmm. A most amus ng theory," Courtney red. By the expressions and blinking around the table, Matt di t think anyone else thought it was funny. "And I do suspect Inquisitor Choon has the right of it," Courtney decided. "But that leaves the motive still in question. Why stop us from approaching the Grik capital, while remaining aloof from the Grik?"

"Because, whoever it was, they didn't necessarily want to *help* the Grik—as much as they wanted to prevent us from decisively hurting them," Herring proposed, rubbing his cheek.

"Very good, Commander Herring! Precisely," Courtney agreed enthusiastically. "Someone out there, besides the sodding Doms of course,

seems to think they have something to gain as long as we and the Grik keep tearing away at each other."

"But we killed 'em," Gray said. "So that's an end to them!"

"I would not be so sure," Choon murmured, his eyes blinking rapidly in contemplation. "Behavior such as has been proposed implies considerable understanding of the conflict underway. Understanding that must have taken time to achieve." He lowered his ears in apology. "I know little of military matters," he demurred. "I am no general or legate, after all. But even I cannot escape the conclusion that such a vessel and its crew should not have been willing to follow your fleet so far, expending valuable fuel and ultimately munitions—not to mention the final, fatal risk it undertook—unless it had some expectation of replenishment. Lingering animosity from a lost world does not strike me as sufficient reason to do these things. There's more here than meets the eye, and I suspect more 'French Naazzys,' or whatever they are, *must* be out there somewhere."

There was dead silence for a moment as they pondered that.

"So what do we do now?" Gray asked, his frustration evident.

Matt looked at them, examining each face. Finally, he squeezed Sandra's hand beneath the table and looked at Adar's expectant, pleading blinking.

"We proceed with the plan," he said at last. "*Carefully*," he stressed. "And unless these new guys have a *fleet* of subs, which I can't imagine, we've eliminated them from the equation. At least for now. We might as well do what we set out to do. If there are more enemies waiting for us out there, all the more reason to settle up with the ones we know about. Especially if that's what they least want us to do."

///// *Allied Expeditionary Force*
Indiaa
July 24, 1944

eneral Pete Alden slapped the tent flap aside
and bowled into his HQ like a rampaging bull.
He stopped just inside, blinking his gummy
eyes. He'd been up all night and had stretched
out at dawn—maybe twenty minutes before—
to have a short nap. *Perfect timing, as usual,* he
thought glumly. Comm-'Cats and staff person-
nel scattered when he stepped, frowning, toward the big table in the
center of the tent where General Muln Rolak sat with "General" Orochi
Niwa. Niwa still looked terrible, but the Japanese confidant of Halik, the
Grik general, was clearly, finally on the mend. Man and Lemurian both
stood, joined by Hij Geerki, who'd been crouching by Rolak's side.

"What the hell's going on?" Pete demanded, addressing Rolak. He
could hardly look at Niwa. The Japanese former special naval landing

force lieutenant was perfectly willing to tell them whatever they wanted to know about their enemy, and he'd supplied a lot of information. He was a lot like Geerki in that respect. He almost seemed to consider himself Rolak's "property" now. But Pete couldn't get over the man's making no bones about his *friendship* with Halik—a Grik!—and that whole notion gave Pete the heebie-jeebies.

"It would seem that Col-nol Daal-i-bor Svec and his disobedient Legionnaires have managed to provoke a real battle this time," Rolak replied, urbane as always.

"I did tell you," Niwa said, almost apologetically. "General Halik is no fool. He was bound to find a pattern to their raiding sooner or later. He has done so, and prepared a reception for your multispecies Czechs." He shook his head. "I would have thought that you should have convinced yourselves by now that he is no ordinary Grik, and done more to restrain Colonel Svec."

Pete glanced at Niwa impatiently. "Sure, we know that. That was why we *sent* Svec in where we did. Just didn't expect Halik to bite so quick." Niwa blinked at him in surprise, and Pete looked at his watch.

"Don't be offended, General Niwa," Rolak said soothingly. "*I* know you are trustworthy, but Gener-aal Aalden still harbors resentments from another war. He is not quite ready to unburden himself as freely around you as perhaps he should." It was more than that, of course, and even Rolak didn't trust Niwa as far as he could throw him when it came to planning actual operations against his friend. Whatever warped sense of duty had formed in Niwa's heart was such a confusing thing that Rolak wasn't entirely sure the man even remained sane, but he tried to foster the impression that he accepted Niwa at least as much as Geerki. Pete gazed at the map on the table and then stepped to the larger one painted directly on the wall of the tent.

"Have you alerted Sixth Corps?" he demanded.

"Of course. And Gener-aal Taa-leen moves my First Corps as we speak."

"Svec's movements are a deliberate deception? A *trap*?" Niwa asked as realization dawned. "You *lied* to General Halik about being unable to control him!" He shook his head. "The Grik are terrible creatures, but they do not lie—and you are breaking the truce!"

Pete's eyes bulged with fury when he turned on Niwa. "You listen to me! Don't you dare compare anything we do to those monsters out there! *We* didn't start this war, and *we* don't run around slaughterin' and eating everybody we run into, including our own. You need to snap out of whatever spell they've laid on you and shake back out into being a man! I know you're a Jap, and Japs are weird, but I've learned they're not all crazy either. Look at General Shinya! He's my friend not only because we fight on the same side, but because we're fighting on the *right* side." He took a breath. "I know you admire this Halik lizard, and maybe he's a peach compared to the rest, but that's also what makes him more dangerous to real people like us . . . and you! You've helped us because deep inside you know it's right—I hope—but you ain't a Grik, see? You just *ain't!*"

Pete turned to the map. "Svec's raids have always been part of the plan to keep your buddy off balance, keep him jumping and guessing. Based on what you've told us about Halik, and our own observations, we figured he'd get serious about slamming Svec sooner or later, especially if he thought we didn't care if he did. In doing so, he's left a gap, a big one, right in front of our very favorite pass that Svec never raided through, and we're about to jump right in it." Pete rubbed his face, cooling down. "And as for breaking the truce, and 'Grik don't lie,' what a load of crap! Halik lies at least as good as I do, and our air's confirmed he's been getting ready to hammer *us.* There never has been any trust! Good Lord, what a thought! This is *war*! All we're doing is getting on with the fight that got called off, on our terms, before Halik does it first." He cocked his head and looked at Niwa. "So, are you finally ready to shake off the scales, or feathers—whatever—and get on the team? The team with *people*? Or are you going to keep wallowing in the notion that they're just as good as us, only different? Who knows what we—or maybe Halik—might make of the Grik after we kill most of 'em, but right now killin' 'em is all we got." Pete sighed. "My question is, are you ready for that? We could use your help figuring out what Halik'll do next. And who knows? That might be the only way *not* to kill the bastard!"

Niwa sat silent, staring at Pete for what seemed a long time, and there was no way to know what thoughts clashed behind his dark, solemn eyes. Finally, he nodded. "I am ready," he said quietly. "And I will do what I can. I do know General Halik better than anyone, I suppose. But I must suggest you do your best *not* to kill him. You can't ever kill all the Grik in the world. You have not seen . . ." He shook his head. "In any event, someday you will need to speak to one again. Better that it should be one that has a grasp of reason."

General Halik snatched his breastplate off and checked himself for a wound. He was far enough from the fighting that he doubted he'd been deliberately targeted, and suspected the projectile that struck him must be a stray—but he could no longer be certain of that. There was only the slightest graze, but when he looked at the breastplate, he was stunned to see the terrible hole, low on the side, where it rode just above his hip. He slung the bronze object away. "Of what use is armor against such weapons?" he snarled. Nearly all the enemy he faced here now were armed with the curious breechloaders his friend Niwa once showed him, and Niwa had rightly foretold how dangerous they would be. The enemy had always possessed better weapons, but Grik numbers made up for that. Halik had grown to dislike such equations in a most un-Grik-like fashion, but had no choice but to embrace them. Now, for the first time, he was beginning to wonder if it would be enough.

"Armor makes the hole in your body bigger," General Ugla replied with a familiarity he would've never dreamed of using just a few months before. "I have seen it. Even the leather armor of our Uul warriors does the same. The enemy missiles distort when they hit, but do not stop."

"As do ours," Halik defended.

"But ours take much longer to shoot, are less likely to hit, and as you can see, this enemy—Alden's 'Czechs'—wear little armor at all," Ugla pointed out.

"His other, more numerous warriors wear leather over their brush-colored clothing," Halik maintained, "but all this is beside the point. It is the effectiveness of their new weapons that is significant. And even the 'uncontrollable' Czechs have them now," he added. "Further proof that Alden could not be as displeased with them as he implied. It is well that we are almost ready to end this farce of fierce opponents that do not fight!"

"We shall have the Czechs this time, Lord General," Ugla assured, gesturing at the battle. "There are but a few thousand of them, and the supply carts lured them out precisely as you predicted. We have cut them off from escape."

"Have we indeed?" Halik mused, looking back at the fighting himself. His plan to trap the raiders had gone almost too well—and it really shouldn't have. With the strange horned creatures they rode, they had far greater mobility, and Halik shouldn't have been able to catch the entire force. He couldn't have, he knew, if those that might've escaped hadn't chosen to remain with the others. Such was _loyalty_, a concept he'd learned from Niwa, and he actually admired his enemy just then. He knew _he_ could never abandon the army that had become his only real purpose in life. That was loyalty as well. "And at what cost?" he added. "Niwa was right about their weapons all along, and we shall lose three or four times as many Uul to destroy them as we would have before."

"We have more to lose," Ugla stated simply.

Halik glanced sharply at him. "Yes," he said at length, "but for how long?"

Ugla shifted uncomfortably and flicked his eyes nervously at the sky. "At least they have no artillery, and if they truly are not under Alden's control, we need not fear the enemy's flying machines. They have never interfered in our scuffles before."

"This is somewhat more than a 'scuffle,' General Ugla."

The firing intensified to a virtually continuous roar, and they stared down the gradual slope toward the surrounded force. It had formed into a rough square, as Halik had seen the enemy do before, and all the animals that bore them were inside the formation. White smoke drifted skyward in a solid cloud, and Halik could only guess at the dreadful casualties this, his northern force, was taking. They were shooting back, of course, with matchlock and crossbow, but even with his heavy corps—as Niwa had described this number of troops—all Halik's could do was mob around the enemy, and couldn't bring many more weapons to bear than they. Far inferior weapons. There could be only one outcome, particularly once the Uul came to grips with sword, spear, tooth, and claw, but these Czechs—human and Lemurian—were gutting Halik's northern force!

"Lord General!" cried a runner, as it flung itself at his feet.

"Rise," Halik ordered, "and report!"

"Lord General," the creature, a First of Two Hundreds—or "captain" by Niwa's definition—rose and pointed to the southeast. "General Shlook begs your attention! More Czech riders emerge from an undiscovered pass, and move to cut between the northern force and the hatchling host that stands before the enemy works in the gap!"

"There cannot be many of them," Halik said in a curious tone. "Why does he not simply destroy them?"

"But there *are* many, Lord General!" the captain almost wailed, and Halik examined him for signs he'd turned prey. *No,* he decided with satisfaction. *He is afraid, but* not *prey. I have formed this army better than the treacherous Kurokawa ever dreamed. All the more reason not to let it die!* "Far more than you surround here," the runner continued desperately, "and they advance before an even larger force of Alden's cavalry!"

Ugla hissed. Halik's crest rose, and he turned narrowed eyes back to the fight. "You must finish this quickly, General Ugla. If you can. I must see what is happening behind us. Show me!" he barked at the runner. Together, they sprinted off.

Halik stopped his guide at the top of another rise a little over a mile away. From there he had an excellent view of the vast prairie all around. The hill where he'd destroyed Colonel Flynn's courageous force (he allowed that ungrudgingly now) was another mile to the southwest, and beyond was Halik's entrenched and static middle force, composed of the hatchling host. His southern force was beyond, but it was the smallest of the three in direct contact with the enemy. A company of musketeers, likely sent by Ugla to protect him, joined them and deployed. Halik knew in an instant that there was no immediate threat to his person there, but his carefully planned strategy to deny Alden his superior mobility and open-field capabilities by keeping him bottled in the forests below the gap was doomed. Czech "raiders" and Allied cavalry were deploying in a line that extended almost to Flynn's hill, and unlimbering scores of guns! Even worse, dense columns of infantry were rushing up in support. Recognizing the flag of Rolak's I Corps in the lead, he hacked a bitter laugh.

Another runner scrambled up and flung himself to the ground. "Oh, do get up!" Halik groaned. "What is it now?"

The runner pointed behind to the north. He was just Uul, and his speech was awkward. "Lord General Ugla tells the . . . Chsshekks is git away! They git on their critchers an' break out our traph, lak they could has did when-epher they decide! He ask he come here?"

Halik hesitated. The enemy line was growing stronger by the moment, with ever more infantry swelling the position. Thousands of shovelfuls of dirt filled the air and began heaping up in front of it. Lemurian runners raced along, driving stakes and unspooling the insidious spiky wire as well. If he hit them *now*, he could beat them—but it simply couldn't happen. It would take more than an hour for Ugla to gather his already-battered northern force and bring it up—and it would be exhausted after the run and the previous fight. It wouldn't be in any kind of shape for another. And though the force was probably still more numerous than the enemy here, mere numbers meant nothing anymore.

The hatchling host was twice as big, but it was dug in to defend the high prairie of India from its trenches across the gap. They were utterly useless defenses against an attack from *this* direction! And no doubt, a large enough enemy force remained in the gap to exploit its flank if he changed its front. The southern force might come up . . . but where could he use it? Nowhere, in time. The enemy line was preparing to attack or defend, to the north or south, and there was nothing Halik could do! To underscore that, the drone of many motors became audible, and he looked up to see a large number of flying machines approaching from the east. He sagged and shook his head, realizing that this was the end. General Alden and General Rolak had already destroyed his army in his mind, and it was just a matter of moments before they began to do so in fact, on the field below. He was somewhat surprised that Rolak's artillery hadn't already opened up, to the south, at least. No reason why it shouldn't have; full batteries of six guns each (he'd learned that was how they reckoned such things) were poised to commence firing, their crews standing ready. He'd watched them load! Why didn't they just get on with it? In frustration, he started to command a general assault, of everything he had, at whatever was in front of it. It was an instinctual response, he knew, but what else remained? Suddenly, a strange thought struck him, however, and he paused, considering. *Could it really be?*

"Tell General Ugla"—he looked at the captain who had first fetched him—"and tell General Shlook, that Generals Alden and Rolak seem to have invited us to leave this place. If they do not attack, we will not, and we will withdraw to the west where we can reconsolidate all our forces."

"But Lord General!" the first runner protested.

"Do not question me!" Halik snarled. "We cannot prevail here. But Alden has taught me yet another lesson, I think, and we will find a place, eventually, to face him again!"

"We should pursue them! Slay them! Burn them!" Colonel Dalibor Svec ranted, spewing spittle on his luxuriant beard. Pete and Rolak dismounted from their meanies and approached the commander of the Czech Legion. On closer inspection, Svec's beard looked more battered, as did the rest of him and his officers. This was not unexpected considering the morning they'd had.

"You had the fight you've been spoiling for," Pete pointed out. "You should be happy."

"My legionnaires were the *only* ones who fought!"

Rolak glared at him and his tail swished menacingly. "Perhaps today, but our army has fought the Grik quite fiercely for a long, long time—at great cost, I must add—while your little band was content to watch and do nothing. Do not pose aggrieved before us!"

Svec was taken aback by Rolak's tone. Usually, the old Lemurian was so calm and reasonable.

"Rolak wants to chase 'em too, Svec," Pete said. "We all do. It might even be the best time for it. I'm sure we'd tear 'em up—for a while. But it'll take time to get the weight we need to finish the job up through the Rocky Gap—and that's the only way to really bring it." He gestured around. "It's taken weeks to plan this breakout, and stage this much artillery in the passes—and it just isn't enough. We do have a major advantage over Halik in the open. He can't maneuver near as fast or coordinate as well. We can catch him whenever we want and force a fight if we have to."

Svec waved at the sky, and by implication all the Nancys and Fleashooters that still swooped about. "But why just let him go? You can still savage him as he retreats!"

"Sure, and lose a lot of planes and pilots to his antiair mortars. They're getting a lot better with those things. What it boils down to is that he's going to be too strung out for a while to make it worth the losses we'd take. Let him bunch back up." He paused. "Besides, I've got some thinking to do about Halik. He could've made it hell for us here if he'd wanted to, even if he lost in the end. That makes me think he's taking a long view of things—and maybe losses don't appeal that much to him either anymore. We might use that. He also has to know we could've clobbered him as he withdrew, and he's got to be wondering why we didn't. He's way too sneaky, and I like to keep him guessing." He shrugged. "And something Niwa said just before we came up has left me wondering," he confessed. "Our blockade of western India's holding pretty tight, and not much is getting through. A lot of what the Grik are sending him might even be getting snapped up by Kurokawa, if he really has run wild. Either way, Halik's essentially cut off, except from supplies that might be arriving overland, across Arabia. He knows about radio, but has no rapid communications of his own, so he won't know squat about anything else that's going on—particularly the results of Captain Reddy's raid. We might use that too. In the long run, with his hatred of Kurokawa and his way different notions of things than other Grik we've run into, it's just possible Halik might wind up more dangerous to our enemies than he is to us!"

"You can't be considering an *alliance*!" Rolak rounded, incredulous.

"Of course not. And Colonel Svec and our cav can keep dogging him all they want, if they haven't had enough fighting today. I've no doubt we'll eventually have to kill General Halik, but in the meantime it might be interesting to see what he does on his own for a while."

att watched Tikker's half-dozen Nancys straggle in from their various scouts over Madagascar and set down, one by one, alongside *Big Sal.* They were recovered as they arrived, and none had been lost. Just sending them to have a look was a very big risk, but they had to have *some* idea what was waiting for them. There was a chance the planes had alerted the Grik, but even if they'd been seen or heard, there was bound to be considerable confusion over their sudden appearance in sacred skies. As far as they knew, nobody on Madagascar had ever seen an airplane before, and if they had, or from descriptions had figured out what they were, Matt hoped it would take some time for the shock of actually seeing them to translate into any real action.

Donaghey had been sent once more—still painted red—to cruise along the Grik coast and report any contacts. She'd also served as a waypoint for the planes. No report from her was considered a good thing, and now that the last Nancy had returned, she was finally free to proceed south on the next leg of her mission. The fate of *Sineaa* was still unknown, but she was presumed lost. Matt hated that *Donaghey* would be so alone, but hoped he could send one of Des-Ron 6's DDs to join her at the Republic's capital of Alex-aandra after this operation was complete. He couldn't help but feel a pang of worry for Greg Garrett and his crew. The kid was the best they had, and if anyone could weather the cape in a dedicated sailor, Greg was the guy. But he'd forever remain the somewhat gangly, anxious young man Matt first met as *Walker*'s new gunnery officer in the mind's eye of his former skipper. *Well*, he thought, *we'll be able to use the wireless again in a few days, one way or the other, and I can send him a proper good-bye.*

"That's the last one, Skipper," Gray proclaimed as the final plane was lifted, dripping water, onto the flight deck of the mighty carrier/Home. Matt stepped away from *Walker*'s starboard bridgewing and moved back into the pilothouse. "Bring us alongside *Salissa*, if you please," he told Rosen, who had the conn. Then he turned to Minnie. "Pass the word for Commanders McFarlane and Herring to join me in the wardroom, and have the cox'n stand by the motor launch. We'll be going aboard *Big Sal* directly."

This would be the last meeting before the first Lemurians in uncounted centuries set foot on the ancestral land of Madagascar, and Adar was practically giddy with excitement. He was seated beside Keje at the head of the big table in Keje's conference room. Matt sat with Sandra in their usual place nearby, and Spanky and Simon Herring were beside them. Farther down was Major Alistair Jindal, the Imperial commander of the 21st AEF Regiment, attached to the 1st Raider Brigade. His counterpart, Risa-Sab-At, commanding the 3rd Regiment, wasn't present, but she could rely on her brother, Chack, to brief her. She was busy preparing the brigade for its role in the upcoming operation. Nial-Ras-Kavaat, of *Haakar-Faask*, sat awkwardly on the stool beyond Jindal. He was to be in charge of a detachment of the DD squadron, and bold as he was known to be in battle, he appeared somewhat nervous in this setting.

On the other side of the table were Kapitan Von Melhausen, finally well enough to attend, and Kapitan Leutnant Becher Lange. Atlaan-Fas, *Salissa*'s nominal commander, and Sandy Newman, his exec, were next. Sitting beside them were Lieutenant Colonel Chack-Sab-At, General Queen Safir Maraan, Tikker, and Irvin Laumer. At the foot of the table were Courtney Bradford and Inquisitor Choon, engaged in a lively discussion about burrowing insects. Crowded in beside them, and oblivious to everything but the great map of Madagascar on the bulkhead behind Keje and Adar—the map he'd helped draw—was Lieutenant Toryu Miyata. It was a compilation of old American charts, from *Walker*'s meager reserves, Grik maps and charts captured at Madras, and Toryu's memory. He was fairly familiar with the capital, where the Celestial Palace lay. Describing it had been his greatest contribution. He didn't know the Grik name for the place, but that hardly mattered. Everyone was calling it "Grik City," anyway. He noticed there'd been some hasty additions since the scouting mission returned, and was glad some of those reinforced his earlier assumptions.

Nothing of significance had been discussed so far; that was the way of things at Keje's table. But the meal was over and the stewards were removing the remains and filling mugs with refreshments those in attendance were known to prefer. Now would begin the final briefings and deliberations concerning Operation "Skuggik Nest," and Matt felt Sandra's hand find his under the table. He looked at her. The strange distance that came and went between them wasn't in evidence tonight, and though he was glad, he wondered why. He still couldn't imagine what he'd done to upset her, and when pressed, she either said it was "nothing," or hadn't seemed able to explain. It wasn't important just then. They were together, and that was all that mattered.

"A toast!" Adar proclaimed, standing and raising his mug. "A toast to victory!"

Matt hurried to rise and extended his mug. As usual, there was nothing in his but the rich Lemurian beer. "I'll drink to that," he said pleasantly, "as long as everyone remembers that our definition of 'victory' is to raise as much hell as we possibly can, with the fewest losses in troops, ships, and aircraft," he stressed again. Everyone stood and took a sip. "Indeed," Adar agreed with slightly tempered enthusiasm. "But surely, after the return of COFO Tikker's scout, there is reason to hope we might accomplish much more."

"Maybe," Matt allowed, looking at the commander of *Salissa*'s 1st Air Wing. "But we've got to remain cautious." He held up a hand. "Sure, I know I haven't always been the one suggesting that in the past. . . ." There were polite chuckles. "But this *is* a different deal. We don't *have* to do this to survive. But this task force and its people . . . Well, it just can't be replaced. I'm not talking numbers alone; I'm talking experience and talent." He glanced around, smiling, but blinking fond sadness in the Lemurian way. "This is the cream of the crop in so many ways, and we can't spare any of you." He took a breath and started to say more; then he shook his head and sat.

"My brother Cap-i-taan Reddy is right, of course," Keje growled, blinking at Adar, "and we must bear that always in our thoughts." He'd remained standing, and now paced to the great map. "If I may?" he asked, and Matt nodded. "According to Grik charts, and now direct observation"—Keje blinked at Tikker—"we know the enemy maintains four separate, um, enclaves, upon our ancestral homeland, all in the North and West. Apparently Lieuten-aant Miyaata was correct when he surmised that the vast majority of Madagaascar has been maintained as a kind of preserve. For what purpose, remains unclear."

"Most welcome news indeed," Courtney Bradford enthused. "Perhaps even some remnant of the indigenous population still remains. Certainly there must be a few examples, at least, of native flora and fauna!"

"That *is* an exciting prospect," Choon agreed.

"Um . . . of course," Keje allowed. "But the most pertinent point at present is that the enclaves are relatively isolated, not only from the mainland of Africaa, across the strait to the west, but even from one another. Cap-i-taan Jis-Tikkar?"

Tikker stood and joined Keje at the map. "We were careful," he said, "and though I can't guarantee it, I don't think we were any of us spotted.

Ahd-mi-raal Keje is correct, however. Of the four Grik population centers we observed, only the two in the far north are within reach of each other. The other two are farther down the coast."

"You used the term 'enclave,'" Von Melhausen observed, his ancient eyes staring at the map, his fingers twisting his white mustache. "What do you mean by that?"

Tikker shrugged and looked at Keje. "Precisely that, if my understanding of the term is correct. Each city is surrounded on its inland side by a great, tall . . . well, wall of some kind, made of mighty trees, in the same way we have protected Baalkpan from the predators of the jungles of Borno. Only these are much larger, and many miles long, in fact."

"Like the big wall erected to protect the natives from King Kong," Herring muttered thoughtfully. "Except this one's not made of stone. . . ." Tikker didn't understand the reference, but nodded. "One must assume it is designed to keep Grik within, or something else out," he agreed. "That would add further credence to Lieutenant Miyata's theory that the bulk of our homeland remains a preserve of some sort." He blinked consternation. "A great many large monsters were reported grazing on the central plain, but nothing of the interior of the jungle could be seen. There is no telling what abides there."

"Whatever it is, we can handle it," Chack assured, and Matt stared at him. Chack caught his gaze and shrugged. "We *can*," he added forcefully.

"Tell us more about these 'walls,'" Matt instructed.

"They're big," Tikker repeated, "heavily constructed of what look like Galla trees, and as I said, they go for miles."

"Do they look like Chack's command will have any difficulty scaling them?"

"I shouldn't think so, sir."

"Which means Grik can climb them too, so they're most likely designed to keep things out, not in. Maybe big things," Sandra mused, speaking for the first time, while absently stroking Petey's small head. The ridiculous creature had been sated by a constant stream of morsels from Sandra's plate during the meal and had behaved himself amazingly well under the circumstances. Now he lay curled, in his usual spot around the back of Sandra's neck, fast asleep.

"I guess so," Tikker concurred. He looked at Chack. "I hope you really can handle whatever that stockade is meant to keep out!"

"The First Raider Brigade will avoid whatever it is, or kill it," Chack said simply.

Matt hoped he was right. "What other defenses did you see?" Matt questioned.

"Not much," Tikker admitted. "No trenches or barricades, if that's what you mean. And we stayed high over the cities, as ordered, so it was hard to tell. There seem to be more guns around the main harbor than Miyata remembered, and there were quite a few Grik milling around in the city. No telling how many were warriors. There do seem to be a number of new parade grounds, though. Many more than Toryu remembered."

"They may be training grounds for the 'new' Grik that General Alden has reported in India," Jindal suggested. "If so, they could provide a nasty surprise indeed."

Herring frowned. "Yes," he said. "And why not? They must come from somewhere, and it strikes me personally that it is more likely they'd come from here than other parts of the Grik Empire."

Matt looked at him questioningly, and Herring chuckled darkly. "We know so little, but whatever training regimen they have established simply cannot be available to all Grik yet, and our man Niwa is certain Halik came from here." He looked speculatively at Tikker. "You saw no massed troop movements?"

"No, and I overflew Grik City myself."

"Hmm. I don't suppose he could do it again?" The question was directed at Matt.

"No. Once was potentially warning enough. I'd rather face ten thousand of 'em with surprise on my side than a hundred who know we're coming." He looked back at Tikker. "You'll keep scouting the proposed landing site for Chack's Brigade, but stay away from Grik City. Now, what about the ships you saw in the harbor. What were they?"

Tikker blinked displeasure. "I believe six of their ironclad baattle waagons were present there, at least. There may have been more."

"I doubt it," Courtney proclaimed. "Like most evil things, they do tend to come in threes. Or multiples of three!"

Matt nodded. "Seems pretty universal with them. What else?"

"A couple hundreds of those Indiaman-type ships, so there probably are some troops. And at least a dozen of their ironclad cruiser things."

"Hmm. Those bother me as much as the BBs," Matt allowed. "Their guns are nearly as big, and they're more maneuverable. We've never had to face them ship to ship before either. Not at close range. We'll have to take care of those."

"So the plan remains essentially unchanged?" Adar pressed.

"We'll have to tweak it a bit, and I'm less sure about the role we envisioned for Chack's Brigade. It seems riskier now. But yeah, we'll still land Second Corps as originally planned, and *Walker* will lead our surface elements into the bay to neutralize the enemy fleet and provide artillery support for the ground forces."

"But what about me?" Keje demanded. "What of *Salissa*?" Matt looked at Keje and couldn't stop a grin from forming. "You, Admiral, will stay the hell out of range of anything they can throw at you from shore, and keep your planes in the air."

"And me, Skipper?" Laumer asked, his tone quiet. Matt's grin faded. "You'll take your PTs in with me. Our first priority is the BBs."

"And we will join you in the fight with *Amerika*, just as soon as we off-load the troops!" Von Melhausen exclaimed.

"No, Herr Kapitan, I'm afraid you mustn't do that. I need you to stay with *Salissa* and help protect her from anything unexpected. Your ship is faster than her, and she may need you." He paused. "And besides, if we need to get everybody out in a hurry, we'll need you for that as well."

"The plan remains as sound as when we first discussed it," Adar gushed before Von Melhausen or Lange could object. "And your cautionary points are also well taken, Cap-i-taan Reddy." He looked around the room, blinking his large silver eyes. "But despite what you said earlier, I propose that we *must* do this thing in order to survive, and we have no more choice than we did in the Battle for Baalkpan. Only the immediacy of the outcome is at variance here. You have said yourself that we cannot be forever reacting to the Grik. We must force them to react to us. What better way to make them do that than to savage their seat of power? Our cause, and most likely our very lives most assuredly do, eventually, depend on how successfully we prosecute this operation." He looked back at Matt. "That is my . . . counsel, for what it is worth. My *order*, as chairman of all the Homes united beneath or beside the Banner of the Trees, the 'Union' Mr. Letts has made, is that we proceed with the original plan, but watch closely for . . . opportunities to press the attack!" He glanced at Matt's growing frown. "If you see any such, report them to Cap-i-taan Reddy at once, so *he* can decide whether or not to pursue them." He sighed deeply. "I have a definite . . . sense, an almost heavenly conviction, that if we *can* press this attack, we will break the Grik here—and possibly everywhere!"

Matt and Sandra visited the stateroom set aside for them to change out of their formal dress before taking a stroll together on the hangar deck. The din was just as great as before, maybe greater, since Keje had declared he wanted every plane aboard ready for the upcoming fight. Squads of Raiders or Marines double-timed through the live and inanimate obstacles, just as they did so often. Neither Chack nor Safir wanted to take any chances that their troops had grown soft during the long voyage. Whichever unit they belonged to, there was no doubt they were in for a strenuous time ashore. Matt pointed at a vast opening in the side, and they eased that way so they could talk without being run down or otherwise interrupted. For a long moment, they just stood together, side by side, watching the sea churn away from *Salissa*'s mighty bulk. In the middle distance, *Walker* doggedly loped along, the gentle swells making her ride seem much more boisterous. Soon, she would ease back alongside, and Matt and the others who crossed with him would go back aboard the old destroyer. In the meantime, he was content just to spend a few moments alone with his wife. He would have been, at least, if he had the slightest idea what it was that had come between them. He contemplated just asking her—but what should he ask? "What's the matter" was far too broad, and invited any number of responses that likely wouldn't get to the bottom of things. "Are you mad at me?" was equally vague. Matt knew that, due to circumstances beyond their control, Sandra always harbored some slight resentments. That was only natural. She was unhappy with Matt's regulations that prevented her from joining him on *Walker*. She disliked *Walker*'s role in the upcoming fight. Most of all, she hated the war that kept them apart and forced them all into harm's way so often. Asking what she was angry about would not be productive. Finally, Matt just put his arm around her and sighed, deciding not to bring it up at all.

"Adar might be right," he said at last, giving voice to the other subject that was bothering him, "but I wish he'd quit sending mixed signals like that."

"Me too," Sandra agreed, leaning into him. "There's always a difference between what he says and what he implies lately," she added. "He says, 'Follow the plan,' or 'Captain Reddy's orders,' but then implies that he wants everybody to go for broke."

"Can't really blame him."

"No, but it . . . worries me, and leaves me confused about what he really expects out of all this. We all know what he *wants*. I think everybody wants the same thing. But what does he *expect*?"

"What do you think?"

Sandra frowned. "I think he expects to take the place—and keep it. No matter what." She looked up at him, her eyes searching his. "You've given him so many victories, Matthew, he's *expecting* another one, the biggest one of all."

"It could happen," Matt murmured in her hair. "But at least he stressed that any modifications to the basic plan had to come through me. I've been a little worried he was encouraging everybody to just have at the Grik on Madagascar, on their own, and the devil take the hindmost."

"He *has* been, Matthew," Sandra whispered. "Not in so many words, but his . . . enthusiasm has been contagious."

A chill went down Matt's back. He thought over what Adar said, and it did suddenly sound, in his mind, more like a pep speech with an arbitrary "oh, by the way" thrown in. "He gave an order, and all those commanders, Chack, Safir, they're our *friends*. They'll do the right thing."

"Will they?" Sandra asked sadly. "*Can* they, this time? Madagascar's like the Holy Land to them, and if they . . ." She stopped herself. "Just be careful, darling," she said, "and be watchful."

"I will."

They settled into a companionable silence for several moments, but then Sandra suddenly took a step away and faced him. "I'm pregnant," she blurted defiantly, and Matt almost jumped out of his skin.

"What?" he demanded, incredulous.

"I'm pregnant," Sandra repeated more softly.

Matt could feel the blood rushing in his ears. "Okay. Wow. I mean, how?"

Sandra snorted a laugh. "The usual way, I assure you!"

Matt's face turned beet red. "Sure, I know. I mean . . . well, sure. I meant to ask *when*, I guess. How long have you known?" A smile started to spread across his face. "A kid! Me! I'm going to have a kid! I mean, *we're* going to have one. . . ." He shook his head and grabbed her, squeezing her tight against him. "So that's why you've been so sore at me!"

"I haven't been sore," Sandra denied, then shrugged. "Just maybe a little . . . uncomfortable, for not telling you for so long."

"How long?" he repeated. "I mean, when did you figure it out?"

"About the time we left Andaman Island, before the second Battle of Madras."

He stared at her. "And you didn't tell me for . . . shoot, nearly *two months*! Why?"

She looked squarely at him in the deepening gloom of the setting sun. "Because you would've made me stay behind," she said simply, and Matt knew it was true. She usually got her way when it came to most anything, but he would've put his foot down about this. And here she was!

"You're damn right I would have," he admitted. "Still should! I should send you home right now!"

"In what? One of the DDs you're about to need so badly? That's just silly!"

"And it was irresponsible of you to come along in your condition!"

"Irresponsible?" Sandra flared. "I'm pregnant, not crippled! And since I'm a doctor, it would've been irresponsible to stay behind." Her temper was beginning to mount, but then she caught herself and sagged hard against him. "Maybe it was," she admitted softly. "Maybe I should've stayed behind, at least at Madras. But I wasn't about to let you run off on this stunt without me—without us," she emphasized, patting her stomach. "We've always been in it together, through thick and thin, ever since the start. Our child will be in it too, eventually, one way or the other. Might as well get him—or her—used to the idea right from the start."

He put both arms around her and hugged her to his chest. "Irresponsible," he repeated softly, "but maybe right too. I always do better when you're around. Just promise you'll stay aboard *Big Sal*! No running off ashore to field hospitals and such, not this time."

"I promise, Matthew," she whispered into his collar. "There'll probably be plenty to do aboard here before all's said and done anyway."

He released her and took a step back, his face finding it impossible to decide whether to smile or frown. He finally clenched his jaw for a moment to get control of it.

"What's the matter?" Sandra asked.

"Oh, nothing." He waved around and managed a wry smile at last. "Everything. This isn't exactly how I ever imagined getting the news that I'm going to be a father—and damn sure not the circumstances I ever figured my wife would be in when she told me!"

"Are you really upset?"

"No!" he assured her firmly. "And yes," he admitted. "I'm still mad you didn't tell me sooner, and I'm scared to death for you, our child— for everything! I'm not used to that. Going into a fight with all that on my mind . . ."

"This isn't the first time the stakes have been high," Sandra pointed out.

"Yeah, but what you told me makes them a lot higher for me personally. You know that."

Sandra shrugged. "Maybe telling you now was my way of making you be more careful this time!"

Matt nodded thoughtfully, then sighed. "But Jesus. What if we lose? What if everything finally comes unwrapped? It could, you know. We know less about what we're jumping off into than ever this time!"

"Maybe. But again, you've done it before," Sandra told him confidently. "You'll sort it out."

"But what if, this time, it just can't be sorted out?"

Sandra cupped his face with her hand. "Quit saying that. You'll do it. And if you can't? You get out. Period. Don't put yourself in a *position* to lose!"

Matt nodded, but he knew it wasn't always that simple. So did Sandra.

Spanky appeared behind Matt, and Sandra nodded at him.

"Sorry to interrupt, Skipper, but our ride's back." He looked over the rail at the gathering darkness. "Crossin' the water in an open boat on this freaky sea gives me the creeps at the best of times, but it's getting dark. Wind's freshening too, and I'd just as soon we hurry up."

Matt chuckled. "Right behind you, Spanky." They moved to the long stairway that had been lowered almost to the water and gazed down at the barge. Chief Gray had taken personal charge of the boat and Silva was with him, armed with a BAR "just in case the fishies get frisky." Spanky and Herring trooped down the stairs, and Matt paused a moment to embrace his wife once more. Petey chose that moment to wake up, and blearily scrambled onto Matt's shoulder.

"What?" Matt reached to dislodge the creature, which, now probably more awake and suddenly disoriented, bit him. "Damn! You little . . . ," snapped Matt, and jerked his finger away. Idiot that he was, Petey didn't think to turn loose of the offending finger until it slung him out over the water.

"No!" Sandra cried.

"Noooooo!" Petey screeched, extending his limbs and catching the air with the membranes stretched between them. He tried to glide back around and make the deck, but he didn't have the altitude or airspeed.

"Make for the stairs, you lizardy little gnat!" Silva boomed up from below. Petey apparently tried but couldn't turn that sharply. Instead, he dove for the boat. "Si-va!" he chirped, obviously recognizing the big man.

"No! You ain't comin' aboard *here*!" Silva protested, just as Petey slammed into his shoulder, digging in his claws.

"Si-va!" Petey chirped with relief, just as he squirted a foul-smelling stream over the side from a slit on the bottom of his tail. Dennis grabbed him. "God-*damn*! Leggo, you little creep!"

"Goddam creep!" Petey wailed.

"Here, Mrs. Minister, uh, Reddy!" Silva shouted, still tugging at Petey, trying to disengage him. "I'll flip him back up there by his legs!"

"No, Silva!" Sandra cried down, just as Petey shrieked, "Noooo! Goddamn!" and fastened onto Silva's arm as well.

"Let go!"

"Pitch him over on the stairs," Gray griped. "Quit foolin' around with that thing!"

"He won't let go, I tell ya!"

Above, Sandra began to laugh, both hands covering her mouth. "It seems the Governor-Empress Rebecca McDonald's little friend has chosen a new playmate!" she managed. "You keep him for a while, Chief Silva. He'll definitely enjoy himself more in your capable hands."

"My hands are about to twist his little head off!" he hollered back. "Beggin' yer pardon. But . . . what the hell am I gonna *do* with him?"

"Now, now. Remember how the Governor-Empress dotes on him," Sandra warned. "I expect you to take good care of him. And who knows? Maybe he'll even make himself useful!"

"But . . . ," Silva started, attempting to reply.

Matt was laughing too, when he joined the others in the boat, waving back at his wife. He knew he hadn't fully absorbed the news he was going to be a father, but his spirits were still running high. "Maybe he'll come in handy for *something*," he said aside, his happy mood crushing Silva's even further.

"As a snack for Larry, most likely!" Dennis warned darkly. "If I don't eat him first," he added more softly, finally prying the little tree-glider off his arm.

"Eat?" Petey inquired, a little more politely than usual.

////// *The Celestial Palace*
Grik Madagascar

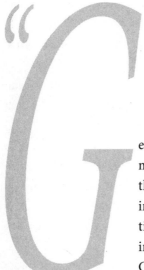

eneral Esshk has arrived, and craves to be admitted into your divine presence," mumbled the Chooser against the stone steps approaching the massive, saddlelike throne of the Celestial Mother of All the Grik. The Chooser had increasingly become the closest advisor to the Giver of Life, with the death of Lord Regent Tsalka, the absence of General of the Sea Kurokawa, and with Esshk himself most often on the continent. He'd been expanding the training grounds where they formed "new" warriors for the Great Hunt, either elevated or bred as such, for some time. The Chooser considered himself poorly equipped for the task. He was the High Doyen of his order, but his former duties had always been limited largely to choosing which hatchlings had the greatest potential to become aggressive warriors, and designating the rest to be culled for food. That occupation had largely ended with this current hunt, this "war," for which formerly culled hatchlings were raised and trained for defensive combat— something that had never occurred to any Grik before Kurokawa suggested it.

The Chooser retained influence by pretending to have the ability to divine further specialties the hatchlings might be suited for, as well as pretending—again—to possess Kurokawa's trust, and special insights into the creature's character. That was becoming problematic since no one, least of all the Chooser, had any idea what Kurokawa was up to now, or even if he lived. All they knew was that all the Grik forces in India had been dealt a severe setback. They wouldn't even know that if a couple of zeppelin crews hadn't escaped the slaughter of airships and somehow made it to the northern reaches of the Sacred Lands. No ships had returned, and no one had anything like a complete picture of the current disposition of Kurokawa's fleet, or General Halik's army. More forces and supplies continued to be sent, but it wasn't even known if they were getting through.

"General Esshk is here?" demanded the Giver of Life. The Celestial Mother was an immense creature, easily three times the size of an adult male Grik. Her plumage was a deep, reddish gold, almost copper, and covered a form so majestically obese that the slightest movement had to be remarkably difficult. Her long, unused claws were gilded just now, though they were often painted with amazing skill and artistry. Her teeth glistened, like iridescent pearls, and great jowls drooped alongside her toothy jaws, quivering with each word she spoke.

"Indeed, Your Magnificence. He just arrived."

The Celestial Mother considered that. "I wonder what brings him," she pondered aloud. "Of course you must allow him into my presence, but I do hope he produces no more tedious speculations!" She rolled her eyes to one of her female attendants, nearly as large as she. "I do *so* mislike tedious speculations!"

"At once, Your Magnificence," the Chooser cried, rising to his feet. "I shall fetch him myself!"

Shortly, General Esshk, first general of all the Grik, strode into the chamber accompanied by a small escort, all disarmed, and cast himself on the worn stones at the foot of the throne with a soft chink and scrape of armor. The Chooser joined him on the floor once more, and after an appropriate moment for the Celestial Mother to scrutinize his appearance, and sufficient dread to rise in his breast, she waved a taloned finger. "Rise, First General Esshk!" she said imperiously. "All of you. Rise and face me."

The visitors complied, and Esshk swept his scarlet cape aside with a courtly flourish that left it hanging down the left side of his tail. He'd already removed the ornate bronze helmet and equally well-crafted sword he usually wore. The Celestial Mother paused, her eyes absorbing his familiar, powerful frame. He'd always been her favorite littermate, after all. As such, it was such a terrible shame he could never become a regent consort himself. . . . When she spoke again, her voice was more congenial.

"It is *good* to see you, my general," she said, "but I must ask why you thought it necessary to come here yourself. The trainers you designated are proceeding competently, are they not? The greater armies in the Sacred Lands surely need you more?"

"I come bearing news, observations, and impressions. Perhaps now a warning, based on what I learned when I arrived. None of this would I trust to the tongue of another. The greater armies on the continent are secure at present, though one of my observations involves reports of curious activity on the part of the other hunters in the south. We never received a reply from them regarding our offer that they join the Great Hunt, yet it appears their meager armies are massing on the frontier! Most curious."

"Perhaps they still mean to join us?"

"It must be so, for they cannot hope to harm us. I will continue to monitor their movements, and watch for an overture of some sort. We know so little about them!"

The Giver of Life shivered dramatically, imagining the, to any Grik, frigid wasteland the southern hunters called home. The only reason the Grik had not swept them away long before was that they simply didn't want their land. "Perhaps they come slowly to the hunt, accustoming themselves to a more reasonable climate?"

"Perhaps. In any event, I shall wait and see what they do. There is no point in going to them if they are coming to us." He glanced at the Chooser. "Otherwise, the trainers here do seem competent, from what little I have seen," Esshk allowed. "Though most of the warriors they form are dispatched directly from here to General Halik in India. That is another of the reasons I desired this meeting—besides simply craving your lustrous gaze upon me."

The Celestial Mother shifted with pleasure on her throne. "Very well then, General Esshk. Bask in my favor, and explain what troubles you about our current deployments."

Esshk bowed. "Of course. Essentially, in light of our having heard nothing from Halik or Kurokawa, I believe we should *stop* sending elements of the new host to join them, at least until we know more of the situation there."

The Celestial Mother leaned away. "You suspect disaster there?" she asked tonelessly.

"I must *suspect* it, Your Magnificence," Esshk said. "We already know General of the Sea Kurokawa suffered an . . . inconvenience, at sea, and we have heard no more from him."

"You think he was destroyed?"

"I cannot know what to think," Esshk confessed, "but we have long suspected"—he glanced at the Chooser again—"that Kurokawa possesses a means of communication he never shared. I suspect another of his devices, that somehow sends and receives messages of some kind across . . . impossible distances. I am reinforced in this belief by the fact that, even before word first arrived of the battles in India, nearly all the Jaaph hunters that had been supervising our industrial toils suddenly vanished—presumably to gather at their sovereign nest at Zanzibar. I cannot help but think that, whether Kurokawa was destroyed or not, his Jaaphs may know something we do not."

"Should we investigate?"

"Surely," Esshk said, "but that brings me to my warning. I have heard upon my arrival here of a possibly more pressing concern."

"Indeed?" the Celestial Mother inquired.

"Indeed," Esshk agreed. He was not surprised the Giver of Life had not heard. Who would tell her? "One of the trainers of the new Host here was part of the Invincible Swarm that accompanied me to the enemy lands and fought as Uul at the Battle of Baalkpan. He has since been elevated, of course, but retains memories of his earlier life." He paused. "I have often described the flying machine the enemy used in that battle, and compared it to those the Jaaph hunters have designed." The Giver of Life gestured him to continue. "Well, by reports we received from General Halik early on, he faced similar, if smaller machines in India that were most troublesome at times."

"Yes, yes, I am aware."

"But you obviously are not aware that such a machine might well have been seen, soaring high above this very city just days ago."

The Celestial Mother leaned forward again. "That I did *not* know," she acknowledged. "Was this sighting confirmed?" she demanded, staring at the Chooser now.

"No, Your Magnificence!" the Chooser cried in distress. "I did not see it, nor did any Hij of note. Most of those who *thought* they saw it were ridiculously unreliable creatures, and it—whatever it was—remained so high that describing it in detail was impossible." He glared accusingly at Esshk. "Only a very few seemed certain, so it was not worthy of your concern."

"Those 'very few' were the only ones who had seen such a thing before," Esshk shot back. He faced the Celestial Mother once more. "If it was a machine of the enemy, I am informed that it cannot have flown by itself from where they are known to be, all the way to this place. They require fuel, just as our airships do, and a place to be when they are not flying. That can only mean that some force, possibly considerable, has drawn near enough to establish, or serve as its base!"

"Impossible!" the Chooser stated emphatically. "The prey—I mean, the 'enemy' cannot possibly have eluded detection all this way along our very coast in a single ship, much less a force of any size sufficient to cause alarm!"

"I agree," Esshk said mildly, "but you underestimate our enemy. I shall never do so again. I submit that they may have crossed the center of the terrible sea to come at this place, and we must prepare accordingly."

"Crossed the terrible sea!" the Chooser chortled. "How? Nothing and no one can do such a thing. Even if they were so foolish, barely one ship in ten—two tens!—could have survived the passage! There are not enough prey in all the world to sustain such losses and remain a threat to us!"

"Nevertheless," Esshk said, "I believe I should remain here for a time and supervise the latest levy of the New Host. Consider it an exercise. We will pretend that the enemy has somehow managed to find its way here, and I will act as though our warriors must quickly prepare to meet an equal force. We cannot leave such a thing to chance."

The Celestial Mother growled deep in her throat. "Oh, very well, First General Esshk. Do as you will. No doubt the New Host will benefit from the further training at the very least." She paused. "But what if you are right? What should we do?"

"Slay them as they land," Esshk said simply. "I have never personally designed a 'defensive' battle before, but the description General Halik sent some months back of the enemy 'trenchworks' in India does interest me. Halik considered them formidable, so I may employ them here." He paused, trying to imagine *how* an enemy might attack the Celestial City. Never in his life had he even contemplated such a thing. The trackless jungle beyond the Great Barricade to the south was impenetrable, of course, and there was a powerful fleet at anchor in the bay. It struck him that if the city was vulnerable, it could only be from the east or west. He'd have to split his forces and dig trenches to guard both directions—or would he? Grik were accustomed to launching multipronged attacks, and apparently so was the enemy. But the western approaches teemed with shipping, and they'd surely get *some* warning if the enemy came from that direction, even if only by an absence of ships entering the harbor. He decided to concentrate his better warriors east of the city, where they'd get no warning at all, and try to keep them ready for anything.

He'd fortify the western trenches with ordinary Uul warriors and leaven them with thoughtful, "elevated" leaders. There they would stay unless desperately needed. Defending would confuse them enough, and they were far more difficult to move in any case. There should be sufficient warning to shift other warriors to bolster them if the need arose. *Designing a defensive battle is not so hard,* he thought, *once one puts his mind to it. Quite similar to simply blocking an enemy's blows in combat. One should be able to do it without thinking, with a little practice.* He looked at his Giver of Life and practically shivered with a strange foreboding. *But what if it is not so simple as it seems?* He coughed politely. "As a further precaution, Your Magnificence, I must advise that you move your throne to the Sacred Lands on the continent. Just until these concerns are past. Enjoy a pleasant respite from your duties here."

The Celestial Mother managed a gurgling chuckle. "Really, General Esshk! I am the Giver of Life. I shall not flee from fantasies! And besides," she added cheerfully, "I would never fit through the passageways to board a ship! Such a movement would be most tiresome and uncomfortable!"

CHAPTER

22

////// *First Fleet South*
July 29, 1944

USS *Walker* eased slowly, carefully shoreward on a calm sea, beneath a meager moon. The only sounds within the confines of the darkened pilothouse were the rumbling blower and soft commands and acknowledgments of Spanky McFarlane, who had the conn, and the Lemurian helmsman. Periodic, muted cries rose from the fo'c'sle declaring the depth Chief Gray's detail found with the lead. Steaming in column in *Walker*'s wake were the DDs of Des-Ron 6, now carrying the entire 1st Raider Brigade. Soon they would anchor, and swarms of broad-beamed boats that looked (and stacked) much like dories would pull for the beach. The motorized landing craft, now stowed aboard *Amerika* and *Big Sal* would carry Safir Maraan's II Corps ashore at Grik City, since it was assumed they'd be most likely to face opposition.

Matt was on the port bridgewing with Chack and Courtney Bradford, anxiously glassing the silver surf that broke upon the forbidding shore the 1st Naval Air Wing had described and Chack had chosen. Beyond the shore was a dark, junglelike forest of tall, broad trees unlike any Matt had seen except perhaps for the Great Tree in Baalkpan. The things were *huge*! Matt's companions were aboard because Chack would lead the landing in *Walker's* motor launch, since she was the most capable ship to close the beach during the landing operation. Bradford had insistently declared that he must accompany him and be among the first to set foot on this almost holy, if equally evil land.

"I think this is it," Matt practically whispered aside to Chack.

"Yes, Cap-i-taan Reddy," Chack agreed formally. "I believe you are correct." Matt looked at the brindled Lemurian he was so fond of, knowing how nervous he must be. Chack had seen a great deal of action and was amazingly capable, but this was an entirely different situation for him. He was in complete command of this element of the operation, and the operation itself was risky beyond anything they'd ever tried. Matt was tempted to pat his arm, but he knew that was out of the question. Instead, he turned and spoke to Spanky. "All stop. Stand by to anchor. Have the launch made ready in all respects."

"All stop and stand by to anchor, aye," Spanky replied. "The launch is already swayed out and ready to lower as soon as you give the word."

"Very well." Matt looked at Courtney. "Last chance," he said, then shrugged. "It's really kind of, well, stupid for you to go. You're not a soldier. And what if something happens to you?"

Courtney eyed him. "What if something happens to any of us? The assignment you have set yourself is not without risk! Besides, if I was once of some importance, I am no longer—I mean, to the 'cause' of course! I remain quite important to me! But this is a moment I have dreamed of as ardently as our dear Adar, if for slightly different reasons." He grinned. "And besides, who are you to say that I'm no soldier! I've been training with Chack's Raiders these last weeks, and if I'm no physical match for them, I daresay I shan't slow them down too dreadfully. I've never felt more fit! And I still have the Krag Jorgenson rifle I carried about so uselessly during the Battle of Baalkpan! I assure you, I know much more about it now, and Chack still has a similar arm."

Matt nodded reluctantly. Essentially, Courtney had stated the simple fact that they were *all* soldiers now, and he was ready to do his part. Matt had no doubt the man had become proficient with the Krag, and Chack still kept his own as a constant companion. He found that a little odd. They didn't have a lot of '03 Springfields, but they were shorter and more powerful than the Krags. If anyone "rated" one, it was Chack. But he still stubbornly clung to the old Krag he'd been given—right after the Battle of Aryaal, if Matt remembered rightly. He smiled and nodded. "Okay, Courtney. If you say so. Just be careful, will you?"

"'Careful' is my very favorite word, Captain Reddy!"

The splash of the anchor hitting the sea distracted them, and they all glanced forward.

"I will take my leave now, Cap-i-taan Reddy," Chack announced, still speaking formally, "and I wish you the best of luck."

"Sure, Chack," Matt replied, falsely cheerful. "And you be careful too! I'll see you back aboard—or on the steps of that creepy, dumpy, palace in Grik City!" He silently cursed himself, realizing *he'd* just encouraged Chack to go beyond the parameters of his mission! All the 1st Raider Brigade was *supposed* to do was provide a diversion in the Grik rear to take pressure off II Corps when it became time to disengage. The brigade would then filter back into the jungle and be withdrawn by the DDs that would steam back down the coast to take it off. *Damn it! What's the matter with me?* Without a further word, Chack took a step back and saluted. Matt returned it as sharply as he could, and then Chack and Courtney were gone.

"I hope they're okay," Spanky grumbled softly.

Dennis Silva himself served as coxswain aboard the launch, and Gunny Horn went along as "security" with his BAR. Silva had left Petey clutching to an indignant Lawrence, who'd gone down to the firerooms to try to "give" the ridiculous creature to Isak Reuben. Isak probably wasn't a good choice to take care of him either, but he'd always complained when anybody aboard had any kind of "pet," and they didn't get one for the firerooms. If nothing else, the heat belowdecks might cause Petey to pass out, Lawrence had reasoned, and get him to let go.

Silva waited patiently while Chack and Courtney, and twenty other Raiders slid down the falls into the boat, before turning it toward shore and advancing the throttle with practiced ease. Chack watched him. "I didn't know you could steer a boat," he said at last. Silva rolled his eye. "Lotsa stuff you don't know about me, Chackie. Just 'cause a fella don't do a thing ever' damn day don't mean he can't." He nodded at Horn. "Why, me an' ol' Arnie there have tumped over a en-tire Jap *destroyer* with our bare hands, now! You missed that one."

"I heard about it," Chack said, blinking amusement. "And perhaps, in the future, you will remember not to 'tump' Jaap ships over on top of *yourselves!*"

Dennis slapped his thigh. "That's what I told Arnie, but he never listens."

"What a load of crap. I *always* listen to that maniac," Horn mumbled, "and always get a whole cargo of hell dumped on my head too." He stuck out his hand. "Gunnery Sergeant Arnold Horn." Chack chittered a chuckle and shook the offered hand. He knew exactly what Silva and Horn were doing: trying to lighten the mood for him and all the troops in the boat. It was an effort he would've considered uncharacteristic of Silva, at least, for most of their acquaintance. But whether he'd admit it or not, Dennis had changed. He glanced around. The ploy was working too, he realized, judging by the other faces he saw in the moonlight.

"Kinda wish we was goin' with you fellas," Silva added a little whimsically. "I know I've said I was retirin' from the jungle hee-roin' bizness, but a fella gets melancholy for his adventurous youth, from time to time."

Horn snorted.

"You will have plenty to do at Grik City," Chack reminded, just as the keel of the launch touched the sand amid the gently breaking surf, and Lemurians returned to their ancestral lands for the first time in . . . well, it was impossible to say. Chack hopped out without ceremony, and his troops filed out of the boat to join him. "Take this line," Silva called, throwing a coil of rope at a 'Cat before he and Horn stepped out of the boat. He saw Chack's questioning blink and shrugged. "Just figured we'd hang around an' watch the goose pull for a while."

"Oh dear," Courtney, the last in the boat, exclaimed, looking at the water. "You don't suppose you might, um, pull me in just a bit closer? Hmm. I thought not," he added a little petulantly when there was no response. He jumped over the side and crashed quickly through the shallow water to join them on the beach.

If Dennis expected to be amused by a chaotic landing, he was disappointed. The 1st Raider Brigade had practiced landings on every kind of shore at the Baalkpan Advanced Training Center (ATC), and the boats rowed ashore by platoons and quickly formed into companies. They weren't under fire, of course, but the whole thing was accomplished with a speed and professionalism Silva and Horn could only admire. The only problems came from the animals. Barges of cavalry, mounted on restless, grumpy me-naaks, practically disintegrated as they neared shore and the irascible creatures, fed up with their long, confining voyage, spilled out in the surf. Fortunately, whatever predators cruised these beaches were like most of those elsewhere and stayed out of the shallows at night. There were a few light injuries, but no losses. The paalkas, large, somewhat moose-shaped animals, came next with greater dignity, but then they had to haul the guns and wagons off the barges and out of the surf with cables before they could be properly harnessed. This caused considerable aggravation, and the mournful mooing of the paalkas echoed back at them from the trees.

Eventually, however, Chack's entire brigade of roughly three thousand officers and troops, eight 2-gun "company" sections of light six-pounders, and a full communications company had managed to assemble on the broad beach. The comm company had a short train of wagons and its own section of guns. It would follow the shoreline with two complete TBS sets and the associated paraphernalia, pacing the brigade's advance, so they could maintain communications with a single DD offshore. That ship could, in turn, keep the rest of First Fleet South apprised of Chack's progress. It was intended that silence be maintained for a while, until the "main" show kicked off, but Chack had strict instructions to call for help if he ran into anything he couldn't handle, or if he believed his advance had been discovered by the Grik.

"Well, Chackie, ol' buddy," Silva said after a while, "it looks like you've got things straightened out here. Doubt I coulda done much better myself. I guess Arnie an' me'll shove off." He started to offer his hand for a final shake, when the woods erupted with the deep crackle of Allin-Silva breechloaders, and the stutter of a single Blitzer Bug. "What the hell? Sounds like your pickets've already run into something!" A thunderous screech echoed in the forest, followed by more shots and a terrible commotion of crashing, snapping trees. "Somethin' purty big," Silva added.

"I wonder what it might be?" Courtney murmured eagerly.

Chack's sister, Captain Risa-Sab-At, hurried up to join them. She flashed a quick, friendly, Lemurian grin at Silva, then turned to Chack. "Major Jindal seems to have encountered some kind of resistance," she reported unnecessarily.

"Indeed," Chack agreed, moving out in front of the troops that flanked him. "Action front!" he bellowed. "Fix bayonets! Front rank kneel, and prepare to receive . . . the enemy!"

His command was relayed down the long row of raiders, formed into four ranks in preparation for moving, by column, into the forest. Another roar reached them, and it was closer now, the flashes of rifles visible, and shouts audible in the darkness. The guns were quickly unlimbering and being pushed through the sand to join the infantry in line, their loaders already slamming charges down the moving barrels. Silva unsnapped the holder of his 1911 Colt, wishing he'd brought his monstrous "Doom Stomper" along. Horn readied his BAR.

Walker's two powerful carbon arc spotlights suddenly snapped on and illuminated the tree line with their glaring beams. Apparently the flashes of gunfire had been seen since no message could've been relayed. The lights probed quickly around until they settled on . . . something, emerging from the forest.

"Gawd," Silva blurted. He'd seen "super lizards": giant allosauruslike carnivores, according to Bradford, that inhabited Borno. He'd even killed a few. But this! It made a super lizard look like a chicken.

"Goodness gracious!" Courtney chortled.

The monstrous beast that crashed out of the jungle onto the beach and paused, squinting in the painfully bright beams of light, looked like a giant me-naak at a glance. It went on four legs and had a large head full of vicious teeth like a meanie, but it stood perhaps twelve or fourteen feet high at the withers. It also had a trio of forward-facing horns kind of like the mounts the Czech Legion rode, which was ironic as well, but it also boasted a horny crest that swept back along the top of its head and neck to provide a dangerous mouthful for anything that went for that vulnerable area. Probably only Courtney Bradford reflected on the implications of that just then, however.

"It's a tripto-serpent-top!" Silva exclaimed. Horn glared at him, amazed as always by how quick Silva's irreverent wit could be at times like this.

"Chief Silva! You will kindly let someone *else* provide a thoughtful, scientific name for something we meet for a change!" Bradford challenged hotly.

"Stand by!" Chack trilled loudly.

Just then, the air shattered with the sound of tearing canvas, and three orange flashes lit the area around the monster amid geysers of earth and a stuttering boom. Moments later, the reports of *Walker*'s three landward-trained 4"-50s reached them.

"Good boys!" Silva crowed triumphantly. He turned to Chack. "Our friends'll hammer that booger to pieces before it gets too close to your fellas!"

He was right. Another salvo was already shrieking in on the suddenly confused beast. At least one struck, and mighty gobbets of flesh rocketed into the sky, surrounding a massive, tumbling foreleg.

"Such a pity," Bradford mourned, even as a third salvo convulsed the roaring beast and the ground around it. The roaring snapped off.

"Sure, it's a helluva thing that you didn't get to gawk at the scary booger longer than you did," Silva scolded sarcastically. "Maybe next time you'll get a good look at its innards from the inside!" He looked back at Chack, just as the searchlights dimmed out, their job obviously done. "Hope nobody heard that. Sure you don't wanna call your little hike off?"

Chack shook his head angrily, staring out at the old destroyer. The Morse lamp aboard her was apparently asking the same question. "We will continue our mission," he stated emphatically. "Have each section of guns join its assigned company in the marching order at once, Cap-i-taan," he told Risa, "and we will place a section at the head of the column, behind the scouts, as well, if you please. We are far enough from Grik City that the enemy shouldn't have been alerted if it truly is as isolated as our reconnaissance has reported, but other things like that"—he motioned at the wreckage of the creature *Walker* killed—"may wish to investigate. Form a detail to check on our scouts in the forest to ensure that none were wounded by that thing—or *Walker*'s shells!"

"Ay, ay, my brother," Risa replied, and Chack nodded. "Carry on!" he said. With a last look at Silva, Risa scampered away.

"Okay, then," Silva said. "Have fun, Chackie, and don't get ate. C'mon, Arnie, let's get back to the ship."

"Have a care for *yourself*, Silva," Chack warned, "and tell Cap-i-taan Reddy to look for the First Raider Brigade in the enemy's rear—when he needs us most!"

"You bet. So long, Chackie, Mr. Bradford. Watch out for 'skeeters, an' don't stump yer toes! If you do get yer stripy tails in a jam, I'll try to come a'runnin—but who knows what I'll be tangled up with. May get awkward for me to just drop ever'thing to save your silly asses this time!"

Chack grinned at his big friend. "I will bear that in mind."

"C'mon, Arnie," Dennis repeated. "We hang around much longer, Skipper'll figure we decided to stay with these nuts an' leave us here."

////// *Chack's Brigade*
Northeast Madagascar
July 31, 1944

*T*he me-naak Chack rode was a poor substitute for the horse he'd grown so fond of in the New Ireland campaign, but he was increasingly glad they hadn't brought any horses here. Madagascar might be the ancient homeland of his people, but whether it ever had been or not, it was certainly no place for horses now. The strange and terrifying monster they'd encountered when they first landed had been but a taste of the . . . unreasonably dangerous predators that infested this land. Most were relatively small and quickly dealt with by recon squads that probed ahead of the brigade, but some were larger, and a few were much more clever. All were a menace, and the 1st Raider Brigade was advancing at a frustrating crawl.

The marching column had been essentially abandoned the very first day, since Chack had been forced to move behind battalions that remained largely deployed for battle. This was an incredibly tedious arrangement in the virtually trackless coastal forest, and the alignment of the battalions was extremely difficult to maintain. No one was ever supposed to lose sight of the troopers to either side of them, but the woods echoed almost continuously with sporadic firing, particularly on the flanks, and there was a steady trickle of casualties, dead and wounded, that was bleeding Chack's Brigade at an alarming rate. Worse, the monsters stalking them had quickly closed in behind, snatching any stragglers they could. This kept straggling to an unprecedented minimum, but also prevented Chack from sending his reports—and his wounded—back to the beach without a significant guard. The farther inland they moved, the more difficult that was becoming.

"I have never seen anything like it," Chack's sister, Risa-Sab-At, stated, saluting as Chack and his small staff rode up behind her currently deployed 1st Battalion of the 11th Imperial Marines. She marched with the "Impies" whenever she could because they'd never faced Grik before, but nobody had ever encountered a situation quite like this. "It is like we move through a land of walking flasher fish!"

"The closest situation I have heard of might be Mr. Cook's—and Silva's—expedition through north Borno," Chack agreed, "but their party was much smaller and drew far less attention."

"They weren't discovering a new species with virtually every step either!" enthused Courtney Bradford, waving his sombrero to cool his red, sweat-streaked face. He'd been walking with Risa that day, inspecting the various slain creatures. Risa had been forced to detail a few men to place the manageable carcasses on a cart and bring them to him, so he wouldn't keep scampering toward every shot he heard to have a peek at what provoked it. He was taken, under guard, to see the larger monsters the advancing riflemen brought down.

"Such an astonishing variety of predators!" he continued. "Almost nothing else has been seen! They certainly must prey upon one another if nothing else is to be had. If this truly is a sort of zoo, or preserve for the various 'worthy prey' or 'other hunter species' the Grik have encountered over the ages, it is quite fascinating, of course, but the nature of their existence here would seem to minimize any opportunity to study the beasts as they previously existed, if you get my meaning."

Chack simply stared at the man, blinking tolerant amusement. "And why might that be, Mr. Braad-furd?"

Bradford blinked back. "Why, with predators being forced to subsist on other predators, many behavioral, and even physiological changes, will have had to occur—particularly over long periods of time, of course!" He gestured at his latest acquisition, weaving through the trees beside him on a cart drawn by four resentful-looking Imperial Marines. The thing looked vaguely similar to a Grik, though it was larger and more colorful. Its arms weren't as well developed, and its tail was considerably longer. Interestingly, its teeth were very different from a Grik—more like those of a rhino-pig, complete with wicked tusks, than anything else Chack could compare it to. Courtney frowned, and flapped his hat more vigorously. "I may be wrong, of course," he conceded. "I'm *so often* wrong these days, it seems! There's no reason to presume there aren't any prey animals on Madagascar. They'd naturally flee our approach, as well as the concentration of predators we invite. And if the Grik truly brought these creatures here, they could certainly bring others for them to feed upon." He paused, peering at the creature on the cart. "And now that I think about it, this specimen, among others, displays a credible capacity for omnivorism. Most interesting indeed."

"But you would say that most of the monsters are somewhat Griklike in form?" Chack asked.

"Most," Bradford cautiously confirmed. "At least the majority that seem most inclined to attack. I haven't seen them, but other creatures, some armed with primitive weapons, in fact, have been reported. Those appear content to merely scrutinize us for the most part, and almost timidly avoid prolonged observations."

"Indeed?" asked Chack, blinking curiosity. Then he shook his head. "But most that attack are somewhat Grik-like?"

"In the pertinent respects."

"But not Grik?"

"Certainly not like any *true* Grik we've encountered."

Chack nodded at Risa. "Then our Imperial troops will have some small experience of the enemy before we ever meet him. That is a 'silver lining,' as I have heard such situations described. The less good aspect of this constant, low intensity combat is that we are being badly delayed." He shook his head. "I see no alternative to severing our lines of communication to the coast—and pushing more aggressively forward despite the possibility of increased casualties." He blinked determination. "This brigade *will* arrive on time to accomplish its mission, regardless of the cost!"

There was more shooting suddenly, to the left, out in front of Major Jindal's Respitans. A chorus of shouts arose as well, insistent and incredulous. Chack stared in that direction but couldn't see anything through the trees.

"Oh my!" Courtney chortled. "They sound quite excited! I wonder what they've found!"

A few moments later, a Me-naak-mounted courier galloped to join them along a twisting path, saluting as he reined his snot-slinging animal to a stop. "Major Jin-daal's compliments, Col-nol," the 'Cat said with his slightly different Maa-ni-la accent, "an' he begs to report a 'curious development' to his front. He asks if you'd care to join him."

Chack looked at Courtney, then at Risa. "Of course," he said to the courier. "My compliments to Major Jindal, and we will come directly."

"They're quite obviously *people*," Jindal whispered aside to Chack as the two stood, conferring, a short distance away from a fairly large group of men who lingered, only vaguely visible, in the forest ahead. "I meant to say 'human' people, of course," Jindal quickly added. "Though judging by their appearance, it's no wonder they were fired upon when first seen."

Chack agreed that the beings were clearly men—of a sort. They were dressed entirely in animal skins, and their hair and beards were long and matted. All carried spears or longbows, and projected a confident air concerning the world they inhabited that must've taken generations to achieve. Some, more exposed than others, stared back with open curiosity, while others kept a constant, almost casual vigil against the approach of other creatures.

"I believe they've been watching us for some time," Jindal added. "We've had glimpses now and then, but I scarcely credited the reports that there were *people* out there! Even when my Respitans fired at them, I probably wouldn't have had them cease—I couldn't see them myself— if someone hadn't cried out that they were shouting *English* back at us!"

"English?" Chack asked.

"I'm not in the least bit surprised," Courtney exclaimed. "It only stands to reason, after all."

Chack blinked at the man, then huffed. "We should speak to them, I suppose. If we truly can understand them, they may be able to advise us on how best to proceed."

Chack, Courtney, Jindal, Risa, and half a dozen troopers stepped forward and waited while the strange men seemed to discuss this move excitedly among themselves. Eventually, a like number of skin-clad . . . hunters? . . . warriors? moved forward to meet them. A few paces apart, both groups stopped to appraise the other. For a long moment, no one spoke, but finally, awkwardly, Major Jindal took another half step forward and introduced himself. "And this," he added, gesturing at Chack, "is Lieutenant Colonel Chack-Sab-At, commander of our expedition. His people and ours are allies against the Grik."

"Gariek?" one of the bearded men spat, pointing north. "Ya min the Gariek? Nastee buggers beyan' the wall a' trees?"

Jindal was startled that he understood the man—and his accent was so bizarre that he only *barely* understood him.

"Why yes. We—our alliance—are at war with them and mean to destroy them." He pursed his lips. "I do hope they are not friends of yours."

A gale of laughter erupted that extended back into the trees much farther than they could see.

"We's nae friends a' thars!" the same man proclaimed. "Theys came huntin' us, naw an' thens, fer fun we's reckans, but nat fer a lang tyme anaw." The man's face hardened. "We's makes it hard fer 'em." He shrugged very normally. "We's hunt theys when theys came anow!"

There was a chorus of agreeing growls.

"That's excellent news," Chack said, and the group drew back slightly.

"Ya spake Ainglish!" another man blurted.

"Of course he does!" Risa said, scowling. "Better than you!"

"Nae affense," the first man said. "Is jest that nae a' the mankey falk we's ever knawn'd spake it, an' unlike ya's, theys dannae much lak tae fight. Theys all live as far that way as theys can git!" He pointed south.

"Other Lemurians! Here? Still? My God!" Courtney gushed.

"So it would seem," Chack agreed uneasily. "May I have the pleasure of your name, sir?" he asked the man who'd spoken the most.

"Aye. Aym Will. This here's Andy, that's Sam. . . ." He proceeded to name the rest of those closest, then called out to those behind to shout their names as well. Chack began to fidget. "It's a great pleasure to meet you, particularly under these circumstances, but we really must push on toward the, um, wall of trees. Can you suggest a better way than we are taking? Or a better mode of advance? We have another army scheduled to land beyond the wall in a few days and would very much like to meet it there."

Will looked closely at Chack.

"Ya's rilly mean ta' kill all the Garieks?" he demanded, then nodded at the Respitans beyond. "Ya's is armed fer it, an' that's a fact, wit yer maskits an' big gannes."

Chack was just as startled as Jindal when he figured out that "maskits" meant muskets, and "gannes" meant guns. "Killing the Grik is our sole purpose here," he replied.

"Aye. Weel, ay'll hafta spake the cap'n, but it may be we's can halp. We's may not be much help aganst the Garieks theirsefs, but we's can keep these ather buggers af ye's an yer march—an' ye's'll need ta' keep yer maskits shushed as ye's get claser tae the wall. Ay's reckan ya's wants ta snake in behind, er ye's wadneamarch thray the farest?"

"Indeed," Jindal agreed. "Any help you wish to provide would be much appreciated!"

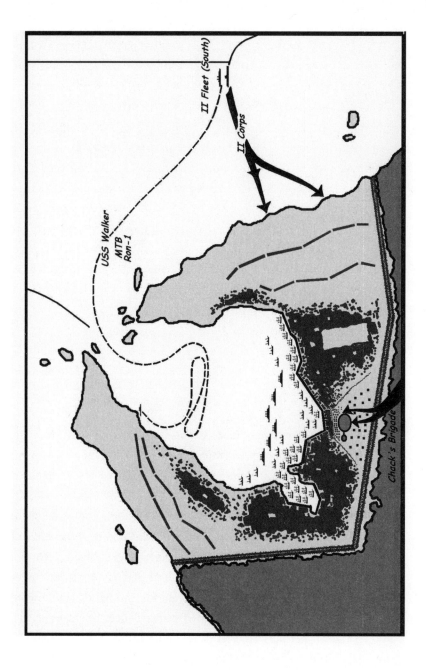

II Fleet (South)

II Corps

USS Walker

MTB Ron-1

Chuck's Brigade

////// *The Great Raid*
Grik Madagascar
August 4, 1944

*T*he sea was choppier than General Queen Safir Maraan would've preferred as she approached the almost mystical homeland of her people in the jet-black, predawn darkness. Grik City was dimly lit by indoor lighting, much like the Grik outpost at Raan-goon had been, but even by that meager illumination, she could tell this place was much, much larger. She'd seen the drawings made by Miyata from memory, and the aviators from observation, and knew they were as precise as minds and hands could make them. She'd seen what the human destroyermen called "photo-graaphs," however, and for perhaps the first time she understood why the failure to make the little machines that produced them, and the "film" they required, had recently become such a sore subject with her friends. They had some of the machines, probably enough, that had belonged to nearly every human American from any of their ships, but the film had just never been the priority they all now recognized it should have been. She shook the thought aside. Her friends had performed enough technical miracles, in her view. Sometimes the simplest, overlooked things could be decisive, but with everything else they'd been focused on, she forgave them—and the "backseaters" in the Nancys were chosen largely for their artistic skill, after all. . . .

She glanced around. Almost a hundred of the broad-beamed little landing craft surrounded her in this first wave of nearly four thousand troops. She couldn't see many of them, but their four-cylinder engines rumbled in the night, and the turbulent foam kicked up by their dory-shaped hulls churned purple-gray around those nearby. She doubted they could possibly be seen from shore, but they might be heard when they drew near enough for the engines to drown the brisk surf here. Behind her, she saw no sign at all of the small fleet supporting them, not a light, or anything else that might give them away. Having disembarked the first wave, *Salissa* would be moving away, preparing to commence air operations. *Amerika* and the smaller support ships would join her when their similar task was complete. She was satisfied, and suspected they'd achieve surprise—at least for the critical time it took to establish a beach head. She hoped so at any rate. There was no telling what kind of Grik they'd encounter in this place.

She stared hard to the northwest, trying to observe the least glimpse of *Walker* and her little "mosquito fleet" of PT boats headed for the mouth of the harbor, but they were just as invisible. She missed the comfort of seeing the old four-stacker moving to attack the enemy fleet at anchor, but knew that whether she saw the sleek ship or not, it was there. That was better from the perspective of surprise, and good enough for her. Like most, she had absolute faith in Captain Reddy.

"It is not far now," she said to General Grisa, whose 6th Division, minus the 3rd Maa-ni-la Cavalry, had won the honor of being the first ashore on what they were calling "Lizard Beach One." It wasn't a very imaginative name for such a momentous place; they'd used the designation before, on Say-lon. But they weren't at Say-lon now, and there was no need to confuse the enemy—or the troops—with new code names. Besides, it somehow seemed appropriate.

"Yes, my gener-aal queen protector," Grisa replied tartly. He was still distressed that she'd insisted on coming along with this first, and likely most dangerous element of the assault. Not even Captain Reddy or Adar had been able to prevent it. She still took her role as "protector" very seriously. Besides, Chack—the male she loved with all her soul—had been ashore for several days now, fighting northward against terrible monsters by all accounts, and nothing under the Heavens could've prevented her from joining him in danger after all the time they'd lost. A sense of uneasiness gripped her when she thought of Chack. Nothing had been heard from him for two days now. The communications division that was supposed to shadow his movements along the coast was still in contact, but Chack's Brigade wasn't. It had reported unexpectedly serious delays imposed by ferocious creatures. No Grik had been encountered, but apparently Miyata had been right about the bulk of Madagascar being kept as a preserve for examples of the many predators the Grik had discovered over time. She wondered why that would be. In any event, Chack's last report had stated that he meant to strike hard and fast away from the coast by an avenue he'd discovered, and doubted he'd risk more runners, or even small groups, to carry further dispatches. Safir remained supremely confident that Chack would meet his objective, but she didn't like his brigade being entirely on its own.

She blinked away that anxiety and focused on Grisa's form in the darkness. "Do not sulk, Gener-aal," she chided gently. "It does not suit you. I will not take a rifle and lead a charge of bayonets against the Grik, I assure you, as long as you do not either."

"I will not," Grisa answered in a clipped tone. "I am fully aware of my duties and responsibilities!" he jabbed. Safir laughed. "Indeed! I am most glad to hear it—though I already knew that, of course!"

They settled into silence as the beach grew closer, and the muted lights of Grik City sprawled beyond. One thing they knew about this place that was different from any other beach they'd landed on was that precious little cover was to be found between the city and the water's

edge. Much would depend on what, if any defenses the Grik had ar-
ranged, and how quickly they reached the outskirts of the rat maze of
Grik City itself. If they were contested or delayed, their only hope would
be to quickly dig in and wait for the successive waves to reach Lizard
Beaches Two and Three, to disperse the defenders. And the shock of
Captain Reddy's attack on the harbor, of course.

Barely a hundred tails separated them from shore when there was a
sudden series of flashes, like musket fire, not far beyond it. Bright, white-
green meteors arched into the sky, casting a dull, flickering light on the
surf as they fell. Immediately, more of the eerie flares went up. *The Grik
are shooting them from muskets!* Safir realized. The Allies had always
used flares, as well as signal rockets. But the color of these was utterly
wrong, and none of her people would've used them now, in any case.
There were murmurs of alarm in the boats, and the tension ratcheted up.
"What other surprises has Kuro-kawa given them?" she wondered aloud.
Raising her voice, she yelled as loudly as she could. "Quickly! Quickly!
Surprise is lost! To the shore as fast as we can, and *at* them before they
gather what wits they can find!"

A mighty muzzle flash blossomed in the night, then another, raising
greenish splashes among the boats. Throttles roared all around her as
the landing dories accelerated into the teeth of a growing number of
cannon that spat fire and shrieking iron.

"Something woke them up," Chief Gray observed, standing beside Matt
on *Walker's* port bridgewing. Like everyone else, he already wore his
helmet, and the web belt with his .45 and cutlass. *Walker's* crew had
been at battle stations ever since she turned to close the harbor. The
lookout had just reported flares and cannon fire from the northwest
coast of the city, in the vicinity of Lizard Beach One, but his alarm had
been unnecessary; the flashes were obvious to all.

"We'll be opening the harbor mouth any minute," Rosen called from
behind the 'Cat at the big brass wheel.

"Very well," Matt replied, glancing at Lieutenant Toryu Miyata,
who'd joined the ship as the closest thing they had to a harbor pilot.

He'd been a navigation officer aboard *Amagi,* and had actually sailed in and out of this very port, but he couldn't tell them much about the channel other than that it was marked. He shrugged apologetically at Matt. "Maintain your course and speed for the moment, Mr. Rosen. We don't know these waters at all. Any faster than one-third, and we're liable to ram smack into the 'Celestial Palace.'" He spoke to Minnie. "Have the lookouts keep their eyes peeled for Mr. Miyata's channel markers, and tell Mr. Palmer he's free to transmit on the TBS. Whatever Safir's running into, our objective remains the same. Mr. Laumer will continue to advance his boats in line abreast of us, watching for shoals, then break off to go after the Grik BBs on the fringe. We'll launch port torpedoes at the ships in the center of the enemy formation, but when we turn to give 'em the other side, Laumer needs to be out of the way!"

"Ay, ay! Cap-i-taan, lookout says he glimpsing Grik waagons in cannon flashes! They still right where we marked 'em!"

"Good. I hate surprises," he answered wryly. "Mr. Sandison," he said to Bernie, "everything set?"

"Yes, sir," the torpedo officer replied anxiously. The Mk-3 Baalkpan Naval Arsenal torpedoes he'd helped design had proven themselves once before, but they'd also shown they could be dangerously fickle. He was far more used to faulty weapons than ones that worked, however, and he'd been tweaking and tinkering with those aboard ever since they left Madras. He looked back and caught Matt still watching him in the dim bridge lighting. "They'll work, Skipper," he defended.

Matt forced a smile. "I know."

"Exec says the PTs to staar-board is lagging," Minnie announced, and Matt crossed to look. Visibility was gradually improving, and he could see the uneven wakes of the three boats off *Walker's* starboard quarter. It wasn't that bad, but Spanky was probably nearly nuts with frustration on the auxiliary conn on the aft deckhouse. "Very well. Signal Mr. Laumer to get his ducks in a row."

Matt knew Irvin Laumer would take the mild reprimand too much to heart. The kid still thought he had something to prove. But they did need to emphasize the necessity of keeping the torpedo boats glued to their predetermined attack patterns. Better to jump on them now than run one down once the shooting started.

"Jeez! Look at that!" Bernie murmured, barely audible over the blower. Matt crossed back to port. The fighting on Lizard Beach One was boiling up into what looked like some kind of surrealistic lightning storm, and Matt felt a pang of loss, realizing how many of his friends were catching hell over there. It wasn't going all one way, however. Enough of Safir Maraan's forces must have landed to keep steady fire on the defenders, and even a few light guns were joining the fight.

"Havin' a hard time over there," Gray remarked simply.

"There can be little doubt now that they did indeed see our reconnaissance flight and plan accordingly," Commander Herring stated sourly, joining them. Matt looked at him. "No criticism, Captain. None at all!" Herring hastened to add. "We *had* to see what we faced, or we could've planned nothing ourselves. No, I was merely making an observation, and the conclusion it draws me to is somewhat unsettling."

"They knew we were coming," Gray interrupted, impatient with Herring's manner.

"Indeed," Herring said, "and they are obviously *defending* the beach, which implies that the enemy here is composed, at least partially, of the 'new' Grik that are capable of doing that!"

"But why would they have 'em *here*?" Matt asked, frowning. "Sure, they pitched in when they knew we were coming, but they couldn't have known for long."

Bernie scratched his jaw. "And why keep such a valuable force here— unless they knew we were coming all along, which I doubt too—to defend a place they'd never suspect needed defending?"

"They must *train* them here!" Miyata said, suddenly certain. He hadn't spoken much since he came aboard, sensing a measure of hostility—mostly from Commander Herring, who, he understood, had been a prisoner of the Japanese—but this might be important. "They train them here where they can keep an eye on them—I saw Kurokawa's first, vile experiments with my own eyes, but only now did the significance of that return to me! These 'new' Grik are very different, as your

General Alden has reported, and I suspect they keep them separate from the vast majority of other Grik on the continent!"

"Makes sense, Skipper," Gray grudged, "which might mean that maybe there's not an endless number of 'em . . . but why? Why keep them from the others?"

"That's obvious as well," Herring said, bestowing a strained nod in Miyata's direction, and earning a resentful glare from Gray for his condescending choice of words. "According to the AEF in India, their General Halik has turned his whole army into something more than 'ordinary' Grik. That might pose a problem, eventually, for their more, ah, traditional hierarchy."

"You mean they're afraid to teach most of their peon warriors to think," Gray guessed.

"That's exactly what I mean."

The fighting on the northeast shore flared and strobed ever brighter—and began shifting south as well, as the reconstituted 5th Division came ashore at Lizard Beach Two. Whether there were numberless Grik here or not, Matt's friends, his *people* were landing on a terrible shore, barren of cover, and invested with far better defenses than they'd ever dreamed. He ground his teeth.

"Well, I hope you're right. But it won't be long before we maybe give them a little something else to think about," he said, his voice tight and sharp.

6th Division
II Corps

"We cannot just crouch here and take this forever, General Grisa!" Safir cried over the thunderous sound of battle. The division was dug in behind a hasty mound of sand, firing independently at the Grik cannon crews when they saw them in the flare of the flashing muzzles. "They will eventually chew us apart!"

"We are taking few enough casualties, now we are ashore," Grisa said evenly, apparently trying to calm her. "The Grik have no exploding shells, and if they have canister, they have not used it yet. Our own artillery is now in place, and we do have exploding shells and canister. The enemy cannot close with us without suffering a terrible slaughter!"

It was then that Safir suddenly decided that, despite his worth, General Grisa had spent far too much time in the trenches around Alden's Perimeter in India. "That is unacceptable! We cannot lie here and exchange jabs all day! And though Grik artillery practice remains poor compared to ours, either through inferior training or equipment, it is much better than it has been! We are too exposed, with nothing but the sea at our backs!"

"Exactly! With daylight, our navy will join the bombardment, as will our air power. That should discourage the Grik sufficiently to allow the fleet to pull us off the beach." Grisa gestured at the slowly brightening sea. "Too many of our landing craft have been destroyed, so we must wait for more!"

"Pull us off?" Incredulous, Safir coughed, pointing to the south where the 5th Division was still leaping out of its own powered dories and scattering, prone, in open order. Roundshot was beginning to shower them with geysers of sand. "We are still only just *getting* here! We did not come all this way to drench this damp ground, however revered, with our own blood, take up handfuls of sand, and then depart! Are you mad? Soon the Grik will respond to our presence with *firebombs* as well as guns. We cannot survive that all day. We must move!"

"Where, my queen?"

"Toward the enemy, fool! While there remains some darkness. We must push the attack now or we *will* die here!" Her voice softened. "You are a good gener-aal, Grisa. One of the best. You have proven yourself many times, and your courage is not in question. But if you do not get these troops up out of the sand and attack this instant, I shall relieve you and do it myself! Is that clear?"

Grisa stared at her, stricken. "Y-yes, my queen. Very clear. But . . . I thought the whole point of this raid was to simply do it, to show the Grik that even their most important places are vulnerable, so they will slow their own attacks. If we press forward, might not our 'raid' grow into something more, unprepared for by other elements?"

Safir realized he was right, and finally recognized the great mistake that had been made. The specific objective of the operation had always remained a simple, careful, hopefully destructive raid. But too many of the various hearts that conceived it (even hers, she admitted) had their own opinions of how the raid should *progress*, and had simply assumed all others would come to share them when the moment was at hand. Adar's ambiguous exhortations, despite his insistence on strategic control, and Captain Reddy's desire to support Adar's position, while sticking to the original concept in the vacuum of further discussion (that Adar had discouraged all along, she remembered now), had doubtless precipitated the current confusion. Grisa's reaction was a prime example.

The apparent readiness of the Grik was a surprise, and to him that meant they must resign themselves to what was achievable with the fewest losses. The stated, strategic goal of the raid had already been realized as soon as the first shots were fired, and now it was time to protect his troops. But Safir Maraan had bigger aims, as did many others, she knew. Adar's intent was utterly clear to *her*. She *believed* Captain Reddy, and even his mate, the Lady Saandra, ultimately shared Adar's desire, whether they were prepared to admit it or not. Most important, she was completely certain what *Chack* meant to do, and as long as he was somewhere on the island, enduring whatever his brigade was facing, she simply wouldn't leave. That left only one option for her, and by her next actions, every single soul engaged in the raid. She supposed some spontaneous act such as hers was what Adar had hoped for all along and she suddenly resented him for his unwillingness or inability to make it plain. *Adar has been right all along,* she decided. *Someone has to be in charge. But Adar quite possibly isn't the best choice for the job after all, at least not at the "pointy end."* She felt a wave of sadness. What did that mean for them today? More important, perhaps, what did that mean for the entire Alliance, the new "Union," tomorrow?

"Is the TBS up?" she demanded.

"Yes, my queen—and we are already connected to the Fifth Division by the new field tele-phones. The comm section was the first ashore."

"Very well. You will inform everyone within range of our voices, regardless of what devices are required, that our 'objective,' the 'objective' of Second Corps and every Allied being here today on land, sea, or in the air, is to kill Grik, General Grisa," she stated without inflection. "We will kill them until there are no more—or until there are no more of us. Now carry out your orders!"

"Orderly!" Grisa snapped, his tail swishing excitedly.

"Gener-aal?" replied a 'Cat nearby.

"You heard?"

"Yes, Gener-aal!"

"See that the order is sent at once! Whistler!" he added to another 'Cat crouching beyond the first. Lemurians couldn't manage bugles, but they made do with shrill whistles and drums. "Blow a preparatory call! Then, when I give the word, you will sound the charge!"

The sky over the harbor lit up, painfully bright, with a series of monstrous flashes. A few seconds later, there came another and another. Moments after that, the rumble of heavy detonations reached them where they were, all but silencing the Grik guns for an instant.

"Now, Grisa!" Safir cried. "Cap-i-taan Reddy has commenced his attack on the Grik fleet in the harbor! Sound the charge now!"

The whistler didn't even wait for Grisa to repeat the command.

USS Walker

"My course is one two zero, Skipper!" Rosen cried, staring in the dimly lit pelorus. The flashing explosions amid the anchored Grik dreadnaughts actually made it harder for him to see the dark numbers on the card.

"Very well! Steady as you go! Mr. Sandison, stand by for torpedo action starboard! All lookouts will keep particular watch for shoaling water! Have Mr. Campeti commence firing at the cruisers with the main battery!"

Walker had just finished her turn after launching her port torpedoes, and that first salvo had been stunningly effective. At least two Grik ironclads had been completely destroyed by solid hits at a range of a thousand yards. One fish had missed, but apparently hit a pier where ammunition and other inflammables were stored, and the resulting concussive display was a magnificent thing to see. The PTs were doing good work too, having accounted for another pair of enemy dreadnaughts already, and their racing wakes were clear against the calm harbor waters as they jockeyed to make more attacks. Minnie was reporting Ed Palmer's play-by-play account of overheard TBS traffic as Irvin Laumer coordinated his little mosquito fleet with a calm professionalism that made Matt proud. The biggest problems *Walker* faced now were the discovery that the deep water channel was much narrower than they'd assumed from the aerial recon, and the old destroyer had already actually dragged her groaning bottom across an unsuspected sandbar. Now, everyone was afraid they'd find another, more tenacious one—particularly when Commander Herring stated that, according to his calculations, the tide was on the ebb. Even more critical, the Grik were starting to "get their shit in the sock" faster than anyone had ever seen them do before, and *Walker* was taking return fire from undamaged dreadnaughts, as well as from a few of the cruisers nearby.

The salvo bell rang, still a little strange to those who'd served aboard from the beginning, since the old buzzer had been replaced by a Japanese alarm bell. The bright bloom of the salvo that followed was familiar, even if the converging tracers weren't quite the right color anymore. The new "common" shells performed just fine when they hit the first cruiser, however, causing a series of bright yellow-orange flashes along its side.

"Cap-i-taan!" Minnie cried. "Mr. Paal-mer says Second Corps is chargeen the Griks! They goin' for broke, and Generaal Queen Maraan says we *takin'* this place!"

Matt took a deep breath. He felt a little sick, but had to admit he wasn't really surprised. He'd known it. *Known* it, all along. Adar's hints, Safir's enthusiasm, Chack's drive . . . It had been inevitable that when they actually got here and got stuck in, there'd be no stopping them. He sighed. He'd warned, he'd cautioned, he'd practically pleaded—but deep inside, he'd known. Despite how close he'd grown to his Lemurian friends, there remained a fundamental difference between them. He hated the Grik, and the war had turned very personal for him after all the people he'd lost, but to him, Madagascar remained just a place, another strange chunk of land occupied by the enemy on a very strange world. He'd go there and fight the Grik because that was where they were, and the place was important to them. Ultimately, though, Madagascar was far more than just a "chunk of land" to the Lemurians; it was their sacred, ancient homeland. There'd never really been a realistic chance they wouldn't try to wrest it away once they returned at last.

"Very well," he acknowledged, rubbing his eyes. The churning in his stomach was passing, crowded out by a familiar exhilaration he never could explain. "Make sure everybody got that, and knows we just went all in. Oh, and send to Adar that I'm okay with it—nothing I can do about it now, anyway—but we need to have a long talk when all this is done." He hoped his failure to confront Adar, to confront *any* of his friends and force a commitment to stick to the plan or confess their true intentions, wouldn't come back to bite them in the ass.

"Stand by!" Bernie cried. "Fire one! Fire three! Fire five!"

The ship jolted slightly with each impulse charge from the rigged-out torpedo tubes, and Matt saw the concave splashes of the weapons. It was much lighter now, and he even saw the churning, bubbling wakes rise to the surface and lance toward the enemy. Then, without even the warning of near-miss splashes, several heavy shots struck *Walker* almost simultaneously in what was likely the greatest example of Grik gunnery ever performed. The lights went out, and the ship staggered beneath Matt's feet with an audible screech of pain. A bright flash aft lit the right side of his face, and he suspected the fuel drums for the Nancy had been hit. The plane itself had been launched some time ago and was orbiting now, sending reports of the action. He looked toward the stern. Sure enough, at least one drum had ignited, and even as he watched, hoses tried to spray the burning fuel over the side. Spanky's gun crew on the aft deckhouse had probably been singed, but wasn't even paying attention, so fixed on plying the number four gun. "Damage report," he demanded.

* * *

TAYLOR ANDERSON

282 Lieutenant Tab-At had been at her preferred combat station near the throttle control, but now she bolted aft through the forward engine room, undogged the hatch, and ducked into the aft engine room. The only light was the dawning gleam coming from the overhead skylights, and it wasn't much. As her eyes adjusted, she was immediately met by a body, facedown, lying on the grating at her feet. There was a tremendous amount of noise in the space, mostly yelling, but some screaming too. All came to her over the thunder of rushing water. "What the hell's goin' on in here?" she roared.

An ex-pat "Impie gal," machinist's mate 3rd, named Sitia, met her with wide eyes and a bloody forehead. "We took two rounds in here!" she cried. "One was high in the side, an' didn't do much damage, but the other came in at the waterline right behind the aft main junction box! Pieces o' that hit me—an' others."

"Reroute all power through the forward main!"

"We tried!" The girl seemed close to panic. "There's nothin' left to do it with! I already called damage-control parties aft. There's a bigger leak in ship's stores, under the guinea pullman, an' we had to send guys. We musta took another hit there!"

Tabby trotted on until she saw the wound in the compartment. A lot of water was coming in, pouring directly down on the still-spinning 25-kilowatt generator that was atomizing the spray. She swore. "Close the steam line an' secure the damn generator! Call the guys back. Seal off stores, an' get 'em to work patchin' *that*! We gonna lose the engine room an' starboard shaft, we don't stop this water!" She moved toward the heavy Bakelite handset but swore. Instead, she dashed to the voice tube. "Bridge!" she shouted. "Aft stores is gone, an' we got floodin' in the aft engine room! I need more help back here, an' 'specially EMs if you want 'lectricity back!"

"How bad's the floodin?" came Minnie's tiny, tinny voice.

Tabby gauged the inrushing water. The hole was *big*, and the more water they took, the more they'd take. If the weight pulled the stern down low enough, they'd take water from the higher puncture too. "We don't stop it in ten damn minutes, we gonna lose the space, the engine, an' maybe the whole goddamn ship!"

"We must break off, Captain Reddy!" Commander Herring insisted. "We have crippled the enemy fleet, but your ship is badly damaged and we can't afford to lose her!"

"I'm well aware of that, Commander," Matt replied, still staring through his binoculars at the effect of their salvos on the "cruisers." Some were burning, but a few had raised steam. Bernie shouted, "Now!" and Matt redirected his attention to the BBs they'd targeted with their torpedoes. Several seconds later, tall columns of water rose alongside two more of them and collapsed down across the armored casemates. Even as he watched, a flight of Nancys stooped on the remaining ships, protected from his fire by their sinking sisters, and bombs tumbled away from the planes, impacting with yellow flashes and white clouds of smoke.

"We're running out of room, Skipper," Rosen reminded.

"Very well. Right full rudder. Come about to course two six zero."

"Right full rudder, aye. Making my course two six zero!" Rosen acknowledged without inflection.

"Captain Reddy!" Herring persisted. "That course will take us even closer to the enemy!"

Matt took his eyes from the binoculars. "One more gun pass, then we're out of here. Those cruisers are getting underway. If the planes don't get 'em, they'll cream the PTs that are out of torps. Signal Mr. Laumer to break off," he called to Minnie. "We'll cover his withdrawal."

Herring gestured out to sea. "Let the sailing DDs handle the cruisers!" he suggested.

"They probably can," Matt agreed, "but they're not as well armored— and it's already too tight in the channel to let them in here. They'd have to wait outside, and if just one or two of those cruisers get past them, they can clobber the transports off the beach!"

"Order *Amerika* to join them."

Matt shook his head. "*Amerika* stays with *Big Sal*. If everything does go to pot, we'll need her to pull our people out of here."

"My course is two six zero," Rosen reported.

"Very well."

With the electricity out, *Walker*'s guns were firing in local control, which eliminated their ability to concentrate on a single target, but at the speed and range they were engaging the enemy, it didn't much affect their accuracy. The ship was growing logy, though, as more water gushed into her aft spaces despite Tabby's, and now even the Bosun's best efforts at shoring. One of Irvin's PTs had been destroyed, speeding too close to a fire-vomiting dreadnaught, but other than that, and *Walker*'s wounds, the battle that began so chaotically seemed to be getting under control. The Nancys and Mosquito Hawks of *Salissa*'s 1st Naval Air Wing were fully engaged, now that it was light enough for them to tell friend from foe. No enemy zeppelins, or other unsuspected aircraft had been encountered, and they were free to punish the Grik ships in the harbor, or the warriors still massing to face II Corps. Under the command of the recently promoted General Mersaak, 3rd Division had gone in as a reserve for 6th Division on Lizard Beach One, instead of where originally planned, when Safir Maraan charged the enemy formation in front of her. That charge had been initially successful, and Grisa's division had managed to push the Grik out of their forward positions and capture a number of guns. It had required bitter fighting, though, of a sort somewhat like what they'd seen on the Madras Road in India. Never had the Grik shown such stubborn resistance to a charge! Now 6th Division was largely spent, for the time being, and had to wait for the 3rd to move forward. Interestingly, once they were on its flank, the Grik in front of 5th Division pulled back as well, and Safir Maraan wasn't at all happy about what that implied.

All this information came to Matt via TBS as his ship steamed west, across the mouth of Grik City Bay, booming away at the Grik cruisers trying to sortie against her. There was little incoming fire at present since most of the cruisers' guns were mounted in their sides and they were coming straight for her. Matt thought there were only three left, and they were all damaged to varying degrees. He grunted. Laumer's surviving boats had just sped past at last, and now it was time to take *Walker* out as well. He looked ahead at the shoaling water and frowned. The lookout in the crow's nest high on the foremast behind the bridge hadn't passed a warning, but they were cutting it much closer than he'd have liked.

"Right full rudder, Mr. Rosen," he commanded. "Make your course zero four zero. Minnie, what's Tabby's status? We'll make for *Big Sal* and add her pumps to ours if we need to."

"My course is zero four zero, Captain," Rosen announced several moments later while Minnie consulted with Tabby.

"Very well," Matt said, staring aft now. He felt a little better. He knew there was desperate fighting on land even then, and it was likely to get worse, but regardless of how that turned out, his "little raid" had been amazingly successful already. Vast towers of smoke piled high in the morning sky, and with just his ship, a few small PT boats, and a little help from Keje's and Jis-Tikkar's naval air, they'd laid a whole fleet to waste! It was a heady moment. Now, if things went well ashore, there was no telling what they might accomplish—or what they'd do next, he suddenly brooded.

"Tabby say she's gettin' ahead of the floodin' at last, an' we have 'lectricity back shortly," Minnie proclaimed. "She not bitch—'scuse me, Cap-i-taan! She not *complain* if *Big Sal* help pump us out, though."

"Very well," Matt agreed, gazing out over the fo'c'sle. They'd pass fairly close to the western headland as they exited the bay, but the channel markers—great tree pilings driven into the sea bottom with faded red pennants fluttering in the freshening breeze—were clear.

"Look at that, Skipper!" Bernie said, pointing out to port. Hundreds, *thousands* of Grik were beginning to line the shore, waving weapons and clashing them together. They'd probably started coming out of their defenses west of the city at the sounds of battle behind them. Most of *Walker*'s crew had seen similar sights many times now, and even from their perspective of relative safety, the ravening mob just a few hundred yards away stirred anxious feelings. The Grik cries were muted by the wind, sea, and the blower, but the familiar hissing roar raised goose bumps and hackles. Impulsively, Bernie made an energetically rude gesture at them, then glanced apologetically at Matt. "Sorry, sir."

"That's okay. I was tempted myself. Maybe we can throw something more harmful at them, though." He stepped back into the pilothouse and addressed the talker. "The number four gun will continue firing on the cruisers aft, but have numbers one and two commence firing on that enemy concentration."

"What about the secondary baattery?" Minnie asked. The frustrated Grik were in easy range of the ship's 25 mm, .50 cals, and even .30s.

"The twenty-five and thirty cals can play, but not the fifties." Matt gave Bernie an encouraging smile as the torpedo officer joined him by the captain's chair. "Despite Mr. Sandison's other miracles, we only recently got the brass drawing process for the fifties sorted out. There's still a shortage." He looked at Rosen as Minnie passed the word and the salvo bell rang to warn all hands that the main guns would fire and they should cover their ears. "All ahead two-thirds," Matt ordered. "Let's join *Big Sal* as quick as we can. Tell Tabby to holler if she needs us to slow down."

"Ay, ay."

Even with the sporadic jolts caused by her 4"-50s, the crackle of the .30 cals, and deeper booming of the 25s, *Walker* still felt sluggish beneath Matt's feet, but he sensed her speed begin to build as her shafts dutifully wound up. Still, the old destroyer hadn't quite reached seventeen knots when she slammed hard aground on a shifting sandbar that even the Grik probably hadn't known was there.

Matt and Rosen were the only ones on the bridge who managed to keep their feet during the abrupt deceleration. It was a somewhat mushy impact, thank God, due to the nature of the bottom she struck, but it was intense enough that nobody with nothing to hold on to could possibly remain standing. Matt had his chair, Rosen had the wheel, but nobody else in the pilothouse had anything at all. Minnie slid across the deck strakes, her headset ripping free, and tumbled into the forward-bridge plating near Matt's legs. Bernie practically somersaulted over the back of the chair and smacked his head on the footrest. Herring and a couple of the 'Cats went down and slid forward as well, grabbing for anything they could. 'Cats on the bridgewings managed to hold on, but their feet went out from under them.

It was worse on the fo'c'sle. To Matt's horror, a couple of 'Cats were actually pitched, headlong, over the side, and those not sitting on the "bicycle seats" on either side of the number one gun cartwheeled into the splinter shield or the low spray shield just in front of it. All firing had stopped. Matt lurched to the lee helm and slammed the lever to "all stop" before anyone else had a chance to rise. He didn't feel the telltale vibration of the screws churning the bottom, but they had to stop the engines before they did. He also knew that, as bad as things had been among those he could see, the surprise stop would be most painful to those in the hot, machinery-filled, engineering spaces.

"Up! Up! On your feet!" came the bellow of a Lemurian bosun's mate in a creditable imitation of Chief Gray's manner, if not tone. "Get back to your stations!" the 'Cat continued. "This ain't no time to loll around on deck!" Minnie scrambled for her headset, but Gray's distinctive voice was already blaring out of the speaking tube.

"What the hell?" he demanded. "Tabby's shutting down the engines, but all hell's broke loose down here! Hell, an' everything else! Everybody's hurt, and we got at least two dead!" The repeater on the lee helm clanged to "all stop" even as the rumble of the shafts started to fade.

Matt limped slightly to the voice tubes. He must have strained his old thigh wound somehow. "You okay, Boats?" he demanded.

"I'll live," came the somewhat aggrieved reply. "And Tabby looks okay, but some ain't."

"We must've hit a sandbar," Matt explained. "Too much glare on the water. The lookouts couldn't see the bottom coming up, and we were moving too fast for soundings." He paused. "My fault."

"Don't even think about that silly crap right now," Gray scolded. "What've we gotta do to get off? We had the low hole in the aft engine room just about stopped up, . . ." He paused. "But we've ridden up a little forward. That'll press the stern lower, put more pressure on the leak. We might've sprung some bottom plates too. What're the tides like around here?"

Matt looked at Herring, who was dabbing at a cut on his chin. Herring caught his gaze and shrugged. "I'm not sure, Captain. Perhaps half a fathom? Maybe more."

"Not good, Boats," Matt relayed, "and it's ebbing. We have to back her off now, or we're stuck until the next high tide, at least. Bring the engines up slow," he said to Gray, and the bridge in general.

"Skipper!" Bernie called, back out on the bridgewing. "Those Grik cruisers are getting closer!"

Matt nodded. "We need to get some air down on those things," he told Minnie, who was trying to arrange her helmet back over the headset.

"I already tell Ed to call *Big Sal*," she replied.

"*Big Sal* could pull us off," Herring suggested, then pointed east toward where the new day had revealed the DDs of Des-Ron 6. "Or they could."

"None of 'em can get here before those Grik cruisers do—and I don't want 'em tangling with them in any case. Hopefully, our air or our guns can sort them out before they become a bigger problem. What's Campeti got to say about the main battery?"

"He just report that all guns is manned an' ready again, but we got problems with the gun director." Minnie blinked confusion. "It 'jump its track,' er somethin."

"Tell him to have all guns resume firing at will, in local control," Matt ordered.

Two of *Walker*'s four guns reopened against the closing cruisers while numbers one and two resumed a more leisurely fire on the growing Grik horde packing the beach. Muddy water churned up along the destroyer's flanks as her screws strained to pull her off the sand. "All astern, full!" Matt said calmly, even as it became increasingly clear that his ship was badly stuck. He contemplated having the crew rock the ship, but doubted it would do any good. Smoke piled high in the air, slanting downwind of three tall funnels, joining the brown-gray puffs from the guns. The deck throbbed in time with the groaning shafts, and the windows rattled in their panes, even as the main blower impotently roared behind them.

"Spanky—I mean, the exec, Mr. McFaarlane, say the number four gun has did for another cruiser, but they all gonna drown, aft, as much water as the screws is throwin' up!" Minnie alerted them after what seemed a very long time, but was probably just minutes. "He say we might as well save the fuel an' the strain on the old gal."

Matt nodded reluctantly.

"Captain," Herring called quietly, but urgently, from the port bridge-wing.

"Signal 'all stop,'" Matt ordered. "Tell Mr. McFarlane and Mr. Gray that we'll have to think of something else. Where are those planes? We've still got another cruiser out there!" he added when a series of splashes caused by a skipping shot rose alongside. "What is it, Mr. Herring?"

"Sir, you need to see this. I think we have another problem!"

"Surely not," Matt replied, unable to mask the sarcasm as he joined Commander Herring.

"Yes, sir." Herring lowered his binoculars and pointed. "You may have noticed that the Grik on shore are closer now."

Matt shook his head, but then realized it was true. "My God. With the tide going out, the sandbar's rising above the sea!"

"Yes, sir!" Herring hesitated. "Ah, surely the sandbar won't allow them to actually reach the ship, will it? I mean, there's bound to be some distance of water left between us and the shore . . . at low tide . . . isn't there?"

"I'd hope so, Mr. Herring," Matt answered grimly, "but even if there is, it might not matter much. The shallows'll be full of flashies for a while yet, but they'll go deeper as the day progresses. Even then, if these Grik here are the 'old style,' they won't much care about losses if they think they can get at us. Our most pressing concern remains that last Grik cruiser, but we might start thinking about preparing to repel a helluva lot of boarders, shortly."

Herring gulped. "I've, uh, never fought the Grik—like that—before," he reminded.

Matt rubbed his face. "You might just get to today."

////// *USNRS Salissa (CV-1)*

A pair of rearmed and refueled P-1 Mosquito Hawks hurtled into the air, one after the other, from the front of *Big Sal*'s flight deck. These carried a fifty-pound bomb under their centerlines in addition to ammunition for their wheel pant–mounted "Blitzer Bug" machine guns. They'd discovered it was possible to get the little planes in the air with that much weight if they were launched into a sufficient wind, and the wind was certainly freshening. The Nancys were operating from the sea alongside a stationary *Amerika*. The old liner had sufficient cranes to lift damaged planes from the water, and a maintenance division had gone aboard with plenty of ammo, fuel, and spares to get the job done. *Salissa* and her escorts were steaming in circles around the big iron ship, launching planes when they came into the wind.

Admiral Keje-Fris-Ar turned to regard Adar as the roar of engines diminished, and two more of the little pursuit ships were wheeled over to the catapults. "The situation is spinning out of our control, my brother," Keje gently told his lifelong friend, "as I warned you it would." These words he added with a blink of vindication.

"As the Amer-i-caans would say, you 'told me so,'" Adar agreed. The hood of his Sky Priest's robes was thrown back over his shoulders, and his ears lay flat. "But why did not Cap-i-taan Reddy press me—us— more closely about our ambitions? He could have planned better had he known!"

Keje glared at him, blinking reproof. "You dare blame *him*—after you demanded stra-tee-gic command so you might take the blame for any failures? He gave you, all of us, ample opportunities to specifically state our ambitions, even as he counseled caution. We were afraid to tell him the truth, so he prepared for what he knew would be the least of our aims, as always agreed. Yes, he could have pressed. Perhaps he should have. But that would have diminished your position, the position you were so emphatic about. He does not want to rule us, my brother, so he could not challenge you more forcefully than he did! You *will not* blame him for that!"

Adar bowed his head. "It would still have worked," he said dejectedly. "Everyone was prepared for what they suspected would happen, even Cap-i-taan Reddy himself! But no one could predict a sandbar might trap his ship!"

"War is full of 'sandbars,' Mr. Chairman!" Sandra said hotly, storming up behind them. She'd clearly heard most of the exchange. "And Matt's dealt with a lot of them before. Now he's stuck on one, and my question to you is, what are we going to do about it? You've got everybody out there fighting to conquer Grik City now, and one way or another, that's become the objective. Even Matt acknowledged that! We can't just pine away and lament how it would've still worked. We've got to *make* it work! We can't just pull back now. Even if we wanted to, the Grik won't let us. Second Corps is in close contact, *Walker*'s stuck, and nobody even knows where Chack is! If we're 'all in,' let's go all in!" She paused, looking Adar in the eye. "You wanted to be in charge. Take charge!"

"What would you have us do?" Adar asked.

"I don't know!" Sandra practically yelled. "I'm *not in charge!*" She gestured around at the surrounding battle group. "But there are an awful lot of people and ships out here that aren't doing much."

Keje nodded thoughtfully. "Cap-i-taan Reddy might not approve," he considered.

"It's a little late to worry about that now, isn't it?" Sandra demanded. She looked back at Adar. "Matt gave you the lead, so lead!"

Adar blinked, then nodded slowly. Finally, he took a breath. "Ahd-mi-raal Keje," he said formally, "we will continue to try to contact Chack and his brigade of raiders, but regardless of whether we do or not, it is my order as chairman of the Grand Alliance that we shall capture Grik City at all costs! Assemble every ship in the fleet except those DDs directly supporting Second Corps. We will advance into the harbor and when it is secure, we shall land every soldier, sailor, or Marine from every ship capable of bearing arms. Is that clear?"

Keje blinked amazement. "Of course," he said, almost eagerly. "But what of air operations? And *Salissa*'s batteries are much reduced."

"By all accounts, there is little left in the harbor that will require *Salissa*'s guns. Besides, she still retains her original five thirty-two-pounders per side. She once performed well enough with only those if I recall. General Queen Safir Maraan shall capture that broad expanse that we suspected had been used to operate Grik zeppelins at one time, though none are present. There is evidence they have been, and perhaps there is fuel. Even if there is not, or what there is will not work, we can move some there and the Fleashooters will have a place to land."

Keje's eyes grew wider. "What of the Naan-cees? *Amerika*, at least, should remain outside the harbor to operate them."

"Very well, but just outside, where her guns may be of assistance, and her people may join the fight on shore as well." Adar blinked anxiously. "I only pray to the Heavens that I have not dithered too long!"

"Admiral," called Lieutenant Newman, Captain Atlaan-Fas's exec, "Laumer's come alongside with his PTs. He wants fuel, Marines for all his boats, and mortars, sir!" He cast a worried look at Sandra. "He says he's headed back to *Walker!*"

"We will give him whatever he wants," Keje ordered.

Sandra hesitated only an instant. "I'm going with him!"

"I do not think that is wise," Adar said, glancing significantly at her midriff.

Of course he knows! Sandra realized. *He's "in charge," and many of my medical division on board are bound to have seen the signs!* "Probably not for me," Sandra agreed tightly, "but all *Walker* has are Pam Cross and a few assistants, pharmacist's mates, and SBAs. She's liable to need more than that before this is done. I'm going!"

USS Walker

The final Grik cruiser had led a charmed life during its advance, and it seemed like nothing could touch her for a while. Her skipper was particularly skilled when it came to evading bombs from diving Nancys, and she'd even shot a couple down with her antiair mortars as the planes bored in ever closer to have a better chance of hitting. Even *Walker*'s guns seemed to have less effect than normal, firing straight at her oncoming bow. The shots caromed off the armored, angled sides, and exploded in the water, or splashed into the bay far beyond, flipping end over end with a manic *whirr.* Maybe she was a newer, more heavily armored class, or maybe they'd all been as well protected from the start, and they'd just been lucky enough to catch them with plunging fire on their decks. Either way, the thing had gotten way too close with her one big, forward-mounted gun that would bear, and with the armored ram they saw between the feathers of seawater she kicked up as she closed. It was the machine guns, hastily carried to the fantail, that finally did for her. They chopped up her little flying bridge and slaughtered her apparently talented officers, sending the ship careening into the sandbar herself, just inshore and a little aft. *Walker*'s guns finished her then, firing straight in at point-blank range. The frustrated Nancy pilots helped, and soon the other beached ship was a flaming wreck.

But the tide was inexorable, and they had only a brief respite before it became abundantly clear that the ever-growing Grik force on shore probably could reach the ship when the sea achieved its lowest ebb. Matt was pacing the deck, his sword and pistol belt clasped about his waist, watching Chief Gray heap abuse on those who couldn't handle the companionways as effortlessly as ballerinas—while carrying mattresses up from below. Spanky, a Springfield rifle slung on his shoulder, was with him, grimly viewing the Grik who'd decided to stay back until they could swarm forward in force. Following along behind was Lieutenant Miyata, looking nervously around, unsure what to do.

"I don't see any guns over there," Spanky commented. "Prob'ly have 'em all massed against Second Corps and can't move 'em all the way over here."

"Maybe," Matt allowed. He'd been pausing periodically to view the desolate landscape around Grik City and create a proper mental image of the place in daylight. The city itself was a filthy, sprawling, low-lying hovel, and Matt was strangely reminded of the dried mud mounds that rose around crayfish holes when the creeks around his childhood home ran low. *Thousands and thousands of wood and adobe crawdad holes,* he thought. Miyata had indicated the "Celestial Palace" to them; compared to the rest of the city, it was certainly impressive, at least. It was immense, for one thing, rising like a mountainous, stone cowflop in the center of the city. *Not a cowflop, exactly,* Matt thought, rejecting the first metaphor that came to mind. *More like a gigantic dome—or the top of a monumental cowflop-colored toadstool.* A broad stairway led up the northern flank to a broad landing and arched entrance about a third of the way to the top. There was apparently no other way in, higher than that, but there did appear to be openings, like skylights or vents here and there. Beyond the "palace," they could see the top of the great peaked wall that separated the city from the jungle to the south. *A helluva lot like the wall in* King Kong, he mused, *but Chack's the most dangerous thing on the other side of* this one, he decided confidently. He blinked and stared southeast where clouds of white smoke rose above II Corps's pitched battle, to join the darker smoke rising above the ruined Grik fleet in the anchorage. *What a god-awful, terrible place. Not worth a single, solitary life, but as good a place to kill Grik as any, I suppose.* He looked back at his companions.

"They want to *take* your ship, Captain Reddy," Miyata said, nodding at the Grik on shore. "That is the most likely explanation to me, why they have not brought more artillery." He shrugged. "You must understand that to Kurokawa, USS *Walker* has been the symbol of all that has thwarted the Grik, and no doubt the Grik commanders, perhaps even their First General Esshk in particular, would like nothing more than to have her."

"That's not gonna happen!" Spanky seethed, and Matt nodded. "No, it's not," he said with certainty. He flinched slightly when the number two gun barked above them, from atop the amidships deckhouse. The bright, off-colored tracer slammed into the Grik on shore and blew many of them into the sky when it burst. The main battery was still slaughtering Grik, but ammunition was beginning to dwindle. Matt accepted that. When the Grik got too close, they'd be "under" his guns. Better use the ammo while they were bunched up at a distance. The machine guns would have to do when they got close. *Walker* had virtually no protection against boarders—or their muskets, which the Grik horde apparently possessed in considerable numbers. There were only the rail and the safety chains, and the crew was busily lashing mattresses to them, as many deep and as fast as they could. It didn't look good, but it was clear by everyone's attitude that there was no way the Grik would capture USS *Walker* while anyone aboard her lived.

"Captain!" cried Ed Palmer, catching up. He hadn't bothered with a message form, but if he came in person, Matt knew he had important news.

"What've you got, Ed?"

Palmer gulped at the sight of the Grik, and a frown spread across his boyish face. He jerked his gaze away from the enemy. "Uh, Keje's comin'. The whole fleet's comin'. All we have to do is hold on."

Matt shook his head. "I'd be happy to see the DDs, but what the devil is Keje doing, bringing *Big Sal* in the bay? I'd rather have her planes." He gestured at the channel. "Besides, with the tide this low, I'm not sure he can even get *Big Sal*'s fat ass through the deep part!"

Palmer shook his head. "He's not just coming for us. They're going to land everybody and kill every Grik in the city!"

Matt rubbed his chin. "Okay. I guess that makes sense. No half measures anymore. I'm still worried about the channel, though."

Palmer's face fell. "No reason to be, sir." He hesitated. "It'll be a few hours before they can sort things out. Tide's liable to have turned by then."

Matt nodded. At least his friends weren't being idiots, but that wouldn't help *Walker* much in the short term. "Any good news?"

"Uh, yes, sir. They'll keep as much air on the Grik here as they can. There might be a lull while they shift *Amerika* . . . but Mr. Laumer's comin' in."

"What good can he do? His boats don't have any guns."

"No, sir, but he's bringing us reinforcements and some mortars."

"That'll help," Spanky grunted.

Matt noticed that Dennis Silva and Lawrence had drifted closer while he talked with Palmer, and that big Marine named Horn was with them. Petey was clutching Silva's neck much like he had Sandra's and Rebecca's before him, but he didn't seem nearly as relaxed as in the past. His head kept jerking toward the explosive sounds of the guns, and his eyes were huge, and constantly darting. Silva didn't even seem to notice him now, and he was grinning that special, gap-toothed "Silva Grin," that implied he thought he'd just come up with the greatest idea the world had ever known.

"Good Lord, Silva," Matt practically groaned. "What've you got in mind?"

"Oh, nothin', Skipper. Just a notion."

Matt couldn't help but roll his eyes. "Spill it!"

Dennis shrugged, and gestured east with his chin. "Queen Maraan an' Second Corps' got the main Grik army facin' off with her, right?"

Spanky nodded.

"We got what looks like the rest o' the Griks in the city waddin' up yonder to come tromp on us. . . ."

"What's your point?"

"Why, somethin' purty obvious. Hell, even my little lizard buddy here seen it before I did." He ruffled Lawrence's crest, and the Sa'aaran hissed at him. "With ever-body off fightin' us, er getting ready to, I wonder who's left downtown to babysit the Sequest'ral Momma?"

"He's got a point, sir," the Marine said earnestly. "But it might be a fleeting opportunity. When the whole fleet steams into the bay, the Grik are bound to pull something back, beef up that palace thing they keep her in. If we're going to go, we need to do it soon!"

Matt looked hard at Silva. Did he know what he was asking? He nodded slightly to himself. Of course he did, despite that goofy grin. "What do you want to do?"

"I want one of the PTs when it gets here, a few sacks o' grenades, a Thompson, and a BAR. I'll leave my Doom Stomper here. You might need it. Oh, and I'd like to take a few fellas, if you can spare 'em." He looked at Toryu Miyata. "Might need him too, o' course. He knows a little of the layout, an' has a idea where they might keep the puffed-up, lizardy queen," Silva said.

Matt looked at Miyata, and the Japanese sailor jerked a tense nod. "Very well. What then?"

"Why, we haul ass straight to the dock in front of the palace, run in, an' kill that big fat lizard bitch, once an' fer all!"

"Lizard bitch!" Petey echoed querulously.

The arrival of what remained of Laumer's little mosquito fleet, burbling up alongside *Walker*'s starboard quarter, must've stirred the Grik on shore to action. They probably would've come soon at any rate; the tide was almost out. There remained only about thirty yards of water between the damp, sandy bar and the dry side of the ship that was now visible well below the boot topping, all the way down to where it curved away toward the keel. The Grik waved gaudy red and black pennants, bordered with macabre trinkets, and their impatient roar rose to a shattering crescendo. Suddenly, the strident, bellows-operated horns they relied on sounded the note everyone had come to dread: the signal to attack.

"Here they come," Gray shouted, unnecessarily, pacing behind the sailors and Marines lining the mattress breastworks. With Irvin's arrival, there were close to two hundred defenders now, about half armed with the 1903 Springfields the destroyermen had jealously guarded. A few Krags remained aboard, but most of the reinforcements were armed with the increasingly ubiquitous Allin-Silva breechloaders and a sprinkling of Blitzer Bugs. Long, triangular bayonets on the Allin-Silvas glistened occasionally in the beams of sunlight that avoided the smoke and the rapidly clouding late-morning sky.

Matt was standing with Sandra as Silva's party clambered down the starboard side onto the waiting PT boat. He hadn't even been surprised when she showed up, and couldn't really summon any genuine anger either. Somehow, he'd known she would come. She always had. Anxious as he was for her and their unborn child, he knew that whatever they faced that day, they'd face together. It had been building to this, he guessed, since the very day they met. Chief Gray had been furious when he discovered that Diania had accompanied Sandra, however, and had ordered her back on one of the boats that would return to *Big Sal*. She refused. He did manage to get her armed (she hadn't thought of that) and sent down to the wardroom where Sandra would take over as chief surgeon.

Silva's shore party consisted of him, Horn, Lawrence, Pack Rat, and Isak Reuben—of all people—who'd just jumped down on the PT without permission. He had a Krag, and hadn't paid any attention to Spanky's orders to get back on the ship. He just kept muttering something about his boilers. Spanky gave up and quit yelling. Commander Herring had volunteered and was in nominal command, but everyone knew who would really be in charge. He stepped aside and said something to Ian Miles before joining the others, and the China Marine lance corporal just looked at him incredulously. Irvin already had sixteen Lemurian Marines crammed on the boat.

"They'll need a doc!" Pam Cross shouted, running up with a Blitzer Bug slung over her shoulder, and pitching a backpack down to waiting hands.

"Not *you*, doll!" Silva roared back. "Not this time!" He'd been tugging at Petey, trying to get the little tree-gliding lizard to let go so he could toss him back to Sandra. Maybe Petey was too terrified, but he wouldn't be budged. The harder Silva tugged, the deeper Petey's claws sank through his T-shirt. Blood was starting to soak through. Pam stuck her tongue out at Dennis and glared at Sandra, daring the other woman to refuse her. Sandra just shook her head and looked away. What *could* she say? With her here, Pam had more real business going with Silva than Sandra had coming to *Walker*.

"Skipper?" Dennis demanded.

Matt took a breath, then shook his head as well. "She'll be safer with you, Chief Silva," he said at last. "Good luck to you all, and God bless." He hesitated, as if he wanted to say more, but then turned toward the roaring Grik horde, now sprinting across the sandbar. "Get below," he ordered Sandra, and strode toward the 'Cats and men who would defend his ship.

Pam climbed down and defiantly faced Silva, fishing in her pack. "Here, stupid. Fatso Lanier gave me this for you." Dennis took a battered, stainless steel butter knife from her hand and looked at it, remembering. Up where the blade flared into the handle was a deeply inscribed U.S. "Yeah," he said softly. "I got promises to keep." Inwardly, he thought Captain Reddy might be right about Pam being safer with him, and he felt torn between an instinctive urge to defend his ship, his *Home*, and doing what he knew he had to do. Pam's presence might complicate that, but there was no point arguing with her. With an artificial nonchalance, Dennis Silva took a last, long look at USS *Walker*. Abruptly, he turned to Ensign Hardee, standing at the wheel beside Irvin Laumer. "Let's get on with it!" he grated. "What the hell are we waitin' for now—the goddamn Easter Bunny?" Resignedly, he quit tugging at Petey and glared at the big eyes staring back at him. "Maybe you'll be safer with us too, you little creep—or catch a sword swipe for me."

"Creep!" Petey shrieked.

The twin six-cylinder engines rumbled noisily as the crowded boat backed away from the ship, her crew watching for snags in the shallow water. Above them, they heard *Walker*'s machine guns start to roar.

////// *USS Walker*

rik fell like dominoes under the withering fire of four machine guns lining the rail, and the twin 25-mm gun tubs in the waist. A downy fuzz rose above the charging swarm, mixed with spattered muddy sand, sprays of red, shattered weapons, and gobbets of flesh. White puffs of smoke rose as well, from matchlocks, sending whirring balls over the heads of the defenders, or flurries of mattress stuffing drifting downwind.

"Riflemen, hold your fire!" Matt yelled, when a couple shots answered the Grik. Crossbow bolts were starting to thump into the mattresses too, or sleet by overhead. The 4"-50s were still firing, spitting long tongues of flame, but they were having more and more trouble engaging the closest targets. They'd keep after those farther behind when they couldn't depress their muzzles anymore. "At one hundred yards . . . ," Matt continued, gauging the distance. He wanted his first volley to slam them. "Take aim!" he cried, echoed by the Bosun.

"Fire!"

It was impossible to miss. At least two hundred Grik fell with that first volley, the heavy 450-grain bullets of the .50-80-caliber Allin-Silvas often plowing through one target to hit another. The Springfields and Krags had a similar effect. The mortars Laumer brought began thumping, but their baseplates tended to skate across the ship's steel deck, leaving scars in the paint, and their crews immediately started looking for ways to wedge them in place.

"Fire at will!" Matt roared, echoed by the Bosun and others. Then he drew his 1911 Colt and moved up beside Juan Marcos, who was busily working the bolt of his Springfield and selecting targets between competent shots. The one-legged Filipino had proven himself with a rifle before. Juan cursed when his bolt locked back, and he fished another stripper clip out of his ammo belt. Inserting it in the guide with practiced ease, he slammed the five .30-06 cartridges into the magazine with his thumb, tossed the clip away, and resumed firing. Matt peered over the mattresses and saw the Grik were still getting closer. The first volley must have slowed them, but they continued surging forward in "the same old way." Scattered Blitzer Bugs ripped into them with dull *buraaaps!* and bodies literally poured into the shallow water alongside the old destroyer. There were no flasher fish yet, but Matt was sure they'd come. Unfortunately, there was no way they could eat the entire causeway of flesh that was beginning to form—not nearly as fast as the Grik built it with their own bodies.

"Campeti!" Matt roared at his gunnery officer, atop the amidships deckhouse. Campeti stuck his helmeted head over his own breastwork of mattresses to look down. "Sir?"

"Shift your machine-gun fire farther back! We're helping them build their damn bridge! Have your riflemen do the same."

"Aye, aye, Captain!"

"Boats!" Matt called aft. "Have the twin twenties chop 'em up farther from the ship!" Gray relayed the order with a nod, but then hurried to join his captain. "It's not gonna do any good, Skipper. Look what them devils are doin'!"

Matt peered through a gap between the mattresses and the deck-house. At first he didn't understand. Then he did. As fast as dead and dying Grik fell in the water, others were hurling *more*, those killed behind, in on top of them! "Good God!" A big musket ball slapped the steel beside his face, dishing it in like a hailstone on a car. The lead spattered, and hot fragments gouged his cheek. He reeled back.

"You okay Skipper?" Gray demanded. Matt nodded, touching his face. For the first time, he paused long enough to measure what they were taking. The tightly stuffed mattresses, at least doubled in most places, were absorbing the enemy projectiles amazingly well, and they quivered like live things under the onslaught. They couldn't stop everything, however, and 'Cats in a steady trickle were limping or being carried forward toward the companionway to the wardroom. Half a dozen or more bodies lay where they'd fallen. Most of those had grisly head wounds, he noticed. A ball blew through and smacked against the number three funnel, reminding him that even the mattresses couldn't hold up forever. "Cap-tan!" Juan called. "They're nearly to the side of the ship! Right here below me!"

"Go, Boats. Round up anyone far enough aft that the Grik can't reach and bring 'em forward! We've got to keep them off the ship!"

"Aye, aye, Skipper!" Gray growled, and trotted aft, keeping his head down. Matt heard a twin roar above his head and watched a pair of P-1 "Fleashooters" swoop down and scythe into the Grik mass with their own wheel pant–mounted Blitzer Bugs. The sound of their weapons was different from the handheld versions, and barely audible over their motors, but each plane left twin streaks of writhing Grik in their wakes as they pulled up and circled around for another pass. The Grik wailed in pain and terror, but aircraft didn't have the same effect on them that they once had. Matt wondered about that. These particular Grik had probably never seen an airplane before. He shook his head. He needed Nancys *right now*, with their antipersonnel fragmentation firebombs! Where were the damn Nancys? A 'cat torpedoman, acting as a talker, had his headset plugged in at the mount. "Ask Mr. Palmer to find out where our air support has gone! We need bombs, not bullets. We've got plenty of bullets of our own!" he ordered.

Palmer must've been working on it already, because the talker immediately repeated what Ed replied. "Nancys is working over the Griks in front of Second Corps. They gotta fly out to *Amer-i-kaa* an' rearm before they come here. We got all the Fleashooters, an' more o' them is rearming with bombs on *Big Sal,* but it take a little before the Nancys get here. They is movin' *Amer-i-kaa* closer, an' she ain't fuelin' an' armin' *nothin'* right now!"

Matt ground his teeth. The Grik were almost on them, and it would soon be down to the bayonet. "Tell Mr. Palmer to inform Adar, Captain Von Melhausen, Keje, or anybody he can get ahold of, that *Amerika* needs to stop right now, wherever she is, regardless of whatever scheme they're cooking up. If she doesn't start getting our air support turned around as fast as she can, there won't be anything left of us to support!" The 'Cat blinked wide eyes and then spoke quickly to Palmer.

The pair of Fleashooters came back, their blue paint difficult to distinguish against the darkening sky. There were none of the antiair mortars, like giant shotguns mounted on a baseplate and aimed by hand, among the mobs surging against *Walker,* but the incoming fusillade of musket fire paused while what must've been nearly every matchlock in the horde puffed smoke at the diving planes. The little pursuit ships had to get low for the short-range Blitzers to be effective, and countless crossbow bolts rose as well. It was impossible to say which weapons were responsible for savaging one of the planes so badly that it sprouted flames and spun into the burning remains of the Grik ironclad cruiser. A ball of fire roiled into the air, and flaming gasoline spattered the Grik crowding forward, closest to the beached wreck. The other P-1 clawed at the sky and staggered away, trailing a thin stream of smoke.

There remained a lull in the fire directed at the ship while the Grik reloaded, and the defenders rose up and poured it in. Rifles flashed. The 25 mm pounded with a metronomic booming, machine guns and Blitzer Bugs chattered, and the big 4"-50s roared defiance—and still the Grik came. There'd be no stopping them, Matt realized. It was as though they somehow knew that USS *Walker* was the heart of the Allied fleet.

These warriors were mostly young and almost crestless, so maybe they actually believed that, having been taught it since birth. Their motivation hardly mattered in the grand scheme of things. What did matter was that they were about to reach the deck of Matt's ship, over the mounded bodies of the slain, and it didn't look like there was a thing in the world he could do to stop it.

"Marines!" Matt roared, mostly addressing those who'd come aboard from the PTs. "Take shields and move to the front!" Allied Marines had gone back and forth between using their bronze-faced shields and discarding them, but it had been shown that, in fights like this, shields still served a valuable purpose. "Riflemen, behind them! Bayonets forward!" He looked at the excited torpedo talker. "Everyone on the ship, but the seriously wounded, a minimal watch in the firerooms, and the repair party in the aft engine room will report to the point of contact, between the bridge and the port torpedo mount! Secure all hatches from the inside and keep them that way until further notice!"

"Even to the wardroom?" the 'Cat asked. "Where'll we take the wounded?"

"*Especially* the companionway hatch to the wardroom!" Matt ordered. He suddenly noticed Earl Lanier standing just under the overhang, between the aft galley bulkhead and the number three 'stack. The obese cook had a Thompson, but was just looking around, wide-eyed. "Lanier! Get your mates and what corps-'Cats you can find, and set up a dressing station on the starboard side of the galley! The amidships deckhouse, the bridge, and the aft deckhouse will be our battlements, and the last places we retreat to. Spread the word!" he added for the talker.

"But Captain!" Earl finally managed. "I never got my Coke machine struck down below! It's still sittin' where you want the dressing station! There'll be a buncha m'lingerin' bastards tryin' to get away from the fight with a scratch er scrape wallowin' all over it, dentin' the lid!"

Matt shook his head, struck by the weird things people thought of at times like this. The Coke machine was usually empty, but despite repeated battle damage, it still worked. It had become a kind of talisman for many of the old crew—and particularly Earl Lanier.

"If it gets in the way one little bit, you'll heave it over the side! Is that absolutely clear? Now *go!*" Matt snapped at Earl's hesitant nodding.

"You want my riflemen down there?" Campeti called from above.

"Not yet, Sonny. Use 'em to try to keep the Grik off us. Otherwise, you're our last reserve. You can see where they'll be needed better from up there than I can!" Matt racked the slide on his Colt, chambering a round, then flipped the thumb safety up. Releasing the magazine, he thumbed an extra .45 ACP cartridge on top of the remaining six before slamming it back in the well. "It's about to get a bit frisky, as Silva would say," he added to those around him, managing a slight grin despite the turmoil in his chest. It had been a long time since he'd faced the Grik at such close quarters. He was better with his sword than he'd been before, he reflected absently, but fervently hoped it wouldn't come to that. An instant later, the first Grik began swarming up, over the mattresses, and somehow he knew it would.

CHAPTER

27

////// *PT-7*

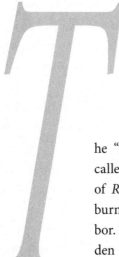

he "Seven boat," or *Lucky Seven*, as Irvin Laumer called her since she had, after all, survived the sinking of *Respite Island*, crept slowly through the jutting, burning remains of the Grik fleet in the shallow harbor. It was a surrealistic sight, even blurred by the sudden downpour drenching everyone aboard. Blasted carcasses of mighty ships, laid open and gutted on their sides, bore stark testimony to the quality of Bernie Sandison's Baalkpan Naval Arsenal Mk-3 torpedoes. Between them, *Walker*'s new armor-piercing shells and the work of *Big Sal*'s 1st Naval Air Wing, it didn't look like a single capital ship had survived the predawn onslaught. It was possible a few cruisers remained, anchored beyond the cluster of Grik "Indiamen" deeper in the harbor, but none were reported by the flyboys. Many of the Indiamen themselves were burning too, but they hadn't been priority targets. They were crewed by warriors, and it was most likely they were abandoned while their crews fought on shore.

Besides, considering the growing strain on Allied supply lines, captured Grik Indiamen, once despised, were now prized for their cargo capacity— and easy conversion to better ships, of course. They were helpless right now, and wouldn't all be destroyed until it was decided whether the Allies could get them or not.

Lieutenant Irvin Laumer had taken the wheel of the Seven boat himself, coaxing her through the treacherous anchorage like a trout in a rocky stream, while crewfolk on the fo'c'sle warned of hazards such as underwater obstacles or floating debris. It was hard to see. The rain was churning up the surface of the water, and the flashies were doing the same as they feasted on countless Grik corpses. All the nearby ships were burning brightly, and there wasn't a live Grik to be seen on any of them.

"Lawsy, what a awful place!" Isak Reuben muttered, clutching his Krag close to his skinny chest with one hand while he lit one of his vile, soggy cigarettes with the other, under the shelter of his helmet. "I bet I shouldn't'a come," he added.

"Why *did* you, you nutty twerp?" Silva demanded, taking a chew. "Tabby'll have your skin when she finds out!" he mumbled around the yellowish leaves he stuffed in his cheek.

Isak shrugged. "She don't need me. *Walker* don't even need me anymore," he added miserably. "Least not with her all scrunched up ashore." His voice firmed and he glared up at Silva, the rain trying to quench the butt dangling from his lips. "An' besides, that sequittal, lizardy grub worm all the Griks is so worked up over has been havin' her nasty critters tryin' to kill my boilers ever since the day we brung 'em here." He shrugged. "Gilbert's my half brother, you know." Silva nodded, surprised by the sudden confession. Everybody knew, though the Mice had never openly admitted it before. "Well, he ain't here. He's off engineerin' in *Maaka-Kakja*, with Second Fleet, fightin' the Doms." He took a long drag and coughed. "Just seems *one* of us ought'a try to hit a lick against the damn thing, after we come all this way." He waved his hand helplessly.

"You're gonna get ate, Isak," Silva stated matter-of-factly.

Isak shrugged again, but glanced back the way they'd come. *Walker* was barely visible through the smoke and rain several miles away, but her guns still flared against the dreary day and the deadly shore. "Could be," he answered quietly, "but I bet I would have back yonder, anyway. Least this way, if I get ate, it'll be doin' somethin' different. Ever'body's always on me to try new things."

"*I* didn't come along to get eaten," Gunny Horn stated, and Silva looked at him.

"Why'd *you* come? You at least could'a been of use on the ship. I thought Marines always craved fightin' on ships!"

"He came for the same reason as me, stupid," Pam snapped, speaking for the first time since she presented Silva with the knife. "Because you did."

Horn regarded the woman strangely. She had a Blitzer Bug slung over her shoulder, and a bulky bag of magazines hung from a strap. The rain had turned her T-shirt translucent to the point that she might as well have worn nothing at all. Like the rest of them, she wore a "tin hat" helmet, but her dark hair was soaked and strands were plastered to her face. He knew how tough she was, but right then, she looked very small and vulnerable. "Maybe, in a way," Horn admitted. "Me and that idiot ape have a long history, all the way back to the China Station, of getting into scrapes together." He fingered a little leather thong around his neck that was threaded through a tooth with a hole in it. "Kind of unnatural, come to think of it, considering I'm a Marine, and he's . . . whatever the hell he is," he continued. "But I surely doubt the *real* reason we both came is exactly the same." He scratched his thick black beard. "I'm here because Dennis always throws a helluva party. I figure you tagged along to make sure he doesn't have too much fun."

Pam looked away. "Just shut up, wilya?"

Laumer coughed. "*I'm* here to get your crazy butts ashore. Lieutenant Miyata? You've been here before. Point the way, if you please, to the best place to land."

Miyata complied, indicating a long section of dock, crowded with small boats a little beyond the jutting funnels of another dead Grik ship. This one had some survivors, crowded atop the exposed casemate, but they weren't any threat. As far as they could see, the dock was deserted.

"It looks like you may have been right," Herring told Silva. He hadn't said much either. Now he was looking through an Imperial telescope. "I don't see any Grik at all, ashore."

"There may be quite a few in those warehouses and shops beyond the dock," Miyata advised, "or in the—I think you would say 'shantytown'— between them and the palace."

Herring grunted. "What does the Jap say about palace guards?" he asked. He'd rarely been able to bring himself to address Miyata directly.

Miyata bristled. "Commander Herring, we are about to go into action together, and if you want my best assistance, I hope you will remember that my name is not 'the Jap'!"

"Settle down, Lieutenant," Silva soothed. "Mr. Herring's only met the kinda Japs that murder pris'ners. He ain't as forgivin' an' open-minded as me an' Larry are. Hell, I even got a Jap friend! Gen'ral Shinya's a right guy!" His face turned serious and his tone hard. "Now, that said, you an' me don't know each other very well, but anybody'll tell you that if I do get a notion you're settin' us up for any Grik or Jap buddies o' yours, I'll feed you to Petey a strip at a time!"

"Eat?" Petey chirped happily.

"I am on your side!" Miyata objected. "Surely Becher Lange has convinced you of that by now."

"Don't personally know the Kraut neither," Silva replied reasonably.

"Leave Lieutenant Miyata alone," Irvin Laumer ordered with an authority Silva didn't remember. "He's okay."

Silva sniffed.

"The 'palace guard,' as you call it, is quite numerous," Miyata said crisply. "But its members are dispersed between several levels, and more entrances that we can see from here. I doubt they have ever considered a need to practice massing in one part of the palace to prevent an actual attack, and they may not know how—or even be able to." He considered. "There *is* another possible reserve the palace might call on that could prove even more problematic, if it has not already been sent to the fighting."

"What's that?" Irvin asked.

"The 'sport fighters.' Consider them like 'gladiators.' They are all skilled warriors with considerable experience. It is that experience, in fact, that makes them 'entertaining' to watch, I understand." He looked at Herring. "You may recall that I reported that it was from that group that Kurokawa initially selected leaders for their 'new' army, and their General Halik rose."

Herring nodded. "I remember," he said, finally looking straight at Miyata. "How many?"

"I cannot say. There *were* several hundred, at least." He glanced at the gloomy palace growing near. "There may be even more now—or perhaps there are none, if they have all entered their armies."

Lawrence looked from one man to the other. He hadn't said anything at all, but had observed his friends and all the strangers on PT-7 with considerable interest. He'd learned a lot about humans and Lemurians in the last couple of years and recognized that there were a lot of differences between his kind and theirs. His folk were much less emotionally complicated; that was certain. He sensed many emotional undercurrents on the boat just then, and like the predator he was, he wondered who might be the weak link in their little pack of "hunters," and how that might affect their mission. He sensed a lot of fear, and that was normal. He was afraid himself. He didn't remember when he hadn't been afraid, on some level, since he'd set out on his "awakening," or "rite of passage" voyage so long ago. That was what brought him in contact with humans and Lemurians in the first place. It was also what truly "awakened" him to what he could become, and he was wholly devoted to his friends. He wasn't worried how *they* would perform—even Pam. He already knew. As usual, he was utterly content to follow Silva's lead while he watched for the weak link. If necessary, he'd cut it out himself before it had a chance to break.

They motored closer to the dock in silence, always on the alert for threats. Laumer coaxed his boat between a pair of smaller vessels that looked a lot like Lemurian feluccas, and a pair of 'Cats leaped across to the dock. One had a coil of rope, and the other stood by to fend off, as Laumer cut his throttles.

"Single up there," Laumer called in a loud whisper, wondering as he did it why he was trying to be so quiet. The rain and the battle raging

behind and to the east were sufficiently loud to keep his voice from carrying far. Almost immediately, Lawrence scampered ashore, his head
bobbing as he tasted unfamiliar scents. Silva jumped after him, followed
by the rest of the party in a rush. After a moment, and without a word,
Laumer chose a shortened smoothbore Allin-Silva from the rack beside
him in the cockpit of the boat and slung a bandolier of 20-gauge shells
over his shoulder. The shells were made of thick, waxed paper with a
brass base, and were loaded with a dozen roughly .30-caliber balls on
top of one hundred grains of powder. Initially called "buckshot," the
shells had quickly been renamed "Grikshot." The weapon that fired it,
so similar to the standard issue rifle in every other way, was simply
called a shotgun. Winny Rominger had lobbied for their issue to the
PTs in addition to some of Chack's Raiders on the grounds that if one of
his boats ever lost power, its small crew would need all the antipersonnel firepower it could get.

Ensign Hardee looked at Laumer with wide eyes. "You're not going
with them, are you, sir?" the sixteen-year-old boy almost squeaked.

"Yes, I am," Irvin replied. "You can handle the Seven boat as well as
I can, and they might need the help." He frowned. "Besides . . . I have to.
For S-Nineteen, and, well, other reasons too." He patted Hardee's shoulder. "You're in command. Back her off and keep station by that wreck
we passed—not the one with the Grik on it!" He grinned. "Keep an eye
on the dock here. If you see us running back, we might need a lift in a
hurry!" He paused. "Get on the TBS and report that we're ashore, and
anything else you see, got it?"

"Aye, aye, sir."

Irvin Laumer nodded, then trotted forward and hopped off the boat,
joining the others as they prepared to enter Grik City itself.

///// *II Corps*

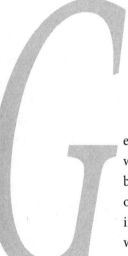

eneral Queen Safir Maraan and 6th Division were in the first Grik trenchline now, and the bright morning had been strangled by an opaque haze of smoke and dust beneath a growing pall of darkening skies. A few raindrops were beginning to fall, as if shaken from the air by the concussive thud of artillery and constant crackle of rifle fire. She'd lost track of General Grisa somewhere on the long, corpse-strewn beach behind, between their initial landing point and here. But a pair of signal 'Cats with one of the new field telephones remained beside her, unspooling wire. The charge across the naked beach had been one of the most unnerving events of the entire war for her thus far. She knew her beloved Chack had done much the same against equally implacable foes in the East, and she'd run into a defensive Grik position herself once before, but this was the first time she'd ever slammed a charge home, directly into bristling spears, cannon muzzles, and withering crossbow and musket fire. The 6th was fortunate that these Grik, though clearly able to defend, didn't have much practice at it, and the wild melee in the trench itself had been equally awkward and terrifying for both sides. The better discipline and firepower of Safir's troops had been the only, final, advantage.

She looked around at the panting faces nearby, and saw the furtive, fearful blinking of those who were scampering back and forth, rejoining their companies and squads, all while nervously wading through the carpet of dead in the bottom of the trench. Fortunately, most of those corpses were Grik, but many troopers bayoneted bodies as a matter of course before moving along. She understood how they felt. These were veteran troops, but though they'd fought from trenches before, this was the first time they'd ever captured one. With so many Grik this close, actually *touching* them, after what they'd just been through . . . it was only natural they wanted to make sure they were all entirely dead.

She looked back to the front, taking a small sip from her canteen, and noticed her hand was trembling. She quickly lowered it, hoping no one had seen. By the Sun above, she wished Chack were beside her! Or perhaps even better just then, her old nemesis turned virtual father, General Lord Muln Rolak! Doubtless he'd be chatting away about the situation in his calming way. She took a deep breath and almost gagged. The stench of the dead, of the gore and voided bowels, was bad enough, but the reek of the *place* itself was beginning to get to her. It was an ancient, all-pervading thing that she'd begun to notice as they advanced farther from the cleansing shore. The Jaap, Mi-yaata, had warned them of it, proposing that it was caused by eons of Grik, defecating wherever they liked outside, and Safir uncomfortably wondered how much of the dusty soil she'd breathed was composed of age-old Grik dung. She shook her head and coughed.

"If it rains, it might settle this dust, and perhaps some of the smoke," one of the comm-'Cats suggested hopefully, as if reading her thoughts.

"Let us hope so," she replied. "It may render their matchlock muskets useless as well. Contact the comm section on the beach and have them move the TBS set forward to the trench where it will be better protected. I also want a line to all other division commanders as soon as possible, so we may better coordinate our next advance. The Grik have retreated, but only to another defensive line. I want naval gunfire from the frigates offshore placed on that position, and as much air support as can be spared." She paused. "Any word yet on General Grisa's whereabouts?"

"I will ask if he has . . . gone back to the beach," the 'Cat said, and Safir nodded solemnly. The wounded and dead were being taken there to be carried out to the ships in their remaining landing boats.

"Please do, and have someone look for him specifically if he has not been seen." She felt a twinge of guilt over the harsh words she'd spoken to Grisa. He'd only been doing what he thought was expected of him before, but he'd charged just as enthusiastically as anyone when she made his orders more specific. She prayed he was well. A squall marched across the anchorage in the distance, but didn't quell the smoke; it only added vast plumes of steam to the impenetrable curtain over the remains of the Grik fleet. She was satisfied with that, at least. As always, Captain Reddy and USS *Walker* had done their part. She suspected that Irvin Laumer's "mosquito fleet" had done much as well. She heard the comm-'Cat talking but was too absorbed by the sight of the destruction they'd wrought on this vile, ancient city, and her gaze was drawn past the next enemy trenchline to the vast, round-topped structure south of the harbor, just beginning to appear through the haze. *There you are,* she thought. *And we are coming for you!*

Mortar crews were clearing bodies and hacking at the earthen trench to give themselves a better angle, but at present, no Allied cannon were firing except those out on the ships, their smoke-tailed case shot beginning to explode on or above the enemy. Safir's light guns couldn't be brought down in the trench, and even if they were, they couldn't fire westward. Not yet. For now they stood in the open, having been brought up by hand, their crews safely under cover while they too labored to clear emplacements for them. Quite a few Grik guns had been captured, but even as they turned them against their former owners, they faced a similar problem.

"My queen!" the comm-'Cat said urgently. "*Waa-kur* is aground at the mouth of the bay! Thousands of Grik are massing to attack her across a low-tide sandbar! Chairman Adar asks if we can press the enemy here more vigorously to prevent more Grik being sent against Capi-taan Reddy! He also desires to know if we can secure the zeppelin field closer to the city for our planes with fixed landing gear to use."

Safir blinked concern, but then her tail slashed the air indignantly. "Tell Chairman Adar that we already press the Grik as hard as we can, and will resume our advance as soon as we reorganize from the last one!" She regretted her harsh tone as soon as the words left her mouth, but continued without altering it. "More air and naval artillery support will help, as would the reserve division aboard *Amer-i-ka*! Our losses have not been insignificant!"

The comm-'Cat repeated her words, then listened for a moment. He looked at her, blinking, his own tail swishing back and forth. "Chairman Adar says it is imperative that we take the airfield, because *Salissa* may not be able to launch or recover aircraft much longer. In the meantime, we will get all the air support that can be spared," he told her, "but there will be no more ships than those already at our disposal—and no reinforcements either. Every other ship, and anyone able to bear arms, in fact, will make another landing in the harbor itself, after the tide turns! Chairman Adar says that he would be . . . obliged if Second Corps might meet him there!"

Safir Maraan swore softly, closing her eyes. Then she looked at the strengthening enemy position about two hundred tails away, and knew the airfield lay a few hundred tails beyond. The new line didn't have as much artillery as the first one, it didn't seem, but their attack would be costly. The Grik might not have proper canister—which suddenly made a kind of sense to her. Canister was a strictly defensive weapon, and if the enemy was just learning the concept of defense, the proper tools might take a while to be employed. But it *had* learned to stuff its barrels with whatever was at hand, from nails, to rocks and musket balls. There were many more Grik awaiting them now as well, and the next line was all that remained between II Corps and the bizarre warren of mud hovels that was Grik City itself.

"Tell Chairman Adar that we will try," she said at last. Just then, several sputtering arcs of flame hurtled skyward from the Grik posi-

tion, almost simultaneously, trailing large, burning spheres. With un-
canny, unprecedented accuracy, all of them came down right in the very
trench the 6th Division occupied. The spheres burst on contact, washing dozens of Lemurian troops with a viscous, flaring, saplike com-
pound they'd always called "Grik Fire." Horrible screams tortured
Safir's soul, and many screamed in sympathetic pain or outrage. "They
knew we would take this trench!" Safir cried in fury. "They knew—and
they already had it targeted!" She spun to the comm'Cat, who'd essentially become her personal talker. "Inform the other commands immediately!" she shouted, then turned in time to see another pair of flaming
spheres climb into the gray sky. "Tell Adar we will meet him at the harbor or *die* trying. We certainly cannot stay here!"

Grik City

Silva's landing party trotted carefully, watchfully, through the empty
warehouses bordering the waterfront. Their shoes and the sandaled feet of
the Lemurian Marines on the concrete-hard earth inside echoed loudly in
the cavernous buildings. There was a jangle of equipment and weapons
too. Silva was as well armed as usual, even if he'd left his precious "Doom
Stomper" behind. He had a Thompson SMG, his 1911 Colt, trusty cutlass,
and 1903 Springfield bayonet. He also carried a shoulder bag full of grenades and had magazine pouches all over him. Oddly, as always, an or-
nately made, long-barreled flintlock pistol dangled from his belt by a hook.
Only a few people knew why. Gunny Horn was actually more heavily
laden for once, with a BAR, pistol, and just as many magazines and grenades. Herring and Pack Rat both had Springfields, Pam carried her
Blitzer Bug, and Laumer had his shotgun. Like the Lemurian Marines that
accompanied them, Lawrence carried an Allin-Silva breechloader. Everyone had cutlasses, pistols, and a bayonet, if their weapon would accept one.
Isak carried the only Krag, which didn't make sense from a perspective of
ammo interchangeability, but he liked it because it didn't kick much.

At first, they'd advanced in rushes, covering one another as they
did, but so far they hadn't encountered any Grik at all, not even the "ci-

vilian" sort that were a kind of nonmilitary Hij. They'd first encountered such as those when they "captured" Hij Geerki at Raan-goon, but
there were many more in Colombo at Saay-lon. Strangely, most of those
had been slaughtered by their own kind, or took their own lives. Nothing like that seemed to have happened here, though; the warehouses
were just empty of life. That didn't mean they were empty of other
things, and first Herring, then Pam and Pack Rat, stopped to gaze about
at the tons and tons of crudely made but now-familiar Grik ordnance
arrayed within the recently constructed buildings.

"Quit loafin'!" Silva called back from the lead. "So there's a bunch o'
cannons and such. Whoop-te-do. We got a chore to attend to!" He
coughed. "Gaad, Larry! Was that you?"

Lawrence stared daggers at Dennis. "No! It's not I!"

"Wull . . . *somethin'* sure stinks!"

"Somethin' Stinks!" Petey whined on Silva's shoulder as he gaped
nervously about.

"I told everyone at a meeting Commander Herring attended that the
city had an . . . unpleasant odor," Miyata informed him. Herring had
raised a cloth to his nose when they stopped.

"Did you tell 'em it stinks worse than a dead skunk's ass? 'Cause Mr.
Herring didn't see fit to pass that along."

"I meant to say something about it," Herring gasped. "I'm afraid,
under the circumstances, I entirely forgot."

"Hard to forget," Horn hacked.

"I personally would not know to compare this smell to a, um, 'dead
skunk's ass,'" Miyata said, "though I am pleased to defer to your greater
knowledge, Chief Silva."

Dennis looked at the Japanese officer, stunned. Then he barked a
laugh. "I'll be damned! I *like* you."

"Si-vaa's an expert on all kinds o' stinky stuff," Pack Rat supplied,
blinking amusement.

"Shuddup, you. I know you're the stinkiest 'Cat I know." He cocked
his head back at Miyata. "Never met a Jap with a sense of humor before,
not even Shinya," he complimented in his way. "Is it as bad as this in the
palace?"

Miyata considered. "No. I only ever visited the lower regions—the 'dungeon,' perhaps?—and even there it was not as bad. It was not really *better*, but it was more bearable."

"At this rate we'll be used to it by the time we get there," Pam said with a snort. "I thought we were in a hurry."

Dennis ignored her jab. "Not many more o' these warehouses up ahead," he judged, looking through a gaping opening before him. There were no doors on the buildings. "Just adobe-like huts an' such like they have ever'where else we been. Kinda tangly lookin' too. If they're gonna jump us, in amongst that rat maze is where I'd expect trouble."

Laumer hefted his shotgun. "Then we may as well get on with it."

Grik City really was a maze in the sense that there was no organization to the various pathways at all, and the "rat" part of the description was reinforced by the profound and comprehensive nature of the filth and detritus they hurried through. The rain had stopped, but the hard-packed ground had turned to a sticky, slippery caliche that clung to their shoes, weighting their steps, and making their footing treacherous. Pam constantly murmured about disease and warned them all against cutting themselves on the shards of bone as thickly mixed with the dull mud as gravel might've been. Despite all that, the 'Cats finally removed their sandals with her reluctant blessing. They blinked disgust at the thought of what they were treading through, but it was getting between their feet and their hard soles, making injuries more likely, not less. There was no help for it.

Every so often they saw a Grik, or a small group of them hurrying in a generally eastward direction, and those in the party slammed to a stop or flattened themselves against one of the muddy buildings. Few of the Grik they saw appeared to be warriors, however, and all were moving with an apparently single-minded purpose that helped prevent them from noticing the intruders. Of course, they were deep within the very loathsome center of all Grik existence, and it likely never occurred to any of them that there might possibly be intruders there. Dennis, Laumer, and Commander Herring all concurred that they must not shoot unless absolutely necessary. With all the tumult, the firing might never be noticed, but if it was, they could be badly surrounded very quickly. At the very least, they might get cut off from their objective.

Eventually they saw no more Grik, and they quickened their pace through that part of the city. None of the structures was particularly tall, but the tracks were narrow enough that they often lost sight of the imposing palace. Without the sun to guide them, Silva relied on his trusty compass: a small thing the size of a pocket watch, with USN engraved on the push-button lid. At least until they got close enough that the palace loomed over them regardless of the obstacles. All they had to do then was keep moving in its general direction. On they went, as fast as they could, panting in the vile, dank air; all thought of stealth rapidly fading as they struggled through the mud and fug. Above all, the dull booming and muffled crackle of battle urged them on.

"Buggers the mind," Silva gasped, breathing hard for the first time in anyone's memory. Most of them, and Herring in particular, couldn't have said anything at all just then. "To think they wanna turn the whole world into a shithole like this. They can't *all* live like this!"

"They don't," Lawrence replied around his lolling tongue, nodding forward. Just ahead, beyond a narrow alley, stood a mixed rock and adobe wall about six feet high. It was clearly a demarcation between the "slum" the majority of Grik infested, and a region of more angular, less congested architecture sprawling at the foot of the mountainous palace.

Everyone crowded forward to see. "It has long been known that there are two basic 'classes' of Grik," Herring managed, still breathing hard.

"You don't say?" Pam quipped sarcastically.

Herring ignored her and continued. "There are the warrior-worker 'Uul,' and the 'Hij,' who do all the actual thinking. No Uul would have any sort of separate dwelling of its own, even as execrable as those we've just passed through, so some level of Hij had to inhabit that area. Obviously, there are various subclasses among the Hij as well, and the more prominent among them, for whatever reason, must reside beyond that wall."

"Very astute, Commander Herring," Miyata observed, "and I could have told you all of that. You seem to keep forgetting that I have been here before!"

Herring looked at the mud-spattered officer and finally nodded. "Indeed," he allowed. "You could have told me if I asked. My mistake . . . and my apologies." He looked at Laumer, Silva, all of them in turn. "My apologies to you all. This is no time to harbor grudges against any but our current enemy. Please tell us what you can, Lieutenant Miyata."

"Very well. As was apparent, the larger part of the city was at least mostly deserted. That is because it serves as a kind of 'base housing,' if you will. All the yard workers, artificers, carpenters—anyone, in fact, with any productive skill—resides there. I suspect a large percentage of upper-level NCOs and junior officers live there as well. Since the various battles raging around the city seem to be everyone's focus today, it stands to reason that they would be elsewhere."

"I can see the fighters bein' all gone," Isak croaked, still gasping. "There's, well, a fight. Stands to reason. But where'd all the yard apes go?"

"I get it," Silva said, snapping his fingers at Isak. "Griks is almost as specialized as you an' Gilbert, but they can do other stuff too."

"Right," Laumer agreed. "They stampeded everybody else off to help prepare the defenses in front of Second Corps! They'd need the low-level Hij to supervise the Uul in doing stuff as simple as digging a trench!"

"I can do other stuff," Isak grumbled. "I'm here, ain't I?"

"I suspect you are right," Miyata agreed with Laumer.

"Right or not," Lawrence said urgently, pointing with his rifle, "they didn't take *all* the Griks a'ay."

They looked and saw a crested head peering at them over the wall, just before it disappeared.

"Let's go!" Silva urged. "Bigwigs or not, armed or not, all Grik got claws an' teeth! Over the damn wall as fast as you can!"

Lawrence vaulted to the top and helped Silva scrabble up behind him. Standing on the wide, flat top, Dennis saw the Grik racing away—past a lot of other Grik. "Uh-oh," he murmured, raising his Thompson. "Hurry it up! Get your ass up here, Arnie, an' cover us with that BAR!" Horn gained the top of the slippery wall, his eyes widening at the number of Grik they were about to wade through. Again, these were obviously not warriors, but there were a lot of them. Silva reslung his Thompson, and he and Lawrence, then a couple of the 'Cat Marines, started practically pitching their comrades over to the other side. Through the apparently panicked mass, Horn saw a column—a *column*—of about a dozen Grik warriors shoving its way in their direction. With a grim expression, he racked the bolt back on the BAR and very professionally hosed the small force to extinction. The rest of the Grik around it broke into a panicked rush in all directions.

"Goddamn, Arnie!" Silva yelled, working his jaw to pop his ears.

"Goddamn, Arnie!" Petey squealed, fluffing his gliding membrane and hunkering back down. He'd very nearly launched himself. "Why don't you just toot a bugle an' say, 'We're here!'" Silva demanded.

"As some big idiot destroyerman once told me, sometimes it's time to quit pussyfooting around and get on with the killing!" Horn retorted.

"Idiot's right," Pam snapped as Silva handed her over last.

"Enough!" Irvin Laumer decreed in a new tone that brooked no argument, and it would occur to some later that it must have been then that the young former submariner more or less officially took command of "Silva's" mission. "This isn't a game. Get down from there," he instructed Silva, Horn, and Lawrence, who were the last ones on the wall. When they complied, he nodded forward, toward the palace. "We'll run for it. Shoot what you have to, but we must reach the entrance before they have a chance to fortify it!"

"Right." Silva nodded, accepting Laumer's authority as a matter of course. "Me, Arnie . . ." He paused. "And Pam, with the automatic weapons, will take point. The rest o' you lugs keep the bastards off us on the flanks. They might jump at us outa any o' these alleyways." This new part of the city was clearly more geometrical. There were nods, and Silva looked at Irvin. "Whenever you say, Mr. Laumer."

There wasn't that much shooting as they practically sprinted the remaining half mile to the palace. A few Grik lunged at them, but the vast majority only wanted to get out of their way. These they left alone, conserving ammunition. It was a little disconcerting. They'd never seen so many "civilian" Grik before, and it was stunning how little fight they had in them.

"What a buncha pansies!" Silva panted, still having trouble with the heavy, wretched air. Three Grik had nearly fallen over themselves trying to clear his path when he menaced them with the Thompson. Its barrel was still smoking after a long burst he fired down a congested alley where another column of warriors was struggling to get at them. Those that followed fired into the writhing mass as well, the heavy booming of their rifles much louder than the stutter of the Thompson.

"Pansies!" Petey cawed. "Pansies! Ack! Goddamn!"

A swarm of musket balls from Grik matchlocks, like barely subsonic bumblebees, thrummed around them, and they ducked and flinched. "That group at the base of the palace steps seems a little more determined," Laumer warned, pointing at around thirty Grik deploying to block them. "Not to mention competent, to keep its weapons working in this damp."

"Yeah," Horn replied. "Let's get behind something to think this through."

"The hell with that," Silva roared, charging ahead. "At 'em while they're loadin'!" Lawrence and Pam raced after him, and the rest, faced with both the fact and the logic of what Silva did, followed with a shout, and chittering Lemurian yells. Silva's Thompson blatted, and Pam's Blitzer Bug burped short bursts, spraying helpless, frightened Grik, caught in the process of loading their long, fishtailed weapons. Many quickly sprawled in bloody heaps on the narrow steps. Others continued loading with half-panicked fingers and were cut down by Horn's BAR. Lemurian rifles roared at the rest with white smoke and stabbing slashes of orange fire. Maybe half a dozen Grik dropped their weapons and bolted, but the rest drew their curved swords and charged. Laumer blasted one in the face with his shotgun, and it fell past him, its head a shattered wreckage of blood and bone. Pack Rat shot one with his Springfield, then drove it to the ground with his bayonet. The 'Cat Marines met the others with their bayonets as well, and made short work of them. "C'mon!" Laumer cried, sliding another paper and brass shell into his weapon. "Up the stairs! More Grik are gathering at the entrance above!"

"No grenades," Silva cautioned Horn. "They'll roll back down at us!"

"Tell somebody that doesn't already know that!" Horn snapped back. He and Silva were the only ones who *had* grenades. Under cover of the automatic weapons that sent showers of blood, fuzz, and pulverized stone drifting away from the Grik in the high-arched opening, they puffed and gasped up the remaining forty yards or so to the opening in the north side of the palace. Grik tumbled down around them as they neared, and Dennis did throw a grenade from right below the entrance. It disappeared inside and exploded with a harsh thump, followed by a chorus of wails.

"More!" Laumer yelled.

Dennis and Horn each tossed two more grenades in the opening, and ducked when smoke, debris, and pieces of Grik vomited out around them. "In, in!" Laumer cried. They all rose up and leaped the little stone rail around a broad landing. A 'Cat screamed, dropping his rifle with a clatter, and fell back with a crossbow bolt jutting from his chest. Pam fired blindly into the smoke-choked passageway until her bolt locked back, and Horn and several 'Cats kept up the fire until they were empty as well. Then they listened. Aside from a few moans, there was no sound besides the frantic panting of the attackers themselves.

"Get our guy," Laumer instructed the Marines, "and his weapon." A pair hopped back over the rail and dragged the dead 'Cat and his rifle back to the group. For a moment, they all paused, listening and catching their breath. Silva looked back over the city and the harbor, and was stunned by the view. *Walker* was under her own rainsquall now, and was barely visible in the distance beyond the smoldering Grik cruiser. Bright flashes in the rain encouraged them that she was still in the fight. To the east-northeast, the battle continued to rage in front of II Corps, but all they could see was the Grik rear; a mass of confusing motion. Beyond the smoke of battle, most of which had to be Safir's, they couldn't see much of her force either. Silva grunted with satisfaction to see that the me-naak mounted cavalry had finally reached shore and assembled directly east, just to the left of the Allied infantry. The Grik didn't seem to have noticed it yet.

"We've got to leave some guys here," Laumer wheezed. "Enough to keep the Grik off our ass if any try to follow us in."

"How many?" Herring asked.

"We can't afford to leave too many, but a few have to stay."

Herring nodded. "I'll stay. Leave me . . . Gunny Horn, a few Marines, and half the grenades."

"We're gonna need Arnie in there," Silva said, nodding at the interior of the palace. "He's a good bayonet man, and he won't need his BAR. You take it. Take Isak too. He ain't good for nothin' outside a fireroom."

"Now wait just a damn minute!" Horn objected, holding his BAR close.

"Yah!" Isak protested.

"Hand it over, Gunny," Laumer ordered. "We'll have the Thompson and the Blitzer. The BAR's better for long range, and Herring'll need it."

Frowning, Horn handed over his bag of grenades and exchanged the BAR for Herring's Springfield. "You know how to shoot that thing, sir?" he demanded.

Herring nodded. "It's been a while," he admitted, "but I remember how."

Isak Reuben stared sullenly around, then nervously cleared his throat. "Herring ain't gettin' me neither," he stated. "I'm on my own hook here, an' by God, fer once, I'm gonna fight this war the way I want! Ever'body else gets to." He shook his head, his skinny chest still heaving from unaccustomed exertion. "I'm goin' in there, fer me, an' Gilbert, an' Tabby—an' all the other snipes that always got to do their fightin' blind, in the hot, dark, engineerin' spaces. I'm goin' for all them who the only glimpse they ever get o' the enemy is one o' their shells er cannonballs shootin' holes in our goddamn hulls!" He fumbled at his side, then drew the '03 Springfield bayonet and shakily affixed it to the muzzle of his Krag. "I'm . . . I'm goin' in there," he repeated determinedly.

Silva just grinned. "You're gonna be a Grik turd, Isak. This time tomorrow!"

"Gonna be a turd!" Petey confirmed.

"You're already a turd, Dennis!" Pam scolded. "Leave 'im alone. You always get to fight the way *you* want. It's my turn too!" She looked at Herring. "We'll try to get our wounded back here to you before, you know, we get in too deep." Herring frowned, but nodded his head. "Five Marines, then?" he asked Laumer.

"I'll stay too," Pack Rat almost sighed, pushing more .30-06 shells into his magazine. "My feet hurt, an' I got this Springfield. Might come in handy out here."

They heard a commotion in the passageway behind them, gurgling cries and the clatter of equipment, and Laumer nodded toward it. "More coming," he said. "Let's go meet 'em!"

////// *The Celestial Palace*

eneral Esshk joined a very nervous Chooser in the throne room of the Celestial Mother. His armor was spattered with mud and blood, and his once-bright red cape was torn and singed. The Chooser regarded him with horror.

"What is happening?" he demanded in an anxious near whisper.

"*War* is happening, my Lord Chooser," Esshk replied, still somewhat bemused himself. "Of a sort I have only witnessed once before." He raised a corner of his ruined cape and gazed at it. "Most unruly." The first general of all the Ghaarrichk'k simply did not personally engage in battles; he designed them for others to fight. He was beyond such things himself. Esshk had spent most of his life suppressing the passions that drove a warrior in combat so he could more clearly use his better mind. He'd done his best to apply his new understanding of the principles of defense to prepare for the attack underway, but was beginning to suspect that even the enemy couldn't have specifically designed the very . . . odd battle sprawling all around the principal city of his kind. It had just happened, as far as he could tell, and his own ability to influence its outcome had been quickly overwhelmed.

Of course, he'd very nearly been killed as well, when one of the flying machines of the enemy prey dropped a stunningly forceful firebomb rather close as he surveyed the chaotic fight an appropriate distance from the point of contact. He'd been indignant. Designers of battles did not *slay* one another! They planned the game for their Uul to play! Then he'd fretfully thought again, reminding himself of the dreadful stakes he'd forced himself to consider ever since the terrible setback at Baalkpan two years before. He'd been away from the fight too long, relying on Halik and Kurokawa to carry the load. Now he had no idea how they fared, and he'd been forced to revisit his earlier impressions of this unprecedented war. This was not a territorial battle between friendly regents, intent on reducing their numbers and entertaining their Uul. This was a *war*, a real war for the survival of his race. The singed cape drove that forcefully home once more.

The Giver of Life herself still slept—it was not yet midday—and her attendants glared at Esshk and the Chooser for speaking in her presence. Esshk didn't care. The fight was reaching a tipping point, and contingencies had to be explored.

"Your Magnificence," he said loudly, "I must report!"

The Chooser recoiled from him, stunned by the hideous breach, and hurled himself to the stone floor. The equally startled attendants leaned toward Esshk, ready to seize him if ordered.

The Celestial Mother, draped heavily upon her saddlelike throne, opened an eye and regarded him. "You have awakened me, First General Esshk," she said simply. "Have you decided to destroy yourself? I will certainly command you to do so if you do not have sufficient reason to disturb me."

"I will gladly destroy myself, but I beg you to hear me first," Esshk said. He did not even join the Chooser on the floor. The Celestial Mother noticed that as well.

"I will hear you," she said in a curious tone. "What has happened?" She paused, contemplating the dull rumble leaking into the chamber through the overhead light portal. Normally, the warming rays of the sun were allowed to wash upon her during the day by means of mirrors set along a convoluted shaft that admitted light, but not rain. There was no light now, but she'd been aware of thunder for some time. "Surely you do not awaken me for a storm?"

"I do, Your Magnificence. A dreadful storm indeed." He showed her the cape. "The dire proposal I made you, concerning the significance of the enemy flying machines, has descended upon us. The enemy is here, and has come in force. I don't know how they did this, but it has happened. Even now they threaten this very palace on its eastern side with perhaps ten thousands."

"That is not so many," the Giver of Life said, deflecting, "and hardly worth my attention. You are the first general! Destroy them!"

Esshk bowed his head. "That has been my aim, but the enemy prey has not cooperated," he said with some irony. "The force that threatens the palace had barely landed before the small iron ship that Kurokawa so desperately loathed stole into the harbor . . . and destroyed the entire fleet at anchor."

The Celestial Mother sat up, her eyes wide with indignant astonishment. *"One ship did that?"* she raged.

"Perhaps not all alone," Esshk murmured. "The details are unclear. Some flying machines certainly helped. The ship itself has suffered damage as well, and is currently grounded at the harbor mouth. Sufficient warriors have converged on it that I am confident it will trouble us no more—but the force that presses here is most tenacious."

"So few cannot be a threat," the Celestial Mother insisted.

"They can and are, Your Magnificence. Our new warriors fight well, better than I have ever seen, but the enemy has better weapons and obviously, greater experience. These are doubtless veteran warriors, Your Magnificence, and there is only one place that so many could have gained their skill."

"India!" the Celestial Mother snapped.

"So we must assume, which means they must have won an even greater victory there than we dreaded, to be here now. That also implies that India is entirely lost, and Kurokawa and Halik with it!"

"It does indeed," the Celestial Mother mused. She jerked her head to the side, and her jowls quivered. "What must be done?"

"I have already taken the liberty of having the sport fighters released into the palace." Esshk licked his teeth. "They cannot fight together, but in confined passages that should not matter. Individually, they will fight very well to protect you, their God."

"It will come to that?" the Celestial Mother asked, a trace of fear touching her disbelief. "Not even this prey would dare threaten me directly!"

Esshk sighed, realizing that the eons of absolute power enjoyed by an uninterrupted procession of Celestial Mothers had not well prepared them to deal with reality. "Obscene as it may seem, Your Magnificence, not all creatures revere you as do your own. I consider it possible these might even *slay* you if they can."

"Impossible!" the Giver of Life almost chortled. "No *thing* could possess such hubris!"

"It does seem absurd, Your Magnificence," the Chooser finally ventured, "but in the event they may even accidentally harm you, I most humbly recommend you—all of us—should go from here!"

"Go? Where? *How?* You have always been a most pretentious and ridiculous creature, Lord Chooser, but now you have lost your senses."

"With all my worshipfulness," Esshk interceded, "there *is* a way, Your Magnificence."

Two members of the palace guard, competent if unimaginative lower-level Hij, threw themselves through the entrance to the throne room and sprawled on the dank stones.

"Such a day for unseemly visitations," the Celestial Mother observed, amused by her own wit. "Speak!"

"The prey!" the senior guard cried. "The prey has forced the north entrance to the palace!"

Without consulting the Celestial Mother, Esshk simply said, "Release the guard beasts!"

"*I* rule here, Lord First General! What right have you to give such a command?" the Celestial Mother rumbled indignantly.

"The right of any first general, Your Magnificence, to protect his

Giver of Life. We must release the guard beasts on the north entrance level!"

"My pets," the Celestial Mother lamented. "They might be harmed! And it is always most difficult to return them to their pens!"

"Nevertheless, it must be done, and we must evacuate the palace at once!"

The Celestial Mother gave a great sigh. "How very tiresome you have grown, General Esshk!" She glanced about, realizing for the first time that *she* really couldn't leave if she wanted to. She couldn't possibly move herself. Even if she had the strength, it wouldn't be seemly. And she'd grown too large for the number of attendants it would require to move her, to fit through the narrow passageways of the palace. "Very well. Prepare to evacuate my sisters, but if these intruders dare annoy me in my own chambers, I will confront them myself!"

////// *SMS* Amerika

"What the hell!" roared Captain Jis-Tikkar, commander of Flight Operations for the 1st Naval Air Wing, as SMS *Amerika* got underway and began moving toward the distant, smoke-crowned harbor. His Nancy had been idling along, wallowing in the growing chop alongside the big steamer, waiting to be refueled and rearmed. Now his and several other planes had been left bobbing and spinning in the rising wake. "What the *goddamn* hell!" he bellowed again when another clearly leaking Nancy pirouetted dangerously close to his. He spun to face his backseater. "Get on the wireless and find out what they think they're doin'! They tryin' to kill us all?"

"I try!" the backseater yelled back. "They's too much traffic!"

"Stomp on it," Tikker ordered, meaning for his observer-copilot to hold the transmit key down, essentially jamming all other messages on the frequency. A few moments later, the 'Cat reported. "*Amer-i-kaa* says they is ordered to move closer to the harbor, to turn planes around quicker!"

"What about the planes they just ran off on!" Tikker cried incredulously. "They don't care to turn *us* around?"

"Uh . . . Kap-i-taan Leut-naant Becher Laange begs our forgiveness, an' says Kap-i-taan Von Melhausen got the order an' maybe got a little ahead o' himself."

"I'll say," Tikker griped. Even as he watched, the liner-turned–commerce raider in a more-distant war than he could imagine began to slow. "Send to the other planes to motor over to her," he instructed. "They'll never get that thing turned around." The backseater acknowledged, and Tikker advanced his throttle. Packets of spray wet the two 'Cats as the pitching bow of the little seaplane tossed it back. It took nearly thirty minutes, by the clock on Tikker's instrument panel, before the half-dozen planes were back in position. By that time, nearly as many more had landed in the water.

"Keep an eye on things," Tikker ordered, dropping his goggles on the wicker seat and swinging up the cable that supported the fueling boom. He reached the deck of the big ship even before his ground crew—hesitant to meet his eye even though they'd had nothing to do with the fiasco—scrambled down to service his plane. Another boom was lowering a basket of ordnance. "What a screwed-up mess," Tikker growled, disgusted. "The whole damn fight's gonna go in the crapper just because everybody wants in on the show so bad." He stopped one of the Lemurian crew of the Republic vessel. It dawned on him that he'd never spoken to one of the "foreign 'Cats" before, and he hesitated. "Hey," he finally demanded. "Where's the bridge on this tub? I gotta see your crazy skipper!"

"Kap-i-taan Von Melhausen is not crazy!" the 'Cat defended uncomfortably in a strange accent, even though he was clearly aware of the situation. He'd hesitated as well, and Tikker briefly wondered if the other Lemurian had trouble understanding *him*. His speech was laced with so many Americanisms now that he doubted he'd have understood himself just a few years before. "And you cannot just go to the bridge whenever you decide!" the other 'Cat added indignantly.

"Yes, he can," interrupted a voice from the deck above. "Seein' as how he outranks both of us!" Tikker looked up and saw a burly man with a gray-blond beard, dressed as an officer in the Republic Legion. "Please come along, Cap'n Tikker. I know who you are. Doocy Meek's my name, and we've got a proper knot to unravel here!"

Tikker nodded and trotted up the stairs to join the man. "I know you," Tikker said. "What's going on?"

"Orders came from your Adar to move the ship closer in. Kapitan Von Melhausen's rather keen to prove the Republic's bound to the Alliance in this fight, and he complied just a bit too quickly." Meek tapped his head. "Von Melhausen's a fine man and a damn good seaman, but he's a bit far along, if you get my meanin'. Tends to get a bit . . . overly focused. Follow me, if you please."

Meek wasn't a young man, but the pace he set proved he remained in top form. Just a few minutes passed before he brought Tikker to the bridge. The scene there was . . . unexpected.

"Kapitan," said Kapitan Leutnant Becher Lange, obviously still in the middle of a confrontation with the much older man, "we will proceed to our appointed station as soon as is practicable—but we can't simply leave the planes already fueling in our wake!"

"But our orders!" Von Melhausen insisted. "I swore I would obey all signals from the flag! You have prevented me from keeping my word!"

"No, sir! I have not. And I have already sent an explanation that will amply explain our delay. This ship is supposed to serve as a tender for the flying boats in this action, not a surface combatant. What use are we if we do not 'tend' the planes, as we were entrusted to do?"

Von Melhausen blinked, and Tikker caught Lange's pleading glance. "Kap-i-taan Von Melhausen," Tikker said, his anger dying away, "I am Cap-i-taan Jis-Tikkar, COFO of the First Naval Air Wing aboard US-NRS *Salissa*. Do you remember me?"

Von Melhausen looked at him and blinked confusion in the Lemurian way. "I'm not sure. How did you come to be aboard my ship?"

"I arrived in one of the planes now floating alongside—the planes that must have fuel and ordnance to continue our attack." He was still standing adjacent to the port bridgewing and pointed down and aft.

"One of my planes is sinking now, a plane that might have returned to action if it had not been forced to lie so long in the water. Please, sir, all I ask is that you allow my planes and the ground crew personnel that transferred to this ship to complete their current evolution. After that, you may certainly proceed to the station appointed you."

Von Melhausen blinked doubtfully and removed his hat from his balding head. "But Chairman Adar ordered me to move my ship," he complained.

"Which you may quickly do, as soon as my aircraft have been serviced," Tikker stressed. "I swear to you by the Heavens above that this is the intent, if not the specific wording of the orders Chairman Adar sent. He does not want your ship to move closer to the fight so you may tend aircraft that have been left so far away from it!"

Von Melhausen looked at Becher Lange. "Was this your understanding when you countermanded my orders?"

"It was, *mein Kapitan*," Lange fervently assured the old man. Von Melhausen shook his head and smiled wanly, his white mustache arching upward. "Very well. I believe I shall retire to my quarters. Would you be so kind as to have some of that wonderful pudding Admiral Keje sent brought there for me?"

"Of course, *mein Kapitan*!" Lange said with relief as Von Melhausen shuffled off the bridge. Immediately, he turned to Tikker. "Please accept my most profound apologies! Kapitan Von Melhausen is an old man, and he is not often . . . like this."

When Tikker replied, the soft voice he used with the elderly officer was gone. "You should not have allowed him to be 'like this' now. Precious time has been lost, not to mention an equally precious aircraft! The Heavens only know how many lives those things might cost us! I understand your desire to spare the feelings of an aged one, but a battle is underway! You wished to participate in it, and lives depend on you." He gestured at the departed captain. "Not him, who cannot help himself, but *you* who must!" Lange nodded miserably, and Meek cleared his throat.

"You must understand Kapitan Von Melhausen's position, and Mr. Lange's as well. The old man has been like a father to him—to many of us. . . ."

"Then you should have *protected* him from himself—and us from him!" Tikker lashed out. "I swear, by all the stars, if this . . . idiocy has cost us this fight, I will drop a bomb down the stack of this useless ship myself and save us all from any further 'assistance' it may inflict on us! Good day!" With that, Tikker spun and stalked back the way he'd come. Doocy Meek spared Becher Lange a rueful glance and chased after him. "Captain Tikker," he called, "I've a request."

"What is it? I must get back in the air."

"Just so—an' I'd like to fly with you."

Tikker paused, beginning to regret how harshly he'd spoken to their allies from the Republic. "How's your fist on a wireless key?"

"Smooth as breathin'."

"Very well. You will relieve my OC. Perhaps it is time someone from your nation saw just what kind of war you've joined."

When they reached the bulwark under the fueling boom, Tikker glanced over the side and saw his plane. Its engine already idling, it was preparing to cast off. "Wait here," he ordered, and dropped down on top of the wing. Meek winced at the nonchalant way the 'Cat performed the feat with a spinning propeller just a few feet away. "Go aboard up there," Tikker shouted at his OC over the motor noise. "I gotta carry a passenger on this run."

Reluctantly, Tikker's backseater climbed the handling line, leaving the trailing edge on his seat. When he reached the deck, he granted Meek a surly series of blinks while he stripped out of his parachute and handed it over. "That's the rip cord there," he said, pointing, "but if you get knocked around bad enough you gotta jump, I wouldn't pull that if it looks like you gonna go in the water, if I was you. Better you go *spaack*! Die when you hit, er get knocked out an' drown than get ate to death by flashies!"

Meek nodded his dubious thanks and donned the chute. Then he had to negotiate his way out on the boom before sliding down to the seat below—again, just a few feet from the whirling prop.

"Strap in," Tikker called. "It'll be bumpy." The engine roared and the prop blurred. Moments later, the plane was wallowing away from the ship, picking up speed. Tikker had the most time in Nancys of any man or 'Cat, and he was familiar with all their idiosyncrasies. He quickly had the plane bouncing over the swells and clawing into the sky. "Raise the wing floats!" he ordered. "It's that crank down by your left leg. Wind 'em up smart!" Meek complied. When he finished, gasping from the exertion, he realized they were already high in the air. He looked around. A fat bomb, an antipersonnel incendiary he supposed, hung beneath each wing, secured by pins. He quickly deduced that the lever by his right leg provided the mechanical advantage to release them.

"I assume that I am your bombardier?" he asked loudly into the voice tube.

"Right. But you just leave that lever alone until I tell you. Right now, you send to all Second Bomb Squadron planes to form on us, over *Big Sal*. We're gonna have a look at *Walker*. All other squadrons is to make theirselves useful to Second Corps."

Meek gazed at the unfamiliar wireless set in front of his right knee and saw that it was on. Grasping the key, he sent the message. Belatedly putting on the headset, he caught the replies.

"I, ah, believe I've accomplished that."

"Good. Now we gotta wait."

Meek glanced down and saw *Salissa* proceeding toward the harbor, wisps of smoke hazing the tops of her funnels. A pair of DDs preceded her, and another pair brought up the rear. Tikker had banked the plane slightly, setting up a leisurely orbit of the flagship. Eventually, three other Nancys joined them as they lifted off from *Amerika*'s lee. A terse signal from the last informed them that there'd be no more at present.

"I guess we're it, then," Tikker announced, peeling off to the south. The other planes quickly followed, forming on Tikker's starboard wing. With nothing to do for the first time since they'd lifted off, Doocy Meek had a moment to view the spectacle of the battle from his lofty perch. He'd never ridden in an airplane before and was experiencing a strange tightness in his chest. The closest he could come to describing it was as a kind of excited anxiety. He shook his head. He'd asked for this, damn it! Smoke from the fires still raging in the harbor towered high in the sky, much higher than they were, before blending with the overcast sky or dissipating in the wind. More smoke rose above what he assumed must be II Corps's position to the southeast, but the plane was headed toward a lone column of smoke rising above a grounded Grik steamer. He didn't have a telescope—Tikker's OC must have taken his—but even he could see the slender shape of the stranded American destroyer not far from the burning enemy ship. What took his breath was the crowded swarm of Grik funneled up against it, their reserves curling back and around on shore, beyond the burning cruiser. It looked like a tightly focused stream of ants picking at the innards of some great, helpless insect.

"There's thousands of 'em," he observed, "and *Walker* has what, three hundred crew?"

"Maybe, with the reinforcements that went aboard." Tikker grunted. "It don't look good, huh? Hold on, and stand ready with that bomb lever. When I say 'Now,' don't think, just do. We gotta make these bombs count, or some really good folks are gonna buy it!"

////// *USS* **Walker**

A dense column of rain swept across the stranded destroyer at the same time the Grik managed to scramble over the disintegrating barricade in significant numbers. They seemed a little stunned they'd actually made it, and most lost their footing on the suddenly—unexpectedly— slick deck. Many were quickly killed by bayonet thrusts, but more of the defenders were falling back now, wounded or dying, as the once-protective bedding was torn away. The Marines still fought from behind their shields at the main point of contact just aft of the amidships deckhouse, but bayonet-tipped rifles didn't make good spears for stabbing downward one-handed. Most of the killing was performed by the Marines behind them, but the frustratingly helpless shield wall was starting to buckle. Here and there, Marines even pitched their precious breechloaders behind them and drew their cutlasses as they would be more effective in this kind of fight.

The machine guns were split between firing down on the boarders, clawing their way over the causeway of corpses and chattering at the larger mass beyond, waiting their turn to cross. The 25s were still mulching the enemy farther out, but their rate of fire had slowed, as had the 4"-50s forward. The gun on the aft deckhouse had ceased firing completely. Matt ducked a thrown spear and shot at a Grik trying to vault the shields, his Colt bucking in his hand. The Grik shrieked, then fell backward onto his comrades. Matt trotted to where the Bosun and half a dozen others with Blitzer Bugs were holding the Marine's left flank, anchored on the torpedo mount. Gray was bleeding now, from a couple of cuts, but the rain washed the blood away so quickly, it was impossible to tell how bad they were. Probably not too bad, Matt judged. Gray hadn't even noticed them. The older man was resting his Thompson on a Grik corpse draped over the rail, sending short arcs of hot brass clattering off the Marines' helmets to his right. He fired like an automaton—*Braap! Braap! Braap!*—quickly choosing targets between his bursts. After every sixth squeeze of the trigger, the smoking barrel came up, and Chief Gray replaced the twenty-round magazine so he could do it again.

"Been killin' those ones on the edges," Gray explained matter-of-factly, noticing him there. "Bastards are heavin' the dead down in the water on either side, tryin' to increase their front an' get more warriors up against the ship! Damnedest piece o' combat engineerin' I ever saw!" He spat. "Course, I'm helpin' 'em do it too, since half the ones I shoot just roll in the damn water anyway! Shit!"

Matt saw what he was talking about and realized it was working too. Then he looked beyond at the seething horde and felt a terrible heat in the back of his neck. The rain obscured much, but it was clear that the numbers trying to swarm his ship were growing all the time. Silva must've been right. Nearly every Grik in the city not facing II Corps seemed to be surging to reach the sandbar—and USS *Walker*. The rain had eliminated the most dangerous Grik weapons, but there were just too many of them. Sooner or later they'd get a firm toehold on the ship, and that would be that. Matt shook his head, slinging water off his helmet. *No!* He emptied his pistol into the mass. "Keep at it, Boats!" he cried. "I'm going to see what's clogging up the ammo supply to the guns."

"We're gettin' low here too, Skipper," Gray said. "Just thought I'd mention it." Matt nodded, turning to where the torpedo talker had been, but the headset now dangled from the wires. The 'Cat who'd stood there so long was lying on the deck with a crossbow bolt in his eye, the blood on the deck quickly diluting and running away. Matt grabbed the headset.

"This is the Captain," he said. "What's the holdup on the ammo train?"

"No holdup, Captain," Spanky replied immediately, and Matt looked up at the man atop the aft deckhouse a hundred feet away. His gun crew was firing rifles now. "The fact is, we're out of common shells in the aft magazine. Nothing but AP left. I figure my guys back here can take better cover and kill as many Grik with rifles."

"Out already?" Matt demanded, then realized how ridiculous he sounded. "The AP will still explode, if you shoot it at the *planet!*" he shouted angrily.

"Sure, but most of the force'll be deadened by the dirt it penetrates first. And besides, it looks like you could use a hand. I've released the shell handlers to take rifles and assemble behind you as a reserve."

Matt finally nodded. Spanky was thinking clearly—more clearly than *he* was, right now. "Very well, but what's the holdup elsewhere?"

"That's what I was tryin' to find out—an' for a little more good news, the twenty-fives already have all the ammo they're getting. It *is* all gone."

"Skipper?" It was Campeti, using the comm even though he was close enough to shout. He might not be heard, though, over the racket of battle.

"What's the dope? I know the forward magazines aren't dry."

"Not quite, but we're gettin' jammed up. Too many wounded crammed under the deckhouse and getting carried down the companionway to the wardroom. Getting replenished through there is becoming a big problem." Despite Matt's concern over leaving that particular hatch open, they'd had no choice after all.

"Small arms ammo?"

"I've rerouted the handlers through the firerooms—I hope they don't drop any!—and they'll bring it up the escape trunks." Matt glanced back just as the hatch rose and clanged against the deck. He also watched the mortar 'Cats grimly heave their weapons over the starboard side. He hadn't heard them firing for some time now and they were obviously out of ammo as well. He nodded at them as they retrieved their personal weapons.

"Half you guys, over here," he shouted, pointing at the Marines fighting at the rail. "The other half, help with that ammo coming up from below. And keep a watch on that hatch! If the Grik get aboard, down you go, and secure it behind you!"

Heavy crates of ammunition, stenciled BAALKPAN ARSENAL .50-80-450, started appearing out of the trunk, and 'Cats, their rifles now slung, started grabbing and dragging them away.

"I need some of that up here!" Campeti roared down, ignoring his headset. "And we need forty-five, an' belted thirty too!"

There was a roar beyond the shield wall, and Campeti whirled. Matt saw the stunned look on the man's face and raced back to Gray. "What's happening?" he demanded. Gray just pointed. A dense *column* of Grik, several hundred strong, was sprinting up the bridge of flesh, directly at the ship. Grik caught between them and their objective were either swept up in the charge or thrown aside. The number one gun, depressed as low as possible and trained around to the stop that prevented it from hitting *Walker*'s bridge, blew great, bleeding swaths out of the gory slope. Machine guns and riflemen redoubled their firing and bodies tumbled into the water, but the roar only built as the leading edge of the column, ablating flesh and bone, churned up the slope of dead and slammed into the shield wall with a mighty, rain-muffled crash. Then, with a furious flurry of shots and exhausted, forlorn screams, the shield wall protecting USS *Walker* cracked.

Chief Bosun of the Navy Fitzhugh Gray grabbed Matt by the shoulder as Marines fell back under the onslaught. When Matt's eyes went to the face of his old friend, they saw that he was smiling. "Tell Miss Diania I love her," he shouted. "I never could do it. Too damn chicken, I guess. And tell Silva he can have my good hat. If he finishes his job, he'll have earned it."

"What?"

"And God bless *you*, Skipper! It's been a helluva run!" Before Matt could even contemplate what Gray meant, the powerful old man practically *threw* him under the torpedo tubes as the tide of Grik washed over them. Even as Matt scrambled to his feet on the other side of the mount, his pistol up, he heard a long, final burst from the Thompson.

Matt shot his pistol dry, killing Grik as they came for him. Fortunately, somebody else took up the slack while he reloaded, but then he emptied his pistol again. Without conscious thought, he pushed the magazine release, dropping the empty to clatter on the deck, and slammed another in the well. As he thumbed the slide release, his pistol automatically chambered another round, and he aimed as carefully as he could. An anger, a *hatred* so sharp and focused had overwhelmed him so completely that, for a brief moment, no thought entered his mind but the necessity of killing Grik. The notion that he might take even a single step back never occurred to him. He *must* stand; he *must* kill—because somewhere under that terrible horde climbing over the rail and dashing toward him across the top of the torpedo mount was a man who'd become more than a friend.

"Cap-tan!" gasped a familiar voice as a body slammed into him. It was Juan. Matt didn't know how the one-legged Filipino had done it, but he'd somehow managed to get out of the crush. There was blood all over him and he was hopping—his wooden leg was useless on the rain-and-blood-slicked deck—and using his Springfield as a walking stick. "Cap-tan!" Juan repeated, his tone contrite, "I hate to impose, but I find myself in the awkward position of having to ask you for help."

Matt blinked. "Here, take my arm," he said, firing again, but moving toward the galley.

Lanier was shooting his Thompson, flanked by a growing number of bandaged 'Cats, who also fired into the Grik as they filled the waist of the ship. "This way, Captain, if you please," Lanier bellowed. He hadn't been out in the rain, and for some reason, the bloated, cantankerous cook's grimy face was streaked with tears.

Matt had a near-panicky thought and spun to look at the escape trunk. It was already closed, thank God, surrounded by shattered crates. "We're coming!" he yelled back. Suddenly, Juan's good leg wasn't working as well as it should, and he slumped. "Somebody help me with this man!" He heard a clang, and watched a spent 4"-50 shell casing crush the skull of a Grik that suddenly lunged to cut him off. Shell and Grik clattered to the deck, and he looked up to see Sonny Campeti firing a pistol while his gun's crews all started throwing shells, empty magazines, even *wrenches* and other tools, at the enemy.

"I think this is gonna get bad, Cap-tan!" Juan gasped as Earl Lanier unceremoniously dragged them through the new defensive line coalescing on either side of the galley.

"Mark your targets!" Matt managed to shout. "Don't forget we've got people aft!" Only then did he look around. The bridge must be nearly deserted because joining the destroyermen and Marines who'd been defending the ship from the start, Chief Quartermaster Paddy Rosen had arrived, leading Bernie and the rest of his torpedo 'Cats, Wallace Fairchild, and even Matt's bridge talker, Minnie. All were armed with the Springfields that had been issued to the bridge watch. Matt pushed Minnie back, slamming her into Ed Palmer who was also just arriving with a Springfield—and very wide eyes.

"You two get back to the comm shack," he ordered. "Get on the TBS and yell your lungs out! If we don't get air support right damn *now*, we're going to be overrun. Got it?"

Ed nodded thankfully, but Minnie raised her chin. "I can fight!" she insisted.

"I know," Matt agreed, more softly, "but not yet—and not with *that*." He took her Springfield for himself. With the sixteen-inch bayonet in place, the rifle was longer than she was tall. "Now quit arguing and help Mr. Palmer. You know the comm gear as well as he does, if he buys it." He turned to Rosen who, though junior to Bernie, had more experience at things like this. "You're in charge down here. If you have to fall back, try to get the wounded out first, then take everybody forward to the bridge. Double-check that every hatch below is secure before you leave it behind, got it?"

"Aye, aye, Captain . . . but where will you be?"

Matt pointed up. "With Campeti. If we keep the high ground and keep 'em the hell out of the lower decks, we might have a chance. The damn tide'll be back in eventually. If we can just refloat her..." He shook his head. "Good luck!"

Spanky saw it all with a sick, sinking heart and unashamed tears. Across all his years on *Walker*, even before the Old War, he and Fitzhugh Gray had quarreled, bickered, and generally carried on their traditional "ape-snipe" conflict without even thinking about it. Even after he'd become an officer, and Gray became something far more than a regular bosun, they'd kept at it, out of habit. Right then, he'd give anything if he could just look the other man in the eye once more and simply shake his hand, because he knew Gray, that magnificent, towering example of strength, fortitude, and all that it meant to be a destroyerman, was gone. For an instant, he was sure Captain Reddy was too. Then he saw him, standing all alone between the torpedo mounts, firing his pistol at what seemed to be all the Grik in the world charging right at him. "Pour it into those bastards!" he'd roared. "They're gonna get the Skipper!" Smokeless and black powder cartridges boomed and crackled, and Grik spun and tumbled to the deck, writhing or still, with thumps or clatters of weapons— and somehow there was Captain Reddy, still on his feet, helping Juan toward the amidships deckhouse. A moment later, he was lost to view as more and more Grik poured into the waist. Some of the things even started climbing the searchlight tower, though none of those had crossbows, and Spanky had no idea what they hoped to accomplish. They probably didn't either. "Corporal Miles," he shouted, his voice rough, "you're a Marine. Quit screwin' around and organize a line below, on the starboard side of the deckhouse. We've got plenty of guys and gals crammed on the fantail right now. Just a few determined men or 'Cats behind a rifle and a bayonet should be able to keep the Grik back. Hell, one fella can barely pass there without falling overboard."

Miles wavered, looking resentful, and Spanky's eyes narrowed. Despite his diminutive size, nobody *ever* hesitated to obey one of Spanky's orders. "What the hell's the matter with you?" he thundered. "Get going before I kick your worthless ass to the fish!" He looked around. "Jeek? Where's Jeek?"

"Here," said the burly Lemurian chief of the Special Air Division.

"You do the same to port. One thing: everybody at deck level has to watch where they shoot! We don't want to hit any of our people under the amidships platform!" He considered. "See if you can rig a fire hose. If we've got pressure, maybe we can *squirt* some of the sons of bitches off the ship!"

"I try," Jeek confirmed. "An' we not worry much about hitting our own guys much longer—we nearly out o' ammo!"

Spanky nodded grimly. "Right. Oh well, enough Marines made it back here with their shields. We'll fight behind those with cutlasses when we have to." He took a moment to gaze forward. A few crossbow bolts zipped past him, but most of the apparent "shock troops" that made it aboard hadn't carried them—and now they packed the waist so densely that there wasn't room for more Grik to squeeze aboard. An eruption of mangled flesh and body parts alongside coincided with another blast from the number one gun, which continued to perform admirably, with its uninterrupted ammunition train, but the number two gun on the amidships platform had fallen silent. Closer, Spanky heard shots from within the 25-mm tubs and realized some of the guys stationed there must not have been able to clear out in time. The shots diminished and quit under the rising and falling swords and spears of Grik that leaped into the tubs. For an instant, there was a slight pause; then a mass of Grik turned aft and began lapping at his own platform, trying to get past or over it. "Kill 'em!" he bellowed, firing downward. "Kill every damn one! Give 'em some grenades!" They'd been saving the hand grenades expressly for a situation like this. It was then that he heard a terrifying sound: the clang of the hatch just below that led into the torpedo workshop, laundry, and aft crew's head! And, of course, there was a companionway in the deckhouse that led down into the guinea pullman, or aft berthing spaces, and ultimately to the engine rooms themselves. He thought all the hatches had been secured, but maybe the Grik had jimmied the thing. It didn't matter. Grenades thumped as his comrades pulled the pins and rolled them into the mass, sending sprays of blood and fuzz back in their faces. He turned to grab some himself, from a bucket near the number four gun. A bolt struck him high in the thigh. *Awful close to where I got shot in the ass when we fought Amagi,* he realized with dark indignation, through the waves of pain. "Goddamn it!" he roared, snapping the shaft off and hurling it at the Grik trying to scrabble up and onto the leading edge of the deckhouse. He grabbed several grenades and hooked them on his belt, then fired his '03 into a slathering face that rose above the deck. Cursing, he lurched toward the speaking tubes by the auxiliary conning station.

"Tabby!" he shouted into the tube that terminated at the throttle station. "You're gonna have company, aft. . . . I'm sorry, doll." He looked around. "Quick! More grenades! We gotta keep the rest of these critters away from the hatch!"

"Grenades!" Campeti roared, seeing what Spanky was doing aft.

"No!" Matt shouted. "Belay that! We've still got people below us around the galley!"

"Not much longer!" a 'Cat gunner squeaked, pointing forward. Wounded 'Cats and a few men were making their way to the companionway to the left of the foremast, trying to get below to the wardroom where Sandra and her medical division waited. Matt suspected many would return to the fight once their bleeding had been stopped. No one, particularly the Lemurians, would want to die down there. If they had to die, they'd rather do it in the open. With a rush, most of Rosen's remaining sailors and Marines pulled back, forming another line just aft of the stairway leading up to the bridge. A few clambered up to join Matt, including Bernie Sandison, chased by a flurry of clattering spears. Bernie's helmet was gone, and his dark hair was matted with blood that the rain washed down his neck in pink rivulets. He also had a deep cut on his left shoulder, and his shirt was mostly torn away. He still had his rifle, though, and the bayonet was clotted with reddish black blood.

"It's good to see you, Mr. Sandison." Matt smiled. The incongruity of the greeting was profound, there on what was rapidly becoming a rectangular island of steel in a sea of Grik.

"It's good to see you too, sir," Bernie gasped. "Sorry we couldn't hold them longer. . . ."

"Nonsense. You did very well. What happened to Lanier? I didn't see him fall back with the others."

Bernie blinked. "He dragged his damn Coke machine in the galley and shut himself in with a couple of the mess attendants," he finally managed, and Matt barked a laugh.

"He should be safe enough in there, for a while. Mr. Campeti, go ahead and throw all the grenades you want. The Grik'll be coming up the stairs directly, I suspect."

As if his words had summoned them, Grik surged up the stairs, and even leaped at the platform from the tops of the vegetable lockers alongside the number three funnel. The twenty-five or so defenders immediately re-directed their aim, or met the charging enemy with bayonets. Some continued throwing shell casings or the jumble of spears that had accumulated at their feet. Matt and Bernie rushed with the others, roaring and slapping away spears with their rifles before driving their bayonets into bodies that wildly squirmed to avoid them. Matt jerked back, sending a Grik tumbling down amid its comrades, and lunged again. Another Grik yanked the rifle from his grip, the wet stock slippery in his fingers, but managed to impale itself on the blade. Either way, the rifle was gone, and Matt took a step back, face set, and drew his academy sword. Somehow, he'd known it would come to this.

////// *II Corps*

ith the help of the new field telephones to coordinate the attack, General Queen Safir Maraan prepared to take what was left of her entire II Corps into the next Grik trench. Almost nothing was ready; everyone was growing short on ammunition, and they'd been waiting for the Nancys to come back and plaster the position with incendiaries one more time. Apparently *Walker* needed some rather badly just then as well. Of course, *all* the Nancys had been delayed by some monumental screwup having to do with where they should refuel and rearm . . . but that only made it more imperative that Safir move as quickly as she could. She couldn't wait any longer, air or not. The Grik firebombs were cooking her out. She wasn't sure exactly when they'd need it, but with *Big Sal* and the rest of the fleet coming in with the tide, she had to secure the airfield for the Fleashooters or they'd start setting down wherever they could—on the beach if they had to. She did finally have quite a few mortars up and running, and a number of guns had been turned, so the Grik weren't having it all their way, but she could sense that the time had arrived when the momentum of battle was about to begin cascading—in one direction or another. In her experience, such moments rarely favored those who sat and waited for them. She saw her chance with the approach of one of the virtually opaque rainsqualls that had been marching about the area all day long.

A furious fusillade of mortars and cannon churned the enemy trench at a rate she couldn't sustain, but nothing could resist it either, and nearly all fire from the Grik position came to a stop. Further substantiating her notion of "cascading momentum," the rain struck.

"Up!" she cried. "Up and at them!" Prepared by the telephones, the whole corps was poised and waiting when hundreds of whistles shrilled damply under the downpour. Safir had promised General Grisa she wouldn't charge the enemy with a bayonet, but Grisa was gone. *Besides,* she told herself as she drew her brightly polished sword, *I shall keep my promise regardless. Bayonets are such awkward things.* A terrible roar arose in thousands of wrathful, frustrated throats, reflecting all the misery II Corps had endured that day, and to some degree, an inherited consciousness of what all Lemurians had endured at the hands of the hated Grik since before time was ever measured.

Up they went, out of the suddenly rain-slick trench, like a swarm of furry demons. There were 'Cats from Baalkpan, Maa-ni-la, and Sular; Aryaal, B'mbaado, and all the various seagoing Homes that had contributed a few troops, here and there, throughout the Allied armies. There was even a sprinkling of early arrivals from the Great South Isle, and a few liaison officers off *Amerika.* All Lemurians in the Alliance were represented in that dark tide that rose against its ancient enemy on their—and his—most sacred soil. Some Grik obviously saw the move, even through the lashing rain, and tried to rise and meet it. They were scoured down from the lip of their own trench by pounding swaths of canister. Then, even as the infantry surged to the attack, some of the lighter artillery pieces were heaved forward as well: six-pounders mounted on the lighter, improved carriages that had become standard in the Alliance. These continued to send murderous cans full of musket balls at the enemy—and beyond, at the milling mass of Grik behind the front line—just as quickly as they could be slammed down hissing barrels.

"Forward! Don't stop!" Safir cried, waving her sword. "Fire as you go—but make sure you're loaded when you reach the trench!" The last was a tactic that Chack had developed in the East against the Doms. A last, withering volley down into the cowering, unprepared enemy had been shown to produce most satisfactory results. The Grik had spears, but their musketeers didn't even have plug bayonets so they'd be helpless against the final fusillade, and the ingeniously offset socket bayonets that followed.

Crossbow bolts slammed into her troops in a hail of iron-tipped wood, but there was almost no firing from the Grik. The rain had seen to that by dampening their powder and wetting their match cords. Safir breathed heavily in the sodden air, and the visibility was virtually nil. The rain gave everything a dull, blurry aspect, and the gunsmoke clung to the ground like a heavy fog. Even more quickly than she expected, she reached the Grik trench and saw Grik heads rise up and stare back at her with open-mouthed astonishment. Flashes of booming Allin-Silva rifles rippled in the smoke, the jets of flame angled downward, as the first wave of attackers gained the position. With another mounting roar, the leading edge of 5th Division leaped down in the trench, and the terrible sound of weapons crashing together mixed with the screams caused by triangular bayonets and broad-bladed Grik spears piercing flesh.

Safir stomped on a spear pointing at her, and vaulted over the Grik wielding it. She landed in the muck behind the creature and slashed back with her sword. Other Grik were packed close around, barely conscious of her, and she slew them with little effort. More rifles fired down around her, and she was somewhat amazed no one hit her by accident, but more Lemurians quickly joined her in the suddenly corpse-choked pit—she couldn't distinguish regimental or division devices in the rush. They fanned out protectively around her, killing as they went.

She paused then, for a breath, and watched the fighting rage around her. There was little shooting now, only a desperate motion of bayonet-tipped rifles stabbing, thrusting, parrying, or battering with a maniacal level of spastic violence she'd rarely seen before. The squall was passing and the visibility began to improve, showing her an unbroken mass of Grik still behind the trench; she felt a rush of terror. If they came on now, they'd smother her entire corps under numbers alone . . . but they weren't coming! With a moment to scrutinize them, she realized that the Grik behind the trench weren't warriors, weren't even armed, and instead of rushing to join the fight, they were running away! Most were, at any rate.

A few were advancing from the horde in a disciplined line that made her stare as they carried leveled spears and their customary small shields. She roared for the troops around her to prepare, and they barely did so in time. A big Grik with a young crest protruding from a gap in his helmet almost fell on top of her, slipping as it came. She thrust upward with her sword and felt a hot rush of blood course down her arm. The creature wailed but carried on, almost crushing her under its dying bulk. Claws groped at her, gouging her silver breastplate with a rasping scrape she could feel in her spine, and teeth gnawed at her helmet. Her breastplate protected her from the weight of the thing, but her face was jammed in the reeking muscle of its powerful forearm. She could barely breathe and tried to bite down, but couldn't even move her jaw. With a chill she realized the thing was sinking her in the muck, and she *would* suffocate if it didn't shift enough to shred her first!

"My queen!" came a voice as the flailing corpse was dragged off and hacked apart. Hands raised her up and steadied her solicitously as she took deep, gasping breaths. Renewed firing had erupted in the trench, and she was dizzy and a little disoriented. When she focused on the one who spoke, she realized it was her "personal" comm'Cat! The Heavens alone knew how he'd kept up with her in all of this. A different EM crouched beside him with a muddy spool of wire, and she suspected the other must have fallen in the advance.

"What are the Grik doing?" she demanded, appreciatively taking her sword from a sergeant who'd retrieved it.

"They flee!" the sergeant trilled with glee, pointing at the retreating mass. "They run away! Courtney Braad-furd's 'Grik Rout' has finally taken them!"

She stared. The sergeant seemed to be right at a glance. Clearly many of the Grik were running in abject panic . . . but many may not have been. She groped for her glass but couldn't find it. She'd lost it somewhere, either in the charge or here in the slurry of the trench. "They are moving back toward the palace, or temple—whatever that monstrous great structure might be!" she said.

"Ah, my queen," the comm'Cat said with some hesitation, "I have received a signal that roughly detailed an attempt by a small party from *Waa-kur* to use the diversion of the various fightings to make an attempt against the palace! It seems the great Si-vaa and others mean to slay the High Chief of all the Grik herself!"

"And now all the Grik we just faced in their thousands are moving in that direction!" Safir breathed. She blinked sudden determination. "We must not give the enemy time to retreat within the palace! Not only might they thwart the courageous plan of our friends, but we surely have nothing that can batter down such a massive structure." Her tone was granite when she continued. "This victory has been bought with too much blood for it to remain incomplete! Does your communication device—your 'phone'—yet function?"

"Yes, my queen!"

"Very well. First, if you cannot contact COFO Tikker yourself, please ensure that enough people know to spread the word that his First Naval Air Wing is *not* to attack the second Grik trench when it finally arrives, as we are in it already. I do desire that he attack the concentration of Grik out in the open between here and the palace as vigorously as he can. In fact, an effort to divert the enemy's retreat away from the palace would be ideal." She waited for a moment while the comm'Cat spoke into his handset. When he blinked at her, indicating the task was complete, she took a long breath. At least the stench of the place had been deadened by the rain. "Now," she said, "send to Col-nol Saachic to charge his cavaal-ry into the flank of that mob; drive it north and keep it in front of us! To all other commands: Second Corps shall pursue the enemy at once. Our foremost objective is to press him *past* the palace, and deny him an opportunity to escape within! If Adar can manage to land the rest of our forces in the harbor, he may be of great assistance to that task. Regardless," she continued with complete resolve, "we shall kill every Grik in this city if it destroys this entire corps to do so!"

1st Allied Raider Brigade

To Lieutenant Colonel Chack-Sab-At's anxious dismay, his exhausted brigade had been rushing to the sound of distant guns since before the dreary dawn. Clearly, the attack on Grik City had begun without him, and he had no way of communicating his presence, or even knowing the situation he was hurrying toward. His only consolation was, whatever was happening, the battle still raged and he hadn't missed it entirely. He looked at Courtney Bradford, riding awkwardly on a borrowed Me-naak beside him in the damp forest gloom. He had no doubt they *would* have missed it if not for the strange humans they'd met. Courtney had proclaimed that they were obviously descendants of the third East India Company ship that had ventured west so long ago, when the other two had gone east to found the Empire of New Britain Isles. The Grik had preserved them here, like so many others, as examples of "other hunters," or "worthy prey," to help identify more they might yet meet—or simply for sport. It was impossible to say.

Jindal had been skeptical at first that they actually sprang from the same source as his own ancestors, but there really was no question. No matter how far they'd regressed, Courtney insensitively argued that they actually *looked* more closely related to the founders of the Empire than its current subjects—after generations of female additions from the Dominion. But Imperial histories maintained that none of the women in that ancient squadron had sailed with the westbound ship, whose ultimate goal had been a return to England, so either Will's forebears found other women somewhere along the way or the histories were in error. Courtney leaned heavily on the latter explanation, further exasperating Jindal, but even Jindal finally had to admit it was possible. Chack still found it hard to believe their benefactors had survived at all, but their language was further evidence. They spoke strangely, to be sure, but they could be understood. They'd maintained a number of nautical traditions as well, including that of calling their leader "the captain."

True to his word, the one named Will had secured permission from their "captain" to help them reach this place, and they'd largely replaced Chack's skirmishers and scouts. Somehow, they kept the local denizens away with great skill and bravery, accompanied by superior, age-old knowledge of the monsters. As far as Chack had been able to learn, they'd managed it without losing a single man. That amazed him, and the service had been invaluable since it had allowed the brigade to travel much more swiftly. That morning, however, their escorts began to melt away, and the one called Will joined Chack on the march. "We's leavin' naw," he'd said with some apparent embarrassment. "Thar's few beasties 'tween here an' the wall a' trees. Garieks keep 'em killed back." With a wistful glance at the marching brigade, back in column now, he'd continued. "I'd love ta gae an, but the Garieks hae maskits naw, an' we's daint." Then he added hopefully, "I reckan ya's dadn't brang enaw ta spare?"

"If we had, I'd gladly share them," Chack lied. He appreciated the help Will and his people gave, but wasn't about to arm them with modern weapons. Not only did he prefer to learn more about them first—not least what their relationship might be with other intelligent "predators" the Grik preserved here, possibly even including members of his own race—but with so short a time to train them, he feared the weapons and ammunition would be wasted in the fight to come.

"Indeed?" Will asked, possibly guessing some of Chack's concerns. He finally shook his head. "We'll nae fight Gariek maskits an' gannes, but yan thunder is prafe enaw that ye's dae indeed hae anather armee pawncin' an the buggers. I'll wish ye's gad fartune, an' pray far yer success. My falk'll be watchin', an' we's halp ye's haw we's can—in ather ways, praps—an when the fight is wan."

"You have my most sincere thanks, Will, as do your people. I hope we meet again."

Will had nodded, and without another word, melted away into the dark forest.

Now, Chack's Brigade, minus some three hundred casualties of the trek, was poised just inside the forest before a clearing at the foot of the wall of trees.

"Goodness gracious!" Courtney gasped. "It looks so much larger from this perspective than the sketches drawn by Tikker's scouts implied." He cocked his head and smiled. "Of course, 'perspective' is the thing. Even mighty *Salissa* looks quite small from high above. I really should fly about more, you know; air travel often stimulates me to philosophy." He blinked. "As has this tiresome but fascinating trek just completed. Amazingly stimulating, particularly from a philosophical perspective!"

Chack looked at Courtney and controlled the almost reflexive blinks of amused affection the man's interesting but often random thoughts inspired. He was glad Courtney was there, to contemplate things beyond the immediate necessity of getting over the massive obstacle they'd encountered.

There were many mighty trees, true Galla trees, no doubt, on Madagascar, but to see so many thousands stripped and incorporated into such a monstrous barricade simultaneously struck Chack as sacrilegious and ingenious. Galla trees were sacred, to various degrees, to all Lemurians, and to have countless numbers of them stacked side by side for as far as the eye could see in either direction revolted him. No doubt they leaned against an equal number on the city side of the wall, the pinnacle forming the jagged ridge of an artificial mountain range. How the Grik ever cut and moved such enormous trees, many as tall as a hundred tails, was a mystery, however, and the sheer scope of the construct was awesome to behold. Adding to the mountainous impression, Galla trees were virtually immune to wood-boring insects, and it might take them centuries to rot. This had enabled the wall to foster its very own thriving ecology, and though built on the skeletons of long-dead trees, the wall was alive.

"I don't see any Grik," Risa said, scanning the peak with her glass.

"No doubt their attention is elsewhere at present," Courtney observed. "The battle beyond sounds quite vigorous!"

"Cap-i-taan Risa," Chack said, "I'd be obliged if you personally led a mounted squad to the top of that . . . construct, to view the situation beyond. It appears the slope is not too extreme for our beasts. If all seems clear, do not send a runner, just signal us forward. We will be watching, and I will bring the entire brigade."

"What if it's not clear?"

"Then you may send a runner, with your recommendations."

"Ay, ay, Col-nol!" Risa wheeled her somewhat reluctant mount and dashed off to recruit her scouts. Shortly, she and a dozen riders were loping toward the wall, and they quickly, if a little clumsily, managed to scrabble to the top. Chack was watching intently through his own glass, and when he saw his sister wave her arm, he spoke to an aide. "Pass the word—the brigade will advance to the summit yonder. No one will proceed farther, regardless of what they see, without further orders."

It took nearly an hour to get the entire brigade started out of the woods, across the clearing, and up the treacherous flank of the great wooden wall. Impatient, Chack and Courtney Bradford reached the summit before most of the others, despite Courtney's protests and little cries of fearful surprise as his me-naak lunged jerkily upward.

"That was quite invigorating," he proclaimed, joining Chack, who'd already reached Risa and dismounted. "I don't know what to compare it to; I've never frequented amusement parks. Perhaps climbing a mast in a storm? In any event, I must say that our . . . might I say somewhat obscure excursion, has set me up amazingly in a physical respect. Not to mention what it has done to restore my natural curiosity and enthusiasm for discovery!" He paused and looked around, seeing for the first time what had taken Chack's attention. "Oh my," he murmured.

The southern face of the vast palace was directly before them, perhaps half a mile away. A portion of that distance was open ground, broken only by occasional structures that, compared to the rest of the city in view, might have been virtual mansions or estates of some sort. Beyond them was a belt of what looked like barracks, for lack of a better term, before another open area interspersed with garish pavilions lapped against the palace itself. A stairway scaled the side of the palace, interrupted by two arched entrances at different levels, the upper one being more impressively situated in the center of a broad, stony platform overhung by a scarlet awning. Few Grik were in view between them and the palace, and most of those were racing about in a most confusing fashion. Impressive as the palace was, however, a number of other things immediately drew their most intent scrutiny.

Without another distracting word, Courtney dismounted and raised his own binoculars he'd "borrowed" long ago, and scanned the various points of interest along with Chack, Risa, and a number of other officers who'd hurried to join them. The harbor beyond the palace was a strangled mass of burning, smoking wreckage, and the dismal pall that stood above it disappeared into the gray clouds above. First Fleet South and USS *Walker* had clearly completed their objective of savaging the Grik fleet at anchor, but Courtney had never feared otherwise, as long as his friends achieved the surprise they desired. What Courtney hadn't expected to see was the titanic, nearly linear struggle underway just east of the palace. Clearly, the notion of staging a heavy raid had been discarded in favor of something a bit more ambitious. Glancing at Chack, he realized that the commander of the 1st Raider Brigade was not particularly surprised.

"Drive them, my love," Chack murmured quietly, obviously urging on II Corps in general, and Safir Maraan in particular.

"I take it that our dear orphan queen has decided upon a more aggressively ambitious course of action," Courtney mused aloud.

"You truly believed she would not—could not—under the circumstances?" Chack asked him gently. Courtney shifted his weight under the blinking scrutiny.

"Oh, I don't know. Perhaps not, indeed."

"Col-nol!" Risa blurted, still looking through her glass. Like most Lemurians, she had exceptional vision, but the Imperial telescope was still welcome. "It seems that Second Corps is pushing the Grik back toward the palace and the harbor—but if you will note, a number of the enemy closest to the palace are falling!"

Chack raised his own glass once more. Even as he watched, small geysers of mud exploded among the fleeing Grik, checking their dash and sending them sprawling amid puffs of fuzz and sprays of blood. "Someone is shooting them! From the *palace*!" He redirected his gaze. A portion of the east part of the great structure could be seen, and it

looked much like that nearest them except there was only a single entrance. A few Grik milled there, but none were shooting. They probably
couldn't shoot, given the recent rain that had drenched Chack's Brigade,
and probably passed across the battle below as well. "Those have to be
modern weapons," Risa insisted, "the shots are coming from the *north*
side of the palace! Some of our people must have made it there!"

One of the company commanders, Lieutenant Galay, a former corporal in the Philippine Scouts who'd survived *Mizuki Maru*, stepped
closer to Chack. "That's a BAR, sir. Bet my life on it. The rate of fire is
pretty distinctive."

"You can *hear* it over all that?" Chack waved.

Galay snorted. "No, sir, but aside from the impacts—way too powerful for a Blitzer at that distance—what other automatic weapon could
somebody have carried up there?"

"By the Heavens!" Risa groaned with a tone of worried certainty.
"Dennis Si-vaa! What has that insane man done now?"

Chack took a breath, knowing Risa had to be right. Despite
whatever . . . relationship Silva had, or once had, with his sister (he still
could hardly bring himself to contemplate that), Silva was probably his
very best friend. If he was in the palace, rapidly becoming surrounded
by untold thousands of Grik, inside and out . . .

"My God!" Courtney exclaimed. "There's *Walker*! Sometimes you
might glimpse her through the smoke, several miles away beyond the
harbor! It looks . . . Oh dear! I believe she's aground, and has her own
fight on her hands!" He paused. "It looks as though help might be on its
way for her, at least. Some of our ships are venturing toward her. Oh! I
hope they're not too late!"

It suddenly became perfectly clear to Chack what had happened.
He'd been with Silva in such situations often enough to know exactly
what sort of scheme had occurred to the maniacal human. "He's gone
for the Celestial Mother—their High Chief!" he stated with certainty. A
quartet of Nancys suddenly swooped low over the retreating Grik, and
bombs tumbled from beneath their wings. Greasy orange flames roiled
into the sky, and black smoke corkscrewed in the wake of the climbing
planes. Grik squalled and raced everywhere in panic, many toward the

harbor. What could only be a more disciplined formation of several thousand still churned relentlessly toward the palace.

"Uh-oh," Galay murmured. "More Grik, streaming from the west. Didn't that Jap say that big cross between a coliseum and an anthill next to the palace was some kind of gladiator arena, or something? There're a few hundred Grik running across that causeway thing, straight toward what must be another entrance on that side!"

Chack slammed his telescope shut and turned to Galay. "My compliments to Major Jindal, and would he please take the Twenty-first, and two battalions of the Seventh down there, at the double, and interpose his force between the enemy and the palace? He may have all the artillery and mortars."

Galay whistled. "What are you going to do, sir?"

"I," Chack said, "and Cap-i-taan Risa, will take the First Battalion of the Eleventh Imperial Marines and storm the southern entrances. We cannot hope to take more than five hundred men through those arches without getting hopelessly jammed up—and they seem the least well defended in any case. We will maintain communications via the field telephones as long as possible, but must assume we'll lose the line at some point. If Major Jindal finds himself sorely pressed, he—the entire remainder of the brigade—will fall back to the north entrance that, hopefully, will remain in the hands of our friends now defending it."

"We will have only a battalion of *Impies*?" Risa asked doubtfully, and Chack looked at her. "They will do fine," he said. "We trained them ourselves, after all. We and the Impies will enter the palace and engage the enemy 'glaad-i-ators,' and whatever guards there may be. Hopefully we will buy sufficient time for Chief Silva to accomplish whatever it is he is trying to do."

"Aye, ay, sir!" Galay acknowledged, and trotted away, his slung Allin-Silva slapping his side.

"What about me?" Courtney demanded.

"Personally, I would prefer you stay here, under guard," Chack said, then shrugged. "That said, you have a rifle, and may go where you wish."

Courtney Bradford considered this, fingering the sling strap of the Krag he carried. "I've never pretended to be a fighting man, and have yet to fire a shot in this entire war. I've often protested that this modern weapon is wasted in my hands—but of the choices presented to me, tagging along with you does promise to be the most . . . interesting. I believe that's what I shall do, if you've no objection."

"Just so long as you make the most of the 'modern' weapon you've so generously been entrusted with," Chack agreed, shifting his own faithful Krag, slung muzzle down, as always, "and you don't require others to protect you."

"Never fear, my dear Colonel Chack!" Courtney beamed. "I require no protection! I may not have much combat experience, but I am proficient in the use of arms." He blinked. "Though perhaps I remain more proficient with a Lee-Enfield than with the charmingly complex peculiarities of loading *this* one! Such a quaint arrangement!" he added, referring to the loading gate on the side of the Krag's receiver. Lee-Enfields used "stripper clips" just like a '03 Springfield, and had a detachable magazine as well.

"You *can* reload it?" Chack questioned, a little offended by the implied slight against his own cherished weapon.

"Oh, quite well. It's second nature to me now," Courtney affirmed.

Chack blinked discomfort, but turned back to Risa after a glance at the sky. "The drums will likely get wet if we uncover them, and they and the whistles will only draw attention. We have half a mile to cover and cannot possibly do so unobserved, but I would prefer to exploit whatever surprise we may. Pass the word for the brigade to advance—the First of the Eleventh on us!"

///// *2nd Bomb Squadron*
Above Grik City

"O h my God," Doocy Meek murmured as the four ships in the squadron spiraled lower over the target. Rain lashed the canopy in front of him and turned it opaque, and the wind gusts inside the squall battered the little seaplane in a particularly disconcerting way. But looking down to the side, Meek saw the funnel-shaped mass of Grik directly against *Walker*'s side. It even looked like . . . "Captain Tikker," he shouted into the voice tube that terminated behind the pilot's left ear, "I think the Grik have gained the ship's deck!"

"I see it," Tikker replied brusquely. "We're almost too late."

To Meek, it looked like they already were, but after a brief pause, he'd begun hearing urgent pleas for air support on the secondary TBS-tuned receiver again. He couldn't respond, but he could listen. He'd learned the man on the other end was Lieutenant Ed Palmer, and the youngish voice was increasingly desperate. Looking down again, Meek could well imagine why.

"*Some* are holding out down there, Mr. Meek," Tikker continued, as if reading Doocy's mind. His eyesight was certainly better, Meek knew, but from this height, he never would've guessed it.

"Send to the rest of the squadron that we'll approach from the north so we don't have to adjust our aim after flying through the smoke of that cruiser. The first two ships'll follow us in, and we'll lay our eggs as close alongside *Walker* as we can. The second two will drop on more Griks a little farther out."

"Why not make two passes?" Doocy asked, even as he hammered out the orders.

"We got the biggest anti-Grik an' Dom bombs in the Navy strapped on," Tikker explained. "I wanted more, smaller ones, but this is what the geniuses sent over, an' all *Amer-i-kaa* had for us. Anyway, if we only drop one, there's a good chance the 'rolling moment will exceed the aileron authority,' as Col-nol Maallory would say. In other words, it'll flip the plane when the weight goes." He paused. "So we got one shot to save *Walker.*"

Doocy Meek finished his transmission and listened for a moment. He really was a "good fist" after all. "Your orders've been sent and acknowledged by all of your pilots, Captain Tikker," he reported.

"Swell," Tikker shouted back, gauging the angle as his little squadron continued its orbit to the northeast of the battle below. When he decided the time was right, he banked slightly left and pushed his stick forward. "You better start poppin' yer ears, Mr. Meek, 'cause here we go!"

USS Walker
Aft Engine Room

The fight raging just a short distance over Tabby's head had been a distraction for some of the Lemurian and female human snipes under her control, but she'd personally managed to tune it out to a large extent. Only when somebody paused in his work, shoring yet more mattresses against the leak in the hull, did she give it any apparent notice—and that was to harangue the culprit with a creditable impersonation of one of Spanky's more colorful rants. The sound of grenades drumming against the plates overhead caused even her to glance up, however. Grenades on deck meant Grik were on deck!

Chief Machinist's Mate Johnny Parks splashed through the hatch from the forward engine room, nervously wiping sweat from his brow. The EMs had finally bypassed the junction box and generator in the space (Tabby remained skeptical that the original schematics would've made that any easier and resolved to cure that later), but though power had been restored to the pumps and the rest of the ship, the aft engine room remained dark. Parks was looking anxiously for her in the gloomy light of the battle lanterns. "Tabby?" he called urgently.

"Here."

"Spanky says the Grik got past him somehow! They're gonna be down here any minute! What're we gonna do?" Tabby looked at him and blinked. Parks was a good man, but the news had clearly rattled him. That was okay; the very thought of Grik running amok in her engineering spaces rattled her too. She quickly controlled her terror and blinked grim determination. "We can shut 'em outa here, but they'll raise hell in the steerin' engine room, at least." Her eyes narrowed. "We gotta run their nasty asses the hell out!" She looked at her repair party, evaluating which ones would be less useless in a fight. Theoretically, everyone aboard USS *Walker* was required to be proficient in the use of small arms, but she'd taken on a lot of replacements in Maa-ni-la, and the learning curve in engineering was high enough that she'd let it slide when her snipes habitually skipped the drills. That had been a mistake, she realized now. "Take over here, Mr. Paarks," she ordered, then called some names. "You guys keep at it. I want this entire space dry as a bone when the tide comes in. The rest of you, quit your shorin' an' drop them timbers. Take sidearms an' cutlasses, an' follow me!"

The Grik were already in the crew's quarters when the sixteen combatants Tabby chose had scrambled up the catwalk and through the upper-level hatch. They heard them even before they saw them, down the corridor between the aft fuel bunkers, rampaging among the racks in the compartment. Tabby quickly told a pair of smaller 'Cats to seal and hold the hatch behind them, and charged into the fight with her Baalkpan Arsenal 1911 barking in her hand. There were no mattresses left for the enemy to shred, but they'd already made a shambles of the place, hacking the chains that held the racks from the overhead, and slashing bedding with their swords. Nearly all the lightbulbs had been smashed for the apparent amusement it provided. The companionway to the provisions locker was choked with Grik, gorging on what they found down there, and Tabby's bullets turned bedlam into pandemonium. Startled Grik, seemingly convinced they'd fought their way past all resistance, hesitated for an instant while the rest of Tabby's fighters deployed behind her and started shooting as well.

The opening fusillade was stunningly loud in the confined space, but not particularly effective. "Try to *hit* 'em!" Tabby shouted, disconcerted by how poorly her party's marksmanship measured up to their enthusiasm. "At least point your weapons *at* something before you fire!" Her own first shots weren't much better, but she quickly improved. Downy fuzz floated in the dim light around the portholes, and Grik screeched in agony as they crashed against dangling racks. A lot of them charged, but even her snipes could hit meat at a couple of paces. But bullets ran out. A 'Cat screamed as a Grik slashed her open with its claws. "Don't take time to reload!" Tabby cried. "Use your cutlasses!"

Transferring her smoking, empty pistol to her left hand, she drew her own Navy cutlass with the right, and chopped at the Grik that killed the first snipe she'd ever lost in hand-to-hand combat. Her cleft lips peeled back, baring bright teeth in a furious grimace as she waded into the enemy. Led by her inexperienced but ferocious example, the rest of her little party followed with a roar and a rush. Somehow, they beat the enemy back past the companionway and a small, dark-skinned girl who hadn't been able to shoot before, mercilessly emptied her pistol into the helpless Grik crammed on the stairs to the provisions locker. *She* had time to reload and do it again, and before she loaded her third magazine and moved on, nothing remained alive below. After what seemed like forever but could only have been a few terrible minutes, Tabby and her snipes chased a dozen Grik back up the stairs into the laundry. It cost them, though. Tabby looked around, panting, her right arm and shoulder in agony from the unaccustomed exertion of swinging the cutlass, and realized she was down to ten effectives.

"We keep after 'em!" a burly 'Cat water tender insistently coughed through heaving breaths. His fur was nearly the same shade of gray as Tabby's, and just as slick with foamy sweat and blood. Tabby nodded. He was right. Despite her inexperience with this sort of thing, everybody knew that when the Grik ran, you *chased* them. "Okay," she gasped. "Ever'body reload pistols." She blinked determination, and her tail swished sharply. "Nobody stops till the deckhouse is clear an' whatever hatch they come through is secure." She knew that only the efforts of Spanky and those above could explain why they'd faced so few Grik inside—and there was no telling how long they could keep up whatever they were doing. She suspected it was the grenades she'd been hearing, and sooner or later they'd run out. "Okay," she repeated, looking up the companionway, "let's go!"

They clambered noisily up the pierced steel stairs. No Grik met them in the laundry, but several were in the head, apparently looking for a way out. They turned at Tabby's appearance and snarled, but there was something . . . a kind of desperation in their eyes that convinced her then that these *couldn't* be the "new" Grik she'd heard so much about. They didn't charge either, but only scrabbled more fervently to escape, tearing up the seats across the trough and even slamming themselves against the portholes. Tabby and the couple of others who fit in the hatchway killed them with their pistols. A 'Cat's scream and a flurry of shots brought them racing into the torpedo workshop where they found two of their own already down. More than the dozen Grik who'd retreated here were still slashing at them, or fighting the rest of their party who'd been backed against the lathe. Beyond that desperate fight, Tabby caught her first glimpse of another, through the open forward hatch. She'd known the Grik were all over the ship; they had to be to have gotten inside, but to see it with her own eyes . . . "At 'em! Kill 'em! Chase 'em out!" she screamed, shooting at the several Grik still savaging one of her own. More pistols popped in the confined space before the three 'Cats behind her joined the rush with their cutlasses. Her pistol empty, Tabby tucked it in her belt and snatched one of several Allin-Silva barreled actions off a rack. She used it as a club in her left hand after she drew her cutlass again. Bashing and slashing, she helped chase the suddenly terrified Grik out the hatch. She briefly caught a bright flash of fiery light out of the corner of her eye, to port, but something *clunked* on the deck among the Grik just outside, and she slammed the hatch just as a deep *bam!* peppered it with grenade fragments. "Watch where the hell you thowin' them things!" she roared, knowing no one above could hear. The water tender tried to push the hatch open again, his eyes blazing with the energy of the moment.

"No," Tabby said, her own energy suddenly gushing away. "Secure it. We done our job. Now we gotta get this div . . ." She stopped. Three of those by the lathe were badly injured, and two were dead, of course. Her tail went limp. Her division, people she knew and cared for and worked with every day, had suffered a frightful toll. Five members of the party remained unhurt. "We gotta get this division back to work, doin' what we do," she finished.

A gust of orange fire roiled skyward, close enough to Matt that it seemed to sear his flesh. A raucous skirl of tortured shrieks accompanied the ball of blackening flames, and he turned his gaze to view the roaring Nancys that had finally appeared, banking left over the water and away from the burning cruiser's column of smoke. He blinked watery blood out of his eyes and saw a stream of smoke following one of the planes as it dropped out of formation and angled for the water off *Walker*'s starboard side. A yell brought him back to the business at hand, and he thrust his sword down the open mouth of a Grik that had lunged for him with yellow teeth. The sword tip pierced the charging flesh and grated on bone before it suddenly appeared, gleaming red, from the back of the Grik's neck. The creature fell like a reptilian marionette with all its strings cut, and he tried to follow the fall, guiding it slightly as he'd learned to do, so he could retrieve his sword without the blade binding. It had become an unconscious thing. Another Grik battered past a 'Cat to his left, and he shot it with the pistol he'd reloaded at some point and now held in that hand. The Grik took another stumbling step toward him, and his finger tensed on the trigger—but the thing fell under a blow from Bernie's cutlass to the back of its head.

A part of Matt's mind was interested by how the fight had become one of brief, snapshot impressions: the yellow teeth, grasping claws, slashing swords, and wild eyes of Grik and friends alike. Occasional muzzle flashes still punctuated the chaos, and bayonets and spearpoints waved and glittered and leveled and thrust like pale grass on a sunny, windswept day. He blinked. The sun was out; at least a few tentative beams had broken through the clouds and smoke above. That almost distracted him as well, but just then he nearly tripped over a corpse behind him as he took another step back. They'd lost the rails, the only physical barrier they had left, and if he went down now, he was finished. The line between the Grik and the bridge still held, but only because the number one gun had ceased firing and its crew had joined the fight on deck with half a dozen Blitzer Bugs. Their arrival and the fusillade of fire they brought had staggered the Grik for a moment, but when they were empty . . . All Matt could think about was what would happen when the Grik finally swept all the defenders off the upper decks of his ship. Eventually, they'd get below where the wounded were . . . where his wife and unborn child were. . . . The fight on the amidships platform was doomed, he knew, but as long as they held out, as long as they kept some of the enemy away from that line forward . . .

The Grik seemed to know it, and they attacked with a focus Matt had rarely seen, even as the men and 'Cats defended the platform with an equally fanatical desperation. Anything that came to hand was a weapon; Grik spears and shields, even helmets, were wielded and thrown. The Grik were caught up in it as well, using spent shell casings as weapons themselves if they had nothing else, throwing the heavy things at killing, skull-crushing velocities. One such narrowly missed Matt's head, clanging loudly off the open breech of the number two gun behind him. He fought on. No more was he commander in chief of all Allied forces, even if that position had been dangerously undermined by Adar—and himself to a large degree, by his desire to support the precedent Adar was intent on setting. He knew now that had been a mistake; at least the timing of the way it happened had been, and since he'd allowed it, the greatest measure of blame was his. Nobody could've foreseen this situation or the sandbar that precipitated it, but that was no consolation. This, and all the other confused, deadly episodes that had unfolded that day were a direct result of a divided command that left various elements uncertain about what, exactly, was expected of them. Matt suspected *Walker*'s mission was the only one that hadn't changed at some point during the fight, and he wondered if a firmer, single hand at the wheel might have made a difference now—at least for his ship and her people. He'd become merely another soldier in the Alliance, unable to influence anything that occurred beyond the reach of his blade. He genuinely didn't expect to survive beyond the next few minutes, but if he did, there would have to be changes.

A thrown weapon of some sort, he had no idea what it had been, glanced off his helmet and sent colorful stars streaking across his vision. He sagged, trying to remember what he'd been thinking about. Campeti had him, he realized, holding him up by his sore right arm and yelling into his ear. He shook his head. *What the hell's Campeti going on about?*

"What?" he managed. Grik wavered in front of him, and he tried to aim his pistol. He wasn't much good with it left handed, not beyond a few short steps, but that had been enough. Now, the Grik seemed to be holding back, and he couldn't get the sights to stay on any one of them as they turned away, apparently drawn by something else.

"We have to keep them occupied!" Matt ordered. "Don't let 'em go forward!"

"They ain't goin' forward, Skipper!" Campeti rasped. "Look!"

"I *see* them."

"No." Campeti shifted his grip and hoisted him higher. "I don't mean at the Grik!"

The roar of battle had intensified in the waist, and Matt realized there was heavy firing there for the first time in quite a while. More mushrooms of fire climbed to port and Matt felt their radiant heat, but he barely noticed them when he realized there were suddenly quite a few more Lemurian Marines along the *starboard* rail, advancing around the number one torpedo mount and shooting into the milling Grik aft of the deckhouse.

"Where'd they come from?" Matt managed, uncertain if he was seeing right through the bloody rain and sweat in his eyes. Even as he asked, he became aware that one of the DDs had drawn up alongside *Walker* despite the shallow water, and Marines and armed sailors were clambering aboard as fast as they could. Thunderous booming drew his gaze aft, and there was another DD, its sails furled and smoke hazing the top of its 'stack, furiously firing stands of grapeshot into the few Grik still staging to board. It was only then that Matt realized how few of those remained. The firebombs hadn't only burned hundreds of their enemies; they'd cut the bridge of corpses! Even beyond that, hundreds more of the enemy lay or writhed, crawling and smoldering, on the strangely smaller sandbar that had brought them so near. It suddenly dawned on Matt that he had no idea how long they'd been fighting, but the tide must've finally turned.

Ever so slightly, and possibly discernible only to those like Matt and Campeti who knew her so well, *Walker* shifted in her bed of sand and Matt looked to starboard once more. *Salissa* was passing in the deeper water of the channel, her high, massive form displacing a bow wave that caused the DD alongside to roll noticeably—and *Walker* to shift again as another wave struck her. Fierce fighting still raged aboard his ship, but shouts from below, and cheering, trilling jeers from the bridge informed him that many Grik forward of the platform were jumping over the rail onto the bridge of bodies, or even into the increasingly flashy-frothed sea. Matt felt a smile begin to crack his stony visage when he caught the flicker of a Morse lamp high on *Big Sal*'s bridge.

"Keje wants to know if you're okay, and if we'll float if he pulls us off this damn beach," Campeti croaked after clearing his dry throat and spitting on the corpse-strewn deck.

"I saw *that*," Matt told him. "Let's see how quickly we can reply."

More sunbeams found them, shifting and fading in the dirty sky, and the rain had stopped at last. The sunlight still looked rather odd filtered through the dense gunsmoke shrouding *Walker* once more, but the darkness that had been creeping into Matt's eyes and soul slowly began to clear.

////// *The Celestial Palace*

ennis Silva only *thought* Grik City was a rat maze. Compared to the dank, dark, labyrinthine stone passageways through the bitter heart of the Celestial Palace, the shoreside slum had been a bright, cheery garden spot. The halls were narrow, and the ceilings were low and confining. What little light there was came from the meager flicker of small lamps recessed into the walls, and set atop large clay vessels of what was likely some kind of fish oil, judging by the smell. The lamps gave barely enough light to see the little compass Silva resorted to, time and again, to keep their bearings. Not that it helped much. The place was like a hive, with corridors placed at right angles to one another, but with no more sense of direction or purpose than an ant might have used to lay them out. Occasionally, they opened into broad galleries with arched ceilings and lamp-lit walls, but these had no apparent purpose either. Miyata proposed that they were dining halls or places where ceremonies of some sort might be held, but none looked like they'd been used for a long time. But Miyata had also promised them it wouldn't stink quite as bad in here, and he'd been wrong about that. *All a matter of taste*, Dennis supposed. *It is different, but still damn bad. Course, the air ain't exactly wholesome in* Walker's *berthing spaces, but it ain't a patch to this.*

And there were Grik.

Their first encounters came very soon after they entered; a group of "palace guards," most likely, rushing to reinforce the ones they'd killed, came charging around one of the blind turns. Silva hosed the leaders with his Thompson, and they tossed grenades around the corner before they showed themselves. Peering around at last, they saw close to a dozen Grik, wadded together, mostly dead. A few were only wounded, but they'd been stunned by the concussion of the blasts and were easily dispatched by the 'Cat Marines' bayonets. The next ones weren't as easy, probably realizing they needed to proceed with caution. Miyata had warned them that the guards were a "kind" of Hij themselves, and would be a cut above ordinary Grik warriors. Unfortunately, Irvin Laumer didn't think his party had the luxury of taking its time. Whatever they could accomplish in the Celestial Palace had to be done before they were overwhelmed by numbers, or their targets—the Celestial Mother herself, for one—could escape. Of course, it was hoped that her death or capture might influence events outside the palace, and that was another reason they were in a hurry. If the battle for Grik City was lost before they found the Grik leaders, it wouldn't make a hell of a lot of difference in the short term if they killed the Celestial Mother or not. To make matters worse, Laumer and Miyata weren't even sure that killing her was a good idea.

"That's what *I'm* here for, damn it!" Dennis grumped, his words echoing in the passage they searched—an empty passage, for the moment. "I even brung along a special tool for the job!" Petey stirred from his perch around Silva's neck, but was too terrified to make a comment. Instead, he just scrunched down tighter to the big destroyerman.

"But if we kill her, the Grik might just fight even harder," Miyata argued. "Whereas if we capture her—hold her in our power—she may be convinced to force the rest to stop fighting entirely!"

"Yeah." Pam snorted at Dennis. "Killin' her might be the most idiotic thing you ever did!"

"No way," Silva denied with an ironic chuckle.

"I'm with the big idiot," Isak grouched, puffing up behind with the 'Cat Marines. "Not that anybody cares what I think," he added.

"I do," Horn stated, "and I agree with your assessment of our priorities—and Silva. But the Jap may have a point."

"He does have a point," Laumer agreed. "But we've got to find her before we can kill her *or* take her prisoner. Where the hell is she?"

Miyata paused, considering. "You must remember I was only in the palace that one time, and I never saw the creature myself." He frowned. "I came in through the entrance we used, but then I went down. I haven't seen a stairway yet—but I don't remember ever coming this far either. We must have missed it somehow." He shook his head. "I only assumed she was on this level by the amount of activity at the time, but that may mean nothing today. In any event, she may reside on a different level entirely."

"Helluva lot of good you are." Silva sulked. "Our only 'guide' can't even find the fattest Grik in the world—who I doubt would surrender even if the damn thing knew what surrender was! Buncha pie-in-the-sky *crap*, arguin' 'Let's do this! Let's do that' like the goddamn League o' Nations—like anything you decide'll make any difference, anyway. I say we just follow our noses. She's s'posed to be bigger than the rest—and Larry's Tagranesi big mama sure was, so I guess it follows. If that's so, then she's liable to stink worse than the rest of 'em too. We sniff out the worst stink in the joint an' kill whatever we find!"

"Kill what we find!" Petey mumbled intensely.

Laumer had a compass of his own, and he looked at it in the dim light of a lantern. "I bet Miyata's right," he said, ignoring Silva's rant. "I think we've just about covered this level, though I don't think we've seen anything twice. That leaves up or down."

"Up, I would think."

Laumer nodded. "Okay. But how do we get up? Where would the stairs be?"

"If not near the entrance, then toward the middle—I think."

"Grik!" Silva barked, and loosed a burst from his Thompson. Petey squawked and launched himself back down the passageway with another squirt from under his tail. Bullets slapped into two of the charging warriors and they sprawled on the stones, but four more were coming. One threw a spear that narrowly missed the top of Laumer's shoulder—but buried itself in the throat of a 'Cat Marine behind him. Laumer blasted that one with his shotgun, and Pam killed the others with a sustained burst from her Blitzer.

"As we were sayin'," Silva said, suddenly breathing a little harder while Pam checked the 'Cat, "which damn way?"

"This one's dead," Pam announced, helping shift the body so one of the other Marines could take the cartridge box and sling their comrade's weapon.

"I suggest the direction these Grik came from," Miyata offered tensely, watching them do their job. Then he shrugged. "They had to come from somewhere."

"And there ought to be *more* of them," Horn suddenly interjected. "Here we are, running loose in the big house, and all we've run into is a few scattered groups. I don't know. . . . It just seems like it ought to be harder, you know?"

Laumer looked at him speculatively.

"So our strategy is to just go whichever direction offers the *most* resistance?" Silva asked, cocking a brow. Then he grinned. "Sounds good to me."

The blood-spattered corridor suddenly echoed with a monstrous roar that seemed to shake the very stones.

"Whoa!" Lawrence said, his crest rising, and his bright eyes wide. "That sounded like a su'er lizard!"

Petey had reappeared, and he made panicky little chirping sounds as he scrambled up Silva's leg and back and resumed his perch. "Make up your goddamn mind," Silva scolded the creature, then looked at the rest of them. "Relax. That can't be no super lizard! Even if they had one, they'd never stuff him in here."

"It was *somethin'*," Pam insisted. "Somethin' big. Somethin' that might explain why we've only seen these small groups of Grik!" Another *pair* of roars, possibly closer, shook grimy condensation from the ceiling.

"More than one, whatever they are," Miyata observed, "and Surgeon Cross might well be right." He looked at Laumer. "Onward? The way the Grik came?"

Laumer nodded, and Silva, Horn, and Lawrence trotted ahead. It might not've been much of a plan, but at least it was one. The passage took an abrupt left turn, and they followed that for a while. Here, at last, the corridor opened into several dark chambers, but again there appeared to be nothing inside them. There was a fair amount of evidence of recent occupation, however, suddenly interrupted. Finally, after another left turn, they entered one of the larger halls, similar to those they'd seen before. This one was different, however, in that several other passageways opened into it, and there were two broad staircases, hewn from stone, at the far end. One led up, the other down. Another chorus of roars, apparently very close, froze them in their tracks, and they heard a kind of loud snuffling sound as well.

"They're here!" Lawrence warned.

"Up the stairs!" Silva urged. "We'll fight whatever the hell they are from the high ground!"

"Belay that!" Laumer ordered. "We don't know what's up the stairs! We fight here, where we know there's nothing at our backs!"

"With all due respect, sir," Horn said, "we don't know that either!"

The argument was quickly rendered moot when "something big" suddenly flowed out of one of the passageways and into the hall. The first thing they noticed was the head. Long, massive jaws, easily as frightening as a super lizard's, filled with a double row of yellowed, sharklike teeth, gaped at them as small, pinprick eyes swiveled toward them like a chameleon's. The deadly head was framed by a large spiky frill and a pair of forward-facing horns. Another horn, shorter than the others, protruded near the snorting nose. The face, at least, looked like a narrower, "sport model" version of the giant creature they'd seen when Chack's Brigade went ashore. That was about the only similarity. Behind the head, the body was long, almost serpentine, with more spikes down its back and four short, powerful legs. The skin was a mix of scales and fur, very closely matching the stone walls around it, but the scales glittered like inset jewels in the lamplight.

"Jesus Christ!" Horn whispered. "It's a Chinese dragon!"

"Bullshit!" Silva hissed. "It looks more like a giant horny-toad poodle to me!" He grinned. "It's a dragon poodle!"

Whatever it was, it attacked.

Pam's Blitzer Bug and Silva's Thompson sprayed .45 ACP at the thing, amid the deeper booming of the Allin-Silvas. Faced with this unexpected cacophony, the monster slowed its rush. The .45s didn't seem to do much, and some even ricocheted off the horns, frill, and even what were apparently armored casings around the eyes, and whined off the stony walls. Some got down its throat, no doubt, and that might have stung. The heavier bullets fired by the far more powerful Allin-Silvas gave it something very unexpected to think about, however, as they plowed past the facial armor and deep into the flesh beneath. Even Isak's Krag did some damage when it blew the casing off one of the eyes.

"Spread out!" Dennis roared, grabbing Pam by the arm and starting to move to the side. He stopped, feeling something drag him back, and he whirled. Isak's hand was in his bag of grenades.

"Nearly yanked my arm outa its socket," Isak sneered. "I need one 'o these!"

"Well, don't throw it in *here*—it'll just get us!" Silva snapped, still holding Pam. She was reloading. "Me an' her gotta get at the damn thing's sides. Wish I had my ol' Doom Stomper!"

The beast had recovered itself and lunged again. A renewed fusillade from a wider front startled it again, and it roared in pain and frustration. Miyata bolted to the side to get a better angle, and his motion drew its attention. It snapped once on air, but spun as fast as a striking snake and snatched his leg in its jaws. Miyata cried out as the monster picked him up—then dropped him on the stones when two Lemurian Marines drove their bayonets in its side. With no apparent thought, the beast simply rose up slightly and slammed its body down on its tormentors. They didn't even have time to scream. Silva changed magazines again and bored in, chewing a hole in the scaly hide and into the flesh beneath, while Pam began judiciously firing bursts to distract it whenever it focused on another victim.

"Hey!" Isak Reuben screeched, his voice shaky. "Leave it be a second, wilya?"

The firing tapered off as the stunned combatants looked at him. So did the monster. "Looky here, you big, fat, horny-toad poodle dragon! I got somethin' for ya!" Isak spat. He pulled the pin on his grenade and started a classic windup, just as the monster went for him, jaws open wide. With a grunt, Isak pitched the grenade with all his might straight down the dark gullet as it came, then threw himself to the side. Silva yelled, and everyone started firing again, to distract it from Isak. The grenade went off with a muffled thump that would've been anticlimactic— if it hadn't blown the monster's throat out with a sudden cascade of smoke and blood. It must've broken the thing's neck too, because the giant body started flopping and rolling around the chamber with spastic abandon, slamming the slack-jawed, lifeless head against the walls and floor. It almost smashed Laumer as he and Lawrence pulled Miyata out of the way. Slowly, the corpse lost animation, and the diminished group gathered at the stairs.

"You oughta strike for pitcher on the ship's team," Silva told Isak. "Jeek's gonna be jealous."

"Not me," Isak grated.

"Well done, Chief Reuben," Laumer said, just as another roar thundered in one of the passageways.

"Thanks . . . Mr. Laumer," Isak said, flustered by the compliment. "Now let's get along up them stairs!"

"What?" Dennis said. "You mean you don't wanna wait for another one?"

"Hell no!"

"We're gonna hafta carry Lieutenant Miyata," Pam announced, tearing the man's trouser leg and quickly smearing polta paste from her pack on the wound. Miyata didn't make a sound, but he clenched his teeth in pain. "Gimme a hand here!" she ordered one of the seven remaining 'Cats before looking defiantly up at Laumer. "We sure can't leave him!"

Irvin couldn't help hesitating just an instant, considering how dragging Miyata—or any other wounded—might slow them down, before shaking his head. "No," he agreed. "We can't leave him. Bandage him as quickly as you can, and let's get going."

Commander Simon Herring had never seen anything like the battle that sprawled around the great
dome-shaped palace. He snorted. *Considering how
often I realize things like that lately, it's really saying
something,* he supposed. The panorama of the destroyed fleet was awesome and stirring to behold,
but perhaps even more striking was the unrivaled,
ceaseless, surging *noise* of it all. The surflike roar of thousands of warriors, continuous rifle fire, and the blended clatter and crash of weapons
was all-encompassing. The bass *thud* of field guns, exploding shells, and
mortar bombs wasn't as constant, but it was encouraging since few Grik
guns could be firing anymore. And the deeper thunder of bigger naval
guns was beginning to reassert itself. The DDs off the east coast were

hard-pressed to fire over II Corps without risking harm to their own people, but *Salissa* and her battle group were edging closer to the harbor mouth, shrouded in smoke and stabbing gunfire. It looked like much of First Fleet South was finally coming in. As frightened as he was, Herring wouldn't have traded his vantage point with anyone just then.

He couldn't tell how things fared aboard distant *Walker*, but gouts of flame arising alongside indicated that the Nancys were covering her at last. And, of course, she'd have fleet support soon—if there was anyone left to support. He hoped so. He'd grown to admire Captain Reddy and his crew, and believed—despite the cock-up this operation had become—that Reddy had done all he could really do under the circumstances. Perhaps he'd known, even subconsciously, that it would take a fiasco like this to convince Adar and their allies that, much as they needed a single, supreme authority in the alliance, they still required another, *different* authority once the shooting started. Adar—or someone like him—clearly remained the best choice for the one, but he just didn't have the experience or talent for the other. One of Herring's secret early criticisms of Matt had grown out of his inability to understand why the man hadn't simply taken over himself. Now, even he had to admit that would have been disastrous. Reddy was probably the only one who could command everyone in battle, but he couldn't—didn't *want* to—lead the Alliance as a whole, and that created an interesting contradiction that Herring finally understood.

Many would've followed Captain Reddy as blindly as Alexander the Great's Macedonians followed him, but certainly not all. Even Alexander had to conquer many of the peoples who provided a large percentage of his later armies, and not only was that impractical here, but that behavior had led to chaos and the unraveling of most of Alexander's accomplishments after his death. Matt was uniquely suited to lead all the armed forces of the Alliance because he was good at it, and more important, everyone *knew* that—aside from his own "Navy clan"—he had no intention of ruling them! It was suddenly all so clear to Simon Herring now, and he only hoped he hadn't realized it too late. Now that he knew what had to be done, he'd like to live long enough to help it happen.

He couldn't see all of the battle in front of II Corps because the flank of the palace blocked his view, but what he saw was reassuring—and terrifying all at once. It was reassuring because it looked like General Queen Safir Maraan's attack on the last Grik trench was succeeding, and had at least partially driven the enemy from the position. It was terrifying because now it looked like countless thousands of Grik were streaming back, away from the fighting, directly toward him, Pack Rat, and five Lemurian Marines.

"Gunner, um . . ." He paused. "What *is* your real name?"

"Paak-Ras-Ar," the Lemurian gunner's mate replied, then shrugged. "Pack Rat."

"Very well." Herring looked at the Marines. "And your names?" They told him, and he nodded thoughtfully. "I suppose it is an honor to be with you all, under the present circumstances, but I believe we should hurry and finish heaping these dead Grik atop our little barricade, because we're likely to have a great deal of company soon."

Pack Rat glanced down at the tide of Grik, and his tail swished in agitation. "Ay, ay, Comaander. I think you right. You want me on the BAR . . . first? I purty good with it."

"By all means. I can certainly operate it, but I'm probably better suited to a Springfield."

Two Fleashooters strafed the leading edge of the Grik swarming toward them, and a pair of Nancys swooped low in their wake, dropping bombs. High-pitched screams reached them through the rushing, roiling flames. Burning Grik lapped against the base of the palace, falling, curling up . . . but it wasn't nearly enough, and hundreds burst through the flames, leaping the corpses, and starting up the steps.

"To your posts!" Herring ordered, nervously opening his bolt to ensure his rifle was loaded. "Commence firing at will!"

Pack Rat's BAR hammered loudly, launching spent brass and spitting bullets into the surge. Almost immediately, he was replacing the magazine. One of the Marines started rolling grenades down the steps, and they tore steaming gaps in the enemy mass. The other 'Cats fired steadily, as fast as they could, and it was impossible for them to miss, with each bullet sometimes passing through three or more of the enemy. Herring took more careful aim, being less familiar with small arms, and still emptied his rifle more quickly than he would've thought possible. He stared over the grisly barricade as he inserted another stripper clip with fumbling fingers, and any hope he might have cherished fluttered away. They were *slaughtering* the Grik, but they just couldn't possibly do it fast enough to make a difference. One of the 'Cat Marines tumbled back, his helmet spinning away, and Herring stared at the kicking corpse for a moment before he shook himself and closed his rifle bolt. There wasn't much incoming fire of any sort from this mob, but Herring realized that at least a few of the enemy's muskets were working, despite the damp. Unconsciously, he tried to make himself as small a target as possible as he aimed and fired again.

Relentlessly, the Grik charged up the steps.

"We already runnin' outa ammo!" one of the 'Cats cried out, groping in his cartridge box. Pack Rat slammed a fresh magazine in the BAR—he couldn't have many left, as fast as he'd been using them—and looked at the Marine.

"We ain't gonna run out," he said simply. Herring knew he was right; they wouldn't live that long.

Inexplicably, the mass of Grik suddenly shuddered, as if struck by a blow from the side, and dozens dropped or tumbled back down the steps. Another blow slammed into them and more fell away. Herring didn't understand. He looked around, realizing he'd hunched down almost too far to shoot, and saw the Grik recoil back as if physically pushed away.

"Hot daamn!" Pack Rat shouted, rising up and emptying the BAR from his shoulder.

"Are you mad?" Herring demanded, and Pack Rat blinked relief and glee in reply.

"Maad? Hell no! I'm *haappy*! Look!" He pointed with his weapon. A column of 'Cats in the mottled tunics of the 1st Raider Brigade was streaming in from the right to interpose itself between the Grik and the arched entrance—between certain death and Simon Herring. Speechless, he slowly stood and watched. Whistles blew and the column quickly went into line, facing down the steps. Shouted commands raced down the line, and rifles came up—and fired a sharp, stunning volley directly into the reeling mob.

"Chack's here!" Pack Rat trilled, almost capering with excitement. "Chack's here!" he repeated, slapping one of the Marines on her armored shoulder.

A second volley swept the Grik farther down the flank, and a third seemed to turn the tide completely. As quickly as that, it looked as though the Grik, like a great, dark river, had been diverted away from the palace and down toward the city and the harbor beyond.

"Take positions around the entrance," ordered a dark-complexioned man with black mustaches. "Respitans, in you go. Find someplace inside to stop anything coming out, and await further instructions!" Herring stood aside as men—Imperials—rushed past and clattered down the passageway behind him, their hobnailed shoes scritching loudly on the stones. He watched them for a moment, then turned to face a man who'd stopped in front of him, holding a salute. Instinctively, Herring returned it.

"Good afternoon, Commander Herring! We met once before. I'm . . ."

"You're Major Jindal!" Herring managed. "Alistair Jindal!"

"At your service, sir."

"You are indeed!" Herring grinned, grabbing the man's hand and pumping it enthusiastically. "You are *indeed*!" he repeated. "Uh, where's Colonel Chack?"

"He's assaulting the south entrance. We secured the one on the east side of this"—Jindal's eyes flicked around—"this place, and came to your relief as quickly as we could."

"You cut it a bit fine, Major," Herring confided, relief still washing through him, "but I'm grateful all the same."

"My pleasure, sir. If you please, could you tell me what my lads are liable to face in there?" he asked, nodding at the entrance.

Herring's grin faded. "I'm afraid not. Lieutenant Laumer and a small party of sailors and Marines went in some time ago, but I remained here. I can't tell you what's inside, but nothing has come out since they went in."

Dennis Silva and Gunny Horn dashed up the long, coarse-cut stairway and arrived at the top amid a swarm of musket balls that spattered them with lead and stone chips. *Course the Grik's matchlocks work in here,* Silva realized. *It's damp an' mucky, but it ain't rainin'!* He cursed himself for an idiot even as he dove to the floor, firing his Thompson into a *lot* of Grik that must've been waiting for them. "We got a respectable reception up here!" he shouted over his shoulder. Horn's rifle cracked, and then a staccato of shots erupted as the rest of their party joined them, taking cover as well. Pam dropped to Silva's left and fired a stick into the Grik. "Gaa!" Silva shouted. "You're rainin' hot brass all down my shirt!"

"Better that than a musket ball in your good eye!"

"I guess," Silva conceded after a shorter burst of his own that sent several Grik clattering and kicking on the stones. "I mean, what's a little hot brass between us, doll?"

"Not near enough misery for you, after what you've caused me."

"*Now* what are you sore about?"

"This!"

"Hey! This ain't my fault!"

"It was your idea."

"So? We shoulda stayed on the ship?"

"Maybe."

"Let's go!" Laumer ordered, rising up and trotting across the bodies sprawled before them in the lingering smoke. "Make for the center. We should either find the Grik leaders there, or another stairway."

Silva followed, but he could still see Grik down the long corridor in front of them, flitting from side to side. "Lots of Grik here, sir," he cautioned. "Up ahead. They'll come at us from the sides or behind." The lamplight made it immediately obvious that this level was similar to the first in construction, but the layout was entirely different. Where the lower level was a maze of right angles that didn't seem to have any purpose but to confuse, this one was almost perfectly geometrical, like a grid, or more accurately, a series of square chambers separated by long passageways that intersected others at precise intervals.

"They will," Laumer agreed, taking it in as well, "but another monster," he said, smiling ironically, "another 'dragon poodle,' is still behind us. We have to push on."

Silva shrugged and trotted past Laumer. Lawrence was already casting ahead, like a hunting dog, scouting the cross-corridors and urging them on. It struck Dennis that the little guy probably counted on any Grik seeing him thinking he was one of them, for an instant. *That'll make all the difference, him bein' smaller than most Grik, after all. Not that he's at too much of a disadvantage. Little booger's grown up fightin'. Shoulda thought o' that myself, though,* he judged. *I ain't been thinkin' right about any of this little caper,* he suddenly realized, glancing back at Pam. She was covering the rear with her Blitzer, behind the 'Cat helping Miyata. *Jap musta not wanted to be carried after all. Just as well. That'd only get him and two others dead at once.*

They rushed past several of the large squares—they *were* chambers, with arched entrances, Dennis saw—and Lawrence was sniffing and checking inside each as they passed. Once, he fired into one and raced in with his bayonet, only to emerge a moment later and scurry on. When Dennis passed the entrance, he saw lots of blood pooling on the floor, and three dead Grik. None seemed to have weapons, besides the ones they were made with, but ol' Larry could sure be a ring-tooter in a fight, as he well knew. Add the sight of something that looked so much like them bursting in among them, and the surprise would definitely give him a brief advantage. All the chambers stank even worse than the corridor, and Silva began to realize they were finally seeing "how the other half lived." There was dingy bedding inside, heaped in the corners, along with clay jars full of water and who knew what else. There was no provision for a fire, but charred bones were scattered around, so the inhabitants probably ate there after their food was prepared elsewhere. *Not much decoration,* he observed dryly; *none at all, in fact. Grik sure are dreary-minded critters,* he thought. *No landscapes, no pictures of bananas an' grapes heaped up next to a bottle o' booze.* Then he realized there *was* graffiti, or at least some scratches on the walls. He wondered if it was writing of some kind and squinted. *Nope. Well, maybe. Some is pictures, like I've seen scrawled on the walls o' brigs all over China and the Philippines.* He snorted. *I doubt this is a brig,* he decided, *but whoever hangs out here must get as bored as prisoners.*

He contemplated this only an instant before hurrying on, reaching the next passageway. A musket roared in the hall to his left, and a ball *zwing*ed past and showered him with rock chips. *"Goddamn!"* Petey screeched, digging his claws into Silva's neck. He was through gliding off and climbing back up every time he was startled, apparently sure at last that he was safer where he was. That didn't mean he was enjoying himself—and Silva was increasingly aware of his painful presence. *Oughta just twist his stupid head off,* Dennis thought as he threw himself back. "Half a dozen Grik down there!" he shouted accusingly at Lawrence. The Sa'aaran just looked back, holding his arms out as if to say, "There weren't any there when *I* went past." Dennis rolled his eye and tossed a grenade around the corner. "Just like I pree-dicted; they're workin' their way around us." The grenade went off, and he followed it with a long burst from his Thompson, chopping wounded or dazed Grik to the floor. When he fished another magazine out of his pouch, he realized he had only a couple left. *Crap.* "C'mon," he told the others. "It's clear—again. But keep your eyes peeled!"

Pam fired a burst behind them, but Dennis couldn't see her target through the smoke and gloom. *She's my damn problem!* he understood at last. *Her bein' here has me all screwed up! I gotta quit worryin' about her; she can take care o' herself!* Several shots came from the same corridor, from the *right* this time, as the party hurried past. Another one of their Marines fell while Isak and the other 'Cats returned fire.

"See?" Dennis warned. "They got us in the squeeze!"

"Forward," Irvin ordered, "as fast as you can! We're nearly to the center of the palace! We'll end it there!"

For a moment, beyond the crossing corridor, no one moved, and Irvin had to catch himself. "What?" he demanded.

"End it—or start all over again, if there's more stairs!" Horn reminded. Irvin opened his mouth, but didn't reply before more shots sounded. The noise built until all the passageways echoed with almost continuous firing that was amplified and funneled around them as though the noise were coming from loudspeakers. As if in response, the monster from the lower level roared at the top of the steps. It was barely visible in the glimmer of the lamps that had survived the firefight near the landing.

"A helluva squeeze," Silva proclaimed loftily.

"That shootin' is *rifles!*" Isak ranted indignantly. "Where'd the Griks get rifles?"

"Those aren't Grik," Irvin declared, realization dawning. "Some of our people must have broken in from the south!"

"Against the 'all!" Lawrence snapped as Grik started racing past, fixated on the noise from their left.

"Even more in here than I thought," Dennis mumbled, "an' they're pourin' out o' the middle like ants outa their hole, up there." He nodded. "Right from the direction we was headed."

"That's swell," Pam panted from the rear. The 'Cat helping Miyata had been wounded, and the small woman was trying to support them both. Noticing her situation, a 'Cat took her place and she sagged.

Three again after all, Dennis brooded. *Take my eye off her for one damn instant . . .* The monster roared again, then sprinted to its left, toward what it must have perceived as other intruders—or maybe it went after some Grik it saw. There was still no telling if it differentiated between invaders or defenders. Dennis looked back over Lawrence's head, toward the center of the level. The stream of Grik had tapered off. "Okay, Mr. Laumer, how's this? The wounded fort up here in one o' these nasty rooms—with Pam and a couple o' Marines—an' wait for the good guys." He gestured at the nearest arched entrance. "This spot's as good as any, I guess, with the diversion yonder." He nodded toward the firing. "The rest of us leave 'em half the grenades, in case o' monsters—I think there's four left—an' we use the diversion too."

"What for?" Isak groaned.

"To finish the damn job."

Irvin Laumer watched the Grik guard reinforcements slow to a trickle, then looked back at the others. He nodded curtly, curious why Pam was glaring so intently at Silva. "Very well."

"Pour it in!" Risa-Sab-At shouted, pacing behind a platoon of Impies deployed in the eastern corridor off the anteroom to the various divergent passageways. She was somewhat surprised that "her" Impies seemed so poised in this confined space, in their first fight against the Grik, but they were loading and firing their breechloaders mechanically and well. The ordeal of the trek across Mada-gaas-car had clearly hardened them to the visceral shock that staggered so many, human or Lemurian, when they faced the Grik for the very first time. "Cut 'em down!" she continued, her voice as calm as she could keep it. There were suddenly a lot of Grik in front of her, charging in without regard for themselves. They might be fighting the "same old way" in a sense, but these weren't the "same old Grik." Something had possessed them of an unusual desperation. She looked back at Chack, standing in the anteroom while guiding more troops to the corridors that seemed to need them most, as they charged through the entrance. Courtney was beside him, gazing at the walls and ceiling in rapt fascination, as if oblivious to the fight around him.

Something roared beyond the Grik, something big—and definitely *not* Grik. Risa felt a chill in her spine. The Grik surged forward and slammed into her narrow front, impaling themselves on bayonets that stabbed remorselessly into their bodies, their eyes, their throats. "What was that?" she shouted back at Courtney. He blinked at her. "I haven't the faintest idea, my dear. Something new, I expect." Chack was looking at the fighting in the corridors, trying to gauge which ones seemed to carry the roar best. It was impossible. He did notice that all the Grik suddenly fought even harder, though it was hard to tell whether it was to kill more of his troops or to get away from whatever had roared. They had that look in their eyes he had seen before, the one that preceded panic, or "Grik Rout," as Courtney called it, but they weren't trying to run away.

"Something's coming," he said to Bradford. "Something they're afraid of!"

"So it would seem!"

The Grik in front of Risa surged maniacally, utterly wild-eyed now, and those behind them began to scream.

"Here!" she cried. "This corridor *here*!" Chack redirected a crew of three 'Cats carrying a rectangular crate through the entrance. There were wheels on it, but they'd been useless on the steps outside, and for most of the trip for that matter, and they'd grown used to carrying it. Now they slammed it down and opened the lid. Risa felt uneasy as they worked, preparing the contraption. She'd been born a wing runner on *Salissa*, and fire weapons of any sort inspired a special disapproval in her. She didn't know what was coming, but being close to one of the "flame throwers" when it was operated frightened her almost as badly. One of the "firecats" unrolled a hose and attached it to a nozzle equipped with a handle and a trigger mechanism. The trigger would spin a roller against a flint inside, like the Zippo lighters she'd seen. The other two

'Cats erected a pump handle atop the crate that contained a bottle of fuel. They'd pressurize the air in the tank, and that would force the fuel down the hose and out, once the one with the nozzle opened a valve. The valve was particularly important, she knew, because it also—theoretically—kept burning fuel from running back up the hose to the bottle and burning everyone around it alive.

The Grik were being slaughtered, but in their panic, they were close to breaking through anyway. "Get that thing up there!" she yelled. "Up to the line! If you light it in the antechamber, you'll burn us all. Only down the corridor, clear?" The line bulged, and the Grik screams became hysterical. Something was *mashing* them forward! The firecats shifted the crate, and two of them started pumping vigorously. The 'Cat on the nozzle looked at her and nodded. Judging by his blinking, he wasn't much more comfortable with his weapon than she was. "Forward!" Risa ordered her troops. "Push them back, *kill* them back! When I blow my whistle, break to the rear as fast as you can if you don't want to burn!" Those in her squad bellowed with rage and determination, physically heaving the Grik back up the passageway and killing as they went. They couldn't keep it up, but she hoped they wouldn't have to. They'd never practiced anything remotely like this, and she sure hoped it would work. She fingered the whistle around her neck and glanced back at her brother, Chack. He took a last look at the other squads, then nodded.

Her whistle trilled loudly. Some Grik recoiled from the unexpected sound, but most were too far gone with terror to even notice. The wall of bodies her troops had amassed was sufficient to create a slight delay, however, and those in the blocking force streamed past her, almost falling over themselves to get out of the way. The Grik were close on their heels, and so was . . . something else.

"Let 'em have it!" Risa cried, and stumbled back herself to join the line re-forming behind the flamethrower.

The firecat on the nozzle opened his valve, and fuel spurted at the charging Grik. He quickly pulled the trigger in the handle, and the stream of fuel ignited with a smoky bark. As long as the pumpers kept up the pressure, the flames would stay a few inches from the nozzle and *shouldn't* be able to race back up the hose after he closed the valve. That was how it usually worked. Then it was just a matter of waiting for the fuel in the sprayer to burn itself out. The effect on the target was not so benign. The fuel-drenched Grik squealed horribly when the flames found them, and the burning stream wilted the rest like moths. Black smoke gushed out of the passageway and swirled in the high ceiling of the antechamber before belching out the entrance in a boiling rush.

Risa crouched low to avoid the bitter smoke and stared at the ghastly sight of burning, convulsing Grik—then her sickened heart quickened when she saw what was beyond them. She caught only a glimpse of huge flame-lit, yellow-toothed jaws closing on squalling Grik, and horns protruding from an armored shield. There was an impression of comparatively tiny eyes rotating independently to glare brightly at her before the spattering river of fire touched the thing and it went amok.

"Open fire!" Risa trilled.

A ragged volley from the shorter Allin-Silvas favored by the Raiders slashed at the monster through the flames as it rolled and squealed in the passageway. Blitzer Bugs joined the fusillade and pattered the burning head with lighter bullets. The monster lunged, its fiery jaws snapping, but the firecat hosed it again. The smell of burning meat joined the charred canvas, sun-baked-toad stench of cooking Grik. The thing bashed its head against the walls in spastic fury, then exploded down the passageway, away from its tormentors.

"Cease firing!" Risa coughed. "Cease firing!" She looked at the firecats with a new appreciation. "Do shut that thing off before we choke, if you please!"

Wide-eyed and shaking, the Lemurian on the sprayer blinked gratefully and closed his valve. The firing down the other corridors eased a bit as the Grik guarding them began to melt away, or simply bolt back the way they came.

"After them!" Chack ordered. He started to warn them to have a care, remembering how dangerously trapped Grik fought, but realized that, though there were times for "careful" attacks, this wasn't one of them. "After them!" he repeated. "Are you ready, Mr. Braad-furd?" he asked, gesturing at Courtney's Krag with his own as his Raiders streamed down the passageways.

"Not entirely," Courtney confessed. "Not as ready as those other fellows, at least. But sufficiently so to tag along with you in a relatively militant fashion, as long as nothing too terribly strenuous is required." He grinned. "And I wouldn't miss it for all the world!"

Dennis Silva emptied his last Thompson magazine as he and Gunny Horn plowed their way up the stairway to the next level in the palace. Grik fell away, to the side and underfoot, under the hammering bullets—but then the bolt locked back and Dennis used the heavy Thompson as a club. *Tommy guns are hungry boogers,* he lamented between mighty swings that cracked arms and crushed heads. *But Arnie Horn really is an artist with a bayonet,* he reflected admiringly, seeing his old friend parry and thrust almost at will. *Might even be as good as Pete Alden.* "Shit!" he roared, taking another slash across his chest—with *claws,* damn it—and he battered his attacker's head to paste. *Gotta stay on my toes,* he scolded himself. *These Grik're better in a brawl than most.* He'd realized they were different when they first ran into them, milling a little awkwardly at the base of the stairs. None were dressed or equipped just alike, as the palace guards had been. On the other hand, though they seemed to be far more capable warriors, individually, they apparently couldn't fight together very well. A notion struck him. "I bet these are them 'gladiator Griks' the Jap was talkin' about," he wheezed, slamming the Thompson into a toothy jaw and shattering it. The Grik dropped, gurgling on gushing blood, but raked its claws down his side as it fell. "Goddamn it!" Silva roared. "They got me *again!*" He viciously crushed the staring eyes with the butt of his gun.

"Goddamn it!" Petey whimpered, his voice muffled by Silva's neck.

Lawrence battered a Grik away with his rifle, then shot it—and stabbed it for good measure. The little Sa'aaran hadn't said much at all from the start, but he'd been instinctively guarding Silva's blind left side, since the fighting got close. His orangish fur was clotted with blood and he'd been cut a few times, but he was just as lethal as always.

Irvin Laumer blasted a final wavering Grik with his shotgun, then drove his own bayonet past a still-slashing sword into its heaving chest.

They'd reached the landing and there were still a lot of Grik, but they'd suddenly pulled back for a moment, as if actually *appraising* opponents that had fought their way past so many like themselves. "I think you're right," Laumer gasped back, blinking and trying to wipe blood out of his eyes with bloody fingers. He squinted in the gloom. "They all have crests so they're adults, but none seem to be in charge! Each one is thinking for himself, wondering how *he* will kill us, not how *they* will," he added.

"Gonna hafta do better than they done so far," Isak shouted from the steps behind. He and the two remaining Marines were guarding the rear. They'd lost the rest of their Lemurians in the gang fight below, but Isak was satisfied these last two were the best of the lot. "Hewy an' Dewy here is a match for the rest o' these Griks by theirselves."

"That ain't our names!" one of the 'Cat Marines snapped indignantly.

"I don't care," Isak sneered back, opening the loading gate of his Krag and dropping three cartridges into the magazine. "I swear. Give a fella a kind word, an' all he does is bitch. My days o' heapin' praise on undeservin' fuzzballs is *through*!"

"Shut up, Isak. By rights, you shoulda been ate already," Dennis said, watching the warriors before them move and shift, brandishing swords, axes, spears, but no muskets or crossbows. "You know, I figger these critters are the skimmed-off cream—the more experienced fighters that know they gotta defend their lizardy queen, but they let the younger rascals whittle us down a little first." He shrugged. "That's what I woulda done."

"Yeah," Horn agreed resignedly, breathing hard. "So now what? I bet there's a hundred of 'em, and we're about outa ammo."

"We kill 'em, o' course! Look, this level has a whole different layout again, only one long corridor, spirallin' clockwise up."

"Silva's right," Laumer said. "We can't wait for relief because there are a lot of Grik still behind us, and I doubt our hosts here will allow it in any case. We can't go around them. . . ."

"So we gotta go through the sons o' bitches, as Chief Gray once so delicately said, an keep goin' all the way to the twisty top o' this joint, where I bet we'll find their sequesteral mother. I b'lieve I'd like to give her a stern talkin' to," Dennis finished. Regretfully, he let the empty Thompson slip to the damp stones and pulled his Colt out of its holster. "Why don't we play pistols an' cutlasses—or bayonets if you'd rather." He grinned at Horn. "A *hundred* of 'em," he mocked. "There you go again, overestimatin' the odds—just like usual!" Casually, Dennis retrieved the last two grenades from his pouch. "All bunched up like that, I bet there ain't fifty or sixty we'll actually hafta *fight*!" He handed one grenade to Horn and tossed the other to Irvin. "You wanna do the honors, Mr. Laumer?" he asked, drawing his cutlass. "It appears them gladiator Griks is just waitin' for somebody to say 'when.'"

Irvin Laumer looked at his comrades and smiled, realizing he'd been waiting for something like this ever since he came to this world: an opportunity to stand and fight with Silva—or someone like him—who'd been in the thick of it from the start. He didn't expect to survive, but that didn't really matter anymore. He'd finally do his part with "the best of them," and he'd be remembered for it. Maybe Silva guessed what was on his mind, because the big man's grin faded a little. "Fight careful, all of you, 'cause there *is* a lot of 'em an' we're here to do a job, not be heeroes." His grin returned. "Live hee-roes have a lot more fun than dead ones, an' that's a fact!"

Irvin nodded, pulling the pin from the grenade. With a final glance at his little squad, he threw it past the closest Grik and into the press in the corridor beyond. "When!" he shouted. Horn's grenade followed closely behind, and Silva, Horn, Laumer, Lawrence, Isak, and two Lemurian Marines charged forward behind a flurry of pistol shots just as the grenades went off. The pistols were quickly emptied, and Silva, Horn, and Lawrence formed the battering ram at the front as they pushed the startled Grik out of the landing chamber and into the narrow corridor. Silva stuffed his pistol in his belt and drew his '03 Springfield bayonet with his left hand to use as a second, shorter cutlass. His two blades wove a savage tapestry of death before him. Lawrence stabbed with his bayonet, pushing his squalling victims back to crowd others behind them until he could pull his weapon clear and stab again. Horn did much the same, shouting with every thrust, his dark bearded face streaked with sweat that glistened in the yellow lamplight. Ferocious as their attack was, Laumer, Isak, and the two Marines did most of the killing. They were free to reload their weapons and fire past their friends with a relatively careful aim. Their muzzle blasts were painful for those in front—at first—but were quickly easy to ignore.

On they fought, endlessly it seemed, stabbing, hacking, slashing, shooting, climbing over corpses that sometimes came to life and had to be killed again. All of them were wounded, even Petey, who'd finally taken all he could stand and bolted for the rear, only to land on a dying Grik that feebly slashed him with its claws. He hissed and bit his assailant, then scampered and coasted away down the corridor screeching, "Shit! Shit! Shit!" There was firing behind them now; they could hear it, echoing up the passageway from the now-distant stairs, but there was no telling how long it might be before help arrived, or how many Grik might arrive first, fleeing from their friends. All they could do was keep fighting, keep moving forward.

Lawrence's bayonet got jammed. Unable to pull it clear, he let his rifle go and drew his cutlass. He didn't have the strength of his bigger adversaries, but made up for it with a more refined technique he'd learned in the Empire. He remained at a disadvantage, however, particularly against spears, and started taking more wounds. None were serious, but they became debilitating, and Laumer replaced him with one of the Marines. Horn's rifle lost its bayonet when the locking catch in the grip broke. He immediately reversed it and drove the Grik with savage butt strokes until the Springfield stock shattered completely. "Give me your weapon!" he shouted behind at the other 'Cat, but before he could take the rifle, a Grik spear pierced his side.

"Ah!" he grunted, and battered the Grik that stabbed him with his rifle barrel before slinging it at another. Then he pulled the spear from his side and drove it into a Grik trying to snake its sword past Silva's slashing cutlass. "Wow," he said, his eyes going wide, and he sank to his knees atop a Grik corpse.

"You okay, Arnie?" Silva hollered aside, his breath coming in heaving gasps.

"Swell. Just a little woozy all of a sudden."

Irvin fired past him until his slide locked, then grabbed him under the arms and pulled him back as Isak took his place. Isak was immediately, effortlessly slammed aside by a very large Grik. The last Marine skewered it and hurled it past the heap of bodies Silva had been building in the pause.

"I can do it, Dewy, damn yer stripy tail!" Isak snarled through broken lips.

"I ain't *Hewy*," the 'Cat replied with a blink of humor. "The *other* one ain't Dewy!"

"I don't give a shit which one you ain't!" Isak retorted, gesturing with his Krag. "Goddamn it, we're almost *through* 'em!"

It was true, or so it seemed. They'd advanced a lot farther up the spiraling passage than they'd realized, distracted by the all-consuming necessity of fighting and killing and surviving, and only a few live Grik now blocked their way. These were fresh, however, and refused to budge, while Irvin's party was all injured and exhausted beyond endurance. Even Silva's cutlass and bayonet were slow and clumsy now, and the fact that he wasn't yelling, swearing, or making any sound at all other than gasping for air was proof that he was spent. "Hewy" went down, an axe finding him between the neck and shoulder, and Isak got his wish. He returned to Silva's side. Lawrence tried to pick up the fallen Marine's rifle, but for some reason he couldn't seem to hold it. Irvin took it and stabbed past Silva, driving the bayonet into the belly of a Grik that screamed and pulled itself clear. Blood and entrails burst through the gash, and Isak stabbed it again.

"Can't . . . you . . . just . . . shoot . . . these . . . last'uns?" Silva managed, his chest heaving, as he clumsily blocked a hacking sword with his cutlass and thrust the '03 bayonet through his attacker's throat.

"I'm empty!" Laumer yelled in desperation.

"Take . . . mine!"

Laumer didn't understand. Then he realized that Silva still had magazines for *his* 1911 on his belt! He'd been too busy fighting to reload his pistol. Isak bayoneted another Grik, hooting with relieved excitement, but a *bong* echoed in the hall and "Dewy" fell, his helmet dished by an axe. There was no telling if he was alive or not, but he was out. Silva brought his notched cutlass down across the back of the axe-wielder's neck, but shuddered when a Grik in front of him scored with a spear. He knocked it away, but then just stood there, swaying a little. Suddenly, there were only three Grik left, and they backed away, obviously stunned that so small a group could fight its way through so many. They were born fighters, and not about to quit, but clearly recognized it was time to reevaluate things. The one in the middle seemed to realize its most dangerous prey was weakening, however, and took a step forward, crouching to spring.

Irvin was already fumbling at Silva's pouches for his magazines, but he'd never get one out in time. "Aw hell," Dennis grunted, pulling Linus Truelove's ornate flintlock pistol from his belt. Shakily, he pointed it at the Grik. The thing's eyes narrowed in realization and it leaped, but with a *clack-boom!* Silva shot it dead. "Always liked to save that one for somethin' . . . you know, kinda weird. But oh well," he said, tossing the smoking pistol on a corpse and bending over to put his hands on his knees. "Ain't *you* got any bullets left, Isak?"

"Why, maybe I do."

"Then you better shoot those other two before they eat your stupid head . . . 'cause I sure can't stop 'em."

Stunned by such an admission, Isak opened his loading gate and dropped his last five rounds in the magazine. The two remaining Grik charged.

Gunny Horn's pistol barked four times, and both Grik sprawled at Isak's feet. With trembling fingers, Isak finished chambering a round and looked at the China Marine, leaning against the wall, his Baalkpan Arsenal 1911 supported by both hands. Slowly, Horn slid to the floor, looking at the Colt copy. "Got so busy, I forgot I even had this thing till you told Mr. Laumer to take your magazines," he said. His voice was weak and strained. "Are you going to die, Dennis?" he demanded.

Silva managed to straighten, then turned to face his friend. It was the first anyone had seen of his front since they started up the passageway, and he was soaked with blood from his short hair to his shoes. His T-shirt and sodden trousers were crisscrossed with diagonal tears, and there were a fair number of punctures as well. Everyone had seen him weakening, but now they knew it wasn't just from fatigue. It was impossible to say whether he'd taken any mortal wounds, but he had so *many*, he was obviously bleeding to death.

"My God," Laumer said, and caught Dennis before he dropped.

"Shit!" Isak croaked.

"I ain't gonna die, you idiot gyrene," Dennis snapped, sagging in Laumer's arms, "so don't go makin' plans for swipin' my Doom Stomper!" He looked at Irvin. "But I'm sorry. I hate to admit it, but maybe I have had enough fun for one day. You mind carryin' the ball from here, Mr. Laumer?"

"No . . . no."

Silva nodded. "Shift me over by Horn, if you will, then the rest of you go ahead on. We'll watch yer backs. We both got pistols, an' Horn's magazines."

Lawrence helped Laumer move the big man over to the wall as best he could, and crouched beside his friend. "I'll stay too."

Dennis shook his head. "Nope. Mr. Laumer might need you, an' we'll be fine. We got Petey, after all." Lawrence hiss-snorted indignant frustration and spun away. Dennis chuckled, fumbling the magazine Horn handed him into his pistol. He dropped the slide, chambering a round, and then glared at Isak. "You take *care* o' Mr. Laumer, you rat-faced little louse!" His voice softened. "He's a good 'un."

"But who's gonna take care o' *me*?" Isak demanded, almost whining. Silva blinked. "Who cares? We already know *you're* gonna get ate! Live with it."

Awkwardly, Irvin patted Silva's shoulder, and the big man winced. "We have to go. We'll come back as soon as we can . . . or the Raiders ought to be along soon. They'll have rescued Surgeon Cross, and she'll get you patched up. . . ."

"Sure."

Irvin turned to Isak and Lawrence. "Come on," he said.

Their footsteps echoed up the passageway, fading in the gloom, and Silva looked around. He was having trouble focusing, but when his eyes passed over the 'Cat Marine who *wasn't* Dewy—he smirked—he was pretty sure he saw him breathing. *Good.* He settled back, taking his blood-soaked tobacco pouch out of his pocket. For some reason, he couldn't seem to make his fingers fish out a wad of the sweetened leaves, however, and he glanced down at himself. "I'm a mess," he muttered, a little surprised. He didn't really hurt that much, but he'd never felt so weak in his life. He turned to look at the man beside him. "*You* ain't gonna die, are you, Arnie?" he asked, but Gunny Horn appeared asleep and didn't reply. "Better not," Dennis warned, and sighed. "Few enough fellas left to talk with about the old days as it is." He gazed at the tobacco pouch again, now lying in his lap. "I'd kill," he said with a smirk, "even *more* stuff, for a cold San Miguel right now." His voice was barely audible.

Hesitantly, painfully, Petey crept out of the darkness, sniffing and cringing at the growing sound of battle behind them. Focusing on Dennis, he hop-sprinted into his lap. The man usually pretended not to notice him, but this time there was no reaction at all. Staring up with wide, searching eyes, he clawed his way higher, closer to the slack-jawed face.

"Si-vaa?" Petey hissed insistently.

Irvin Laumer, Isak Reuben, and Lawrence had no doubts when they finally reached the entrance leading to the chambers of the Celestial Mother herself. There'd been no other openings in the passageway at all, and they'd reached the end of the line. They advanced cautiously toward this slightly larger, considerably more ornate archway, weapons ready, watchful for guards, but there were none that they could see. Lawrence still couldn't manage a rifle—his right arm wasn't working right—but he held a cutlass in his left hand, cocked to slash, and he instinctively took the lead.

"Easy," Irvin whispered, holding his pistol up. "I'll go first." His voice seemed unnaturally loud. "She's got to have some guards, if she's in there," he explained.

"She's in there," Lawrence confirmed. "I think there's other . . . phee-males too. I s'ell—taste? Taste their hot 'reath—lung air?" He shook his head in frustration.

"Eww!" Isak hissed. "Then they must be the mouth-fartin'est critters that ever was!"

"Taste . . . pharts too," Lawrence confirmed.

"Eww!"

"Come on," Irvin urged, stepping through the arch. The others followed, their wide eyes tensely seeking threats in the gloom.

"Some kinda waitin' room," Isak guessed, pointing his Krag in the dark corners of the chamber. There were a couple of the saddlelike "chairs" that only Grik could love, but light leaked around a thick drapery at the far end of the room. Isak reached for it with the bayonet on the end of his rifle as they neared it.

"Careful," Irvin hissed, his pistol trembling slightly.

"The hell with that, they gotta know we're here." Isak gulped, and slashed the drapery aside.

Beyond was another chamber, considerably larger, filled with what looked like sunlight! For an instant, all the trio could do was blink, as their eyes adjusted, but then they saw at last what they'd come all this way to find. Draped across another one of the bizarre chairs, staring intently at them with large, yellow eyes, was the biggest, most ridiculously obese example of the Grik species anyone had ever seen. Its furry plumage was bright and coppery in the light glaring down from an opening in the ceiling, and it seemed to almost flash with fire as it shifted slightly and rolls of fat moved beneath its skin. Uselessly long, but meticulously sculpted claws flickered on its fingers as it clasped its hands in front of it. With a surprisingly small voice for such a monstrous creature, it spoke.

"What the hell?" Isak demanded nervously. "You picked up some o' that Grik gibberish, didn't you, Larry?"

Lawrence nodded, his crest high and tail stiff, eyes narrowed in concentration. He'd learned quite a bit, in fact, working with the "tame" Grik that went along on the expedition to northern Borno.

"What did it say?" Laumer asked.

"It said to enter and . . . kneel, I think . . . and it'd hear us."

"My skinny ass!" Isak snarled. "Tell it to flop down offa that saddle an' beg *us* not to blow its fat head off!"

Lawrence snatched his gaze from the monster and looked at Laumer. "She's not going to do *that*." He looked at Isak. "Don't you get it?

That's her. That's really *her*! She knows the 'attle outside is lost, 'ut thinks us are just other hunters, here to serph *her*!"

"Bullshit!" Isak spat. "Let's kill her!"

"Us *really* need to kill her," Lawrence fervently agreed. Something about this confrontation had him more worried than he'd been at any time during the fight to get here.

"But if we could take her alive, we might win the whole war, here and now!" Irvin insisted, stepping forward into the chamber.

"No!" Lawrence cried, leaping after him, claws outstretched.

Irvin whipped his head toward Lawrence, stunned, but saw a massive Grik, this one all muscle, lunging toward him from the right, beyond the entrance. His pistol came up just as Lawrence vaulted *past* him—at another giant guard, he supposed with relief—and he started shooting the first one. His pistol barked seven times fast, almost as quick as full-auto fire, and the massive Grik—he noticed it had no crest—slammed into him, trying to bury him under its dying weight. He didn't go down, because something had him by the left arm. He saw Lawrence on the floor near the Celestial Mother, painfully trying to rise, and realized he must've been batted away by the far more powerful Grik—that now had *him*.

"Mr. Laumer!" Isak wailed, lunging past him with his bayonet, just as a wickedly barbed spearpoint erupted from Irvin Laumer's chest. The Grik dropped the dying submariner to deal with Isak—but nothing could have dealt with the berserk little fireman just then. Screeching and stabbing with the long blade on the end of his rifle, as fast and maniacally as a piston released from a blown jug, Isak never gave the Grik the slightest chance. Finally burying the blade all the way to the guard, he drove the bloody monster back and down, then fired the Krag for good measure. Twisting the bayonet clear, he stepped back in time to see Irvin Laumer's eyes, staring up at him, glaze into lifelessness.

"Oh, you sneakin', fuzzy ol' toad!" he whispered, looking back up at the monster on the throne. Its expression hadn't changed at all. Its mouth moved and it spoke again. Without even asking Larry what it said, Isak chambered another round and fired.

The 220-grain cupronickel-jacketed Frankford Arsenal ball wouldn't have much irritated the Celestial Mother if it had struck her anywhere else; her fat was so thick, it probably wouldn't have even reached muscle. Blowing through her curious left eye and exploding into her brain, however, it sent her into a flailing mass of mindless flesh. With a squeaky roar and mounting rage, Isak Reuben charged. "When the *hell's* everybody gonna learn, sometimes you just gotta *kill* shit!" he screamed, stabbing at the convulsing, gelatinous corpse with his bayonet again and again until he managed to miss it entirely. He was blinded by the tears filling his eyes and gushing down his cheeks and the bayonet stuck in the wooden frame of the throne. "Goddamn it!" he shrieked, leaving the Krag swaying, and yanking out his cutlass.

"No!" Lawrence snapped, grabbing his arm. "No!" he repeated when Isak struggled. "Us still *use* her. You don't hack her too 'uch! Co'ander Lau'er 'anted to use her," he insisted more gently. "Us could still can!"

CHAPTER

37

////// *USS Walker*

"Cast off!!" came the cry from a Lemurian bosun's mate, aft.

The heavy hawser *Big Sal* used to pull *Walker* off the sandbar now sagged low in the water of the bay, and the battered old destroyer was drifting free. Matt had made his way through the carnage that littered his ship and now stood with a bloody, grimy, Spanky McFarlane atop the aft deckhouse near the auxiliary conn. *Spanky looks . . . okay,* he judged with cautious relief, discounting the broken crossbow bolt shaft sticking out close to his buttocks. *He'll rant about that later,* he knew, *but at least there'll be a later. Must hurt, though, and he is chewing his 'Cat tobacco more vigorously than usual. . . .* Solemnly, without a word, the two men shook hands. It was a spontaneous, congratulatory gesture. Their ship was free, and they were alive. Together, they watched the end of the hawser disappear from between the depth charge racks with a splash. Spanky sighed, and Matt leaned on the number four gun, smoke stained and blood spattered, still trained out to port. He savored the buoyant feel of the steel beneath his feet.

"Signal Admiral Keje that we appreciate his help and that *Salissa's* now free to maneuver," he ordered softly. "And ask Tabby to light a fire under her damage-control parties inspecting the hull. I want to know if we opened any more seams coming off."

"Ay, ay, Cap-i-taan," replied Minnie's strained voice, and she passed the word to Ed Palmer through a speaking tube. Then she whistled up Tabby. Minnie had shown up shortly before and taken the place of Spanky's dead talker without a word. Though liberally soaked with blood, she didn't seem injured, and Matt was grateful for that. *She's just as exhausted, physically and emotionally, as anybody,* he reflected, *but at least she's alive. Too many aren't.* He looked back at her and managed what he hoped was an encouraging smile. His gaze strayed to encompass the rest of his ship—and the recent battlefield beyond.

The Grik cruiser had finally almost burned itself out, and steam was streaking the smoke as the rising tide reached the hot iron and smoldering wood. The great heap of Grik bodies that had made a ramp to Matt's ship was starting to diminish as well. The water around it was churning violently as the ocean predators swarmed to feed, and watching the mound shift and tumble reminded Matt of a pile of dirt being eroded by runoff. He blinked. The water around *Walker* also frothed, as grim, exhausted details rolled Grik corpses over the side. Too often they discovered one of their own buried in the grisly tangle, and these were carefully laid out beneath the amidships deckhouse. Earl Lanier had emerged from the galley and was helping arrange the dead with an unexpected tenderness. Matt couldn't watch the progress of the detail working where Fitzhugh Gray went down. He clenched his teeth. Alongside to starboard, *Walker's* own Nancy floated, nestled among barges of workers and Marines sent from *Big Sal* to help *Walker's* depleted crew, and manhandle at least a little ammunition aboard. This was being handed up to fill the ship's ready lockers, and nearly every 'Cat that came aboard was draped with belts of ammo for the machine guns. If they fell in the water, they'd sink like rocks, but with all the flashies around, that was probably best. . . . The Nancy's pilot was yelling back and forth with a hoarse-voiced Jeek, who was telling the aviator to get his plane the hell out of the way. The pilot was equally insistent on refueling and rearming from *Walker*. Did they know what a crock it was trying to get replenished from *Amerika*? Jeek screamed back that it couldn't be worse than *here* because they didn't *have* anything! Matt shook his head. Jeek was losing it, which was understandable, and the pilot didn't—couldn't—understand.

Campeti painfully climbed the ladder from the deck below, catching Matt's eye. "How much longer, Sonny?"

"Not long, Skipper. Keje didn't send as much ammo as I'd like." He shrugged. "Better than none, though, and it's all 'common.' We still have a little AP."

"Yeah. Tabby?" Matt asked, looking back at Minnie.

"She say we ready to maneuver now. She only lose some steam while the 'lectrics was out to the fuel an' water pumps."

"Leaks?"

Minnie shook her head, blinking apology. "Sorry, Cap-i-taan. I forgot to tell you. She says we weepin' some under the for'ard fireroom, but *Big Sal* dragged us off real gentle. Nothin' bad new. Aft stores is still flooded, but the engine room's dryin' out, an' no more water's comin' in, now our ass ain't draggin' so." Minnie blinked. "She'll answer bells when you ring 'em."

"Very well. Have her stand by."

Suddenly, Matt's heart leaped with relief when he saw Sandra's concerned face appear at the top of the ladder. He'd known, intellectually, she had to be okay; the Grik had never penetrated down to the wardroom, thank God, and all the wounded that made it there were safe as well. Besides, somebody damn sure would've reported it if she *wasn't* okay. Also, just as she'd been too occupied with her duty of saving lives—doubtless hearing word that he was okay as well—he'd been far too busy to surrender to the urge to check on her himself. But now, actually seeing her in the midst of all this relieved a terrible, constant weight that had lain heavy on his soul. "Hi," he said simply as she stepped up on the platform. Like everyone, she was covered with blood, and it wasn't confined to the apron secured around her neck and waist. She even had it in her hair, and there was a drying smear on her forehead where she'd wiped away sweat with her arm. Without a word, or any hesitation, she advanced and embraced him fiercely.

Just as unselfconsciously, he hugged her back, clutching her tight, but only for that crucial moment they both so desperately needed. Then, reluctantly, Matt released her, and she took a step back so she could make a report.

"It's bad," she said, knowing what his first question would be. "Almost a hundred wounded, not counting those still working who haven't been treated." She pushed her damp hair back with her wrist, spreading the blood on her forehead. "About that many dead, I think, but I don't know how many came aboard, or might still be unaccounted for." She noticed the change in Matt's expression, saw the jaw muscles bulge and the pain in his eyes. "Who?" she whispered.

"Gray," Spanky answered when Matt didn't speak. He nodded in the direction of the number two torpedo mount where the detail was still excavating Grik. Sandra covered her mouth and closed her eyes. "Oh my God."

"And a bunch more fine men and 'Cats," Matt reminded sharply. Sandra looked at him, stung, but she nodded.

"Of course. I'll . . . I better tell Diania before she, well, sees him. It would be better. . . ."

"Sure."

Salissa's big guns roared, and Sandra looked at her. She'd moved away, closer to the heart of the city, avoiding the wreckage of the Grik fleet. Splashes rose around her, so at least a few shore batteries were still in action, and she and the DDs were hammering back, even while scores of barges and landing craft motored in, toward an indistinct battle still raging at the foot of the distant palace.

"It's not over yet, is it?" she asked.

"No," Matt replied. "Not yet. And we've both still got work to do." Sandra nodded, and touching his hand, she climbed back down the ladder. Matt looked at Spanky, and the shorter man was staring at him, chewing hard while waiting.

"You keep the conn back here until I reach the bridge," Matt told him. "Bring us about and steer for where the Seven boat is waiting for Mr. Laumer."

"What then?"

"Then we'll see, Spanky," Matt said with a harsh, thin smile. "You'll go down to the wardroom and get your wound looked at, for one thing. This ship's lost enough of her people today." He looked toward the cow-flop palace. "And if there's any chance she might help save even one of those who left her to go ashore, I want her there to do it."

"Aye, aye, Captain."

Compared to the rest of the ship, the bridge actually looked fairly normal since there hadn't been any fighting there. With the blower rumbling contentedly behind, and the fo'c'sle in front of the hastily formed bridge watch clear of bodies, it was easy to pretend *Walker*, and the lives of all her surviving crew, hadn't been so traumatically violated that day. Perhaps not *easy*; there was too much blood on everyone for that, but it was tempting. Bernard Sandison and Paddy Rosen reported as Matt and Minnie were settling in. Neither man wore a shirt, and both were swaddled in bandages. Bernie's left arm was in a sling. Rosen looked sheepish, but Matt nodded at the wheel. Spanky had turned the ship, and she was steaming down *Big Sal*'s unengaged side toward the waterfront where Silva's party landed. "Tell Mr. McFarlane that I have the conn, Minnie," Matt instructed. "And remind him that he's *ordered* to go to the wardroom."

"Ay, Cap-i-taan."

"Steady as you go, Mr. Rosen. When we're two hundred yards from the docks, come right to unmask all guns to port. Have Mr. Campeti stand by for action port," he added over his shoulder at Minnie.

"The gun director is off line," Minnie replied. "Caam-peeti is working on it."

"Very well. All guns will stand by to commence firing in local control." Matt raised his binoculars. He couldn't see the base of the palace because the bulk of Grik City was in the way, but he saw the steps leading up the eastern and northern flanks where large arched entryways were framed by troops. He adjusted his objective. "All stop," he told Rosen. "Open the shipwide circuit, Minnie!" he ordered with a sudden grin, stepping to take the Bakelite handset from the bulkhead. "Now hear this!" he said, crouching slightly so he could still use his binoculars. His voice reverberated around the ship. "Chack's Brigade has the entrances to the palace!" he said triumphantly, realizing that meant Silva and the others had a chance after all. Cheers roared, and the deck vibrated with stamping feet. "It looks like Second Corps has the enemy on the run from the east and they're flooding past the place, barely stopping long enough to get shot at." He redirected the glasses. "Marines and sailors from *Big Sal* and the rest of the battle group are going in now—and Safir Maraan's cavalry is sweeping in on her left flank to keep the Grik running past the palace! The effect seems to be to herd the whole mob out where we just came from! They'll be trapped!" More cheering shook the ship. He returned the handset to its cradle.

"The Seven boat is coming alongside," Sandison announced from the starboard bridgewing.

"Good. Have Mr. Hardee stand by."

"Sur! There somethin' screwy goin' on!" cried a lookout on the port bridgewing, pointing at the palace. Matt looked. For some reason, many of the Grik—thousands of them—had stopped their mad retreat and were staring up at the palace. Then, as if guided by some internal command only they could hear, they charged straight at Chack's Brigade! "What the hell," Matt muttered. "All guns," he shouted, "commence firing at the leading edge of that attack, on the double!"

"That ain't exactly what I figgered they'd do," Isak Reuben complained loudly, "but it was Larry's idea!"

"I didn't think they'd do that either," Lawrence protested as well.

They'd been lugging the dead head of the Celestial Mother down the curving passageway when they were met by Chack, Courtney Bradford, and a platoon of Raiders. Hearing their scheme for the head, Courtney thought it was "charming," and Chack decided to give it a try. Isak had been relieved to see that Silva, Horn, and the 'Cat who wasn't Dewy were already being removed on stretchers, supervised by Pam Cross, but he'd been forced to tell Chack about Irvin Laumer. Chack sent a detail to fetch him, and they hurried back out the way Irvin's party came, meeting Major Jindal on the way. As far as they could tell, the upper levels of the palace were secure, though no one knew what had happened to the monster Risa's platoon of Impies burned. Apparently, it had gone deep, and they'd look for it later.

Through the entranceway in the bright afternoon sun, Isak and Lawrence, full of nervous energy, supervised the impalement of the Celestial Mother's head on a Grik spear, lashed to another for height, then helped hoist it up for all to see. The idea was, seeing their deity—likely for the first time—displayed in such a way, the Grik would lose heart. Instead, a fair percentage of them attacked with senseless abandon. Chack spared them a scolding blink before instructing Major Jindal to commence firing again. The raiders had stopped shooting some time ago when the Grik started ignoring them. Jindal was glad to oblige.

Volleys fired and walls of white smoke rolled down the steps, sending Grik tumbling back. A harsh, keening wail raised the hair on Isak's back as he stared through the smoke. Suddenly, he saw *Walker* a little beyond the distant dock, and he and Lawrence started waving the head back and forth above them, without thinking. "Hey!" Isak shouted. "Looky there! It's my ship, off the beach! Hey, darlin'! Looky what I brung ya!"

"Quit that!" Chack shouted at him, but it was no use—and there wasn't really any point. He had plenty of firepower to blunt the rush of what were, after all, largely "civilian" Grik, and the ones crowding behind were merely making it easier for their pursuers to catch them. Chack supposed—he hoped—he'd feel more remorse for slaughtering Doms as they then began to do, but he wasn't sure anymore. Besides, it didn't matter. These were Grik. Blossoms of smoke opened aboard *Walker*, and her shells rained down amid the surging mob, snapping with flashes of orange fire and white smoke. Nancys swooped, and fat bombs tumbled from their wings to blow huge, gaping, burning holes in the swarm. The P-1s were done for the day, trying to set down on the muddy strip, but the big guns of the fleet chewed at the Grik even as the reinforcements linked up with II Corps, and they started rolling the enemy up. Even the most maniacal Grik finally broke when II Corps's cavalry slashed deep into them aboard their terrifying mounts.

Above it all, yelling with squeaky incoherence, Isak Reuben, and now Lawrence again as well, waved the dripping, tongue-lolling head. Slowly, the whole army began to answer until the thunderous sound of victory was all that could be heard.

"Cease firing," Chack told Jindal, and sat numbly on the steps to wait for Safir to come, as he knew she would.

"What's all the racket?" Dennis Silva mumbled, some distance away, lying on the steps. "Did we win the damn war?"

"I doubt it. But I think we won the fight—you big jerk," Pam shouted in his ear, her tears wetting his neck.

"Horn?"

Pam nodded past Dennis—he couldn't see at what—but he was damned if he'd move. *Everything* hurt now. "Over there. There was a 'Cat Marine with you guys. He was kinda groggy, but he kept you both from leakin' out worse than you did. Don't know where he went."

"His name's Ain't Dewy." Silva smiled. "I guess I owe him one. Horn?" he repeated.

Pam shook her head and frowned. "He'll live," she snapped. "I just said so, didn't I? Not that he deserves to," she added darkly. "Not that *you* deserve to!" she emphasized furiously, returning to the business of bandaging his many wounds. "But you will," she added, too softly for him to hear, "until the next time."

CHAPTER
38

///// *Ajanga City*
NE Madagascar

irst General Esshk paced the dock, glaring at the fires eating the massive barricade around the Second City of the Principal Isle. *Even the bestial hunters of the interior have turned on us,* he brooded. He'd begun to suspect they might, when they began shadowing his swiftly running column almost as soon as it emerged into the jungle from the catacombs beneath the Celestial Palace. They hadn't attacked; the heavy guard of sport fighters he'd assembled to escort the purest female guardians of the Celestial Bloodline had seen to that. But they didn't have to attack; they saw them leave. Now, heavily reinforced no doubt, they were trying to burn Ajanga.

"Can we hold the city, Lord General?" the Chooser asked anxiously, almost trotting to catch up.

"We could *keep* the city," Esshk replied, stressing the difference, "even with the relatively few warriors posted here—if all we had to concern us were the savage hunters in the forest." He took a long breath. Even now, in the darkness after the long, terrible day, his mind was reeling. They—*he*—had lost the Celestial Palace—and the Giver of Life herself!—to what they'd all once considered *prey*! "If the world had not been turned on its head, I would merely send a pack of hunters beyond the barricade to chase the sport prey back into its preserve." Even that term, "sport prey," almost caught in his throat. Even such as they were now a threat, and therefore true "enemies." Throughout its long history, the sprawling empire of the Grik had never had existential enemies before. Now they seemed to be gathering at every hand. What would General Halik do? he wondered, realizing the younger Hij must certainly have a better understanding of the enemy by now. He wished the one he considered his protégé were here, or he could get word to or from the only being left in the world whose judgment he actually trusted. *How odd that is,* he realized. *Halik was just a sport fighter himself a few short years ago. I must interview the others who helped us make it here.*

Not for the first time he wondered where Kurokawa was, and what he was doing. If he'd abandoned Halik in India, where would he go, if he lived? His Sovereign Nest of Jaaph Hunters on Zanzibar, no doubt. Esshk pondered whether he should consider Kurokawa an advantage or menace now. He certainly *needed* the treacherous creature—or more specifically, he needed his people and their technology. But did Kurokawa still need him? He would have to find out.

He spoke again, as much to organize his own thoughts as to explain to the Chooser: "Against those who drove us out, there is no hope. Even if they do not already know of this place, their flying machines will see the smoke of the barricade fires and find us with the dawn." He nodded at the dark form of the iron-plated battleship in the harbor. There was only one of the apparently useless things here, along with a trio of "cruisers," but the twenty-three females he'd spirited away from the palace were already on board. "We must not be here when they come."

"*Of course* we cannot be here!" the Chooser fervently agreed, "and we must preserve the bloodline at all costs," he added. "It has never been . . . interrupted in such a way before, and we must contemplate how best to proceed."

Esshk looked at him, eyes narrowing in speculation. "True," he agreed, "How *shall* we proceed? You would be the proper authority to 'choose,' I suppose." His tone was heavy with irony.

"That may be," the Chooser whispered, licking his teeth as if tasting each word before he uttered it. He was almost trembling with excitement—and terror—over the previously undreamed thoughts suddenly cascading through his mind. "But I would prefer that we choose *together* how to proceed in such . . . unprecedented circumstances. Surely we cannot simply proclaim an unelevated female as our new Celestial Mother. Such a creature might be deemed illegitimate by the provincial regents, and at the very least, her . . . unbridled judgment would be rightfully questioned as unsound. That is something we cannot risk in these perilous times." Esshk stopped pacing at last, and the Chooser regarded him, increasingly earnest. "And, of course, such a proclamation could be resisted for the implication that I—*we*—believe we have the supreme authority to make it in the first place. We might end up sparking internal conflicts among the regents at the worst possible moment while at the same time casting away the power to do anything about it!"

"What are you suggesting, Lord Chooser?" General Esshk demanded, suddenly very formal, and the Chooser gulped. He might have already gone too far, he realized, but there was nothing for it now but to reveal his entire scheme as it unfolded in his mind.

"I am suggesting that we—*you*, General Esshk, as protector of the guardians of the Celestial Bloodline, and carrier of the Noble Blood yourself—should serve as principal regent to *all* the females until one elevates herself above the others and assumes her destiny in a more . . . natural way. By conquest over her siblings."

"But in the meantime, *I* would rule? Don't be ridiculous! I cannot be the Celestial Mother!"

"Of course not," the Chooser quickly agreed, "but you can be the Giver of Life. In *all* respects . . . eventually. Particularly if you lead us to victory."

General Esshk was silent, thoughtful. Finally he snorted. "A most . . . amusing scenario, Lord Chooser. But before we engage in such imaginative intrigues, let us concentrate on making it to the continent alive, and rousing all our race to the task of avenging the dignity, territory, and Celestial Mother we just lost."

India

"We've got to stop meeting like this," General Pete Alden said. "Folks are gonna talk."

General Halik tilted his head. "*You* asked for *this* meeting," he replied, "not I."

When Hij Geerki finished his translation, Pete snorted. "Kind of a joke. Skip it."

The two were facing each other in knee-deep grass on what Pete's people were calling the "Highland Plain." Pete didn't know squat about what India was supposed to be like, but he'd never pictured any part of it looking like this. *It'd be great cattle country,* he supposed. The big herds of duck-faced herbivores seemed to like it. Pete, General Lord Muln Rolak, and Hij Geerki were alone for this meeting, as were Halik and Ugla, his general. It struck Pete how weird it was that he'd grown to, well, *trust* Halik not to pull something fishy at times like this, even while they were trying to kill each other. He was a Grik, a hateful, despicable enemy, but at the same time, he'd shown he had a sense of honor, and even as Pete had directed the systematic dismantling of Halik's retreating army—something Halik hadn't made exactly easy—Pete had to admit he'd grown to respect the bastard.

Their respective escorts had been ordered to stay back, out of earshot, and beyond their capability to help if things went sour, of course. Pete's guard detail—members of the Czech Legion that day—were sullen about that. Likely they thought he'd robbed them of the chance to rub out the enemy leaders and there'd be complaints. There'd *really* be complaints, from everybody, if Halik agreed to the proposal Pete intended to make.

"We've got you, Halik," he finally said almost gently. "Anytime we want, we can wipe you out." He shrugged. "Hell, it won't even be a fight. Our P-Forties are flying off a grass strip this side of the Rocky Gap now, and we've got Clippers—the big fat planes with four engines—flying out of a lake north of there. You ain't got doodly in the air. We can pound you with heavy ordnance until every last one of you is dead, and all my army has to do now is sit back and watch."

"I do not concede that you can destroy so easily," Halik contended, "and we are but a few days' march from our west-coast base of supply—and many reinforcements."

Pete shook his head. "Sorry, Halik. I've decided not to let you make it there." He saw the Grik's slight nod and wondered if that meant the enemy leader had suspected all along that Pete was letting him run.

"Then why are we talking? Why are you not already 'wiping us out'?"

Pete hitched his web belt up, put his hands on his hips, and stared at the Grik for a moment before exhaling explosively. "I'm not exactly sure, to be honest. I've got reasons, but I'm not sure they're good enough. I'll lay things out as I see 'em, and then you tell me."

Halik jerked a diagonal nod.

"Well, first of all, I ain't sorry to tell you that we just got word that an operation we launched against your capital in—we call it Madagascar—has succeeded." He paused to let that sink in, and noticed the intent glares that stiffened Halik's and Ugla's faces. He wondered what that meant, but apparently they knew what Madagascar was. "Not only have we taken the main city, whatever it's called," he continued, "but your honcho, your 'Celestial Mother,' is dead."

Halik and Ugla snarled and snapped at each other in their tongue, while still glaring at Pete and Rolak with what Pete guessed was a variety of incredulity.

"What're they saying?" he asked Hij Geerki.

"They don't 'lieve you, Lord!" Geerki chirped. "Exce't they do. Halik don't think you'd got any reason to lie on such a thing, 'cause us *can* kill they all." Rolak snorted amusement at his pet's use of the word "we," and Pete was surprised by how that struck him as being, well, rude. Geerki didn't seem to mind, and he listened to Halik a moment longer before continuing. "He guesses you know these things 'cause o' 'raa-dee-o,' an' asks why you tell he. Is so'thing you need o' he?"

Pete chuckled. "Doesn't seem as broken up about our news as I expected," he told Rolak.

"Surprised, surely," Rolak agreed, "but not stricken with grief, no. And he has quite quickly steered us back to the purpose of our meeting here."

"Yeah." Pete looked at Halik. "Okay. In case it takes a while for all the implications of what I told you to hit, I'll help you along. First, any reinforcements you might've been counting on, particularly in regard to your better-trained warriors, working up at Madagascar, just dried up at the tap. We also know that Kurokawa's been rounding up most of those before they get to you, anyway. We're not sure what he means to do with 'em, though I'll bet he's not planning on rescuing you. Either way, you were already about as far out on the limb as you could get." He shrugged. "Captain Reddy and the forces under his command just sawed that limb off at the trunk, and whatever you've got with you and in the coastal cities to the west are all you're ever going to have." His eyes bored into Halik's. "You're well and truly screwed, General Halik."

"If you are so sure of that, why do you not simply destroy us and be done with it?" Ugla challenged hotly.

Pete looked at the other Grik, then spoke back at Halik. "That's the question, ain't it?" He looked at the old Lemurian at his side. "Me and Rolak've been kicking this around for a while. It's still a little mushy in my mind, but here it is. You kind of know me, and I kind of know you. We're never gonna be friends—that just flat can't happen," he interrupted himself harshly, "but that doesn't mean we always have to fight." He waved around. "It's a damn weird world. Probably even weirder for you all of a sudden than it is for me, once you think about it, and there's a lot worse people in it than you"—he grinned wryly—"or me."

"Kurokawa springs to mind yet again," Rolak offered conversationally, and Pete nodded. Halik considered that and nodded too.

"The point, I guess," Pete continued, "is that we don't have to love each other to stop killing each other, and if we can stop because we *decide* to, maybe we can decide not to start up again."

"My friends," Rolak nodded at Pete, "prefer to have a reason to fight. I do now as well, though that may not always have been the case. I wonder what it is that you will fight for, General Halik, now that you have a choice."

"You used this argument with me once before," Halik accused through Geerki, "but then broke the truce we had between us and attacked."

"That was different," Pete defended. "You were getting ready to attack *us*!"

Halik seemed to accept that. "So. What is this 'choice'?"

"That is what we have come to offer you," Rolak said. "A real one, and at the most fundamental level, a very simple one as well: A choice between life and death. You may reject our offer out of annoyance that we slew your 'Celestial Mother,' and die for revenge—for the dead leader of a murderous, wasteful culture. Perhaps you will choose to die because you simply know no better. Whatever your reason, you *will* surely die, as will every member of your species we can find in all of Indiaa. You must believe by now that we have the means of accomplishing that end."

Halik didn't reply, but Rolak hadn't really expected him to.

"On the other hand," Pete said, "you can take our deal and give yourself and your army a new start. A *fresh start*," he stressed. "Maybe the first one you Griks've had in a million damn years, because all the shit that made you what you are is gone. *Dead.* Maybe you can eventually make yourselves into something we don't want to kill anymore."

Halik and Ugla snarled at each other for a while again.

"They are probably lying, Lord General, about everything," Ugla insisted, not caring that Geerki would translate. "And even if they are not, about the Celestial Mother, they broke one truce. Why not another?"

"I fear they are speaking the truth about the Giver of Life," Halik replied, "and also about their offer. Why? Because what have they got to gain by lying? They can destroy us, and we cannot stop them. What do they offer? Simply not to destroy us, I think!"

"They must have *some* purpose!" Ugla objected.

"Oh, they do." Halik looked back at Alden and Rolak, and spoke to Geerki.

"Halik asks you tell he *rest* your deal—and then he tell you his," Geerki repeated.

Pete frowned, but nodded, looking at both Grik generals. "My deal's easy. All you gotta do to live is get the hell out of India, and never come back. I don't care what you do after that. We'll watch you, see where you go. We might even stay in touch, because you never know—with the likes of Kurokawa out there, we might even wind up useful to each other down the line. Other than that, my troops'll stop chasing you once you're out of India. I'll even try to get the Czechs to leave you alone, but they do pretty much what they want. What's your 'deal'?"

"Equally easy," Halik said through Hij Geerki. "If you allow us to leave India with our lives, to make this 'new start,' we will not *force* you to destroy us. I know well that is not something you can do entirely from the air. That will allow you to take a larger force elsewhere, General Alden, which is what I know you desire to do—and the only real reason you do not finish us now."

Pete sputtered and Rolak actually laughed. Halik was largely correct in his assessment, of course, although Pete and Rolak, at least, were genuinely curious whether Halik really could change his army's stripes.

"Whatever I 'desire,' we'll leave plenty here to rub you out if you come back," Pete warned.

"Of course."

"Okay then." Pete gestured around uncomfortably. "So, I guess that's it. Scram."

"One last . . . not condition, but request," Halik said.

"Shoot."

"General Niwa. We . . . *I* would consider it an agreeable indication if you would extend my invitation to him to accompany my army into exile, and if he accepts, that you would allow him to do so."

Pete and Rolak both blinked. "You really do like the guy, don't you?" Pete muttered.

"He is of little use to us," Rolak whispered. "His loyalties are too . . . strange."

"Sure, but damn! Do you think he'd *want* to go?" Pete whispered back.

"I do. He despises what the Grik are, and even what he did for them, but he has a genuine affection for General Halik. I think he might be instrumental in helping *these* Grik discover what they might become."

"Well, shit." Pete looked at Halik and raised his voice. "He can go with you if he wants, I guess. I'll ask him."

////// Grik City
Madagascar
August 7, 1944

s the sun crept skyward on the third day after
the battle, it exposed again the results of the
dreadful victory. Morning breezes stirred the
humid, smoky, night-steeped miasma of festering death that overlay the already-unbearable
stench of the place, and carrion eaters of every
description scurried or swooped amid black
clouds of flies. Exhausted troops trudged through the corpses, heaping
them on carts drawn by paalkas or strutted me-naaks, before hauling
their grisly burdens to the docks. From there, the dead Grik were unceremoniously dumped in the water. The troops wore bandanas tightly
drawn around their faces, scented with anything they could find, and *Big
Sal*'s and *Walker*'s fire hoses were in near-constant operation, washing
down the almost unbearably disgusted workers. Some went to the hoses

whether they'd been working the disposal detail or not, just to wash the *sense* of it away. The harbor flickered and churned with the highest concentration of feeding flashies anyone had ever seen.

Matt Reddy frowned down on his battered, rust-streaked ship, her flag stirring fitfully at the mainmast. Her big battle flag had been taken down to be mended again, and have "Grik City" embroidered on its folds to join so many other names of other fights. *She made it through again,* he thought. *She* brought *us through.* His frown deepened. *But not all of us.* He'd never forget the desolate howls of anguish he heard when Diania first saw Chief Gray's body laid out beside the galley. *She really did love him,* he realized, a terrible, painful lump rising in his chest. *Well, so did most everybody else. I wish to God I'd made him sit this one out—but how many more would've died without him? Me, for sure.* He felt a growing pressure behind his eyes. *So long, Boats.*

Almost violently, he broadened his gaze to encompass the entire panorama below the Celestial Palace. He'd practically insisted that the first full-command staff meeting of First Fleet South scheduled since the battle be convened here on the northern steps Simon Herring had defended. The stench wasn't quite as overpowering, and that was an advantage, but mainly he wanted everyone to see the aftermath of what they'd done, good and bad, while they considered just what the hell they were going to do next. He always felt deeply responsible for those who died under his command, and in this case those losses were particularly painful, specifically personified in his mind by Irvin Laumer . . . and Chief Bosun of the Navy Fitzhugh Gray. For perhaps the first time, though, he now keenly felt that their deaths—and maybe most of the others—were somebody *else*'s fault, at least as much as his. He didn't want to focus on blame because he regarded many who deserved it most as family, but he almost had to, to a degree, because he *did* want them to feel the pain of their mistakes, as he always did. Maybe then they wouldn't make the same ones again.

He became aware that Sandra's arm was around him, slowly moving up and down his back, her hand pausing occasionally to massage tense muscles. He took a tentative breath, tasting the air, before taking a deeper one. Then he turned. Everyone who was coming was there: Adar,

Keje, Safir and Chack, Herring, Von Melhausen, Lange, Tikker.... Spanky had left Rosen in charge of the ship to stump up the steps on a crutch, and he and Courtney Bradford had found a place beside Matt and Sandra. Spanky's face was strained and angry, and even Courtney's expression was as grim as Matt had ever seen it. He was glad to see Adar blinking unrestrained horror as he absorbed the view. Maybe he was starting to see. Matt cleared his throat. "Thanks for coming here," he said, looking at Adar. "Especially you, Mr. Chairman. I know it was inconvenient, and Keje's conference room on *Big Sal*'s a lot more comfortable. But it seems like all we've done in there is talk *past* one another for quite a while." He shrugged and looked around. "*I* came here for a raid. I suspected many of you had bigger ideas, so maybe I should've pushed it, but I really thought when it came down to it, everybody would stick to the plan. The good thing about that plan was, if we pulled it off, we'd have been in position to finish the job here after all, it seems. With a helluva lot fewer casualties. All it would've taken was another, carefully considered plan." He grimaced. "I'm no Pollyanna. I know plans always fall apart, but you gotta have them so you at least have some idea how to sort things out when they do." He held as many gazes as would meet his own before he spoke again. "As it turned out, we didn't have any kind of plan for this—or if we did, we had nearly as many plans as we had separate commands—and it turned into a sick, deadly, costly joke we were lucky to survive." He gestured at the scene below. "You all know that, I think, but I also thought it might not sink in, in the luxury of *Big Sal*'s conference room. We, all of us, needed to come up here together and get the big picture—so we can get back on the *same damn page!*"

Adar flicked a single blink of accusation at him, but then his eyelids fluttered with remorse. *Yeah, he sees,* Matt decided, then removed his hat and massaged his sweaty scalp. "We won," he murmured simply, hollowly, "but as screwed up as everything was, we probably shouldn't have. Considering how many people we lost for no good reason, we damn sure didn't *deserve* to."

Eyes looked down. Safir Maraan appeared particularly miserable; her II Corps had been decimated—again—and in the aftermath of the battle she was taking that very hard indeed. Chack blinked at her and put a supporting arm around her shoulders. *Yeah,* Matt realized, *they* all *see it now.* He cleared his throat and looked at Adar. "You're still in charge, Mr. Chairman. You wanted the whole enchilada, and it's lying in your lap. But being in charge means more than just taking the blame when things fall apart. It means you have to lead, and do your absolute best to make sure everyone knows what you want them to do. You didn't. Instead, you basically yanked the curtain up and let everybody else do whatever the hell they wanted." Matt took another breath. "I was tempted to blame myself for letting you do that, but that would've been pretty stupid, in retrospect. As I've said before, either you're in charge or you're not. As it turned out, you were—but you weren't." Matt's tone turned sharp. "Don't ever do that again. You're chairman of the Grand Alliance—and now this 'Union' that's the biggest part of it too—and it's your job to set strategic objectives. If you'd said, 'In spite of everything, I want Grik City in one fell swoop,' I'd have argued, but I'd have followed orders and"—he waved around—"we could've come up with a real plan with sufficient preparation—and a few backup plans—built in. At the very least, that would've saved some lives, I have no doubt." He looked at Sandra and his voice fell. "Probably nothing could've saved Chief Gray and all those we lost on *Walker,*" he admitted. "That was just the breaks, and you're going to hit snags—or sandbars—from time to time." He looked back at Adar. "But there was almost zero coordination between Second Corps and Chack's Brigade, nor was there any way for Tikker to sort out the mess that kept our air wing from providing proper ground support." He glanced at Von Melhausen and saw the old man was beyond understanding what his thoughtless adherence to misguided instructions had cost. Lange knew, and would probably never let anything like *that* happen again. Matt's eyes bored back into Adar's. "And in the end, after all's said and done, that's on *you,* Mr. Chairman." He paused, letting that sink in. "Now, you can accept it, accept the 'blame' for that, like you wanted, and wallow in self-pity—I know what *that* feels like—or you can learn from all the mistakes that *everybody* made and fix the problem. In your case, you have to decide what you want to do next, then let me, as Supreme Allied Commander"—he looked around—"and all these other people here, figure out—together—how to get it done."

The fur around Adar's eyes was wet. "You wound me, Cap-i-taan Reddy," he whispered.

Matt's eyes narrowed. "No, sir. Maybe I hurt your feelings, but there are plenty of guys around here, 'Cats and men, who can show you what real wounds look like. The question for you, the same question I've faced too many times to count, is are you going to roll up in a ball and feel sorry for yourself, or learn from what happened here, shake it off, and try to do better? That's the choice, Mr. Chairman—and all that's at stake is the outcome of the war and the survival of everything you care about." Matt looked around. "Easy choice, if you ask me."

Adar's eyes blazed for an instant, but then he nodded, thoughtfully. "You make the choice most clear. And you are right, as is so often the case," he breathed. He stood straighter. "Indeed. So. I will endeavor to 'shake it off,' as you say, and since we are all here, let us decide— together—exactly what we shall do next. Let us get on the 'same page,' at long last, and remain upon it."

"Um. Hmm," Courtney Bradford voiced, getting everyone's attention. "I presume our most pressing decision must certainly be whether to depart this dreadful place, or attempt to remain. I, for one, insist we *cannot* leave, having discovered that there are other beings, natural allies, already inhabiting the island. They've already helped us, and we can't just abandon them!"

"We could evacuate many," Becher Lange said, but his expression was troubled.

"But not all," Courtney persisted. "I vote we stay. Enlist the locals into the Alliance—they have every reason to help, after all—and remain a festering thorn in the side of the Grik Empire while at the same time using this place to stage further operations. Much as we use the Enchanted Isles against the bloody Doms." Quite a few of those present growled in agreement, but Matt held up his hand.

"Mr. Chairman," he said, "we really can't take a vote on this. We— all of us—can advise you and express our opinions. Hell, you've *got* to let us do that. But then *you've* got to make the decision that'll become *our* mission to plan for. That's the way it works—the way it *needs* to work from now on." He paused and glanced at Courtney. "But before anybody gets carried away, we better hear from Captain Tikker."

Captain Jis-Tikkar stepped into the circle of expectant faces. "As many of you know, who can still hear," he said, absently fingering the shiny brass shell casing thrust through the hole in his ear, "we finally got the P-Forty floatplane airworthy again, and I took it on a scout of the Grik population centers on Mada-gaas-car—and beyond."

Most nodded.

"I reported to Chairman Adar and Cap-i-taan Reddy that the two other Grik settlements I observed appear to have been laid waste by the 'local beings' Mr. Braad-furd mentioned. The great walls around them were burned—still burning, in fact—and so were most of the buildings that could be set afire." He hesitated. "I saw people from the air—hu-maan people. Most hid, but a few stood where I could see . . . and waved."

"Isn't it bloody marvelous to be liberators!" Courtney enthused.

"Captain Tikker?" Matt encouraged.

"There were no ships in the ports at all," the aviator added, "besides some wrecks. So I bet most of the Griks in those towns had already took off for the continent." He blinked a shrug. "So I went there. I knew I'd be stretching my fuel, on the plane's first flight after we put her back together, but I figured we needed to know, right? Anyway, that's what I did. I flew to the Africaa coast." Tikker seemed fully aware of the significance of being probably the first Lemurian besides those in the Republic ever to see the continent that spawned the Grik.

"What did you see, Captain?" Sandra prompted. Tikker looked at her, and his tail swished in agitation.

"I thought I'd see jungle. That's what Miyata said there'd be. But there was only flat dirt an' rock for a long way inland, and maybe ten miles up an' down the coast. Past *that* there was jungle. I flew north a ways, an' seen another dead spot, like the first." He glanced around. "I figure they stripped the land for buildin' ships, but I didn't see many. Just a few. They must be someplace else."

"Perhaps we sank them all, here and at Madras?" Courtney suggested.

Tikker shook his head. "That jungle's *thick*, Mr. Braad-furd. Each one o' those dead spots coulda built more ships than we ever seen."

"What else did you see, Captain," Matt prompted quietly, "in the cleared areas?"

Tikker shifted on his feet. "Grik, sur," he whispered. "Thousands of 'em. *Hundreds* of thousands of 'em, set up an' camped like a proper army, only there weren't many tents. Just Griks—like dark sand."

"Damn it," Spanky said in the sudden silence.

"Yeah." Matt shrugged. "All the Grik in the world, just like we expected." He measured the expressions he saw. "Now we need to decide what to do next," he said. "*You* need to decide, Mr. Chairman," he told Adar.

"Do you think we should leave?" Adar asked him. Matt glanced at Sandra and clasped her hand. Then he took a deep breath. "No, Mr. Chairman, I don't."

There were murmurs of surprise.

"I know—I started this meeting bitching about how we got this place, but we've got it now. The blood's been spilled and there's nothing we can do about that—except make it mean something. We accomplished our mission, our 'raid,' to the extent that even if we pack up, the Grik'll never be able to leave this place so weak again. But now *this* is the front, with Halik retreating from India, and we've got them by the tail. How can we ever let them go? They'll still outbreed us, as long as we're not killing them faster than they can, but the only way to do that is to stay after them." He shrugged. "I'd rather do that on their territory than ours."

Commander Herring cleared his throat. "I will voice no opinion regarding whether we remain or not, but I do think we shouldn't forget the submarine that attacked us. Someone we do not know could well be invested in the outcome here."

"That's true, Mr. Herring," Matt replied, "and I applaud your caution. But my point remains; I'd rather find out who *that* is, if it's anybody more than who we sank, *out here*. Not back home. If they don't like us, I'd rather keep them reacting to us as well."

Herring nodded, frowning.

"But . . . how? How can we stay?" Safir asked, speaking for the first time.

"General Alden's pretty confident a smaller force can keep Halik out of India, and that leaves him free to bring most of his army here, along with the rest of First Fleet." He gestured around before looking at Becher Lange. "In the meantime, we dig in. We fortify this dump like nothing anybody ever saw, and hold it until Pete gets here."

"So simple?" Lange asked, stunned. "I think not. And what if the Grik come before General Alden arrives? Before we raise significant defenses?"

Matt smiled. "If you'll remember, *your* people should help with that. We've transmitted what we did here to the whole damn world, and that was supposed to be the signal for the Republic of Real People to hit the Grik on their southern flank. That ought to get their attention."

"But that was the *sole* intent: to 'get their attention.' Not begin a major campaign!"

"That *was* the intent," Matt agreed with a final glance at Adar, "but the plan's already changed. They'll just have to push harder than they expected to." His tone grim, Matt added, "As will we."

Keje hadn't spoken at all during the conference on the flank of the Celestial Palace. He still didn't. He merely moved to stand beside his human friend. Chack and Safir Maraan did as well. "I know you said we can't vote on this," Chack said, "but the First Raider Brigade and Second Corps stand ready to remain and fight."

"Hell," Spanky muttered. "The Bosun's gotta stay, planted on this stinkin' heap. I say if he's stayin', I damn sure can't leave! He'd haunt Tabby's engineerin' spaces forever."

Adar nodded slowly, his whole face now wet with tears, and strode to stand before Matt, searching his eyes. He turned. "We stay," he said, a little shaky, then cleared his throat. "We *stay*," he stressed. "That is my . . . stra-tee-gic order. Cap-i-taan Reddy, as commander in chief of all Allied forces, will coordinate the design of a plan to carry it out." He looked about at all these diverse people he'd come to love so much and spread his arms, symbolically embracing them. "This conference is adjourned. And may the blessings of the Heavens rest upon you all."

Madness, Herring decided, staring at the place he'd made his desperate stand. He was proud of that. *Battle madness,* he thought. *I can under-*

stand, I suppose, and it makes a kind of sense, but there's no way on earth we can hold this terrible place against all *the Grik! Am I the only one who realizes that? It'll be just like my situation here, all over again, except there won't be any timely—or at least sufficient—reinforcements to save us.* He hadn't slept at all since the battle, and every time he closed his eyes, he saw the slathering horde of Grik charging up these very steps to tear him to bleeding shreds. He shivered despite the heat. *At least that self-centered bastard Miles made sure my canisters are secure. It may all come down to them after all.* He suddenly wondered if Lance Corporal Miles really did check on the special canisters aboard *Salissa*, or just *told* him he had. He didn't trust the man, and by all accounts, he hadn't exactly distinguished himself in the fighting aboard *Walker.* Miles might say that was so he could go to *Salissa* if all else failed, as Herring instructed, and tip the special casks into the harbor. The seed thorns of the deadly kudzu-like plants would've washed ashore. After that, it would just be a matter of time before all Madagascar was utterly uninhabitable, and Herring considered that a suitable parting gift if the Allies had been defeated or had to leave.

That still remained his personal backup plan, but now that they were staying, he needed somebody else—someone he could truly trust—to ensure it was carried out if he couldn't do it himself. He considered telling Adar he'd actually brought the seed weapon along. Adar had been on board for its development, after all. He shook his head, watching the chairman descend the steps surrounded by the others, still discussing their plans. *No, Adar's definitely not in the proper frame of mind,* he concluded. *He's too pliant and unsure of himself just now. Besides, Captain Reddy has given him hope that we might just pull this off, and that's Adar's fondest fantasy.* Herring frowned. He'd learned to trust Captain Reddy, even like him, and he tried to give him the benefit of the doubt. He *wanted* to believe. . . .

"No!" he murmured aloud. Maybe his ingrained thinking—*was it pessimism or realism?*—sprang from the abuse he'd suffered in Japanese captivity, but that didn't matter anymore. *He* would plan as if he and all his new friends were doomed, and ensure that, whatever happened, they would be avenged.

////// *TFG-2 off Alexaandraa*
The Republic of Real People
Southern Africa

gainst all the predictions of anyone who'd ever heard of it being tried, even those of Inquisitor Choon (who remained aboard regardless), USS *Donaghey* did manage to weather the terrible storms that plagued the cape of Africa. It had been a nearer thing than Greg Garrett preferred to admit, however. The confused winds there roiled in what he could only describe as a perpetual strakka, and the sea convulsed with mountainous, desperate swells that didn't seem to know where they were going. The only thing the sea and sky seemed perfectly agreed upon was that Greg's trespassing frigate not be allowed to survive. True to her record, traditions, and growing reputation, however, *Donaghey* gave them both the finger.

The storm almost snapped it off—along with all her topmasts but the fore, and most of two entire suits of strakka canvas. It started nearly every seam in her stout hull, and took seven of her crew over the side. It sprang every spar and smashed every boat, and almost twisted her rudder off, which would've been the end of her, but *Donaghey* made it through to what amounted to an undying "eye" in the storm. There, she limped into a small fishing village in clear view of the semipermanent eastern tempest that the locals simply called "the dark," and with Inquisitor Choon's assistance, they were welcomed.

For the most part, the people they met were about what they'd expected after spending time with *Amerika*'s crew: mostly Lemurians with a very strange accent, and a large minority of humans of various shades and features. They met the first "hybrids" that Miyata had found so curious—crosses between Lemurians and ancient Chinese explorers, most thought. They looked like pale-furred humans—with tails—and performed most of the dockside tasks with a kind of haughtiness that reminded Greg of Navy yard apes. They didn't speak much, and seemed standoffish around the strangers. Greg's crew stared at them—they couldn't help it—and received resentful glances in return, but generally, their brief stay was friendly enough. *Donaghey*'s mission pressed, however, and they made what repairs were absolutely essential, weighed their anchor, and sailed on.

Through the weaker, colder, western wall of the great storm guarding the strait between the continent and the frozen land to the south, they finally rounded what should've been the Cape of Good Hope.

"We're in a whole new ocean," Greg told Bekiaa-Sab-At, his tone somber. "A whole new world."

"Is it as big as the last one?" Bekiaa asked, leaning out over the rail to watch some strange fish that were pacing the ship, almost sporting in her wake. Bekiaa had never seen fish apparently *enjoying* themselves before, and they fascinated her. Choon had told them "flashies" were rare in these waters, probably due to the temperature, but "shaarks" were plentiful enough.

"Bigger than the Indian—I mean, 'Western Ocean,'" he replied, remembering that Bekiaa hadn't been in the Pacific, or "Eastern Sea" before. "A lot bigger."

"We call it 'Atlaantic,'" Choon supplied cheerfully. He was in on the conspiracy to keep Bekiaa's spirits up, and right then they were all anxious to reinforce the younglinglike wonder that had crept into her tone. Greg was just about convinced that the Republic snoop was sweet on her, anyway.

"And if we sailed all the way across it to the west, we'd eventually come to the land of the Dominion?"

"To the same continent," Greg confirmed. "Maybe they don't rule the whole thing. And apparently we have 'friends' to the north, besides the Impies—if Fred and Kari are right. But yeah, it's the same place, and if we could go around it, or through the 'pass' Fred reported, we'd meet up with Second Fleet."

Bekiaa shook her head and blinked. "All around the whole world. It seems so . . . impossible, to sail west and come to a place that lies so far to the east."

"We're actually closer to Second Fleet here than if we sailed back the other way," Smitty said, joining them at the rail. Greg nodded, but watched Bekiaa.

"I think I should like that," Bekiaa murmured. "To sail all around the world."

"Maybe we will," Greg suggested, then shrugged. "No orders against it." He looked at Choon. "I'd rather have a refit first, and meet your 'Kaiser,' of course."

The storm far behind and the sun beginning to set beyond the horizon, they opened Alexaandraa Bay at last.

"Break out the signal," Choon instructed when they neared the fortress guarding the eastern approach. It was an impressive affair, festooned with big guns, and seemingly sculpted from the living rock. Greg noticed there were also two tall columns of smoke standing above the twin turret "monitors" they'd been told to expect, and the squat, ugly ships were already steaming toward them. No doubt they'd been warned by lookouts stationed high in the rocky, wooded mountains surrounding the bay. As usual, Choon had been ridiculously tight-lipped about the recognition signal until shortly before. Greg wondered what would've happened if they'd lost Choon over the side. Would they've been fired on when they suddenly appeared?

"Run up the signal," Greg ordered his quartermaster, glassing the oncoming ships, then studying the mountains beyond the picturesque city at their feet. He'd never been to Cape Town in the old world, which he already knew was what US Navy charts would've called this place, but he wasn't expecting the forest. "Stand by to fire salute," he called to Smitty in the waist.

"I believe you should hold your fire, Cap-i-taan Gaarett," Choon said, his voice suddenly tense. Greg looked at him.

"What? Why?"

Choon pointed at the signal that had broken at the mastheads of the oncoming monitors. "Because we have been ordered to stand away from our guns, heave to, and prepare to be boarded. Also, if we attempt to send a transmission of any kind, this ship will be destroyed."

Greg goggled at the Lemurian. "What? Bullshit!" He raised his voice. "Clear for action, sound battle stations!" he roared. He glared back at Choon. "I know you're weird, but I thought we were friends. And now this? Damned if I'll heave to, and damned if anybody's coming aboard my ship who *orders* me to let 'em! Stand by to come about!" he ordered the helmsman.

"You can run from the . . . monitors, you call them, and would likely even escape. Their guns are large, but not particularly accurate. I doubt they will fire on you in any case, since it is not my people who make the order. They merely pass it along. From that." He pointed at the west side of the bay where Greg hadn't looked. He raised his glasses now. Anchored just off the principal docks, probably about where *Amerika* was usually berthed, judging by the lack of other shipping around it, was a massive gray form, about 550 feet long at a glance. Two funnels stood, spaced a good distance apart—and there were four massive turrets housing two huge guns apiece. Even as he watched, Greg realized one of the turrets, aft, was turning toward his ship, the protruding guns rising slightly. He gulped. A flicker of movement caught his eye, and he focused on a flag fluttering from a relatively fat mainmast just forward of the aft turrets. His mouth dropped open when he saw the red octagon and blue crosslike symbol in the white field.

"She looks like *Amagi!*" Smitty said, climbing the ladder from the gun deck to see.

"She's not as big," Greg snapped, then added sickly, "But her guns are bigger."

"I *am* your friend," Choon assured, his tone anxious. "And so are my people." He pointed at the battleship—the *real* battleship from another world. "Apparently, they are not. Do you really think your noble *Donaghey* can outrun the projectiles that . . . thing seems prepared to hurl at her?"

Greg Garrett sagged. "No," he whispered. "I guess not."

Chimborazo
New Granada Province
Holy Dominion

General Ghanan Nerino, commander of His Supreme Holiness's Army of the South, lay upon a soft, comfortable bed in a lovely little villa. The home belonged to the alcalde of Chimborazo, which was a picturesque, prosperous village, high in the mountains east of the Puerto Viejo crossroads of the Camino Militar. The temperature at that altitude was very pleasant for most of the year, and the late-summer diseases were not so rampant as they were down low.

I wonder how General Shinya enjoys his accommodations, within the fort he has erected at the crossroads, Nerino idly thought, through the drug-induced haze that kept his agony at bay. *Perhaps his men have discovered El Vomito Rojo by now. The time is at hand. I wonder if his . . . surprisingly dangerous animal friends are susceptible.* He opened his mouth to call for wine, through the gauzy fabric covering his mouth and much of his face. He winced. Against all odds, he was improving, but there were still scabs on his lips, and they cracked so easily. Instead of speaking, he merely sighed—and prayed again for death. He was better, after weeks of agony, but it was so unfair that the pain should fade, only to be replaced by the sharper pain of the punishment he knew must await him. *A quick death now, in my sleep, would be such a blessing! Have I not already suffered enough to enter Heaven? I always knew I might die,* he conceded. *Such is the risk of a military career. But I suppose I expected to be shot with an arrow or ball, struck down by disease, or perhaps even be eaten. I never even imagined being flayed alive for failure—after already being seared by fire from the sky. The Blood Priests will honor me as a model of piety, even in my disgrace!* he thought bitterly.

A young slave woman entered the room, trying not to disturb him, but he heard the small sounds of her bare feet on the stone floor and the swishing rustle of her dress. "I would appreciate wine," he managed, his crusty eyelids still closed.

"Of course, General," the woman whispered, "but the healers advise against it, combined with your medicines."

"To the *darkest caves* with the healers," Nerino wheezed. His lungs had been cooked as well. Then he paused, contrite. The healers had done quite well, as a matter of fact, and were as gentle as possible. It wasn't their fault that they had saved him only for further suffering. "Their doses do help with the pain," he granted, more softly. "But do bring wine, if your other duties allow it." He knew he wasn't the only horribly wounded officer in the villa. "I assure you it will not hurt me."

"Of course."

Nerino finally opened his eyes to watch the slave girl leave the room. He doubted he ever would've noticed her under other circumstances, but she'd been his nurse through all the long nights of misery and pain, and she attracted him. Not in a physical way, necessarily, but her kindness, patience, her very presence, had been the most effective balm to his torment. He wondered about that as he painfully shifted to gaze out the window beside his bed.

He didn't know how long he lay like that. Perhaps he slept. He stirred at the sound of the slave girl returning, and turned to face her with the closest thing to a smile he could achieve. The girl wasn't there. Instead, to Nerino's mixed horror and amazement, he saw the chiseled goatee and darkly benign features of Don Hernan DeDevino Dicha, Blood Cardinal to His Supreme Holiness, the Messiah of Mexico, and by the Grace of God, Emperor of the World. Shrouded in his dark red robes, the man seemed to almost *float* into the room, radiating an aura of what someone who'd never met him might mistake for concerned solicitation. Incongruously, he also bore a large goblet of wine.

"My dear General Nerino, you are awake," Don Hernan said in honeyed tones. "I am so glad to find you so." He smiled benevolently. "Having learned the extent of your wounds, I feared I might arrive too late."

"Too late . . . for what, Your Holiness?" Nerino asked, his heart racing.

"To properly start you on your journey to the next world, of course."

Nerino felt a chill in spite of his burns. "Of course," he whispered. At least, if Don Hernan's tone could be believed (never a certainty), he wouldn't be flayed. But the "Final Cleansing," administered by a Blood Cardinal known to be particular about due form, would be only slightly less unpleasant. He clenched his teeth. It wouldn't be quick, but his misery *would* end. For that, at least, he was grateful. "Of course," he said more firmly. "Thank you . . . for your interest, Your Holiness."

Don Hernan flicked it away. "Do not be so impatient, dear general. I cannot release you to Heaven just yet! Now that I see you so nearly healed with my own eyes, it is clear to me that your duty to God demands that you remain in this world a little longer. You see, I may have need of your observations, from time to time."

Nerino was stunned. "Ah . . . yes, of course, Your Holiness. I will . . . try to be patient. And I will most humbly serve you in whatever capacity you think best." He paused, his mind racing. *I'm not going to die!* "Your Holiness, I receive little news. May I inquire about the state of my army?"

Don Hernan sat on a chair beside the bed, and instead of holding the wine goblet to Nerino's lips, he took a long gulp himself. "Your army, my dear general, no longer exists. It is being absorbed into the greater one I am now assembling—the Army of God." He flicked his fingers again. "Not that there was much to absorb! No blame rests upon you; you were bravely wounded, after all. But after that, your army *fled* the heretics! Abandoned sacred soil!" He shook his head sadly. "I do so *hate* to crucify able men, particularly when we are in such need of them."

"H-how many?"

"Only one in five. As I said, we need them, and perhaps my leniency will return the rest to their duty."

Nerino clenched his eyes shut. "And my officers?" he ventured, fearing the answer.

"Half are being buried alive," Don Hernan replied wistfully. "Again, I deplore the waste, but none can ever be trusted to lead, having once run away. The rest will be reduced to the ranks."

"No," Nerino said before he could stop himself, and cringed. "Ah, I mean, with all my heart I beg you to read the report I dictated. I—I *ordered* the retreat to continue, once it had already begun. There was no stopping it, and few officers are guilty of more than following the orders I gave to preserve the experience gained against the heretics. We . . . *You* will need them, Your Holiness. To advise you regarding enemy tactics and capabilities!"

Don Hernan's expression had hardened when Nerino challenged him, but now it softened again. "Perhaps. I may . . . reevaluate their fates on a case-by-case basis. But that is not for you to concern yourself about! Heal! We will talk again soon!" He stood.

"One final thing, Holiness, if I may?" Nerino ventured. "I thought I would soon have no interest in such things, but my worldly curiosity is restored."

"Name it, General Nerino, and I will grant your wish if I am able."

"I only wish to know how you mean to defeat the heretics. They have weapons, monstrously effective, and they are not fools."

Don Hernan pursed his lips, then smiled. "Of course. First, as I told you, the army I am building, blessed by God, will be invincible both in size and power. Needless to say, I will command it myself, and no one knows the heretics better than I. The outcome on land is not in doubt. At sea, we have assembled the greatest fleet the world has ever seen, and even now it waits, beyond the enemy's view, in the vicinity of El Paso del Fuego. All the small dragons that could be gathered, from as far east as Hispaniola in the Caribbean, will sortie with it. The enemy fleet offshore and gathered at the Galápagos, regardless how powerful, will be ground to floating dust." He smiled more enthusiastically. "And since the small dragons, even in such numbers, cannot assure victory with the enemy flying machines being so effective, His Supreme Holiness has finally given leave for his personal stable of *greater* dragons to be employed! Such a thing has never been done, and I am most excited!"

Don Hernan's eager smile faded into an expression of profound compassion. "Rest now, Nerino. Soon we will purge the heretics from all the world, you and I, and earn our places at the right hand of God."

SPECIFICATIONS

American-Lemurian Ships and Equipment

USS *Walker* (DD-163)—Wickes (Little) Class four-stack, or flush-deck, destroyer. Twin screw, steam turbines, 1,200 tons, 314' x 30'. Top speed (as designed): 35 knots. 112 officers and enlisted (current) including Lemurians (L) Armament: (Main)—3 x 4"-50 + 1 x 4"-50 dual purpose. (Secondary)—4 x 25 mm Type-96 AA, 4 x.50 cal MG, 2 x.30 cal MG. 40-60 Mk-6 (or "equivalent") depth charges for 2 stern racks and 2 Y guns (with adapters). 2 x 21" triple-tube torpedo mounts. Impulse-activated catapult for PB-1B scout seaplane.

USS *Mahan* (DD-102)—(Initially under repair at Madras). Wickes Class four-stack, or flush-deck, destroyer. Twin screw, steam turbines, 960 tons, 264" x 30' (as rebuilt). Top speed estimated at 25 knots. Rebuild has resulted in shortening, and removal of 2 funnels and 2 boilers. Otherwise, her armament and upgrades are the same as those of USS *Walker*.

USS *Santa Catalina* (CA-P-1)—"Protected Cruiser" (initially under repair at Madras). Formerly general cargo. 8,000 tons, 420' x 53', triple-expansion steam, oil fired, 10 knots (as reconstructed). Retains significant cargo/troop capacity, and has a seaplane catapult with recovery booms aft. 240 officers and enlisted. Armament: 4 x 5.5" mounted in armored casemate. 2 x 4.7" DP in armored tubs. 1 x 10" breech-loading rifle (20' length) mounted on spring-assisted pneumatic recoil pivot.

Carriers

USNRS (US Navy Reserve Ship) *Salissa,* *"Big Sal"* **(CV1)**—Aircraft carrier/tender, converted from seagoing Lemurian Home. Single screw, triple-expansion steam, 13,000 tons, 1,009' x 200'. Armament: 2 x 5.5", 2 x 4.7" DP, 4 x twin mount 25 'mm AA, 20 x 50 pdrs (as reduced), 50 aircraft.

USNRS *Arracca* **(CV-3)**—Aircraft carrier/tender converted from seagoing Lemurian Home. Single screw, triple-expansion steam, 14,670 tons, 1009'x 210'. Armament: 2 x 4.7" DP, 50 x 50 pdrs. 50 aircraft.

USS *Maaka-Kakja* **(CV-4)**—(Purpose-built aircraft carrier/tender). Specifications are similar to *Arracca*, but is capable of carrying upward of 80 aircraft—with some stowed in crates.

USS *Baalkpan Bay* **(CV-5)**—(Purpose-built aircraft carrier/tender). First of a new class of smaller (850' x 150', 9,000 tons), faster (up to 15 knots), lightly armed (4 x Baalkpan Arsenal 4"-50 DP guns—2 amidships, 1 each forward and aft)—fleet carriers that can carry as many aircraft as *Maaka-Kakja*.

"Small Boys"

Frigate "DDs"

USS *Donaghey* **(DD-2)**—Square rig sail only, 1,200 tons, 168' x 33', 200 officers and enlisted. Sole survivor of first new construction. Armament: 24 x 18 pdrs, Y gun, and depth charges.

*Dowden Class—(Square rig steamer, 1,500 tons, 12–15 knots, 185' x 34', 20 x 32 pdrs, Y gun, and depth charges, 218 officers and enlisted).

**Haakar-Faask Class—(Square rig steamer, 15 knots, 1,600 tons, 200'x 36', 20 x 32 pdrs, Y gun, and depth charges, 226 officers and enlisted).

***Scott Class—(Square rig steamer, 17 knots, 1,800 tons, 210' x 40', 20 x 50 pdrs, Y gun, and depth charges, 260 officers and enlisted).

Corvettes (DEs)—Captured Grik "Indiamen," primarily of the earlier (lighter) design. "Razeed" to the gun deck, these are swift, agile, dedicated sailors with three masts and a square rig. 120-160' x 30-36', about 900 tons (tonnage varies depending largely on armament, which also varies from 10 to 24 guns that range in weight and bore diameter from 12–18 pdrs). Y gun and depth charges.

Auxiliaries—Still largely composed of purpose-altered Grik "Indiamen," small and large, and used as transports, oilers, tenders, and general cargo. A growing number of steam auxiliaries have joined the fleet, with dimensions and appearance similar to Dowden and Haakar-Faask Class DDs, but with lighter armament. Some fast clipper-shaped vessels are employed as long-range oilers. Fore and aft rigged feluccas remain in service as fast transports and scouts. *Respite Island* Class SPDs (self-propelled dry dock) are designed along similar lines to the new purpose-built carriers— inspired by the massive seagoing Lemurian Homes. They are intended as rapid deployment, heavy-lift dry docks, and for bulky transport.

USNRS—*Salaama-Na* Home—(Unaltered—other than by emplacement of 50 x 50 pdrs). 1014' x 150', 8,600 tons. 3 tripod masts support semirigid "junklike" sails or "wings." Top speed about 6 knots, but capable of short sprints up to 10 knots using 100 long sweeps. In addition to living space in the hull, there are three tall pagoda-like structures within the tripods that cumulatively accommodate up to 6,000 people.

Commodore (High Chief) Sor-Lomaak (L)—Commanding.

Woor-Na **Home**—Lightly armed (ten 32 pdrs) heavy transport, specifications as above.

Fristar **Home**—Nominally, if reluctantly Allied Home. Same basic specifications as *Salaama-Na*—as are all seagoing Lemurian "Homes"— but mounts only ten 32 pdrs.

Anai-Sa (L)—High Chief.

Aircraft: P-40-E Warhawk—Allison V1710, V12, 1,150 hp. Max speed 360 mph, ceiling 29,000 ft. Crew: 1. Armament: Up to 6 x .50 cal Browning machine guns, and up to 1,000-lb bomb. **PB-1B "Nancy"**—"W/G" type, in-line 4 cyl 150 hp. Max speed 110 mph, max weight 1,900 lbs. Crew: 2. Armament: 400-lb bombs. **PB-2 "Buzzard"**—3 x "W/G" type, in-line 4 cyl 150 hp. Max speed 80 mph, max weight 3,000 lbs. Crew: 2, and up to 6 passengers. Armament: 600-lb bombs. **PB-5 "Clipper"**—4 x W/G type, in-line 4 cyl 150 hp. Max speed 90 mph, max weight 4,800 lbs. Crew: 3, and up to 8 passengers. Armament: 1,500-lb bombs. **PB-5B**—As above, but powered by 4 x MB 5 cyl, 254 hp radials. Max speed 125 mph, max weight 6,200 lbs. Crew: 3, and up to 10 passengers. Armament: 2,000-lb bombs. **P-1 Mosquito Hawk** or "Fleashooter"—MB 5 cyl radial 254 hp. Max speed 220 mph, max weight 1,220 lbs. Crew: 1. Armament: 2 x .45 cal "Blitzer Bug" machine guns. **P-1B**—As above, but fitted for carrier ops.

Field Artillery—**6 pdr** on split-trail "galloper" carriage—effective to about 1,500 yds, or 300 yds with canister. **12 pdr** on stock-trail carriage—effective to about 1,800 yds, or 300 yds with canister. **3" mortar**—effective to about 800 yds **4" mortar**—effective to about 1,500 yds.

Primary Small Arms—Sword, spear, crossbow, longbow, grenades, bayonet, smoothbore musket (.60 cal), rifled musket (.50 cal), Allin-Silva breech-loading rifled conversion (.50-80 cal), Allin-Silva breech-loading smoothbore conversion (20 gauge), 1911 Colt and copies (.45 ACP), Blitzer Bug SMG (.45 ACP).

Secondary Small Arms—1903 Springfield (.30-06), 1898 Krag-Jorgensen (.30 US), 1918 BAR (.30-06), Thompson SMG (.45 ACP). (A small number of other firearms are available.)

Imperial Ships and Equipment

These fall in a number of categories, and though few share enough specifics to be described as classes, they can be grouped by basic sizes and capabilities. Most do share the fundamental similarity of being powered by steam-driven paddlewheels and a complete suit of sails.

Ships of the Line—About 180'–200' x 52'–58', 1,900–2,200 tons—50–80 x 30, 20 pdrs, 10 pdrs, 8 pdrs. (8 pdrs are more commonly used as field guns by the Empire). Speed, about 8–10 knots, 400–475 officers and enlisted.

Frigates—About 160'–180' x 38'–44', 1,200–1,400 tons. 24–40 x 20–30 pdrs. Speed, about 13–15 knots, 275–350 officers and enlisted. Example: HIMS *Achilles* 160' x 38', 1,300 tons, 26 x 20 pdrs.

Field Artillery—8 pdr on split-trail carriage—effective to about 1,500 yds, or 600 yds with grapeshot.

Primary Small Arms—Sword, smoothbore flintlock musket (.75 cal), bayonet, pistol. (Imperial service pistols are of two varieties: cheaply made but robust Field and Sea Service weapons in .62 cal, and privately purchased officer's pistols that may be any caliber from about .40 to the service standard.)

Republic Ships and Equipment

SMS *Amerika*—German ocean liner converted to a commerce raider in WWI. 669' x 74', 22,000 tons. Twin screw, 18 knots, 215 officers and enlisted, with space for 2,500 passengers or troops. Armament: 2 x 10.5 cm (4.1") SK L/40, 6 x MG08 (Maxim) machine guns, 8 x 57mm.

Coastal and harbor defense vessels—specifications unknown. **Aircraft? Field artillery**—specifications unknown. **Primary small arms:** Sword, revolver, breech-loading bolt action, single-shot rifle (11.15 x 60R—.43 Mauser cal). **Secondary small arms:** M-1898 Mauser (8 x 57 mm), Mauser and Luger pistols, mostly in 7.65 cal.

Enemy Warships and Equipment

Grik

ArataAmagi Class BBs (ironclad battleships)—800' x 100', 26,000 tons. Twin screw, double-expansion steam, max speed 10 knots. Crew: 1,300. Armament: 32 x 100 pdrs, 30 x 3" AA mortars.

Azuma Class CAs (ironclad cruisers)—300' x 37', about 3,800 tons. Twin screw, double-expansion steam, sail auxiliary, max speed 12 knots. Crew: 320. Armament: 20 x 40 or 14 x 100 pdrs. 4 x firebomb catapults.

Heavy "Indiaman" Class—Multipurpose transport/warships. Three masts, square rig, sail only. 180' x 38' about 1,100 tons (tonnage varies depending largely on armament, which also varies from 0 to 40 guns of various weights and bore diameters). The somewhat crude standard for Grik artillery is 2, 4, 9, 16, 40, 60, and now up to 100 pdrs, although the largest "Indiaman" guns are 40s. These ships have been seen to achieve about 14 knots in favorable winds. Light "Indiamen" (about 900 tons) are apparently no longer being made.

Giorsh—Flagship of the Celestial Realm, now armed with 90 guns, from 16–40 pdrs.

Tatsuta—Kurokawa's double-ended paddle/steam yacht.

Aircraft—Hydrogen-filled rigid dirigibles or zeppelins. 300' x 48', 5 x 2 cyl 80-hp engines, max speed 60 mph. Useful lift 3,600 lbs. Crew: 16. Armament: 6 x 2 pdr swivel guns, bombs.

Field artillery—The standard Grik field piece is a 9 pdr, but 4s and 16s are also used, with effective ranges of 1,200, 800, and 1,600 yds, respectively. Powder is satisfactory, but windage is often excessive, resulting in poor accuracy. Grik "field" firebomb throwers fling 10- and 25-lb bombs, depending on the size, for a range of 200 and 325 yds, respectively.

Primary small arms—Teeth, claws, swords, spears, Japanese-style matchlock (*tanegashima*) muskets (roughly .80 cal).

Holy Dominion

Like Imperial vessels, Dominion warships fall in a number of categories that are difficult to describe as classes, but again, can be grouped by size and capability. Almost all known Dom warships remain dedicated sailors, but their steam-powered transports indicate they have taken steps forward. Despite their generally more primitive design, Dom warships run larger and more heavily armed than their Imperial counterparts. **Ships of the Line**—About 200' x 60', 3,400–3,800 tons. 64–98 x 24 pdrs, 16 pdrs, 9 pdrs. Speed, about 7–10 knots, 470–525 officers and enlisted. **Heavy Frigates (Cruisers)**—About 170' x 50', 1,400–1,600 tons. 34–50 x 24 pdrs, 9 pdrs. Speed, about 14 knots, 290–370 officers and enlisted.

Aircraft—The Doms have no aircraft yet, but employ "dragons," or "Grikbirds" for aerial attack.

Field Artillery—9 pdrs on split-trail carriages—effective to about 1,500 yds, or 600 yds with grapeshot.

Primary small arms—Sword, pike, plug bayonet, flintlock (patilla style) musket (.69 cal). Only officers and cavalry use pistols, which are often quite ornate and of various calibers.